Fallen WOMAN

LINDA KENNEDY

TABLE OF CONTENTS

CHAPTER 1

As the morning broke over the horizon, Catherine stood on the tower, watching. The sun was just rising, and she couldn't believe how much she was going to miss this sight. Since she was born, her whole life had revolved around this land and tower. The sun was burning off the mist, and it was going to be a clear day even though the days were getting shorter and cooler. The sky was so blue over the ocean, and the clouds had started to build; the storms would be here soon. She didn't even understand why she still looked every morning; it had been almost three years. She laid her hand on her chest and fingered the gold cross hidden there beneath her gown.

Looking around at the old stone tower just made her sad, so she might as well not worry about it anymore. The repairs up here were extensive, but she had started them before her refusal at court. There were to be new timbers set, and the stones had to be removed and then reset. Hundreds of years of foul weather took their toll on everything, including stone. She gently fingered the top of the stones on the parapet as she looked out over the ocean.

The front curved around in a circle, with iron gates guarded night and day; it would take a small army to get through them when locked. The towers were made centuries ago for archers to fire from and hot oil to be spilled from. But this place had not been attacked, except once a few years back—that time the Raider from the north attacked the village and changed her life forever. The back of the keep was her favorite place; the gardens were back there, enclosed by high walls. When her father was alive, she wasn't allowed to do anything with it; but when he was gone, she started to plant some roses and bring some of the old plants back from the dead. She had been able to save several of her mother's favorites, and they were beginning to bloom. Some still had blooms on them till they froze anyway. Most of the house was closed up; her father didn't think it prudent to heat and maintain anything that wasn't being used, so she ke pt it closed. She had lived her life like a nun, never having anything extra so she could please her father, but she was never able to please him. So she finally gave up trying.

She had done all she could to protect this land and her child, but she had failed. That didn't make it any easier to take. This land, which had been in her family for over two hundred years, soon would no longer be hers. There was nothing else she could do. She would leave with her daughter as soon as the new lord arrived to take control. She couldn't inherit this land because she was a woman, and that made her less than worthy, and she didn't have a husband to keep it. Her mother had been a Celt, so she could inherit the land in the further up in the North Country; at least they couldn't take that from her.

Catherine leaned over the side rail carefully to see Robert looking up at her. He was holding the horses. Robert was the only man she had ever totally trusted with her life and that of her daughter, even when her father was still alive. She waved down at him and said, "I will be down in a few minutes. Do you have the bags?"

"Yes, we are ready to go. Be careful leaning over that wall. You shouldn't even be up there!" he replied.

"I know, I am being careful."

She said good morning to the men coming out of the stairwell; she had beaten them up here this morning. The head craftsman asked what she thought so far and if there were any more changes to be made.

"You will probably have to ask the new lord if there is anything else. I don't know if he will want changes. Just continue to do the repairs until he arrives."

He just nodded and started to assign the men their jobs for today. She turned to leave. Robert waited for her downstairs.

Robert had guarded her since she was a child; her mother could see her father cared nothing for her since she was not the son he had wanted. Robert was there when the news of her father's death in the Crusades was sent. Since her mother was dead, she was glad it wasn't Robert, for she cared little for her father. They hadn't even bothered to return his body; it was too long a trip. She had a headstone put next to her mother's, but she was glad he wasn't next to her; there was no love lost for him around here. Robert would be the one she would mourn if she lost him. He was tall and dark skinned. He had dark hair, with a curl always right in the center of his head. He was beginning to show some gray in his hair, and even that looked good on him.

They were going to go gather herbs from the meadow before the freeze took everything; she had always enjoyed doing this every year, but this would be the last time, and that took away from her joy. She needed to be in the field taking care of the last of the hay, but her foot swelled up so badly yesterday that Robert insisted she stay off it today. She would check the hay in the barn later when he wasn't looking.

She turned to go down but slowed for the stairs. They were steep, dark, and curved; she had to have a railing built after she had taken a fall last year. She had injured her knee and foot rather badly a couple of days ago when she missed the last step in the dark. The rails made them a little safer, but they still needed to be taken slowly. These old stairs were worn slick, and there wasn't much she could do to improve them. She just needed to be careful because a fall all the way down them would be fatal. She turned to close the door, which opened inward so that a bar could be placed across it in case of storms or invasion. After closing the big door, she sat down on the top step; she just needed a few moments alone. She leaned over to rest her head on the old stone wall; she just needed to not be the head of the house for a little while. Soon, this would be someone else's job, and she would be free.

She stood, and as she walked down the stairs, she could hear Beth laughing in the downstairs room that she shared with her mother; she loved to hear her baby laugh. It was the only thing lately that made her smile. As she walked into the bedroom, Beth came running up with her arms held high. Catherine lifted her daughter up and swung her around; then she hugged her and kissed her neck. Beth giggled as her mother tickled her. She had the light of her life wrapped up in this small bundle she held in her arms. They would be going soon, and she hoped she could care for her the way she wanted to. She never wanted her daughter to feel like she was unloved or a mistake. There was still a lot of work to be done at the old estate, and she hoped she had enough money to keep everything going; there just had to be—there were no options left for her.

Jennie was Beth's nanny and Catherine's best friend. Jennie helped her take care of Beth since she was born. They had been friends since childhood even though Jennie was a little older than she was and a servant of the house. Catherine had been trained to run an estate but didn't have the foggiest how to raise a child, so Jennie had taught her to be a good mother and how to run a household as well as an estate. Jennie was very good with children. Cat just wished Jennie had some of her own. Maybe it wasn't too late. Cat had a plan, and maybe without the burden of all her responsibilities, she could have some time to implement it.

Catherine's father had other plans for her, and that was a big part of the problem around here. Catherine hadn't been a boy, and that had ruined his plans for the keep; he didn't seem to care about what was to become of her, just what happened to the land, which there was a lot of—several thousand acres. Since Catherine couldn't inherit because she was a woman, she petitioned King Charles I for protection and a husband. That had been a huge mistake because nobody had noticed her little part of the world until she asked for help. She should have kept her mouth shut and found some noble who needed money and bought a husband; it would have worked out better.

Catherine couldn't imagine a life without her child, but the price to keep her land was to give up Beth, and no piece of land or the tower on it was worth that; this small little girl was her life. She told Jennie she would be back in a while and asked if the clothes and other items they needed were packed.

"Everything is ready to go when you are!" Jennie said, taking Beth from her.

She headed downstairs past the workers cleaning the great hall to the front door; everything had to be ready when the new lord got here. She didn't want him to be displeased with the house because it needed his protection from the Raiders. She wanted him to be as proud of this land as she was. Even if it wasn't to be her land anymore, it still carried her family's name and always would.

Robert met her at the door and helped her mount her horse; he didn't let her go anywhere alone after what had happened almost three years ago. He still blamed himself for not being there when she needed him. She had never been able to tell him that she sometimes wished he had not found her, but that was her secret, for it would hurt him to know that. After he got her mounted, he asked her if her leg was hurting because she was still limping at times.

"A little bit, but it is getting better."

He knew she was lying. Jennie had told him it was badly bruised, and she thought she had a broken toe.

"You have to stop walking around at night with no light."

"I just slipped. It won't happen again."

As they rode out of the courtyard, several members of her household greeted her; they would be as sorry to see her go as she would be to leave. They rode in silence for a while; then Catherine said, "Jennie is ready to leave. Is everything ready with the wagon and the supplies? I don't want to stay any longer than necessary when he finally gets here."

"Yes, everything is ready. But don't you want to stay and see if Lord Giles might have changed his mind about the arrangement he made with you? He was very drunk the night we left."

"No, he said everything he had to say in court. I can't take many more of his insults. I heard quite enough that night. You heard a good deal of what was said. Would you stay? I have spent my whole life trying to please a man that couldn't be pleased, and I won't do that anymore."

Robert couldn't blame his mistress; the man was drunk and abusive when he had talked to the king about her, and what was so strange was that he had never even bothered to meet her.

"I have often wondered why you had me pull him out of the mud and put him in the stable that night. Why didn't you just let him drown? It would have been fitting end."

Cat looked at him and said, "I don't have the foggiest idea. Maybe I thought they might send someone worse."

Like a man, Catherine rode astride her horse instead of sidesaddle; her father had taught her that was the only way he expected her to ride. She had her skirts made with several gores so she could straddle a horse comfortably. It would have been so much easier if she could dress like the men, but that would never be allowed. Just riding astride was frowned upon; a lady just didn't ride that way.

She turned to him and said, "Are you sure you want to go with me when I leave? You don't have to, you know. Or is Jennie why you are coming?"

He just looked shocked and turned his head to her.

"Don't give me that look. I see how you look at her, and she is looking at you when you don't see. You could have a life with her. You are not that much older than she is."

"That is not a discussion I will have with you. But isn't she coming with us?"

"Yes, she is. Maybe things could be different at the new house for you two?"

"Let's just get to the new land and then see how things work out."

He stopped his horse and looked at her.

"The day you were born and your father left your mother crying because you were a girl; I promised her I would always watch over you. I am not quite through with that job yet."

"Did you love my mother?" Catherine asked.

"Maybe I did, but I knew she would never be mine, so you were the next best thing."

"I wish you had been my father. He always was so disappointed in me."

"Your father was a fool, and he left you alone in an unforgivable position. He should have made some sort of arrangement for your future before he left you. I watch you in the mornings looking out at the ocean. Do you hope to see him?"

"Maybe. I would have liked him to see his daughter."

"Would you have gone with him had I not found you?"

"I don't know. Perhaps. But we can't go back now."

"We could always do something different."

"No, I think it is too late to do anything else. Besides, from what you tell me, we still have quite a job in front of us at the lodge."

Robert rode quietly for a few minutes, then said, "Cat, I am not sure that with just the four men and me, we can accomplish what needs to be done. I don't want to take you somewhere you could be in danger."

"It is the only choice I have left. We will make it work. We have to. There are no more options. I need to make a short trip into the village and see some of the women and check the grain stores."

"Why don't you leave that to Lord Giles? It is his job now, and that priest will give you grief if he sees you."

"I don't know when he is going to show up. Instructions for the harvesting and spring planting still need to be given, and I will try to ignore the priest. I will be glad to leave just so I don't have to deal with him anymore."

When they reached the village, her people came out to greet her, and she knew most by their first name. She got off her horse and walked and talked to several of the women about the food stores for the winter.

Then she went to meet with the village elder, and they looked at the grain stores for when the planting was done. There was still enough of the seed to replant if some of the fields got flooded in the spring rains. She was still walking down the street, talking to the elder, when Father Tomas confronted her.

"Has my lady come to see the common people today and speak of virtue she does not have?" She really did not like this man, priest or not. He seemed to think the proper thing for her to do was put Beth with the nuns as an orphan. Cat had disagreed. She had slapped the man and told him to go to hell, and the war was on from there.

"Well, we will have a new lord of this land soon, and you will be gone. I hear he refused you at court. Did he not want a disgraced lady either?"

Robert dismounted from his horse, and Cat didn't want him to kill the priest—at least not now. So she told him, "Whatever went on at court is my business, but when I leave, at least I won't have to see or listen to you anymore. Now get out of my way."

She turned and mounted her horse and started to leave the village. A pretty and very pregnant woman walked toward them; it was Rachel, the village elder's daughter.

"Rachel, how are you feeling? It is about time, isn't it?"

"Yes, my lady, and it can't be soon enough. I am as big as a house."

At about that time, the priest returned and said to Rachel, "You shouldn't talk to her. She has fallen from grace." Then he looked up at Catherine as if he was the voice of the pope; even her father wouldn't have put up with this abuse.

"Rachel, if you need me, send one of the men. If I am gone, I have taught some of my women what needs to be done as a midwife. They will take good care of you." Then she turned to leave, sitting straight in her saddle; she was not ashamed of keeping her child. Nobody, including this priest, would ever make her regret that decision.

"He really is an ass, and he is one thing I won't miss about this place. You want a real ride, old man? I bet I can beat you to the meadow."

"You can try, little girl. I'm not that old yet."

They raced across the meadow until they reached the stream; then they pulled up their horses. They were both smiling; that was the first fun they had had for some time. He always loved to watch her ride; she was exceptional on a horse. Most people didn't know how good she really was if they hadn't seen her ride. It was beautiful and green, but the weather was changing quickly; it would freeze soon, so she needed to get everything gathered now. She grabbed the apron tied on the back of the saddle and then took the bags from Robert's hand.

She got off her horse, and she walked for a minute, just brushing the tops of the plants; the smells of the herbs were intoxicating. It was very beautiful this morning, and the trees were beginning to lose their leaves to the shorter days. She began to fill her bags with what she needed for her medicines and with seasoning that the cook would need. She carried a small knife in the front of her apron. She would occasionally stop and shake some of the plants to drop seeds for next season and then cut what was left. She was collecting extra to take with her when she left until she could get some of her own seeds planted.

Robert stayed on his horse and watched for any danger to his lady. He watched Catherine walking among the sweet-smelling herbs as he had watched her do since the day they had buried her mother. Her grandmother had brought her out here to get her away from her father. They had a picnic in a small cave near here by the stream. Robert had watched over this girl since she was a small child and expected to continue to do so for as long as he lived; she was the closest thing to a daughter he would probably ever have even though he wasn't that much older than she was.

He wondered why her father had always been so hard on her just because she was a girl. Catherine had always disappointed him. He could never see that she was everything that a father could have wanted. Her father had ignored her ever since her mother died in childbirth trying to give him the son he so wanted, and then he started to train her as his heir until he could replace her with a man, preferably a husband. He couldn't see her as anything but a tool to keep his land. He had been a blind fool. His daughter was an asset to be used to secure this land and maybe a better title if the price was right. He didn't care for her feelings as to what she might want in the matter—she was nothing to him.

Robert watched as she picked the things she needed. She was such a pretty woman that he couldn't understand why the new lord had refused her. She had been well educated and was very good at most things. Lord Giles Broussard had refused and insulted her before he had even met Cat; all he wanted to remember of that night was the trip home. She kept her hood down as they left the castle so no one could see her face. It was raining, but he knew. Giles had belittled and insulted her, and she cried on the way home, but never again—not that he had ever seen her cry. Lord Giles had hurt her, and he hoped he regretted his decision before they left because he was as much a fool as her father had been.

She was down by the stream, pulling up some moss and wrapping it in sheepskin, which she would use as a poultice when needed.

He turned when he saw men coming down the road. They were led by a large man on an even larger warhorse. He assumed correctly that it was the new lord, and he knew they would be leaving sooner than expected. Maybe that was the best thing that could happen to her and Jennie. Catherine was right; he had feelings for the girl and had for some time. He wondered if he was too old to take a wife and have a life of his own.

Maybe it was too late to be a father, but he couldn't stop thinking about Jennie and a night when they had been alone some time ago. She had talked to him for a long time, and then they kissed; she made him want to be a young man again. He just wanted to be able to keep them safe, and the lodge still needed a lot of repair.

Catherine looked up and saw the men as well. At about that time, two riders veered off toward them; she continued to pick her herbs. It looked like this would be the last job of her time here.

Robert didn't look happy about the unknown riders coming this close without more protection; she had better go and reassure him. She couldn't see the rider, but she knew it was the big horse at the king's stable. It was a huge black stallion; this was a warhorse, and he bore a knight in full armor. The man on his back was Giles; you couldn't miss him. He was huge; he had to be at least six and a half feet tall. There wasn't any fat on him; he was all muscle. After all, he had been a soldier for at least ten years now. He was dark haired and very good-looking; he had lost his lands and family to the French while fighting for the king. Fever and famine claimed the lives of his mother and sister and left him a very bitter man, so the king had offered him these lands as a reward. Queen Henrietta Marie had thought it a good idea until he had acted like an ass about the contract. King Charles rewarded him the land anyway. So now he again had some land and a home of his own—Catherine's. At least she had a friend at court—Queen Marie herself. They had been friends for some time now.

Be nice, she thought to herself, *just for a while longer. Then you can go. He is just another man. You can handle this.* She walked toward the oncoming horses and thought, why *do I feel like I am the stranger here now?*

Giles was tired, and his arm was hurting from a cut; he tried to catch a falling piece of armor. The wound had stopped bleeding, but it still ached. They had traveled for several days to get to his new holdings, and he was ready to get off this horse and have a comfortable bed to sleep in. He figured he would have a lot of work to do to get this land in shape because it had been run by a woman for several years. He was afraid he would be disappointed because of the way things had gone between him and the woman he had turned down; maybe this land just wasn't worth the fight. He had been without a home and land for too long, and he hoped it was worth his effort. He wanted to rest; he had been at war so long that he wasn't sure he remembered how.

The lady Catherine had offered herself to him in marriage to hang on to her land, but she had refused to give up her bastard child as part of the agreement, and he wouldn't have it any other way; at least that's what his mistress had talked him into doing. To tell the truth, he couldn't remember much of the night except just fighting with Jane.

So far, everything was in order. The crops were flourishing, and the people seemed content; maybe this wouldn't be as bad as he thought. The tower was not too far ahead, and even it looked in good shape even though they were still a couple of miles away.

The king had offered this land and the lady to him to protect as compensation for fighting for him. There had been some Northern Raiders, and there wasn't a man in charge of the soldiers; there hadn't been for almost five years since the old lord had died fighting in the Crusades. All Giles wanted was a home and land he could call his own; it would have been nice to have an instant wife because he wanted children. He had assumed that the woman wasn't very pretty, which was why she couldn't get the father of her child to marry her. It didn't really matter; he thought he had a mistress to take care of his other needs, and he wouldn't have to see the lady much to have children, so he didn't really care what she looked like. A woman wasn't that important to him anyway; there was always one around that was willing.

Things hadn't gone as he had planned. Jane had gotten him drunk and then talked him into refusing this lady's offer even though he thought it might be a suitable situation. When he went to see the king, he had made an ass of himself when he flatly refused this woman's offer. Queen Marie had been furious at him; the next day, she wouldn't even talk to him. The king said the lady had told Queen Marie that she would leave the land as soon as he arrived, but he talked her into staying long enough to show him the running of the land. He didn't care whether she stayed or left, but he just accepted the king's ruling. After all of this, Jane said she didn't want to come to the country at this time. She would stay at court until he could get things in shape for her arrival.

Giles wasn't stupid; she was just hoping for a better option at court but didn't want to cut all ties with Giles until she was sure she couldn't do better. Giles was mad; she had made him look like a fool in front of King Charles with no intention of going with him. He told her she could do as she pleased because he was through with her; then he proceeded to get really drunk. The next morning, he had been found in the barn, sound asleep and covered in mud. Someone had pulled him out of the mud and covered him up with a horse blanket. He had remembered someone leaving in the dark, but he didn't know whom to thank.

He looked across the green pasture and saw two people picking something. He decided to see what was going on and get a feeling of how he was going to be received.

Gerard rode behind his master; he was his second-in-command as well as a good friend. They had ridden together for more than ten years; they had been squires together and had remained friends. He was not any surer than anyone else about what happened at court, but he knew it went badly. At least it seemed that Giles was finally through with Jane, which pleased him because he had never trusted that woman. As they got closer, he saw that an armed man was watching over a beautiful, tall woman. Giles rode up to the man, and Robert put himself between the woman and the approaching men.

Robert could see that this man was Lord Giles; he had seen him at court with his lady several weeks ago. Giles came closer to the man. It was obvious he was guarding this woman, and he wondered why. The woman looked up at him and wiped a strand of hair out of her face. She seemed disappointed that he was there; this wasn't very encouraging. Catherine began to walk toward the men and around the man on the horse, and as he started to stop her, she just touched his leg and looked up at him. Then he moved out of her way. She was beautiful, with long light-brown hair braided down her back, and it was funny that he wondered how it would look blowing around her face. She wore a plain tan dress with an apron; she was taking her gloves off and putting them in the apron pockets. He assumed she was one of the maids for the lady of the house. He thought the man with her was probably her father, but he didn't act like her father or look old enough. As she began to move toward him, Giles said, "Be careful, my horse can be dangerous. He might hurt you."

Catherine just smiled and walked forward, then reached out to touch the horse and said, "I find most large animals like me, especially horses."

As she reached out to stroke the horse's nose, it walked closer to her so she could touch him. Giles was amazed; his horse barely let him stroke him, and he had been trained to stand even in battle, but he walked to her as if he were a pet. She was quite shapely and had green eyes, and she held herself well. The dress she wore was plain in color but was of very fine material; this wasn't someone's maid. She took off the apron, confirming that her dress was made of very good material. The belt and around the collar had silver thread running through it. She also had a nice gold chain around her neck, but he couldn't see what was on the end of it. "You were asked what you were doing out here," Gerard demanded.

She was suddenly mad but knew it would do her no good to say anything. She didn't even look at him and just kept stroking the horse's nose. The horse knew her as they had waited in the stables the night they left; she had been stroking him and feeding him pieces of apple while her men readied the horses.

"We are gathering herbs for the winter," Robert answered.

Catherine reached in her pocket and pulled out a piece of apple from this morning and fed it to the big horse. She told the horse to stay, and he did as she said. She then turned and walked back to get her bags of herbs and began to load them on her horse. She put the sheepskin behind Robert's saddle as it was wet, and she didn't want to hold it in her lap. Giles began to dismount to help her on her horse, but she swung herself up and was mounted before he could even dismount; then she turned to go. Gerard was incensed at this woman's attitude; she had barely even acknowledged them.

"You haven't been dismissed. A village woman needs to be told when she can go. This is your new master!" Gerard yelled at her.

She turned her horse around so quickly that Giles thought she would be unseated and was surprised when she still sat in the saddle like she was born there.

"I know who Lord Giles is, so you can stop yelling at me. And I don't ask permission to leave of anyone, most especially him or you, for that matter. I am not stupid or dumb. I just don't want to talk to you. Lord Giles made it perfectly clear how he felt about me before he got here. I don't need a repeat performance."

Giles gave him a look as if to say shut up; he already knew this woman was no village woman. He suspected she was perhaps one of the ladies-in-waiting; now he wasn't even sure of that.

Catherine just stared at them; she had forgotten just how rude these people could be. She held her horse still and gave Giles a look that would melt metal, then said, "I will go ahead and see to it everything is ready for your arrival, but I expect more courtesy from you and your men till I leave. This is still my right by the king's order, but believe me, I will leave as soon as I possibly can. You and your men have no manners."

Cat turned and began to ride swiftly away before anyone could see how mad this man made her. Giles watched her ride away and couldn't believe how well she rode; he had never known a woman to ride like a man instead of sidesaddle, and she rode so well. He turned to Robert and asked him, "You guard this woman?"

Robert just nodded.

Before Robert could say anything else, Giles asked, "What is that woman's name? Will she be at the keep tonight?"

This might not be so boring a place after all if this woman was around and willing, but he was beginning to get a bad feeling he wasn't going to like the answer to his question. Robert looked at him as if he wished to kill him; then he said, "That is the lady Catherine Demarco, and you told her a month ago you wouldn't marry her unless she gave up her child before you even laid eyes on her. And your man just called her a whore, and as long as I am alive, she is under my protection. She is still the lady of these lands until you take over, so show her the respect you didn't show her at court. We will be gone soon enough, and if you don't wish her to show you this land and business, we will be gone sooner than that. Believe me, I wish it was sooner."

This was like a slap in the face; he wouldn't even meet this woman at court because he thought she was beneath him. The first woman he had met in such a long time that interested him and he had just managed to insult her even more than he had before. He began to follow her and looked over at Gerard as if to say to keep his mouth shut and wondered why he suddenly thought he had met her before today. This wasn't how this was supposed to go, and now it was a mess. She seemed somehow familiar, but he didn't know why.

He started to follow the man to the keep, then turned to Gerard and said, "Be polite until I get a feel for the mood around here. I don't want to have to fight another war just to be accepted as master here."

As they rode, all he saw were well-maintained grain fields and healthy livestock. Even the tower looked good. It looked to him like this woman knew what she was doing. He seemed to be the one out of place here, and now he had insulted her again; this morning wasn't going as planned.

He followed her to the keep; he had several men who needed a doctor, and he wanted them settled and comfortable until he could find one. His surgeon had been killed in battle, but it had not been a great loss; the man was incompetent and a drunk. He could ask at the keep if one was available. His men had always served him well, and it was time they had a rest, and he hoped this would be the place. It was time for all of them to have some peace; he and his men were sick to death of fighting for land and a religion that wasn't theirs. Most of his men had no families anymore, so this was their last chance for one; all of them wanted what they had lost.

Catherine was furious as she rode into the keep, and one of her men came up to take her horse. There were several men who looked hurt, and she knew her men would know where to take the injured men to get them taken care of. She told them to get them settled, and she would be down in a bit to look after them. She entered the hall and was met by several people, and she told them that the new lord was coming. The orders were given to set the large tables and begin preparing a meal for at least twenty men. She went to the kitchen and told Helen, the cook, that there were hurt men downstairs and requested her to see to it that they had some food. Helen asked if she wanted hot water and bandages. Cat told her, "Yes, I will return in a few minutes."

She headed down to where the wounded men were taken and told one of her men to accompany her. When she got downstairs, she looked over each man's wound and told the man to see to their needs and get them fed and comfortable and she would be back. She was pleasant and friendly to each one, and after she got them settled and had a fire set to warm the room, she headed back upstairs.

After everyone was seen to downstairs, she went to the kitchen. She had already told Helen what she would need, and she was sure it would be tended to; she wanted to get her medicine box upstairs, and then she could go take care of the men.

Several of Giles's men followed her into the hall with four large dogs; she turned and told the men to take the dogs outside because there were pens for them there. One of the men began to object, but the look he got from Catherine put an end to the discussion; she was in no mood to debate. Cat began climbing the stairs until she entered her room. Jennie was there with Beth, whom she was rocking to sleep.

"You are back sooner than I thought you would be. Was there a problem?"

"Yes, Lord Giles is on his way here, and I am not moved out of this room. Can you help me move our things?"

"Of course. Let me put Beth down in the crib next door, and we will get started. You look like you are ready to kill someone. Has something happened?"

"Yes, we have stayed too long. We need to be gone from here."

About this time, Giles walked into the building, and he was impressed with the way everything looked. The grounds and the buildings were very well-kept and clean. When he entered, he could smell venison and bread; his men were sitting down to eat and were being well taken care of. Giles asked about his injured men and was told a doctor was on the way and that they were being taken care of as well. He didn't see Lady Catherine anywhere, so he asked where she was; he needed to do some fence-mending, and he might as well get started. He was told she had gone upstairs, so he headed up. He passed several large chests sitting against the hall wall and assumed they were hers. She was ready to leave. When he got to the room, all he saw was Catherine on the floor under the bed. She was retrieving her box of medicine herbs and didn't hear him come in. She had one leg up in the air as she wiggled around under the bed, and she had very nice legs. He walked over to the other side of the bed and asked her, "Do you need some help?"

"No, I am doing just fine. I will be through in a minute."

"I take it this is your room?"

"Yes, and I should have been out of here before."

"That is really not necessary. I could take another room."

"No, this is the master bedroom, and now it is yours. Besides, I won't be here much longer, so I will take the other room across the hall."

He didn't like the sound of that statement; he had assumed she had nowhere else to go except to the village, but he would debate it with her later.

"I was hoping you would help me get acquainted with your people."

"Of course, but then I will be leaving."

"Where will you go?"

"It is not necessary for you to know my destination. Just know I will be gone soon. This land is yours."

As she climbed out from under the bed, she had a spider web in her hair; he reached down to remove it. She looked up and saw him reach for her, and she scooted back to keep him from touching her. He sat back up on the bed and said, "There is a spider web in your hair."

She reached up, plucked it from her head, and then brushed it away. He reached down to help her stand, and again, she backed away. She turned and stood by herself and began to leave the room; he reached to grab her arm, and she stood perfectly still.

"We didn't get off to such a good start, did we? I would like to remedy this situation and talk to you about the keep."

"What exactly do you want me to do? I can introduce you to your new people and see that you are settled. Then I can go. That was the arrangement you wanted."

"Are you in such a hurry to leave your land? I thought that is why you offered me the contract at court?"

"You said I wasn't suitable for you because I had a bastard child, and you had no use for another man's castoff."

"How do you know what was said that night at the court?"

She looked at him as if he were stupid.

"I was there listening. The queen thought I should see what you looked like in case I wanted to call off the marriage. But that wasn't to be a problem, was it? Please take your hands off me."

He had no idea she had been there, and he wasn't even sure exactly what he had said. He was sure it wasn't good. No wonder Queen Marie wouldn't talk to him the next day; she was angry as well. He didn't remember much about that night; he and Jane had too much to drink before meeting with King Charles. Jane had been so sure this woman wanted nothing more than a man to care for her and her land, so she told him to make the demand about the child. Now he realized she was just making sure nobody took her place until she could decide if she was going with him. He looked down at her again, and all he saw were her eyes, and he knew he had seen them before—if he could just remember where.

"If you don't mind, I need to see to moving my belongings."

He didn't know exactly what to say; he realized he had made a big mistake, but this wasn't the time to have this discussion because she had her mind set on going.

"If that is the way you want it." He was thinking that she should go ahead and move, but he also realized she belonged to this place more than he did. He didn't know how he was going to convince her of that, but he intended to try. He kept trying to remember what he had said about her.

This was going to take some time, so he would just have to stall her somehow till he could figure it out.

She got everything set up in the new room. Beth was still asleep, so she headed down the stairs to check on his men, anything to avoid being around him. When she got downstairs, the men were settled in and having a meal, and they were eating like there was no tomorrow.

"I am having some bathwater sent down so you men can clean up, and then we will get started on those wounds. Do you have clean clothes to change into?" They all shook their heads no, so she said, "I will have clean nightshirts sent down until I can have your clothes washed."

She checked the wounds and decided they could wait until they had eaten. One man's leg was worrying her, but she thought to let him get comfortable before she started on him.

"Try not to open those wounds any more than you have to. It looks like you all have lost enough blood for the time being." She smiled at them as they all thanked her.

"If any of you are still hungry, just ask the man at the bottom of the stairs to get you more food. There is plenty. My man will see to your needs. His name is James."

As she went to leave, she leaned over to James and told him to see that the man she was just talking to was cleaned up first because he was in the most need of her care. She walked up the stairs to the kitchen and checked on everything. It was beginning to get cold, so she grabbed her cape off the peg in the main hall and headed to the stables. She had a mare about to foal, and she wanted to check on her; besides, she felt like she was suffocating in the keep—this wasn't home anymore. She could have already been gone, but she promised to stay until Giles arrived.

The mare was fine, but one of her men said that the master's horse was limping; she hadn't noticed it this afternoon because she had other things on her mind. The big horse was giving her men some trouble; he wouldn't let them touch him. They were afraid he was going to trample them. She came into the corral, walked over to the big horse, and watched him walk around. Her man was right; he had a slight limp. The big horse walked over to her just as he had done this afternoon, and she leaned down to lift up his hoof. About this time, Giles came out and saw a caped figure with a hood looking at his horse.

"What is going on here?"

She didn't even look up at him; she was concentrating on the horse. She seemed to be getting better at tuning him out.

"I was checking your horse. He has a limp. It looks like a stone bruise, or he may have stepped on something. After I get it cleaned up, I can see if it needs a poultice, and he should be better in a few days."

He realized it was Catherine in the cape talking to him.

"All right, if you think you know what you are doing."

One of her men laughed and said, "My lady is the doctor here. People come for miles for her help with their horses. They will do anything for her."

"Really? I have never seen anyone that a horse would do anything for."

"You haven't seen my lady work with horses then."

As Catherine looked up, the cape partially covered her face, and Giles remembered where he had seen her. The night he refused her, she had been leaving with five of her men when he came to the stables. She had looked up briefly from under her hood, and all he saw were her eyes—the same eyes he had seen this afternoon, but they had tears in them on that night. This day was getting worse by the minute.

"I saw you that night, didn't I? You and your men were leaving in the middle of the night your men pulled me out of the mud."

"Yes."

He didn't want to talk to her in front of so many people, so he just watched her work on his horse. "I have men downstairs that could use a good doctor."

"I have already seen to feeding them and then bathing them. After that, I will tend to their wounds."

"I would like to talk to you later."

"Why? Nothing has changed." She turned and walked away.

God, how much had she heard that night, and why couldn't he remember what he had said? He must have made a complete ass of himself to get this reaction from her. Most of the women he knew threw themselves at him, but not this one; she had no use for him at all, and he wasn't going to push it here. He could see by the reaction of these men, they would protect her with their lives, and he didn't want to start out that way.

She walked away to make the poultice for his horse's hoof, and he just stood back and watched her. Her men would help her if she asked, but none of them got too close or touched her. His horse acted like a tame stable horse for her and nobody else; he snorted if anyone else came near him. When she was finished, she reached up and scratched him behind the ears as he bent his head for her to reach. "Come on." The big horse followed her; she didn't even have to hold his halter as she led him to a stall. He walked in for her, and she shut the gate. He turned, and she rubbed both sides of his head.

"Now you rest, and I will see you in the morning, baby boy." Turning to one of the men, Catherine said, "See that he gets some oats and a good rubdown."

"My lady, he won't let us touch him."

"He will now," she said as she turned and rubbed his face again. Then she said to the horse, "Be good and let them rub you down."

Giles then watched the men walk in and start working on his horse with no problems, and he just stared at her.

"It seems you were right about large animals liking you."

"Horses are easy. They don't make snap judgments. They just know whether they like you or not." Catherine walked away without saying another word.

When she got back into the keep, she headed down to the basement area, where the wounded men were. There was a large basin of warm water to clean her hands. She rolled her sleeves up and washed her hands thoroughly, then dried them. Several men had fairly deep cuts, but after cleaning the wounds and wrapping them, she was pleased not to have to do any stitching—yet. One man's cut was deep, but she had been putting cloths soaked in salt water on it, trying to reduce the swelling. It was so swollen; she was going to see if her salve could help. She needed to stitch it closed. She asked the man his name while she worked on him, and he told her it was John Ames.

"Nice to meet you John and you other men as well. I will have to learn your names one by one." As soon as she said that, the other men started to tell her their names.

"I am Mark Travers."

"I am Andrew Summers."

She just smiled and went back to work on John's leg.

At least everyone was fed, clean, and had a warm place to sleep with plenty of blankets. They all thanked her as she rechecked each one of them. She then told her man that if she was needed during the night to call her immediately and to keep an eye on John's injury.

Giles had watched from a distance to see what she would do with his men. He was beginning to realize it didn't matter who it was; she cared for them all equally, and they were grateful to her. They were more comfortable than they had been for some time, and it was very nice as was the lady of the house; it sure beat sleeping on the ground. She seemed to be able to get along with everyone but him, and she was trying to avoid him as much as she possibly could.

She headed upstairs to clean up; she had dirt and blood on her, which wasn't all that uncommon around here. But she wanted to look good tonight. He had seemed impressed with the keep so far, and she was sure he would stay to protect it. Sometimes things just don't work out like you think they should; she just wanted her people protected.

CHAPTER 2

Catherine was seeing to the evening meal; after, she changed upstairs when Giles went into the main dining hall to sit down to eat. She came back out of the kitchen and had on a light-green dress, and nobody would mistake her for anything but the lady of the house. It had a square neckline, which showed her breasts at the top. The dress had bell-shaped sleeves and cream satin pulled out of slits down the sides. She had taken her time to dress and even applied a little perfume to her neck. It seemed important to impress this man; even though he didn't want her, she still wanted to look good. Gerard sat beside Giles and asked what was wrong; he looked like he wanted to stomp on someone.

"Gerard, have you ever done something so stupid you don't know if you can fix it?"

"I assume you are talking about the lady of the house. I think you may have messed this one up badly, and the woman would have been a good match for you."

"You really didn't have to agree with me so quickly, and after this morning, you owe her an apology as well."

"Yes, I know that—unless her man doesn't kill me first. I have been talking to the people around here this afternoon and looking at this keep. She knows what she is doing and is well thought of by her people. You have done well by the king. There is a lot of good land and people to tend it."

"She is smart, competent, and has been taking care of the wounded downstairs. And I think if she asked them to desert, they would. And at this point, I wouldn't blame them. I know they are as tired of fighting as we are."

About this time, Beth made her entrance to the room; and when she saw her mother, she started to run to her. All these men scared her. Catherine hadn't seen it when she entered, but one of the large dogs was still under the table. As soon as Beth began to run to her, the dog started to chase her. Catherine saw the dog, but it was too late before she realized that she didn't have time to reach Beth before the dog did. Giles saw what was happening just in time to grab Beth. He picked her up and got her out of the dog's way; then he pushed the dog away. Beth was screaming, and a terrified Catherine yelled at the man who had disobeyed her.

"I told you to take those animals outside! There are small children in this keep, and they aren't safe with those dogs underfoot."

"My master is the only one I take orders from."

Still holding Beth in his arms, Giles stood up, turned, and backhanded the man; then he told him, "If this lady tells you something, you listen just as if it was me. Does everyone in this room understand?"

A murmur of "yes" went through the crowd of men, but the man on the floor looked daggers at his master. Giles decided then that this man should never be at his back. His name was Kevin, and he had joined them recently, but Giles didn't trust him. Gerard saw the look too and thought he'd better keep an eye on this man.

"Get that dog out of here just as the lady asked and don't bring them back inside."

Catherine came up to get her daughter. Giles looked down at the child clinging to him and thought she was the prettiest little girl he had ever seen. She had the darkest blue eyes he had ever seen and blonde hair so light it was almost white. She went to her mother and grabbed her neck. The look on Catherine's face was enough to say it all. The only way for her to give up this child would be to kill her. Catherine was a beautiful, but when she held her daughter, she was radiant; now he finally understood. He had asked her to give up her beloved child, and she would never do that for anyone or anything. She looked up at him and said, "Thank you." Then she turned and walked away, carrying Beth upstairs.

"Gerard, Jane told me to tell that woman that the only way I would accept her contract was to give up that child, and I agreed with her on that point. I think that is the stupidest thing I have ever done, and to tell you the truth, I don't know how I am going to fix it."

"I have to agree with you on that. Jane has ruined this for you with that one little girl. You were a fool not to have talked to this woman at court, and Jane knew that."

It was the first time he had seen this woman smile. He sat back down to eat, and it was wonderful; he didn't remember the last time he had just eaten a meal with his men.

The food was good, and there was plenty of it. It looked as if his men had been able to clean up and had places to sleep inside. He went see to it that everyone was taken care of for the night, but everything had already been attended to. The keep was locked up, guards were posted at each door, and the house settled into the quiet. Giles headed up the stairs; everything down here was under control. This place was very well run; as Gerard had said, this woman had everything under control.

He went to the master bedroom, as Catherine called it, and walked around. It was a very nice room, large and airy; it had a large fireplace, which had been set, so it was also warm. His robe had been set out for him on the large bed, so Giles began to undress and get comfortable. What little belongings he had were scattered around the room, making it feel like his home or what he remembered a home used to feel like; it had been such a long time since he had a home of his own. Giles could still smell the herbs that had clung to her when she was in here earlier.

He had forgotten about his arm until he tried to take off his shirt, which had become stuck to his arm, and his arm was bleeding again. He looked down at the bloody cut and decided he had better take care of it. Then he realized he had a reason to call on Catherine as the doctor, and maybe if they were alone, he would finally get to talk to her; he pulled his shirt back on and headed to the door. He walked across the hall and knocked on her door, and Jennie answered it. He could see Catherine was breast-feeding Beth; she looked so beautiful holding and feeding her child that he couldn't even speak. Jennie finally asked, "Can we help you with something?"

"My arm is cut, and I think I need your lady to look at it."

Cat just looked up and told Jennie, "Get my box, go next door, and start boiling some water. Put some salt in it. I will be there shortly when I get Beth down."

"Yes, my lady." She saw Giles was still staring at Catherine, and she said, "You come with me."

He followed Jennie back into the room and then watched her prepare the water to boil. He walked to the window and looked out at the land; this was a nice place with several thousand acres of land. No wonder she had tried so hard to hold on to it. It should have been a sizable dowry for any woman; he wondered why her father had not found a husband for her himself.

About five minutes later, she came into the room; she had on a blue gown with a matching robe tied at the waist. She told Jennie, "Go to bed. I will take care of this. I will be back in a little while."

She began to put some clean towels into the pot and let them simmer.

"All right, let's see what you have done here."

She put a dry towel on her lap and laid his arm on it as she sat next to the bed on a small stool; this was as close as he had come to actually touching her since he got here.

The shirt was stuck to the arm, and it wasn't coming off. She took one of the hot towels and set it in a bowl to cool, and then she applied it carefully to the arm and let it set. Giles didn't say anything; he just watched her. He was actually afraid if he said anything, she would leave, and he didn't want that.

"How long ago did you cut this?" Catherine asked.

"Yesterday."

"Why is it men always think they shouldn't care for a cut? You care for your animals better."

"Is it that bad?"

"It's bad enough."

The cloth began to come off from the arm, and Giles could see that it was indeed bad enough.

"What do you intend to do?"

"I am going to get the shirt off, then clean and fix it. I don't think it will need stitches."

She went about cleaning the cut with warm towels and salt water; it was already beginning to feel better. She had taken some herbs out of her box, placed them in a smaller pot, and put it in the fire to warm. When it was warm, she brought it to him to drink.

"What is this? I don't recognize the smell."

"It is an herb that takes down your fever."

"Do I have a fever?"

"No, but you will have a fever by morning and this will help to keep it under control."

"How did you learn to do this?"

"My grandmother taught me after my mother died."

"How old were you when she died?"

"I was six, and then she and my father raised me."

"Your father never remarried?"

"No, I think he thought he had plenty of time and just didn't realize that he would ever die."

"Is that why you were here alone for so long?"

"Yes, he taught me how to run this land and the tower thinking I would take over for him while he was away. He just assumed I had no other choices, looks like he was right."

She changed the towels several more times, and he didn't ask her any more questions. But what kind of man turned his daughter into his successor knowing she would be alone to do it?

"We need to get this shirt off so I can finish."

He sat up and pulled it over his head. She tried not to look, but even she had to admit he was a very handsome man. He saw the look before she turned her face from him; maybe he still had a chance. When she was finally through, she wrapped the arm after putting some vile-smelling salve on it.

"I will leave this on until tomorrow and change it again. Then it should be fine before I have to leave."

"Why are you in such a hurry to leave your home?"

"This is your land now, and I don't want to stay and watch it run by someone else, especially when I am not wanted here."

She finished with his arm and stood to leave; without realizing it, he had a hold on her robe. Then she said, "You can let go now."

Then she backed away from him, but it wasn't just him she backed away from—she backed away from every man who got close except Robert. Then he asked, "Is Robert the father of your daughter?"

She smiled and then laughed. He liked the sound; then she said, "No, Robert is more like a father to me. He has always taken care of me better than my father ever did." She turned to collect her pots and medicines so she could leave.

Then Giles said, "Who is your child's father and why isn't he here?"

"That is my business. You should go to sleep now and rest. I will check on this again in the morning. I appreciate you handling the dog downstairs. He could have hurt my daughter."

"What is your daughter's name?"

"Elizabeth, but we call her Beth."

"She is a very beautiful child."

"Thank you. I will be leaving now."

"What if I said you couldn't leave?"

She stopped and just looked at him.

"You gave up that right weeks ago in no uncertain terms, and I thought your mistress was coming to live with you, so my services won't be needed."

"She won't be coming. I told her not to."

"Well then, it seems you will have to find someone else to fill her shoes and your bed."

"What if I said I had changed my mind and wanted you to stay? Could I force you to?"

"You gave up that right, and nobody forces me. You keep saying you don't remember that night. Shall I tell you what happened?"

"Yes."

"I came to the castle a day early. I have known Queen Marie for some time now, and she wanted to talk to me about this contract. The next thing I knew, I was escorted to the queen's solar. She talked with me for over an hour and decided I needed a proper dress, so she borrowed a dress from one of the ladies in waiting. The next day, I was dressed, and my hair was done to the queen's orders as she watched. When it was time to meet you, she handed me a small pair of diamond earrings and a gold bracelet to wear. She and the other ladies told me I looked beautiful, and we went down to meet you. We stood behind a partition as the contract was read, and as I started out, you started talking. You called me every name in the book—even the queen was blushing. She tried to shoo me out of there, but I wanted to hear it all. You said you couldn't understand why I had come begging for a husband when I already had a child. Was I so ugly or such a bitch I couldn't even get the father of my child to marry me with all this land?

"All I wanted to do was run, so I thanked Marie and told her I would be leaving. I went back to the room and took off the dress, and the lady who loaned it to me said to keep the dress as it looked better on me than it did on her. I refused, but I found it days later in a box in my luggage. The queen walked in before I left, and I gave her back her jewelry, and she made me promise to stay at least for a while and meet you. She thought your mistress had influenced your decision. I told her I would, but I didn't say how long. She was so mad she was ready to strangle you herself, and she couldn't understand your outburst at me either. I lied to her. I left soon after. I couldn't stand a repeat performance. I guess I was a coward.

"We went to the stables. I was feeding your horse, and who do we find? You, drunk and mad. Then you looked up at me and said I had pretty eyes. After that, you fell down into the mud. My men pulled you into the stables so you wouldn't drown, and you think after all that, you or anyone could force me?"

She said all this with no feeling at all, like she was talking about someone else. Her body gave away her emotions; her hands were curled into fists, and she was so angry she was shaking.

"I am sorry. Is there anything I can do to fix this?"

"No, I am finally free to do as I wish. No man is going to push me around or call me names anymore. The land is yours, but not me. I am done with it all and most especially you. Enjoy my home. It is a nice place to live."

She almost choked on the last words, and he knew she was crying, but he couldn't see her face as she was too far in the shadows.

She turned to walk out of the room. *Who is the father to her child, and why did he leave her here alone?* His curiosity was getting the better of him, and she was not going to voluntarily tell him. "I would like to ask you to stay for a few more days until I am updated on the land and people, please."

She simply nodded her head; she wouldn't look back at him.

There was one thing he could say when he screwed up—he did a good job of it. Later, he heard the door to her room open, and then his door opened quietly; even in the dark, she knew where she was. She leaned over him and gently laid her hand on his head, then felt his arm for swelling; then she turned and put another log on the fire. She quietly left the room without saying a word. When she left, he could hear her soft footsteps going up the stairs to the tower and the door open quietly.

It was sometime later that his curiosity got the better of him, and he went to the door; he looked up and saw her standing in the doorway just looking out at the ocean. She turned, shut the door, and started down the stairs; he quietly shut his door, but she didn't go to her room. James was waiting at the bottom and told her that John, the man she had been worried about, was much worse. Then he listened as she headed down the stairs. He wondered what she had been doing up there in the dark.

Good God, what had I done, and is there any way to fix it? But he was too tired to think about it now, so he returned to bed. He would check on her in a little while.

Cat made it downstairs to the man who was hurting; when she felt his leg, she knew why. The swelling was cutting off the circulation. She began to untie the bandage and release the pressure. The cut was worse than before, so she started all over again. She made him drink some of her tea and added a little laudanum to it for the pain.

"It's going to be all right, John. Just lay back."

"Will I lose the leg?"

"Most certainly not! Just let me do my work, and everything will be all right, I promise. Trust me." He looked over to James, and he winked at him, and he knew she would take care of him.

Once again, she started with the hot towels till it stopped pounding. After a while, he became drowsy, and she took a razor and went to really cleaning the dead tissue away. When she was done, it was going to have to be stitched, so she lightly woke him to tell him what she had to do. He looked at her a minute and agreed; then she gave him some more of her brew. When she was again ready, one of her men came to help and held him, and she went to stitching as quickly as possible. He didn't make a sound; he just watched her. When she was through, she looked up at him, smiled, and said, "That wasn't as bad as you expected, was it?"

"No, my lady, it was not. And if you ever need our help, please just ask. We have never been treated better than at this keep by you. James told us you were the lady of this keep."

"Yes, I was until your master arrived. Now the land belongs to him. This should make your leg feel better. I am not quite through. You still have a fever and a ways to go before you can walk, but that is enough for tonight." She started to put cool cloths on his head, and the men settled back down on their beds.

John asked her, "When you leave, how many men are you taking? Just the four I have seen and Robert?"

"Yes, you have been watching, haven't you? That is all I can afford. I don't have a whole lot of start-up money, and my men know that."

"We would like to offer our services. We are all able-bodied men, and we have lived in a lot worse conditions for no money. You have kept us fed and warm, and that is a lot more than some of the men we have worked for have ever done."

"You get to feeling better, and if that is still what you want to do, then we will talk again."

He lay back and went to sleep. Cat kept putting cold rags on his head and checking on his leg; it was beginning to look better. Sometime later, she laid her head on a rolled-up blanket against the wall and fell asleep. James came over, covered her with a clean blanket, and put more wood on the fire.

Hours later, Robert came down to see to feeding these men when he found Cat asleep on the wall; he then looked at James. "She wouldn't leave till he was better."

Robert reached down and gently shook her awake; she was so stiff she could barely move. "Put your arms around me, and I will take you upstairs."

"I am too heavy for you to be carrying me up those stairs. Let me check on the men, and you can help me up the stairs." She checked John's fever and then the other men's wounds; everyone seemed to be doing better. She drank the rest of the tea with the laudanum in it before she started up the stairs. She was so tired that she let Robert hold her arm as she limped up the stairs.

"Your leg is hurting again?"

She just nodded.

"If you wouldn't walk around this keep in the dark, you wouldn't fall."

Cat stopped him right there. "We are not having this lecture again. It was stupid. I just missed the last step and fell."

They had reached the top of the stairs, and she could hardly walk; she leaned against the wall. There were tears in her eyes.

"Just give me a minute." Robert leaned down, and she wrapped her arms around him and laid her face in his neck.

Robert asked, "You aren't sleeping, are you? Is that why you started roaming again?"

"Yes, there are still too many nightmares, and sometimes I can just get lost in the dark. He can't find me there."

This was the scene Giles saw when he came to his door, only to hear Catherine say, "I love you, old man. Don't ever forget that."

Giles was green with jealousy; that was the look Robert had waited for. He would regret ever hurting his lady. Robert put her down on his bed as Giles watched from the door. He covered her with a thick blanket and a quilt; this room was cold, but hers was freezing.

"Go back to sleep, little girl."

Then he kissed her lightly on her forehead.

The dawn was beginning to break, and the household was waking up, but he put her where she could still get some sleep while they worked on her room. Jennie had come to his room late last night with Beth because their room was like ice; they had slept on a pallet in his room until a while ago when he went to check on Cat. He added quite a bit more wood to the fire so this room would warm up some more.

Giles confronted Robert at the door to his room. "Where has she been all night? Did she sleep somewhere else?"

"Yes, she slept downstairs with her head propped up on the wall while she tended to your men. It is too cold in that other room for them to keep sleeping in there. Jennie came to my room with the baby late last night. The masons are going to fill the cracks in the walls so it will be warmer." The room had not been used in a long time, so they didn't realize it needed so much work. Cat hadn't planned on being here this long and hadn't checked it. Then he ushered Giles out so she could sleep. Giles was still looking daggers at Robert, and he couldn't help but smile to himself. Let him wonder; he was a fool to hurt her. He would see to it he regretted ever making her cry. He prayed again he would be able to keep her safe in their new land; it was the first time in his life he was not sure that what he was doing was the right thing. There was so little money and so much to do.

Giles walked into the room Catherine was supposed to have slept in, and Robert was right—it was freezing. It had better be a whole lot better tonight, or he would see to it they slept someplace else, like his room—that's where she should be anyway. If he hadn't acted like a fool, she would already be there. He walked on down the stairs to check on his wounded men, and as soon as he got there, he could see John was looking better. He started talking to each one of them, and all they could talk about was the goodness of the mistress of the keep. John didn't say much; he just kept watching him until Giles finally went over to his bed and quietly asked, "Is there something you wish to say to me?"

"She is such a good woman. Why would you turn her down?" "Did everybody know?"

"Because I am a fool."

"Yes, sir, you are a really big one."

After she had slept a few hours, Catherine went about her chores as usual except that Giles followed her to learn about how the keep was run. He began to notice that she was well liked by all the people around here; he also noticed she was limping today. She kept her distance not only from him but from every man who got close to her; sometimes it was not so obvious, but she didn't like to be touched, and she didn't like crowds. Robert was the only man who ever got close, and he generally kept a little distance, except when her arms were around his neck when he was carrying her to his room. This woman who would walk up to a warhorse was afraid of something, and he wanted to know why.

They went to the rooms where the accountant stayed to do the books and oversee the taxes and the farm accounts. He was a short little man who reminded Giles of a puppy he was so willing to please.

His name was Thomas Morgan, and he had been doing the books for ten years. Giles looked over everything and was pleased with the tallies and the way the books were kept. He decided that the man could keep doing the job he was so well suited for. Cat had overseen the books and land, and it was in very good shape; financially, he was a moderately wealthy man with four thousand acres of land. He hadn't noticed that Cat had left the room quietly some time ago, and he wondered where she had gone.

He went looking for her. He looked in the main hall and the kitchen, where they were baking bread; it smelled wonderful. He already felt like this was home. He finally found Jennie upstairs and asked, "Where is your lady?"

"I think she went to the stables."

He found her looking at his horse's leg and decided he liked just watching her. She was very good with the animals, so it seemed she just had a problem with men.

"I think his hoof is all right now. I will take this poultice off, and we will see." After she removed the poultice, she backed away.

One of her men took the big horse and walked him around, then came right back to her.

"It looks like it is much better. Just watch him and come get me if it gets worse. We need to get all of the animals in the stables or the barns where they will be out of this storm."

Cat just rubbed the horse's ear, gave him a handful of oats, and left the stables; but because she wasn't watching where she was going, she ran into Giles. He grabbed her arm to keep her from falling and then quickly let her go. She looked up, apologized, quickly backed up, and walked around him. He followed her back inside to find that she was having extra firewood brought in and quite a lot of it.

"Are you planning for an invasion?"

"The weather is fixing to turn bad. The clouds are rolling in."

As he turned, he could see the black clouds rolling in; he hadn't even noticed them until now. He was generally more aware of his surroundings than he had been lately.

"Does the weather get bad around here?"

"This time of year, it can get very bad very quickly. I would like to ask your permission to stay a while longer till the weather clears. I don't want to take a chance of getting caught in it with no protection."

"Certainly, but you do realize that things have changed, and you don't have to go at all?"

"As far as I can see, nothing has changed. We will leave as soon as the weather clears. You don't seem to understand the decision you made is the best thing that could have happened to me. I am finally free. I am sure you can find another woman. Maybe your mistress would like you back."

Giles was getting nowhere and didn't really know where to go from there, but he wasn't giving up yet. He had caught her looking at him a couple of times and thought he might still have a chance if he was careful. He looked again at the sky and realized that a storm was indeed coming and soon.

Giles and his men carried in cord after cord of wood and saw to the animals; he saw Cat roaming around in the stables, looking at a small covered wagon like where you would carry hay in.

He asked one of her men what the wagon was used for and was told Lady Catherine was leaving in it when she left. After everything was done, he went back to look at the cart; it wasn't very big and already contained boxes he assumed that had her clothes. He wondered if the pretty dress he hadn't seen her in was in there. Her plans didn't include much of anything to take with her. Where the hell was she going so lightly prepared?

When he went back in, he saw her in the bookkeeper's room going through a pile of papers; as he walked into the room, he startled her.

"I have some papers you need to see. They are papers of sale on two of the horses and a small wagon. I don't want you to think I stole from you."

"You are welcome to take anything you need, but I still wish you would reconsider. There wasn't much in your wagon."

"Robert has been preparing for our arrival at our new land. He has already taken many of our things there."

Of course Robert would know everything about this move.

"Is Robert going with you when you leave?"

"Yes, Robert and four other men I have hired who wish to come with us."

"You are taking the four men who are generally beside you in the stables and house?" Giles asked.

"Yes, I trust all of them, and they wish to accompany me and Jennie." She didn't tell him some of his own men had offered to go with her too; if they were well enough and still wanted to go, she was going to take them. She had learned all about each one while she was caring for them and trusted them as well.

She was going to leave his world, and he couldn't think of a way to stop her.

He read over the paperwork and signed the bottom of the page. She counted out the money agreed on and then asked, "I have two mares in foal, and they can't be taken with me now. Can I leave them here and return later to pick them and their foals up?"

"Yes, that will be fine. How much longer till they foal?"

"It will probably be several more weeks."

"Do you have money for this new home of yours?"

"Yes, when my mother died, left me a small inheritance, which had nothing to do with this land or my father."

He was running out of time, and she could take care of herself; she didn't need him, but he was afraid he needed her. He had never seen anyone who belonged to a place as much as she did here.

As she left the room, she had grabbed her cape and was headed out the front door with Robert close behind.

Giles asked, "Where are you going with a storm coming?"

"I need to go to the village and check on one of the women and make sure everything is protected from the storm."

"Wait, I am coming with you."

Great, all she needed now was a scene with the priest in the village; he was always so charming. They rode in silence. Cat was in a hurry to get back before the storm hit. Giles watched her ride; she rode a horse like she was a part of the animal. He could hardly keep up, and he was sure she was only going slowly because of Robert; she didn't care if he kept up or not. She stopped in front of the elder's house and was dismounting to go see Rachel. The elder met her at the door, and she could hear Rachel crying in the back room.

"Is Rachel all right? Is it the baby?"

"No, my lady, the priest won't let her attend church because she talked to you. And he is punishing her for it."

At about this time, Giles stepped up and asked, "What is this all about with the priest?"

Great, this was not what she wanted to do now—have the priest belittle her in front of him. So she started to explain, "He thinks I am a fallen woman, and Beth should have been given up when she was born. We are both a disgrace, according to him. Somehow, he found out that you refused me at court, and he likes to throw it in my face, and he is very good at it. He was just taking it out on me. Now it seems my villagers have to pay too." At about that time, the Father Thomas came to meet the new lord, and Catherine tried to introduce him to Giles.

"I don't need a woman like you to introduce me to our new lord. I would have thought you would be gone by now." When he turned to look at Giles, he knew he had made a mistake; he just wasn't sure what. Giles was angry.

"How dare you talk to this lady in such a manner? I have fought for ten years for king and church and will not have a priest around who does not respect the lady of this land.

"You will apologize now, and if I hear of you not letting any of the villagers into the church because they honor their lady, I will have your position filled by a new priest. Anything that was said at court is our business and not yours, so I don't expect to hear any more gossip about it from you."

Catherine hadn't said anything; it was the first time someone had put this man in his place, and to tell the truth, she enjoyed it. The priest looked at her with hatred in his eyes and said, "I apologize to you, my lady." But his words still sounded like a curse to her.

Rachel had heard everything and was grateful to this man for protecting her and Catherine from this man's hatred. "I am fine now, my lady."

"There is a storm coming. Is everything prepared? Is there enough food in case it lasts longer than a few days?"

"Everything is taken care of in the village, but you had best be returning before it hits. My lord, we will talk later when there is more time, and thank you. My lady doesn't deserve to be treated like that."

Giles followed Cat to her horse and helped her get in the saddle; then he mounted his horse. She turned to look back, and the priest was still looking daggers at her; this wasn't over between them, not yet.

They began to head home; the snow was beginning to fall, and the temperature was dropping quickly. They reached the keep just minutes before they couldn't see in front of them.

Giles kept looking at her; he didn't realize how much she had to put up with because of this situation, and his actions had not helped. It seemed too many people had heard what was said at court. It was no wonder she wanted to leave; certain people around here had made her life a living hell.

When they returned, she headed down to check on the injured men; she felt more at ease without Giles looking over her shoulder. John was looking better; they all were, and she had brought down a pair of crutches for when he started walking. Giles had followed her but stopped on the stairs so nobody could see him, but he could still hear what was going on. He could hear John talking to her about coming with her to her new home; he didn't know about this.

"Have you thought it over, my lady, about us going with you?"

"Yes, quite a bit. But I want you to realize I can't afford to pay you. My other men know this and are willing to wait until I can collect some rents. I will see to it that you are warm and fed. There is plenty of room in this new building for us all, but it is going to be a lot of work. Do you think that Lord Giles will object to this idea of yours?"

"The wars are over, and I don't think he will need us, but you will."

"All right, it is settled then. You will leave with me when I go."

They all started to get up at the same time. Cat was wondering what was going on, and she asked, "What are you doing?"

"We will swear allegiance to you."

"That is not necessary. You will rip out all my pretty stitches."

Then he reached for her hand. Giles started down the stairs to stop him, but she put her hand out to him, and he kissed it as did each man. Great, she trusted them more than she trusted him. She smiled and just said, "Thank you. I promise I will take care of each of you." Her men watched as they sat back down.

Giles thought, *when this woman gets your loyalty, she gets it all.*

"My lady, we don't mean to be a bother, but we were wondering if maybe there was a chess set around that we could use?"

"You know, I think there is one of my father's upstairs. I will see if I can find it and have it sent down to you. I will check on you men later. If you need me, just ask. I am having some extra wood brought down here. It is fixing to get cold. If you need help getting the fireplace stoked, just ask one of my men."

Even his own men wished to stay near her; that was good if he couldn't stop her from leaving, but now he knew she was going with almost no money, and that really worried him. He had to try and stop her.

He walked back up the stairs, and before anyone saw him or knew what he was doing, he went into the accountant's office. He found her metal box, and he counted the money in it and was appalled at how little she had. When he left the office, the box had several hundred more gold pieces than when he came in. If he couldn't stop her, he wasn't going to let them starve; anyway, he intended to go after her if she left, but they had to survive until he convinced her here was where she needed to be.

After supper, Giles went to his bedroom. Catherine had gone up earlier to put the baby to bed. She kept Beth out of his sight and out of his way almost like she was afraid he would hurt her. She hadn't come to tend to his cut, and he was almost ready to knock on her door when she knocked on his.

"I need to change the bandages on your arm."

She entered and began getting everything ready; the wind was starting to howl against the tower and almost sounded like a moan. She was again wearing the blue robe and gown, and he wondered if she had anything warmer.

"Is your room warm enough? I thought it was a little cold the other day."

"It is much better now." He knew Robert had workmen in there today sealing some old cracks in the walls so it would be warmer.

This was the most frustrating woman he had ever met; you couldn't shut up most of them, but Catherine wouldn't say anything—at least not to him. His men knew more about this woman than he had been able to find out, and he wasn't about to ask Robert.

"By the way, I don't want any payment for the things you want to take with you. I think it is little enough for a lifetime of care on this place. I even think you should take more."

"I don't think that is necessary. I just want to start over and build a home and life for me and Beth—something that is mine again even if it isn't this grand."

"You never told me where you planned to go from here. What are your plans?"

"I have a place to go that was left to me by my mother. She was a Celt, so a woman can inherit some of her land."

"I have already told you that you should stay. We could make some sort of accommodation." He should have looked closer at those papers and seen where she was going; he would look tomorrow because at this rate, he was going to have to go after her and bring her back. She was the most stubborn woman he had ever met. Then he smiled; she would be worth the chase.

"The only accommodation I can see is to be your mistress, and I won't do that for you or anyone else. I really don't know what it is you want from me. I was not good enough at court, and I just don't care what you think anymore." And again, he wondered how she got pregnant in the first place, and he couldn't get that information from anyone. There had to have been a man in her life at some time. She started to remove the bandage from his arm.

She was just getting started on his arm when it sounded like the ceiling was coming down around them. They looked at each other and then to the door; all Catherine could say was, "Beth."

She ran across the hall and pushed on the door; it wouldn't move. She kept pushing until Giles moved her out of the way. He rammed it with his shoulder, and it began to move.

He finally got it open enough to see Jennie holding the baby and standing just inside the door. Giles got her and the baby out of the room and looked in to see the ceiling was cracked open around the fireplace, and water was pouring in; it had sounded like one of the tower stones had toppled off the wall. They were still doing repairs up there. The room was already getting cold because the fire was out.

"Can you take the baby to another room where she will be warmer till we can get this repaired?" He turned in time to see Catherine headed up the stairs to the roof. He yelled at her to stop, but she kept on going. "The door isn't bolted!" He followed her, and they reached the top at almost the same time. The door didn't have the bar across it, and it exploded inward, knocking Cat backward. Giles caught her with one arm and grabbed the railing with the other. She began to struggle with a vengeance. Giles didn't know what to do except hold her tighter, and when that made matters worse, he yelled, "If you won't be still, we are both going down these stairs!"

She realized he was right, and she froze; he was holding on for both of them, and his arm was bleeding. It had to hurt, but he didn't let go of her. Gerard was coming up the stairs two steps at a time; he got around Giles as he held on to Catherine. Then he got the brace across the door.

Catherine finally got her balance and stood on the top step; she turned around and looked at Giles. His arm was bleeding everywhere. She was embarrassed; he had saved her life, and she couldn't even look him in the eyes.

"We had better take care of that before you bleed to death." At least she let him hold on to her arm as they went down the stairs.

"Be careful. I don't want you falling down the stairs again." She just looked at him. How did he know what had happened to her knee? Only Robert knew. They headed downstairs.

"I need to check on Jennie and the baby. I will be back in a minute."

"I had Jennie take the baby elsewhere to keep her warm. She is probably with Robert. You can't use that room until it is repaired."

He told Gerard to bring a pallet into his room for Cat to sleep on; she couldn't sleep in there either. It was already freezing, and they couldn't start repairs until the weather cleared.

He told Catherine, "Grab a clean gown and bring it to my room. You can change by the fire. You are soaked and have blood on you." He didn't leave until she was out of the room; then they headed to his room.

Catherine hung her gown by the fire and prepared to repair his arm. They had pulled her door shut to keep the cold out of the other rooms.

"Catherine, you are soaked to the bone. You have to change clothes. You can wear my robe till we can get your clothes dry."

"I will be fine. I will fix your arm and then change."

"You are already shivering. Just change your clothes and hang them by the fireplace to dry now before you get sick. Don't worry, I won't watch."

"All right, but let me at least bind that arm to stanch the bleeding."

After she had wrapped his arm with a towel and started the water boiling, she took his robe off the end of the bed. She turned toward the fireplace and began to unlace her dress, but she couldn't get the wet laces to unknot. He was trying not to watch but didn't see the problem because when she walked in front of the fire, it made her wet gown transparent; she could have been standing there naked, and he couldn't have seen much more.

She timidly asked for some help with untying the laces, and then she could finish. He got up to help her, but not touching her was going to be a problem; he had never wanted a woman so badly. She grabbed her hair and pulled it to the front of her dress; there was that braid again. He really wanted to see her hair down. He couldn't seem to get the laces started either, so he asked, "Can I cut these top ones? I can't get them loose." She just nodded; there was a small knife on the side table, and he cut through several of the laces before it began to come off.

He was going to let her finish when he saw the scar. She tried to pull away, but the more she moved, the more the gown fell off her back. She grabbed the front to hold it up. He began to peel away the dress, and she tried to move away.

He put his bandaged arm under her breast to keep her still and saw there were lash marks on her back, and the more he pulled the dress down, the more damage he saw. He began to cut the laces lose all down the back of the dress. There were marks on the side, and he realized someone had hung her up to beat her. He couldn't believe what he was seeing. Giles couldn't understand how anyone would have the nerve to punish a lady of the court in this manner.

She was trying to pull away while still holding the front of what remained of the dress as it fell down around her waist. He turned her around, put his finger under her chin, and lifted her head up.

She was trying not to cry, and she wouldn't look him in the face. The gown was literally falling off her; she held it across her breasts to keep it up, but all it really did was give him a view of those breasts he so liked to look at. There was also a filigree gold cross hung around her neck; he hadn't seen before. It must have always been under her chemise.

He was furious, and all he could say was, "Who dared to do this to you, Catherine?"

She had forgotten how bad her back still looked; she was embarrassed for anyone to see it. She backed away then looked up at him. "I am sorry. I know how ugly it is." She was shivering so badly; her teeth were chattering. He grabbed his fur robe and started to put it on her when she started to back away.

He just said, "Stop, Catherine. I won't hurt you. Come here."

She stood still, long enough for him to put the robe on her; then he said, "I am not worried about how it looks. I want to know who did it."

She couldn't look at him as she explained. "Almost three years ago, four women and I were captured by some Northern raiders. It was the wrong time of year for them to be raiding, so there were no guards with us. One of the raiders took offense at my trying to defend my women and began to use a whip on me. They led us to their camp behind them, and when we fell, they dragged us. When we got to the camp, he tied me to a post and continued to beat me. I guess he got tired and stopped, but he left me hanging on the post. When their leader came into the camp, he cut me down and carried me to his tent. He tried to tend to my back."

She was apologizing to him for someone beating the hell out of her; now he understood why Robert wouldn't leave her alone anywhere.

"What else happened?"

"I don't remember much. There was too much pain from my back. All I do remember is he fed me and gave me something for the pain. I seemed to float in and out of clouds of pain, but I remember him telling me I was going back home with him. All I seemed to do was sleep, and I remember him holding me. All the rest is a blur."

There was something she wasn't saying, but he wasn't going to push it now.

"They started to load their boat, and while they were gone, Robert found me and two of the others and got us out of there."

"Is he the father of Beth?"

"Yes."

"Why didn't you tell me this at court?"

"You didn't talk to me, remember? Besides, my back is so disgusting and ugly. I didn't want anyone to know."

"Why didn't the king tell me of this?"

"No one knew except the people here and that condescending priest."

Everything began to fall into place; her reluctance to let anyone touch her and her blonde-haired child. He had wondered since he had gotten here how any man could not want this woman and her child, especially him. He reached out to touch her, and she began to back away.

"You offered yourself to me in marriage feeling like you do about men touching you and kept a child of rape. Why?"

"I thought it would get better, and I wouldn't be so afraid if you were my husband. Beth is my child no matter who her father is, and I was trying to keep my land. I know my back is ugly, but I didn't know what else to do."

"You told the queen, didn't you?"

"Yes, she thought when you got to know me, it wouldn't matter. But then everything fell apart."

He wanted to touch her and comfort her, but he didn't know how. She was very afraid to look up at him; she knew how unattractive she must look to him, and now he knew how she had tried to trick him. If she knew how much he still wanted her, she would still be afraid. He tried to control himself so he wouldn't scare her.

"Don't run from me. I promise I won't ever hurt you or let anyone else hurt you or Beth. I would like to make this right between us. Do you think you could try? Look at me, Catherine."

He reached out to hold her, and this time, she didn't back away even though it took everything she had not to. He held her in his arms while she just stood stiff as a board. He promised to himself that if he ever found who did this to her, he would kill him. He held her as long as she would let him, and then she backed away. She let the wet gown drop to the floor and tied the robe around her.

After a time, she rewrapped his arm; then she put on her dry gown behind the screen he had brought in for her. All he could do was watch because she had managed to stay just out of his reach while she tended his arm. When she was through, she lay down on the pallet Gerard had prepared for her to sleep on near the fireplace. She couldn't sleep in that damp, cold room, and there was nowhere else to go. Beth was already asleep with Jennie, and Cat didn't want to wake her. He watched her for a while and thought to himself, *she is what I have always wanted for a wife and a mother*. Somehow, he was going to convince her of his feelings. He wasn't going to let her or Beth out of his life because he might never find this again, and he would see to it no one would ever hurt her again as long as he was around.

He couldn't sleep, so he just watched her. Sometime during the night, he heard whimpering; he had heard it before and assumed it was just the old keep and the wind. She cried out then mumbled to herself; he couldn't understand what she was saying, but it seemed like she was asking someone to stop. He got out of the bed walked to the pallet and lay down next to her as he put his arm over her and gently pulled her to him. She opened her eyes and tensed up, but he just said, "Go back to sleep. It is all right. You are safe with me, and I won't touch you any further." However, he wanted to, but she was so stiff that he wondered if she would ever be comfortable with him. He would see to it no one else ever touched her; she was going to be his somehow.

He pulled his heavy robe over them and just held her. She relaxed and went back to sleep; it was the first time in a long time that she really did feel safe. She didn't know how long it would last, but it was all right for tonight.

He felt her relax for the first time, and he just wanted to hold her and drink the smell of her in. It was all he could do not to unbraid her hair so he could feel his fingers run through it, but he just lay still and held on to her. Sleep was a long time coming. He had a lot of thinking to do if he was going to get her to stay, so he just held her and thought of ways to convince her that this was the right thing to do.

Cat slept peacefully for the first time in a long time with no nightmares.

He had never felt like this with any other woman he had known; he just wanted to keep her close to him and wanted her forgive him. He fell asleep close to morning but awoke when she began to move out from under him.

"Where are you going?"

"Beth will be awake, and she wants to be fed. So I am going to the other room."

"No, you are not. It is too cold in there for both of you. Feed her in here where it is warm."

"Not in front of you."

"I have seen a woman feed a baby before, even you."

She got up, went to get the baby, and brought her to the other side of the room where a rocker sat. She turned it around and sat down; she opened her gown and began to feed Beth. He could see the baby's hand playing with her gown as she rocked and hummed to her little girl.

He decided it was as good a time as any to talk to her because she couldn't run away.

"I want you to reconsider the contract you proposed to me at court, and this time, I will not only consider it but also accept it with all the terms entailed."

She was quiet for a minute while she thought about it, then said, "Why change your mind now that you know everything about me and Beth? I am still a lady with a bastard child, and now you know that I am disfigured, I assumed you would be glad you made the decision you did and let me leave."

"I am not disgusted by your back. It was none of your doing. It makes me mad that anyone ever hurt you like that. As for Beth, most women would have gotten rid of her as soon as she was born. Instead, you love her unconditionally even if it cost you your land to do it. I don't think I have ever met a woman with your strength or your knowledge, and I would be proud to have you as my wife. I think we would be good together if you will give it a try. Will you at least consider it?"

She closed her dress and burped the baby; then she started for the door. She stopped and turned to look at him and just said, "Yes, I will consider it." She couldn't tell him that last night was the first time in a long time she had actually felt safe and even a little content, and it was because of him. She wasn't sure she wanted anyone to have that kind of control over her life again.

She dressed in Robert's room down the hall where Jennie had spent the night on a pallet with Beth and started her day's chores. She went down to the kitchen first to get the day's menu started. When she got down there, Helen was waiting for her as she had ever since she was a young girl. Helen saw him coming and couldn't imagine a more handsome man. He was so tall that he even towered over Cat, and most men couldn't do that. He reached out to touch Catherine's arm, and she tried her best not to move away from him. Helen saw all of this and was impressed because she knew how Cat felt about being touched. She didn't know what had happened at court; no one ever spoke of it, but it seemed this man was trying to make up for it. She hoped he would be successful because she didn't want her mistress to leave or be alone anymore. Cat had been alone most of her life because her father was always gone and had left her in charge until he didn't come home at all. He had gone off to fight for the king and got himself killed; it was very hard to grieve for a man you didn't like.

Catherine gave the day's instructions to Helen and then turned to Giles and asked, "Is this satisfactory with you, or do you wish to make changes to the menu?"

"The menu is the prerogative of the lady of the house."

He looked at Helen, who was smiling, and just nodded.

She just looked at him and wondered what she was going to do. His proposal was giving her a headache. She began to walk out the kitchen door, and he followed her out.

"I need some time to think alone. I am going out to the meadow."

"Not alone you're not. If you won't let me come with you, then I will get Robert. Wait for him here. I will tell him to go with you, all right?"

She nodded yes, but when he turned to go, she left as well. She went to the front door and opened it and left it slightly ajar; she knew that Robert would know where she was and would leave her alone because the fog was rolling in. She had also brought her walking stick so she could get up the hill to her grandmother's grave, even limping. She started climbing the hill to the gravesite.

Giles had found Robert, and they were headed for the kitchen when Robert saw the front door open and the fog outside and turned toward the door. When he got to the door, he just stood there and listened; and when Giles came up next to him, he told Giles to stop and leave her alone. She was all right.

"How do you know she is all right? Where is she?"

"I know where she is, and she wants to be left alone for a while. She will tell us when she is coming back."

"And how will she do that?"

"Before she leaves, she sings a hymn to her grandmother that her grandmother used to sing, and we will hear her."

He noticed that the entire room was quiet; she had done this before, and they knew she would do it again. "She has been singing to her grandmother since the day she died every time she goes to visit her." Helen was standing at the kitchen door, and the guards out front had stopped chatting and were just listening.

"Why is she out there in this weather? The fog is getting heavier, and it is beginning to rain," Giles asked Robert angrily.

"I was kind of hoping you might have the answer for that. She generally only goes walking in the fog when she has something bothering her, and that seems to be you lately."

"I told her I would accept the proposal with all the provisions, the way she wanted them in the first place, if she would marry me."

"And what did she say?"

"I guess that is what she is deciding." They could hear a soft melody and see her walking through the rain back into the keep; she looked like a wraith with her cape down and dripping rain. Robert looked at Giles and smiled. When Giles looked around the room, it was empty; they all knew she was back and safe. This woman was strange sometimes.

He would certainly like to see his mistress happy, and this man seemed to be a good man even after what happened at court. Something had changed in his lady to even have her consider his proposal.

The rest of the day went as usual; they kept to their schedules even though Giles kept an eye on Cat all the time. She was cold when she got back, so he made her sit in front of the fire till her cheeks were red, and he knew that she was warm. Robert sat down beside her and asked, "What is going on? Are you really considering taking his offer?"

"He told me he would agree to all the terms of the contract if I would think about it."

Robert just looked at her and said, "I will do whatever you decide. Just be sure before you consent that this is truly what you want. Does he know of your feelings about men and the Raider Chieftain?"

"Yes, he knows it all." Robert had his doubts about that because she still wore the Raider cross around her neck, but he would see how this would play out; maybe he was wrong about her feelings toward the Raider.

Giles had made arrangements with Jennie to keep Beth in her room tonight so he could talk to Catherine alone. Jennie went to Cat to make sure that it was all right as she was still her mistress and friend no matter what even if Giles was the new master. Catherine thought it was fine; they needed to get this taken care of before she went crazy.

She still didn't know if she could do this; it took all she had just to let him touch her. She went down the stairs to check on the injured men and discovered the chessboard she had sent down was being used. They were playing on the small table she had brought down. She watched for a bit but didn't want to disturb them; they looked to be having fun.

James turned and saw her and immediately stood up and asked, "Would you like to play, my lady? You can have my place."

"No, you look like you are having fun, and I don't play very well." Several of the men offered to teach, and she politely refused. "Maybe another time when we have more time."

James knew better; he had played her many times and knew how good she really was.

At about this time, Giles had followed her downstairs and saw what was going on and asked, "May I play the winner?"

John answered him, "Yes, my lord. We will be through in a minute. I almost have him."

Cat put her hand over her mouth to stifle the grin on her face because she knew how good a player James was. He used to play her father all the time and he generally won. The two kept playing for a few more minutes, and Cat was right—James won the game. John just looked at her; the young man was very good. Then Giles sat down, and Cat was still smiling; it wasn't long before Robert heard them and came down to see what was going on. The game was a tense one; every time Giles thought he had James, he got around him again. Cat couldn't keep from laughing at Giles when James called checkmate; he looked so confused. He wasn't paying enough attention to the game; he was too busy watching Cat. It was the first time he had actually seen her enjoying herself.

"How did you do that? You are going to have to teach me that move!"

James had a wide grin as he said, "Yes, sir, anytime."

"Keep playing. I have some things I need to attend to." She wasn't sure anyone heard her; they had already started another game so Giles could learn that move. She didn't realize she had a big grin on her face as she left the cellar room to climb the stairs or that both Giles and Robert saw she was limping again.

Giles finally asked Robert, "Catherine is still limping. How bad was the fall she took?"

"I am not sure. She doesn't want me to know. She fell one night in the dark going down the stairs from the tower and hurt her knee and foot."

"What was she doing up there?"

"She walks in the dark when she can't sleep, and that has been happening a lot lately. She has nightmares, bad ones, about the man who hurt her."

"Do you know why the tower? Is she looking for something?"

"That is a question you will have to ask Cat.

CHAPTER 3

The day crept by, and by the time the sun set, Catherine was in a panic; she didn't know what to do. She had already fed Beth and then started to his room when she decided she just couldn't do it; instead, she went downstairs and into the accountant's room, where she knew nobody would bother her. This was crazy. What was she thinking? This fear she had was overwhelming, and she didn't know how to get rid of it. No one else was around, and she just sat there and began to cry. She had enjoyed herself today, but that was different; there were a lot of people she knew around. She wasn't alone with him.

Giles was waiting in his room impatiently until he finally went to look for her. He went to the room down the hall, but she wasn't there. Jennie said she had left a while ago. When he went downstairs, he looked in the kitchen and the main rooms and finally found her in the accountant's office. She was gathering up some papers into a pile to put in the metal box and counting out her money. He wanted her out of here before she realized he had put more money in her box and took it out.

"Catherine, what are you doing down here? I thought we were going to talk."

"I don't think I can do this. Just let me leave, please."

"Not until you talk to me."

"Don't you understand? I can't be what you want me to be." She was crying as she said, "This was a mistake on my part for even starting this. I don't know how to please a man or even let one touch me. I am absolutely terrified of being a disappointment again. The baby and I are leaving tomorrow, and then you can find a suitable woman to be with. This has to be the stupidest thing I have ever done."

He wasn't sure what had happened since this afternoon, but she had worked herself up into frenzy about something since then. There was nothing else to do; he leaned over, picked her up, and started up the stairs. She started to struggle, but he said, "Catherine, be still. We are going to talk, and I apologize for that comment about forcing you. I didn't understand. It was stupid of me to even say it." He carried her up the stairs; and then he pushed open the door with his foot, put her down, turned, and locked it.

She looked like a deer caught by some hunter; she was terrified, and he wasn't exactly sure what to do. Then he said, "You are not going anywhere until we have settled this."

He walked toward her, and she started to back away. He said, "Catherine, stand still. I won't touch you if you don't want me to."

He wondered what kind of father would do this to his beautiful daughter. What could he have been thinking? Then her first man had been a nightmare of pain.

He didn't know exactly how to start, so he took both of her hands in his hands and looked her in the eye and said, "I don't remember much about the night at the castle or what I said about you, but whatever it was, I was wrong. I know that this should have started out all differently. So just let me start again, and I will try to do better."

"How can it be right? I don't know how to change the way I feel about being touched."

"What happened wasn't your fault and can't be changed, and you are not disfigured in my eyes. I know you are scared, but it is all right. We will take this slow until you feel comfortable. It won't be like before. You might even come to like being with me. Just give it a try."

She just looked at him like he had to be crazy. There was no way this could be anything but painful. Jennie had told her it could be fun, but Cat just couldn't believe it. Everything in her life had always been a struggle, even with her father.

She just stood there, waited, and closed her eyes. Then Giles said to her, "Open your eyes and look at me. I promise not to hurt you."

She opened her eyes, and he turned her around and began to undo her hair; he had wanted to see it down since he had first seen her in the meadow. He undid the braid and smoothed it out with his fingers as he ran them down her back. Her hair felt like silk; it was so soft. He turned her around so he could see her face. She was shaking even though it was warm in the room. She was so beautiful, and he didn't know how to take her fear away; then she suddenly asked him, "Do you think I am pretty?"

It was such a ludicrous question he almost laughed; then he saw she was serious.

"Yes, you are a beautiful woman. Why do you ask?"

"My father always told me that I had enough land and title to secure a husband, but those seemed to be the only reasons to marry me. I just wondered."

"Your father was a fool. He was so busy trying to make you his son he forgot to let you be a woman. No man in his right mind would have ever mistaken you for anything but a lovely woman and mother. If I had been a smart man, I would have known this when I met you at court. But as you have seen, I am not always a smart man. There is no one I have ever met that handles horses the way you do. I will never understand how you do that. They trust you unconditionally. And to watch you ride is beautiful. You take my breath away when you are on a horse. Trust me, and I will make this up to you."

"I always wondered what people thought of me."

"From what I have seen and heard, most people think of you as I do, even a Raider chieftain. Does that answer your question?"

He gently leaned forward and pulled her to him; he just stroked her hair and held her in his arms.

He lifted up her face to look at him and leaned down and gave her a tentative kiss. She was still stiff, but she didn't back away. It was now or never, and he had to give it a try. Giles nibbled down her neck, and still, she trembled. But it was somehow different now. He loved the way her hair felt and the taste of her skin; then he put his hands on either side of her face and kissed her, but she didn't kiss him back.

"Kiss me back, Cat. Just try." He leaned down to kiss her again, and she returned the kiss if somewhat hesitantly. He backed up a step or two, and he dropped the robe he was wearing; he just had a loincloth on as she looked at him. She couldn't believe how soft his skin always looked; she wanted to reach out and touch him when she worked on his arm but was afraid to. He took her hand, put it on his chest, and said, "Touch me." She began to stroke the curly hair without even realizing she was doing it.

He stood still and let her explore even though he was about to explode; he wanted to touch her so badly. She ran her hands over his chest and then looked up at him and touched his face. Her touch was so light he wasn't sure she was actually touching him. She ran her fingers lightly over his lips, and it tickled. He was afraid to move until she finally looked up at him and smiled; then he reached up to take her hand and lightly kissed her fingers. A little shiver ran up and down her arm, but for a change, it wasn't out of fear. He smoothed the hair away from her face and stroked her skin. He gently reached down to unlace the gown she was wearing. When it fell to the floor around her feet, she again froze; he then leaned down to kiss her again. She still didn't return the kiss; she just stood there. He took her in his arms, brought her close to him, and kissed her again; this time, she returned his kiss. They continued to kiss till he could feel her relax a bit. He picked her up like she was made of glass and laid her on the bed; he spread out her hair around her, and it looked like a halo of silk. He lay down next to her and began to stroke the skin down her arms and across her stomach. She felt like velvet under his hands even though she was still shaking.

He began to kiss little kisses across her face and down her neck to her breasts; it was all he could do to go slow. He wanted to explore every inch of her with his hands. She began to relax and touch him back.
She ran her hands across his back; just touching him was more than she had ever done with any man. She liked the feel of his skin against her, and she began to feel like she was on fire. She began to get a funny feeling in the pit of her stomach. She put her face against his chest and could hear his heart beat.

"See, just like any other man—only it beats faster when you are near me."

He kissed her again, and this time, she kissed back as she pulled him to her. She didn't know exactly what she wanted, but she knew he would teach her what to do. His hands cupped her breast; he placed a kiss on one of them, and she jumped. He wanted to caress all of her, but she wouldn't let him touch her back, so he didn't push it.

He used his finger to explore and see if she was ready to take him inside of her, and to his surprise, she was. He quickly removed the loincloth he was wearing and gently rolled on top of her. She began to tense up again, and he said, "Just kiss me and let me do the rest. It will be better this time, and I won't hurt you."

He entered her slowly till he was all the way in, and he looked at her. She said, "Don't stop."

That was all it took as he began an easy rocking motion, but he knew he couldn't last long; he had wanted her for much too long. Too soon, he had spent his seed in her, and he began to move off her.

"Catherine, it will be better next time. I wanted you too badly to restrain myself."

"Don't apologize. It was very nice." This was not exactly the enthused response he wanted. "Is that how it is supposed to be?"

"Yes, if you love the one you are with." He then realized he truly meant what he was saying. "I love you, Catherine, and I have never said those words to anyone else."

She looked at him with a crooked little smile and said, "I am glad I was the first to hear those words from you."

Then she began to stroke his face, rock underneath him, and kiss his neck as he had kissed hers. All of the sudden, he was ready to go again. Life with this lady was about to become very interesting because it seemed he had awoken a sleeping tiger. They made love again slowly, and this time, Giles mad sure she got some of the release she didn't even know that she wanted. It was the best lovemaking he had ever had, but she still hadn't said she loved him or would marry him. He rolled off her but continued to hold her in his arms; he could stay like this forever. He pulled the blanket up to cover them and then looked down at her with his head propped on his hand.

"I want you to bear my children. We will give Beth a brother or sister to play with if you will have me."

She didn't answer. She just looked at him. But it really didn't matter right now because she was his, and with any luck, she would already be carrying his child. The next time she used those pretty breasts, it would be to feed their babies. If not, they would just have to keep working on that; he did like that thought a lot.

Now he just had to convince her to marry him. He felt he had at least a chance now; a woman like her would want a wedding to go with this relationship, he hoped.

She closed her eyes and just lay in his arms, and he couldn't think of a time he felt so happy; this was his woman and his land. He would finally have the home and family he had always wanted.

When she knew he was finally asleep, she crept out of the bed, picked up her gown, and put it on. She went to the far side of the room where there was no light shining from the fireplace and opened the window; she just looked into the dark as the wind whipped her hair around her.

She looked out to the sea again and then at the land that could still be hers and she just didn't know what to do. She had secretly thought about trying to find the Raider who was Beth's father, but no one else knew this. She fingered the small cross he had given her and just looked out to the ocean. No one but her knew what had happened in those few days she was with him; all she knew was he had wanted her. It was the first time she had felt like something that her father couldn't use to trade for this land. Truth was she had wanted him too.

Giles now wanted her, but she wasn't sure that was still what she wanted. How do you forget a man you hardly knew but still lingered in your memory and in a small corner of your heart and saw in the face of your child every day? She wondered if he would have been disappointed in his little girl the way her father was of her. There were times she could still feel him touching her and telling her how much he wanted her; it was the first time she had heard those words until tonight. Maybe Giles words were just a lie. The breeze was cool coming off the ocean as she stood there. She had waited almost three years and nothing—she was still alone. Maybe it was time to let someone else into her heart.

Sometime later, he awoke to find her gone, but he could faintly see her at the end of the room. He just watched for a minute; he could see she was thinking about something, but he wasn't sure what. She was crying, and as he watched, he finally figured it out; she was looking for him all this time. He was the wall. He got out of bed and grabbed his fur robe because it was freezing in here. He walked over to her and closed his arms around her with his robe. He put his chin on her shoulder and spoke softly onto her ear, "He isn't coming back, Catherine. If he was, he would be here by now. I think the only thing that would have kept him from coming back for you is death. That is the only thing that would have kept me from you." He kissed her lightly on the shoulder; she leaned her head back against him. Maybe the wall was falling one brick down.

"Let's go back to bed." As they started back across the room, he said, "You have to take off that gown. It is soaking wet." She dropped it on the floor, and he hung it by the fireplace to dry while he put more wood on to heat up the room. When he lay down next to her, he pulled her close. She was cold as ice, but she didn't struggle. "You have got to sleep, Catherine."

She turned to her side, put her hand on his face, and lightly kissed him. Then she said, "Maybe tonight I will."

She wondered if Lars would be in her dreams tonight or if Giles had pushed him away. Maybe tonight she would dream of a tall dark-haired man who said he loved her, but she was afraid it would still be the shadow man who haunted her in her dreams.

All the next day, Giles had a smile on his face; he couldn't stop thinking about last night. Cat had left before he awoke, and he had slept better than he had in years; he felt so good, and it was all because of a green-eyed woman.

Cat went about her chores as if nothing had happened until Jennie came to her in the kitchen.

"I need to talk to you if you have a minute."

"What is the problem?"

"The new lord is having your things moved into his room as we speak."

Catherine just looked at her then turned to go find Giles. She found him outside at the stables, and when she caught up to him, she said, "I need to talk to you now."

He could see she was upset and was sure he knew why.

"Why are you having my things moved into your room?"

"I thought we had everything settled."

"All we have settled is I had sex with you. I still haven't decided about marrying you."

"And what if you are pregnant with my baby?"

"I raised one child alone. I can raise another alone."

"No, you can't. We will be married as soon as possible. Remember you signed a contract, and I have already sent Gerard to retrieve it from King Charles."

She knew that Gerard had left this morning, but she didn't know where he was going.

"I don't want my things moved until we are married. I don't want my people to think I am your mistress.

"All right does this mean that you will marry me?"

She looked like she wanted to stomp on him; this was not the way she had planned this.

"Yes, it seems I have little choice."

"You have a choice, and I hoped it would be to marry me because you wanted to."

"I just wanted to make the decision myself, not have it made for me. Some man in my life has always had the final say in what I am to do."

Finally, he had the answer he wanted. Even though she didn't want to move into his room, she would soon be his, and everything would be all right. He could wait, but not for too long; he wanted her beside him as soon as possible, but he would need to be patient.

Catherine started to walk back to the keep as Jennie came running toward her. Jennie was out of breath and could barely talk as she said, "Mistress, please, I need your help. There is a young boy downstairs, and he has been hurt. The master's men won't let me touch him."

Catherine followed her to the basement of the keep, where there was indeed a small boy bleeding on a stack of sacks with a large cut on his leg.

"Why isn't this child on a bed and someone caring for him?"

"He is not one of ours. The master picked him up at a raided village standing over his dead mother. I don't want this boy's blood on my bed. We just keep him around for errands."

Catherine looked at the boy's leg, and the cut was deep; she grabbed a towel out of her apron and held it over the cut.

"Jennie, can you carry him while I hold his leg? We will take him to the little room at the back of the kitchen." Jennie picked him up and started toward the stairs.

Kevin, the man Giles had slapped with the dog, blocked her way. "Where are you taking the brat? You didn't get my permission to move him."

"Move now."

"Or what will you do?" He didn't see Giles, who had followed her inside when he saw her and Jennie running to the house. Kevin stepped back; he knew better than to mess with Giles. It was the woman he disliked anyway.

"Get out of the way and don't ever talk to Lady Catherine again in that manner."

Giles took the little boy out of Jennie's hands and started up the stairs with Cat holding his leg. Jennie led the way to the room at the back of the kitchen and pulled back the covers of a small bed. Giles laid the boy on the bed and backed out of the way. Catherine pulled back the pants leg covering the cut and looked at the damage; it was a deep cut. Jennie looked pale as a ghost, and Cat directed her to get clean towels and water from the kitchen.

"Is this the child I brought with me to the keep? I wondered what happened to him."

"They were using him as an errand boy downstairs. That man with the dog was responsible for him. Why did you not look after his care if you were going to take him with you?"

"I forgot about him with everything else going on around here."

"Well, Jennie seems very concerned about him even though this is the first I have seen of him, so now he is mine. Would you please keep that man away from me and any of my people? He is dangerous."

Jennie came back into the room with the towels and water, and Catherine started to hunt for the needle in her bag, then looked up at Jennie and asked, "What is his name? Do you know it?"

"His name is William, and I have been watching out for him the last few days. I was going to talk to you about him today, and that is when I found him hurt. That man had him dragging the axes they were using to cut wood back and forth to the keep. They didn't even plan on helping him, just let him die."

Catherine set about getting a needle ready to stitch him up and told Jennie, "You are going to have to hold him. He is hardly conscious, but I don't want to hurt him more." Catherine cut open the little boy's pants so she could get to the cut easier. He was filthy, so she cleaned his leg thoroughly before she started to stitch him up.

Jennie sat down on the bed, pulled the child into her lap, and held him tight to her as if she could keep the hurt away from him. Catherine saw all this as did Giles standing behind her. Catherine started putting small stitches in the young man's leg, and he began to moan, but it had to be done. So she did it as quickly as she could. The rest of the little boy was filthy, and she was trying to wash him when Giles said, "Bring him upstairs. We can bathe him in the tub. I will have warm water sent up." Jennie picked him up, and Giles said, "Give him to me. I can carry him easier than you can."

They carried him upstairs and bathed him as gently as possible, keeping his leg out of the water. Then they dressed him in some clean nightclothes. Jennie made sure he was warm as Cat made some tea for his fever and wrapped the wound with some salve on it. Then she asked Jennie, "Do you want him to stay with you in your room?"

Jennie nodded her head yes.

Catherine could see how much she wanted this little boy who couldn't be more than five or six. She looked at Giles to ask for permission, and he just nodded. "He will have to sleep with you. We are running out of rooms."

"What I was going to ask was if I could take him as my own?"

"I don't see a reason why not. It looks as though there is nobody else looking for him."

"But what about you and Beth, You didn't want to have to stay in these rooms?"

"Well, we will sleep on the pallet on the floor till my room is repaired." Giles started to say something, and Cat looked at him, and he shut up. "We will discuss this later."

Helen had sent up some food for them, and Jennie fed William; the little boy's color was beginning to improve. She had him drink some more of her special tea with just a touch of laudanum for the pain, and he began to doze off. Robert knocked on the door and asked if he could help.

"Take him to bed and come get me if he gets worse. Beth and I will sleep in here tonight."

Robert picked up the little boy and followed Jennie to his room. Cat followed them to the room and got Beth; then she started to leave. Robert followed her; then Cat turned around and said, "Where are you going? They need you tonight. I will be all right alone." He looked at her and smiled as she said, "About time, you stubborn old man. Keep an eye on his leg and call me if you need me." If she had been his daughter, he would have swatted her bottom, but she just reached up and kissed him on the cheek.

As she walked into the room, Giles said, "You could both sleep with me in the bed. There is plenty of room."

"No, this is moving way too fast, and I need some time to make sure this is what I want to do. Even if you do have the contract, I still have to say yes at an altar."

After getting Jennie and William settled, she brought Beth into the room, sat her on the pallet, pulled out her hairbrush, and started to brush Beth's hair. She changed her into a warm gown and was starting to lay her down when Beth said, "Kisses, Mama." Well, that was easy enough to do.

She was aware that Giles was watching, but he didn't say anything; before she could even think about it, Beth went running around her and up to Giles and held up her arms. It was obvious she wanted the same from him. Giles picked her up, and she kissed him on the cheek and then gave him a big hug; then she jumped down and ran back to her mother. Catherine put her on the pallet; then she lay down next to her. Beth snuggled up on her right arm and went to sleep. Giles walked over and covered them both up, then leaned down and gave her a light kiss on the top of her head. She turned, brought up her hand, touched his arm, and then said, "Thanks for your help today. I do appreciate it. That man Kevin scares me."

Well, it was a start, and she didn't freeze when he touched her this time. He went to bed alone, but he was sure he could make this work if he didn't push too hard. He would talk to Gerard about dismissing Kevin; he didn't want him anywhere near Cat again.

He wasn't sleeping, and neither was she. She finally maneuvered the baby off her arm, covered her well, and stood up to go to the fire. She put a couple more logs in and stood back; he turned over and just watched her for a minute. She seemed to be making some sort of decision. She had on a new gown, and it showed the light through it and around her like a weird glow. She had grabbed her brush from the pallet and began to undo her hair and brush it.

"I know you are awake. I can tell by your breathing. Can I talk to you?"

"Of course, anything you want to know."

As she brushed her hair, she said, "Why were you so angry at me at court that you wouldn't even meet me?" She had finished brushing her hair and tossed it over her shoulder.

"I let my mistress talk me into believing all you wanted was someone to secure your lands, and she didn't think it would be wise to see you. I was stupid not to have met with you before, and I don't think Queen Marie will ever forgive me for that."

"Marie doesn't like your mistress, and I think she is going to make her life very uncomfortable at court."

"You call the queen by her first name?"

"Not her first name. It is Henrietta. She likes Marie better. We are pretty good friends. I saved one of her horses a few years ago."

"Oh lord, I am surprised she didn't kill me!"

She walked over to the side of the bed and sat down; she just looked at him as he put his arm around her waist and waited for her to move, but she didn't. Instead, she laid the brush down and put her hand on his face.

"Can you tell me why now, all of the sudden, you think you want me, and why I can't stop thinking about you?" He wasn't absolutely sure he wasn't dreaming, but he sat up and looked at her. Cat put her hands on either side of his face and began to kiss his eyelids and his neck; then she said, "Just be still a minute. I want to touch you."

He didn't have anything but a loincloth on, so she didn't have anything as a hindrance; as she leaned back, she ran her hands down his arms and the front of his chest.

"You can breathe. I don't plan on hurting you."

"What do you plan on doing because I can't take much more of this?"

"What do you mean?" she asked as she rubbed the back of her fingers across one of his nipples, and he liked to have come off the bed.

"I seem to want something from you, and I am not sure what." Her hand stroked his leg, but that was as far as she got.

"Let me show you."

He leaned her across his lap and kissed her like he had never been able to before. He couldn't seem to get enough of just kissing her; it was intoxicating. He put his hand up under the side of her gown and felt her shiver; she stood up, and he was afraid he had blundered again. But she just slipped the gown over her head. She started to sit back down, but he said, "Stand there and let me look at you."

He put his hands on her legs and saw the bruise still visible on her knee. "Why do you walk in the dark and cry out in your sleep?"

"I have nightmares of the man who beat me, and I can't sleep, so I walk in the dark. I can get lost in the darkness for a while."

"And you get hurt."

"Sometimes." He looked up at her again and slid his hands up her body until he came to her ribs; then he could feel the scars. She started to move back.

He said, "Don't, Catherine. They mean nothing anymore except bad dreams."

His hands finally got up to her breasts; then he pulled her back to him. Her breasts had always intrigued him, and now he had a chance to actually touch them. They were large soft, warm pillows; and he knew why Beth always wanted to snuggle up to her. He wanted to do much more than that.

"We have to be quiet, or we will wake the baby." He just grinned and took her in his arms; he would be as quiet as possible, but it might be her that woke the baby. He kissed her, and for a change, she returned his kisses with enthusiasm and began to run her hands down his back and side as she explored him. It seemed like the more she touched him, the more she wanted; she seemed to have an intensity of pleasure that just kept growing. His skin was salty, and she could feel his muscles tighten at every touch; she didn't realize that she was clawing at his back as the new sensations grew inside her. She finally couldn't take any more and said, "Make love to me please."

He didn't need any more coaxing; he rolled her to her back and plunged into her, and she was more than ready. He began to move rhythmically. Cat was consumed with new sensations; she felt like she might shatter. It didn't take but a few strokes to take her over the edge, and she finally knew what it was she wanted. That was a feeling she had never expected and well worth the wait. When she started to breathe again, she felt like he really wanted her, not just any woman. A few more thrusts and he collapsed on top of her, and they were both breathing hard; when she turned her head, she kissed the side of his neck and just said, "Yes."

Finally, she had agreed to marry him. The wall was a little smaller with a few more bricks gone; she rose to go back to the pallet, and he asked her to stay. "No, this is already confusing to Beth. We will wait till later." He was going to have some battle scars in the morning; her nails were sharp, but he didn't even care. It had been worth every scratch. Now he felt she was really his and only his. The bruise on her leg and foot were still bad; he was going to see to it that she didn't make it worse—if he had to lock her in a room. He didn't know how she was walking on it. Her nightmares must be awful for her to walk in total darkness just to try to outrun her demons even for a little while, and that staircase was a death trap.

CHAPTER 4

The morning started out as usual. Then one of his men came to him with news that there was a fire in one of the villages to the east, and it was spreading. He gathered about twenty of his men and got ready to leave to help with the fire. Catherine came into the kitchen to see to the gathering of food to take with them, and Giles found her there.

"I need to talk to you before I leave. I don't like leaving so few men here to protect you and the baby, but we need to take care of this fire and the people hurt."

"Do you want me to come with you? What if you need a doctor?"

"No, if they are that bad, we will bring them back. It is too cold for you to be traveling."

He reached down to kiss her, and she didn't move away.

"Catherine, I want you to promise me you will be here when I get back."

"I thought we just settled that upstairs."

"Please promise me right here and now you will be here."

"I promise."

"And I don't want you on that foot any more than need be. It isn't healing. Will you promise me that you will just stay inside and off the horses?"

She just nodded.

One of the men he had left was Kevin. Giles didn't like him much around Cat and the baby, but he assumed Robert could control the situation because he hadn't had time to see him dismissed. He wouldn't have left him, but his other men were more help to him when he needed them, and he just didn't have the time to do anything else. He waved goodbye, took his men, and left just as it started to snow again.

They had a long, hard ride ahead of them, so he hurriedly left. But he couldn't resist turning around to see if Catherine was watching; she was. The next day was long and cold, but William was improving; his color was better, and he was eating. She watched as Jennie cared for him and began to notice Robert was always close as well; maybe this was the push they both needed. They couldn't see a large glow in the sky anymore, so they assumed most of the fire was out.

That evening, Catherine was called to the village about a baby being born; it was Rachel, and she had asked for her. She took Beth with her because she didn't know how long she would be gone, and the baby still wasn't quite weaned. They had a small wagon that was covered to protect them from the wind and weather; she had it built when she had been planning to leave for protection from the elements. It still contained her chests. They bundled up and left; she didn't realize it would be two days before she got back to the keep.

When she did get back, Jennie came running out to meet her; but before she could say anything, a small woman came out of the keep and walked up to her. She didn't know who this woman was until she said, "My name is Jane Hayes, and I am Giles's mistress."

Then she slapped Cat across the face, and she had on a heavy silver ring. Cat put her hand to her face; she could already feel her eye swelling.

"You were supposed to be gone by the time I arrived. Since you were still here, I took it upon myself to move your things."

When Cat walked into the keep, her belongings were all dumped on the bottom of the stairs like garbage. The large chests had already been moved to the wagon, and they had her papers of ownership in them. Giles wasn't aware that they were there; he hadn't asked about them again.

She didn't say a word; she just began to pick up her clothes and Beth's as Jeannie helped her. Beth was standing beside her mother when Jane tried to reach down to touch her.

"Is this the little bastard you wouldn't give up for my Giles?"

She really shouldn't have tried to touch Beth because Cat turned to her and said, "If you touch my child, it will be the last thing in this life you ever do! Stay out of my way, and I will be gone in a few minutes."

Jane backed away; she was mad, but she knew better than to keep pushing this woman because she was still a lady of the court, and Giles didn't know she was coming. She thought if she was here, she could change his mind about taking her back, and the queen had given her very little choice but to leave.

She had thought she could make other accommodations once Giles left, but nobody wanted to take care of her. Jane was getting too old to entice the younger men, and she couldn't have children after some old woman got rid of one of her unborn children years ago. Giles had sent a note with Gerard that he was marrying the lady of the house. She had made a big mistake and thought she could correct it if she was here. She hadn't realized how pretty this woman was and was hoping she could still change Giles's mind with her gone. She found an ally in a soldier named Kevin who also disliked Catherine; he had told her about what had been going on here since Giles had arrived. Maybe with this woman gone, she could take over the house and Giles.

She saw Robert coming toward her, and she just looked at him, trying not to cry. He helped her pick up her belongings and said to her, "Catherine, the wagon is ready and loaded. We are ready to go when you are."

Helen came out of the kitchen and handed her a bag full of food, then walked back to the kitchen, crying. She thought this wasn't going to happen the way the new master had taken to Catherine.

This woman had come early this morning and told them she was the new mistress. Robert wanted to send a man to find Giles, but Kevin wouldn't let him. They gathered everything up, loaded the wagon, and began to leave.

She looked up the stairs, and Jennie was just looking at her; then she realized why.

"Where is William? Why is he not here? We are going."

Jennie just looked up the stairs. "They said I couldn't take him."

"Go get him and wrap him in a heavy blanket."

Then Kevin said, "I didn't give permission to take the brat."

"First of all, I didn't ask, and Sir Giles gave the care of this child to me." She knew by then her men were standing behind her, and she could hear them unsheathing their swords. At the side stairs, Giles's injured men were coming up, and they began to unsheathe their swords as well. She wasn't sure how John was even standing, but he was.

"I have backed up as far as I intend to, so get out of the way." Jennie was coming down the stairs with William.

Cat waited for her at the bottom of the stairs; then she turned to go. She turned to Robert and asked, "Do John and the other men have capes? It is freezing outside."

Robert looked down at her and said, "That and horses have been made ready for them. Let's get out of here."

"Put John up front in the wagon. He doesn't need to be on a horse."

Catherine wouldn't even look back; it was all she could do to keep from crying in front of this woman, and she wouldn't give her the satisfaction. Giles had lied to her; there was still a mistress, and she was a fool to believe he really loved her. She would have to start over after all.

She had Jennie get in the wagon first and then handed her William; then she got in, and Robert handed Beth to her. She turned and asked Robert, "The strongbox with my papers in it, did you get it?"

"Yes, they are in the chest in front of you. I assumed all of the papers you needed as well as the money are in it?"

She just nodded her head yes. They pulled out of the keep with seven armed men, three barely able to ride, and Robert. They headed to the land her mother had left to her; she couldn't believe how much this hurt. She finally had to admit to herself that she loved him, and he had betrayed her. Why did he have to do this? She had been ready to leave as soon as he arrived. Was it so important to belittle her in front of her people? Everyone knew she had spent the night with him. Jennie was next to her, looking stricken, when Cat said, "It will be all right. We have the children and Robert to help us. We will start again."

She bundled up Beth and held her close as they pulled away from the keep. Once they were away and no one could see, she finally let the tears fall. She couldn't trust anyone, but Robert, Jennie, and the men who protected her outside. She should have known better; at least the weather wasn't too bad. As she left her only world behind, Cat had never felt so tired in all her life. They traveled all the rest of the day, just stopping long enough to feed everyone, and then well into the next day, moving until the sun was setting.

Robert came back to the wagon and asked Catherine, "If you can last a little while longer, there is an inn just a few miles more that we can stay at tonight."

Catherine just nodded her head. They continued to travel for about two more hours until they reached the inn. They got down from the wagon and went inside. Robert had been here before when he was traveling to the old castle to do repairs, and the landlord knew him. Robert asked, "We need rooms for the night for my ladies and the children. We can stay in the barn if you are full."

"We have plenty of room for everyone. Would you like my wife to prepare some food for you?"

"Yes please. It has been a long day."

The innkeeper's wife led them to their rooms at the top of the stairs and made sure the fires were set in the fireplaces; she noticed that the lady had a black eye. Maybe she was running from someone. Catherine fed Beth and set her down on the side of the bed; she instantly fell asleep. Jennie was setting out their clothes to dry for the next day. The innkeeper brought up some soup and bread for them to eat. Jennie ate all of hers as she fed Will; then she got down on a pallet to sleep with William curled up next to her. Catherine just lay in the bed, looking at the ceiling; she couldn't sleep. She felt like someone had ripped out her heart and then left her in the dirt. Now what was she going to do? After a while, she fell asleep and dreamed of Giles holding her; then she wondered if her life would ever be the same. Why couldn't he have just left her alone—at least before she hadn't known what she was missing by loving someone? She was better off not knowing; at least she knew how to handle that. She didn't know she could hurt so badly without being physically hurt; there was no poultice for this.

Why had he made her promise to wait for him? Was that that the final slap in the face?

William's color was getting better, and his leg didn't seem to be hurting as bad. Robert didn't let him out of his sight; it seemed this is what he needed to get him and Jennie together. Jennie looked at Catherine one night when Robert was getting them to bed, not knowing if this was all right. Cat just smiled and nodded her head; she was so pleased. Maybe they would at least get to have some happiness; they both adored William as if he were their own. She would love to see them together and happy; maybe this was how it was meant to be. Maybe it was just her life that she couldn't get right.

The next day was dreary and cold, but they set out anyway. Cat was anxious to be getting on the way. They had traveled most of the day when Robert said, "We have to stop. The men are tired, and it is getting hard to see."

When Catherine got out of the wagon, the fog was rolling in on them, and the temperature was dropping. She looked up at Robert and asked, "Didn't you bring a big tent for such an occasion?"

"Yes, but this wind is going to hinder us in putting it up."

"Lay it out and then roll the wagon over the edge. Then bring it up and over the wagon. That will hold it and make it warmer in here for everyone."

The men just looked at him; they weren't too sure about this, but they tried it, and it worked.

"Now put up the tent poles and weight the outsides with some rocks. That should make it pretty snug." Catherine continued to pull things out to cook supper as she gave instructions.

"Build a fire close to the opening and pull back one side to let the smoke out. That way, everyone can sleep inside and under the wagon, and that should at least keep the wind off us." The men did as she said, and it was working; they just looked at one another as she went about cooking over the fire as if she were home. The men laid out their bedrolls, and Cat had extra blankets for everyone. The tent was warm, and the smoke from the fire was being pulled out through the open tent flap. After a few hours, she heard someone moving around and looked out the back of the wagon to see John putting more wood on the fire. She asked, "Is everything all right? Is everyone warm enough?"

John turned and answered in a whisper, "Everything is fine, my lady. You can go back to sleep now." As he looked around, he could see the men were watching and listening to what was said. Every man here knew then that the decision to come with her was the best decision they had ever made. Whatever hardships were ahead, this lady would see to their well-being as she did to her own people. Robert already knew that his life was always going to be tied to her and now to his Jennie and William.

Late the next morning, she was back on the ground cooking while the men loaded everything, except the tent; that was last. When everyone was fed, they disassembled it; and after it was loaded, they were again on their way. The fog and snow had gone, so they were going to travel as far as they could before it got bad again.

Giles returned several days later after he and his men had put out the fires and tried to salvage as much of the grain as they could for the villagers. It seemed that there had been some raids before he came, but Cat hadn't told him about them. There were minor raids on the cattle and grain, and he left some men to guard this village. There hadn't been anyone seriously injured, so they didn't bring anyone back with them.

When he reached the keep, it was already past nightfall, but he couldn't wait another day to return to Catherine.

When he went inside, everything was quiet, so he headed upstairs to his room. He was going to stop by her room and tell her he was back; they were supposed to have the repairs done in there by the time he got back, and he didn't know if she had stayed in his room after he left. It was so quiet upstairs; he had hoped someone would come to meet and welcome him. Before he could do anything, Jane came running from his room.

"What the hell are you doing here? I told you to stay away."

"I know, but I thought you must be joking. After all, you said the lady of the house wasn't someone you wanted."

"I have changed my mind. That is why I wrote you to stay away."

"Well, maybe that isn't what I want."

"You couldn't find anyone to take care of you after I left? Is that what happened?"

"No, I just missed you and thought you might miss me."

Then he began to wonder why Catherine wasn't there giving him a piece of her mind, so he turned to go to her room.

"She is gone. I sent her and the brat away several days ago. She didn't put up much of a fight."

He looked at her, and if looks could kill, she would be dead. Catherine had to be thinking he had lied to her, and now she was gone. He yelled down at Gerard and told him to come upstairs.

"Gerard, she is gone. Find out where!"

"I don't know if you know what all has happened, but Helen says Jane slapped your lady across the face and threw her clothes down the stairs before she told her to leave."

Giles turned around and asked, "Did you do that to her?"

"Yes, you told me you didn't want her, so I threw her out."

"You will pack your bags and leave as soon as possible. And don't let me see your face again, or I might just throttle you."

He went downstairs to talk to Helen; maybe she could tell him where Cat was going because he didn't have the foggiest idea where to start looking.

Helen was crying in the kitchen when he got there, and he asked her, "Where is this land she was going to? I am going to bring her back home."

"I don't know. She never told any of us. It was like a big secret. I just know Robert has been going to it for some time to do repairs on it."

"Who would know the location of the land?"

"The accountant might know if there are any rents due on it."

The accountant didn't live at the keep, so Giles sent Gerard to find him and bring him back here because he felt like he was running out of time.

It took Gerard some time to find the bookkeeper. He waited for him to dress, and then they left to go back to the keep.

When the accountant got there, he was terrified he had done something wrong. Giles just wanted to know. "Where is this land that your lady is going to?"

"I don't know. She never told me."

"Were there any rents due that you can look up to find the location?"

"Not since I have been here, but I can go back further and look for older records."

"Get to it and find me any information of where she could have gone."

Gerard came in and brushed snow off his coat in the front hall and said, "The weather is getting bad again. You can't see for the snow."

"Be ready to go when I find out where she is. And get Jane out of here as soon as possible. I don't know how I am going to explain this to Catherine."

"Are you sure this is what you want?"

"I have never been more positive of anything in my life."

Gerard just smiled; this was a side of Giles he had never seen before, and it was about time. All he had done for days was tell him about how much he loved Catherine, and that bitch Jane had messed everything up.

The accountant had found some old files on some land in the far north of the country that hadn't paid rents for some time because Catherine couldn't provide protection to them. Now he knew what she was doing down here that night he found her; she was gathering up her ownership papers. He started looking for the metal box, but he already knew she had taken it with her. At least he had put extra money in the box before she left. He should have taken the time to read them; then he would have known where to start looking. He thanked the bookkeeper and told him he had done a good job.

"Do you wish to stay the night, or will I have you escorted back home?"

"I would like to get home. My wife will be worried." She was probably scared to death.

"Gerard, please see to it that this man gets home safely."

The Northern raiders had about run everybody off the land, so Cat didn't go about collecting rents. It wasn't much, but at least it was a place to start. The only problem was they couldn't start until the snow at least let up enough for them to see, and Giles didn't have an exact location.

Giles went upstairs to his room, and Gerard had made sure Jane was gone to another room so she wasn't in his way. Giles looked at the pallet, which was still on the floor, and at the bed they had made love in. Could that have only been five nights ago? It seemed like longer to him. What if he couldn't find her? No, he wasn't going to think that way; he would find her, and they would be married, just as he had planned. That was the only way he could stay sane—to believe this would all work out. He couldn't keep thinking about her and Beth out in this cold; even now he had come to believe they both belonged with him, and he prayed they would be all right.

He picked up the robe and put it to his face; he could still smell her on it and feel her hands on his body. He walked to the window and looked outside at the falling snow and thought to himself, *where have you gone, my love?*

Gerard knocked on the door and asked permission to enter. Giles said yes. "My lord, the weather is too bad for us to leave. You can't even see in front of your face. We will be ready when it lets up. I had one of the men take care of the bookkeeper and to stay in town when he was through."

"Do you think they are all right?"

"Yes, Helen said the weather wasn't too bad when they left, and she sent plenty of food. She also thought Robert had been staying at an inn somewhere, so maybe they got there before the weather got too bad. Kevin was the soldier who helped Jane in this little takeover. He didn't want them to take the little boy, but Catherine wouldn't leave without him. She told him she had backed up as far as she was going to go."

"Did he threaten her?"

"Yes, and I think if her own men and some of ours hadn't come to her defense, it would have been worse. I think he would have hurt her."

"The men from downstairs went with her?"

"Yes, they could barely walk or ride, but they still protected her."

"Where are Jane and Kevin?"

"I don't know where Kevin is. He left as soon as we returned, and Jane is in one of the downstairs rooms."

Giles walked to the door, threw it open, and headed downstairs with Gerard behind him; the king wouldn't approve if he strangled her—at least not in front of witnesses.

When he found the room Gerard had pointed out to him, he pounded on the door, and Jane said, "Go away! I don't wish to talk to you."

He didn't ask again; he just put his foot through the small lock, and the door crashed back against the wall. Then he walked in. She started to back up, and he just said, "Why are you here? You talked me into embarrassing my lady and her child, then proceeded to dump me. I sent a letter telling you not to come, yet here you are. Why?"

"I realized how much I missed you and thought that I could convince you to take me back. I could be your lady and have your children. We could be happy together," she replied as she rubbed up against him. It had not been that long ago that she would have excited him with this action; now he was disgusted.

"Get away from me, woman, and don't ever touch me again! And as far as children go, I have known for some time you are barren. I do want children, and as far as I am concerned, you sent my daughter away with her mother. They are both mine, and if I ever see you again, it will be too soon. So I suggest you leave as soon as possible. I don't want you anywhere near my family or me again. Do you understand?"

Then he turned back around and looked at her again. "What else happened at court? And don't lie to me because I will send a messenger to find out."

"When Gerard came, the queen went to the king. They had some kind of bet that you would be coming after the contract to marry the girl, and Queen Marie won."

"Good for her." But Giles figured there was more.

"She came to see me when she found out I had also been sent a letter and asked me what it said. I told her I was not to come here. I thought she had other plans for me. She did. She wanted me gone. I told her the king might not like that idea, so an hour later, he had me banished from the castle. So you see, I had nowhere else but here to go. Giles, it can be like it used to be. Let me stay."

He turned and told Gerard, "See to it this woman leaves my home and never comes back. And if you find Kevin, you had better tell him the same thing because I won't be so lenient with him."

He walked to the kitchen, where he could still hear Helen crying; and when he saw her, all he could say was, "I will find them and bring them home." Then he just held her while she cried.

They started out early the next morning; they were trying to outrun the weather, and so far, they were succeeding. There was a light mist, but not as bad as last night.

Jennie noticed that Cat didn't say much to anyone; she didn't smile like she used to. There was a sadness she seemed to be drowning in. Beth was the only thing that kept her going, and sometimes even Beth couldn't amuse her. Catherine's father or even the Raiders attack had not affected her like this. She acted like a toy that someone had deliberately smashed. Jennie had watched her go through things with her father that no one talked about ever, but even that hadn't affected her like this had. She had stopped sleeping and was only eating and drinking so she could breast-feed Beth. Jennie was getting really worried, but she assumed that she would soon get past this too; at least she hoped so. Last night, she had seen everyone was fed and warm as she had promised, and Jennie could see these men were hers forever, no matter how bad it might get.

William was feeling much better, and Beth loved her new playmate. They made sure Beth didn't play too rough and that Will didn't pull out his stitches; watching the children play made this ride a little more bearable. Jennie and Robert couldn't have loved this child any more if he had been born to them. Robert looked ten years younger and always had a smile for Jennie.

After five days, they were finally getting close to the old castle, and Robert had gone ahead to prepare the lodge for their arrival. When they got there, Cat looked up at the old castle and was sad; it really was beyond repair. It had spent too many winters fighting the wind and the sea, and it was falling apart. It looked like a skeleton rising up out of the dark. Maybe they could tear it apart and use the stones to build a smaller building.

The lodge wasn't so bad; it was longer than it was wide. It had been used for a hunting lodge by the previous residents. When they got inside, it was warm and clean. Robert had done a good job getting it ready for them to move into.

When they were inside, she complimented Robert on his good work and set about getting a meal ready; they were all hungry and tired, and she was ready to get settled in. Jennie set about getting the beds ready and the outer rooms warm. Their timing was good because the snow was beginning to fall hard, but at least they were inside, and it was getting warm. There was a barn for the animals, and they had timed it just right to get everything under some cover before this weather turned too bad.

After she got everybody fed, she took Beth to the room that was to be theirs and shut the door. Beth was already asleep as she put her in their bed and covered her up. She sat down on the edge of her bed and looked at her daughter. What if he was right and she was pregnant? How was she going to provide for these people and another child? In the morning, she would start seeing about collecting some rents; but for now, she was just too tired. Her head hurt, and her eye was still black and puffy. Why did that stupid woman have to be wearing such a big ring? This would just have to wait until the morning. The only problem was she couldn't go to sleep; she hadn't been able to for two nights now. She walked down to the empty room at the end of the hall and went inside. She sat on the fireplace ledge in the dark; she was so tired she couldn't function, so she just sat alone in the darkness.

Her head didn't hurt so badly in the quiet dark and she wondered what this room had looked like once. Robert watched and waited; he saw her go into the room and wondered what was wrong. After about an hour, she came out of the room and went to her own; he would tell Jennie what he had seen in the morning. At least this building didn't have any stairs.

When she awoke in the morning, Catherine felt like her horse had stomped on every part of her body; she ached. She assumed it was from the traveling and that everyone felt as bad as she did. When she got to the small kitchen, Jennie was cooking eggs, and Cat asked, "Where did you come up with those, and do I smell meat frying?"

"Apparently, on some of his trips up here, Robert had been buying supplies from a farm a couple of miles over the hill. He went early this morning and got eggs, salt pork and fresh milk. What would you like for breakfast?”

“Just some water or milk will be fine for right now. I will eat something later.”

“Are you all right? You don’t look so good this morning.”

“I am fine. It was just a very long trip. I think I will go outside and look at this place in the daylight.”

She headed out the door and saw that Beth was drinking from a cup of milk.

“When did she start drinking milk?”

“She has been for a while. I guess she is going to wean herself. She is as independent as her mother.” Robert had talked to her early this morning and insisted she keep an eye on her. Jennie could now see why she was white as a ghost, and she didn’t remember the last time she had seen her eat.

Catherine was a little sad about Beth drinking from a cup because she enjoyed that special contact between her and Beth; that was their time together. But the way she was feeling, maybe it wasn’t good for her to be too close to her daughter. Robert was waiting just outside the lodge and saw her coming toward him; she didn’t look as rested as he thought she should. This trip had been harder than even he had expected. The extra soldiers were working on the stables before the next storm came in. She looked up at the old castle, in wonder that it was still standing; it was dangerous, and something would have to be done about it and soon.

“What are we going to do about that?” she asked.

“The men and I were talking about that this morning. We think we can attach a rope to the top timbers and start pulling it down in small sections. After it is down, we can use the stones to build a new building.”

“Maybe not a new building. Just add on to what we already have and add a kitchen out back, where it would be cooler in the summer. We also need to build a chicken coop so we can have fresh eggs. You might even check into buying a cow for fresh milk and butter. We will need some pens around the back. Nothing fancy, but something for livestock. Make sure John has some easy labor so he doesn't tear that leg open."

"Already got him marking out where they should go. You can look at the sites later this afternoon. Then we will begin building tomorrow if the weather improves."

"You are always one step ahead of me." She giggled.

She walked toward him and stumbled; she caught herself and kept on walking. Robert didn't know what was wrong, but she wasn't acting right.

"Jennie has breakfast ready in the house. Gather up the men and go eat before it gets cold. This can wait a little longer."

They walked back to the lodge discussing how everything was going to look and what they were going to need in the way of supplies. Cat held on to his arm, and she never did that. They went inside to eat, but Cat didn't have anything; she just kept looking in the different rooms to see what needed to be done. At the end of the old building, there was the room that she had been in last night. The wall was falling down, so the wind was howling through it. It looked to be the master's room from the large size of it. They would have to take care of it first before anything else because the house couldn't be kept warm with the wind blowing through. She had the men take the tent, put it over the hole, and weight it down with stones to hold it; that offered some protection from the wind until they could do a better repair job.

She went to bed feeling like maybe things would be all right; they would start again in the morning. She hadn't eaten, and again, she didn't sleep; she knew she was sick but wasn't sure what to do about it. She cooked some of her tea and drank it after everyone was in bed; she didn't want Jennie to worry.

The next day, the weather wasn't as bad, and Cat wanted to go to the village with Robert to meet with the townsfolk; she knew there would be no rents because there was nothing in the fields to harvest and hadn't been for some time. She was going to have to find some seed for next season. When she got into town, there weren't many people that still lived in the village. Some of the elder men came out to meet the new mistress of the land but were disappointed she had so few men with her. After talking to them for a while, one of the elder men asked, "You have no husband and very few men. How are you going to hold this land?"

"The very best I can, and I will see to it we have some grain to plant in the spring."

The man just looked at Robert and asked, "Can she do it?"

"If anyone can, she will figure out a way." He wasn't sure how she was going to do it either, but on the way back, he would ask.

The next couple of days were about the same, just trying to get the house in order before the weather got any worse. But Catherine still felt awful and couldn't get rid of this headache; she was also throwing up in the mornings and was afraid she was pregnant. The men had constructed some pens for the animals, and Robert had been able to buy a cow so that they at least had fresh milk.

When they returned, Robert found her in the little room she was using for an office, and she was crying; he put his hands on her shoulders and asked, "What is the matter?"

"I just don't know how to do it all with the money that I have. Giles even sent some extra with me and offered some more. I should have taken it."

"You know, the queen said you could always come to her for help."

"I know, but that will be my last resort. I have some jewelry I can sell to her jeweler if I have to. That will buy grain at least for next year."

She didn't realize that John and James were standing next to Robert outside of the office until they came around the door. James said, "My lady, you don't worry about us. Worry about the townspeople. We will get everything planted and going again, and then you can take care of us."

She just looked at them, and then James said, "It is going to be all right."

Late in the day, they heard horses arriving in front of the lodge. Robert and his men grabbed their weapons and headed to the door. It slammed open to reveal Giles—wet, cold, and mad.

He had eight men with him, and he was mad as she had ever seen him; she didn't know why. It was his mistress who had started this.

"What in the name of Christ do you think you are doing, leaving the keep in this weather? Do you have any idea how hard it was to find you?"

"I don't know. Why, were you looking for me?"

"That is the stupidest thing I have heard today."

"Let's talk somewhere else. Follow me to my room. Jennie, please see that these men are fed and find someplace for them to sleep. They look worn-out. Robert, show them where to put their horses while there is still a little light left."

Giles followed her to her bedroom; he couldn't believe she would leave the keep for this place, but before he could ask her, she turned and said, "What are you doing here?"

When he finally had a good look at her, she seemed pale, and then he saw the healing bruise under her eye. "Did Jane do that?"

"Yes, she had on a heavy ring. Now you see why I was in a hurry to leave."

"You promised me you would be there when I got back."

"That woman came into my—excuse me, *your* house and told me to leave. She said that it was part of your orders. She had already thrown everything I owned down the stairs and then proceeded to put me in my place, so I gathered up my belongings and was escorted out of the house at sword point by that soldier Kevin."

"Why didn't you send Robert after me? I could have cleared this up before you left."

"That soldier forced Robert into thinking that woman was the new mistress of the house, and she wouldn't let Robert leave to find you. I just wanted out of there. I assumed you had changed your mind again. Should I have stayed, Kevin seemed ready to kill me. I had to fight just to get William out of the keep. The promise to you was the last thing on my mind. If my men and some of yours hadn't backed me up, I am not sure that he wouldn't have hurt us."

"No, I haven't changed my mind about anything, and you should have known that. By the time I got back, you were already gone, and I thought I would go crazy because I didn't know where to even start looking."

"That was the general idea. I didn't want to look like a bigger fool in front of my people. I seem to have done a good-enough job of that already. Maybe we should leave this as it is and just forget about marriage. I am sure Jane is waiting patiently for your return."

"No, I already have the marriage contract, and you have already signed it. We will leave in the morning and go back to the keep where you will marry me."

"That damn contract! I wish I had never started this whole thing."

"Catherine, listen to me. She was told not to come. I had no knowledge of it, and then the queen had her banished from the castle. Now can we please go home?" She had to smile at that. Marie finally got rid of her and accidentally sent her right into her house; bet she didn't count on that. She would have to tell her about that one.

"We are not leaving tomorrow. My people and I are worn-out. We are staying for a few days, but you can return tomorrow if you are in such a hurry."

"Not without you and the baby. I will wait till you are ready to go." Besides, she really looked worn-out.

"Are you feeling all right?"

"I am fine, just tired. It has been a long few days."

He reached down to kiss her, but she dodged him and opened the bedroom door to usher him out.

"I would like to stay here with you tonight. I want to hold you in my arms."

"Not until we are married. I have made enough of a fool of myself. Besides, you might change your mind again. Jennie will find you somewhere else to sleep." Then she slammed the door. She didn't want him to touch her because by now, pregnant or not, she knew she was sick.

He was furious, but there was nothing else to do. Jane couldn't have done a better job at separating them with a broadax. When he returned, he would make sure that Kevin was gone and away from his family—what he should have done in the first place. Jennie came in after him to see if Cat was all right, only to find her throwing up in the chamber pot. She pulled back her hair to help her and could feel the heat coming off her skin. "You really aren't well, are you?"

"No, not for several days now, but I don't want him to know. Please put the baby in your room tonight. I am afraid I might give her something. I know Robert has been staying with William and you. Can you make room for her?"

"Always. Let me get you in bed. Then I will go make you some tea. Have you eaten anything today?"

Several minutes later, she was back, only to find Catherine again leaning over the chamber pot, barely conscious. She finally got some tea down her, but it wasn't working; she was getting worse. She couldn't keep anything down, and Jennie found out she hadn't eaten in several days. When Cat finally stopped vomiting, Jennie helped her up, then got her into her gown and into the bed. She covered her and quickly left the room to find Robert; she needed help. He was putting the children down. Jennie just looked into the room and said, "Robert, come to Catherine's room as soon as you can. She is ill. Leave Beth in here."

Sometime during the night, Giles heard Cat cry out, and he thought she was having another nightmare until Jennie came to the door and said, "I need some help with my lady. She is sick."

He grabbed his robe and followed her to Cat's bedroom. Robert was trying to hold her down, but she was fighting him like he was going to kill her. He just looked up at Giles to help him. Giles leaned down to hold her and could feel the heat coming off her body; she was burning up. He looked over to Jennie and asked, "What do we need to do?"

"Robert will go outside and fill a pot with snow. We have to get her fever down." Jennie said.

"What about that tea she made for me when my arm was hurt?"

"I already have some more cooking on the stove, but we still have to get it down her throat without choking her."

Catherine was dreaming that she was being chased, and she could feel the lash as it fell time and time again. She could hear someone telling her she needed to drink, and she wanted to; she was so thirsty, but she couldn't seem to get it down. Someone was holding her upright and trying to help her drink, but she kept choking; she was so hot, but she had to keep running.

In her fever, she began to tell them what had happened in the Raiders camp—things nobody had ever known about, things no one outside of this room would ever know of. The Raiders who had taken her had said he wanted her to live with him as his wife, and there would be no discussion on the subject. He had placed a gold cross around her neck to prove to her she was his, and she had never taken it off. She began to tell them that she had often wondered that if she had gone with him, would she and Beth have been better off. At least her baby would have been wanted. She said she had thought of trying to find him after she left the keep. Then she began to talk about Beth, how she had been the light at the end of a black tunnel; she had been the one she could give the love she had never gotten from her father.

The more Giles heard, the madder he got; he just didn't know whom he was maddest at: Catherine's father who had ignored her or himself for treating her so badly in the beginning. He kept holding her as she struggled so she wouldn't hurt herself; they finally got some tea down her, and Robert was putting snow in towels, which he put next to her, trying to lower her fever. Jennie continued to put cold clothes on her head even though she kept shaking them off.

Slowly, she began to cool off; it seemed the tea or something was beginning to work. She slept for a time, and Giles and Robert began to relax. Giles sat in the chair while Robert sat against the wall near her bed; they didn't talk and just watched her. She stopped fighting and rested for a while. Soon, the fever began to rise again, and they had to hold her. Jennie kept telling her that Giles was here; it just didn't seem to be sinking in.

Soon, she began to berate Robert because of what happened at court; she said all she wanted to do was get home and that this was a stupid idea. Then she began to tell about what Giles had said about her in very exact terms. Giles was stunned because he still hardly remembered any of it; he should have. He was a bastard to her. Jane had convinced him he didn't need a wife. He had called her and Beth every evil name he could think of. He looked up at Robert, and he couldn't even look him in the eyes.

"You knew, and you wouldn't tell me. How you must have hated me."

Robert just looked at him and said, "I still don't understand how she came to forgive you. I still can't."

She spoke of the devastation of that night and finally deciding to go to her mother's land and start again. Then she began to talk of him coming to her land and trying to charm her; it galled her that he didn't remember because she did only too well. She spoke of loving him and not knowing if it was the right thing to do. She wanted a family and a life with him, but she just didn't know if she could ever trust any man; she said she was so tired and just wanted to close her eyes and rest.

Giles looked at Jennie and asked, "Is she going to be all right? I don't want to lose her before I can tell her how sorry I am for what has happened and make this up to her and to you." He said all this as he looked Robert in the eye.

"The fever seems to be breaking. I think she will be all right after a few days' rest. She has had so much responsibility for so long. I guess it finally caught up to her. She is worn-out. She has always been lonely, and now she is afraid to let anyone into her little world. You are going to have to convince her that you won't tear it all apart, and that is not going to be an easy job. She is a good lady, and I think it will be worth the fight if you are serious about what you have said to her. If you aren't, leave now before you destroy her. I think she truly loves you and needs you, but she just can't do this anymore."

He continued to hold her as she slept; he was afraid earlier that he was going to lose her to the fever, and he couldn't see a future without her. This was a fight he intended to win because she needed him as much as he needed her. He just held her long into the night until Jennie made him lay her down; then he went to sleep in the chair across the room. He wanted to be there when she awoke; he didn't want her to be alone anymore.

Sometime later, he felt someone watching him, and he realized Cat was watching him; she didn't know he was awake, so he said, "How do you feel?"

"Why are you really here? What do you want?"

"I just want you and Beth and a life together."

"I don't believe you. I wish everyone would just leave me and Beth alone. I am so tired of fighting for every little thing in my life."

She closed her eyes and went back to sleep. He watched Robert get up and start to leave the room. Then he turned and said, "I don't care who you are. If you ever hurt her again, I will kill you. I couldn't protect her from her father all of the time, but I can from you."

Giles knew he would do it; he was more a father to this woman than her father was, and he meant every word.

"You don't have to worry. I will not let anyone hurt her, and that includes me. She will rest and get well. Then we will go home and be married."

"What if that isn't what she wants to do?"

It was an honest question, and he didn't have an answer.

"I will have to convince her I am sincere and that this won't ever happen again, and that it is her choice. I won't force her to do something she doesn't want to do anymore."

"All right then. This is between Cat and you. We will see how well you do at convincing her, but if she says no, will you honor it?"

"Yes, I will honor any decision she makes."

He finally began to realize that he broke the wall she built to protect herself, leaving her very fragile; now he was going to have to win her all over again. He sat in the chair for a long time, just watching her breathe till Jennie came back and told him to go to his room.

He had some thinking to do and some decisions to make; he had made a promise, and he intended to keep it. He just kept praying that he would figure this out because he didn't want to leave here without her.

He came back to her room several hours later after he had cleaned up and saw that Jennie had helped her into a clean gown and changed her bedding. She was still asleep, so he again sat down in the chair.

The sunlight came into the room and warmed it up, and he stood up; he was sore and tired. That chair wasn't the most comfortable bed. Cat was awake, but she just watched him. He got down on his knees in front of her and said, "I think you should stay in bed for a few days. You were very sick last night. You had us all very afraid."

"I thought we had to leave today, or the world was coming to an end."

"I am sorry I yelled at you about that. We can stay as long as you need to get to feeling better. I need to see about getting these people some protection anyway if you decide to stay. I want you to be safe."

"I thought we were to be married? Has something changed?"

"Only the fact that I didn't give you a choice in the matter. It should be your decision if you wish to marry me. Don't take this wrong. I still want you and love you. I just think I don't have the right to order you to do so. I will ask you again in a couple of days what you want to do. And I hope you will say yes to my proposal. Rest, and I will send Jennie in to help you until you are feeling better."

She didn't know exactly what was going on, but maybe Jennie could tell her she was just too tired to care at this particular moment. So she lay back down and went back to sleep. She did like the idea he was still around and wasn't so mad at her. Jennie finally got her to eat, and this time, she kept it down. But she was still so exhausted; just sitting up to eat was a job, and walking was out of the question. Finally, sleep was the best medicine for her; even her headache seemed to be going away. It seemed her nightmares were also gone; she could finally sleep.

Jennie kept coming to her room, and it seemed she was never going to be well again. She hadn't seen Beth for a couple of days now until she was sure she wasn't going to give her daughter anything. Giles came and went to check on her but never pressed about the marriage. They would just talk about the old castle and the surrounding land. After a couple of days, she got dressed and wanted to see Beth; it seemed she wasn't so much sick as exhausted, so she didn't think she was contagious.

Catherine went to look for her little girl and couldn't find her; then she heard her giggle outside. As she left the lodge, she saw Beth being held high in the air while being tickled by Giles. Catherine went toward Beth quickly; she wasn't sure she liked Giles walking off with her daughter. When Giles saw her, he didn't understand the look of fear on her face; then it dawned on him she was afraid he would hurt Beth. She walked quickly up to him and reached for Beth, but Giles kept holding her.

"I am not going to hurt her, Cat. We were just going for a little walk. You can come with us if you feel up to it."

She put her hands down. Beth seemed to be enjoying being with him. So she started to walk beside him as well. They were going toward the old castle; then she looked up to see that part of it was on the ground.

"Your men said that you wanted it down because it was dangerous, so we started to pull it apart yesterday. Is that all right?"

He was asking her opinion as if it really mattered.

"I thought you were in a rush to get back?"

"I am rather enjoying myself here. Beth and I are checking everything out, and we are seeing to it that some pens are raised for some chickens. I am getting some men to protect this place from raiders. If you decide to marry me, I will see to it this place is protected, along with your other lands."

He kept calling it her land; she didn't know that he had already been helping the villagers get extra supplies and animals.

"We could keep this land for Beth if you come back with me because she won't be my child, and as you said, a woman can't inherit. This land would give her a nice dowry and let her decide her own fate."

Cat looked up at him. "Would you do that for her even though she isn't yours?"

"Yes, and she will be mine if you marry me. I am trying to make you see I have changed, and Beth shouldn't be put in the same position as you were if we can help it."

They kept walking, and she was thinking this wasn't the same man she had met at court; he was trying to be a good man, and she wanted him more than she could say.

"All right, it is a good idea. We will marry, and by the way, I love you."

"I will always take care of you."

"Just remember I don't share, and that includes you. She'd better be gone when we get back, or I will have her head."

They walked and looked at the men pulling apart the old castle; the stones could be used to build something else as there were plenty of them. The pens for the animals were in place, and he told her he had animals coming to put in them; all the soldiers were working except for a few that were on guard.

"If you feel like it tomorrow, we should ride down there. It has a beautiful meadow and a small stream. We could take a picnic and have lunch down there."

"That would be nice, but don't you have other things to do?"

"Probably, but I think they can wait. I find I am enjoying being a wastrel."

"Really a side I have never seen of you."

"You are the one who never slows down. I am surprised you haven't checked to see if the barn is repaired yet."

She really had wanted to look; she just hadn't.

"Go on, look. We will wait for you."

So she went around the corner to look inside, and she was quite pleased at how they had cleaned it up and repaired the ceiling.

"Are you happy? Now can we continue our walk? Is everything to your liking?"

"Yes, dear." Then she took his arm, and they continued walking up the hill.

CHAPTER 5

They were all but starving, and he could see they were desperate for help. The village elder was named Brian, and they had talked several times and even rode to several neighboring villages to buy supplies. They now had some winter vegetables and grain for animals as well as for the people to make bread. He planned on taking Cat home, but he couldn't leave these people like this; they needed his help, and he was going to see to finishing what Cat had started. She would have run out of money quickly trying to feed these people and her men, but she would have tried. Robert said she was going to try and sell what jewelry she had for some more money to help these people. He had to get things growing and thriving if he planned to leave this land as an inheritance for Beth, so he was really trying to get this village and its people on the way to supporting themselves again.

When he was in the village today, he had seen a man chasing a small boy, trying to hit him with a stick; this was the second time he had seen the same man trying to catch this child. He was going to find out why. He had stopped and found that there were two children in the village scrounging for scraps and sleeping in a barn; they were a couple of years older than Beth, and when Giles asked about them, Brian told him their mothers abandoned them because their fathers were Raiders. Giles just looked at the man and asked, "How do they survive? They are babies."

Brian looked at him and said, "We try to take care of them, but we have five of our own to feed, and no one else will care for them. There were three. One died last winter."

Giles started to leave the village and realized Cat would have his hide, so he turned around, went back to the barn, and started looking for the children. He got off his horse, found the little girl hidden in the hay, and picked her up; she looked a lot like Beth with her light hair, and he wrapped her in a blanket and handed her to one of his men. The little boy came running, and he went crazy; he thought they were trying to hurt her and attacked Giles. He just grabbed him and held him as the little boy screamed for them to let her go, and then when he calmed down, he turned him around in his arms and said to him, "You are coming with me now. Nobody will hurt you anymore, and you will have a place to eat and sleep, and so will she."

The little boy just looked at him and said, "Really?"

"Yes, what is your name and hers?"

The boy looked at him and said, "We don't have names."

One of Giles's men was on the ground by then and handed him a blanket, and the look between the two men said it all: how have these children survived this long? He wrapped the boy in the blanket and handed him to his man.

Before he could mount his horse, the man who had been chasing them before came around the corner of the barn and said, "Good, you caught them. Hand them to me, and I will hang them from the rafters. The little bastards won't steal from us again."

Giles didn't even think he started to beat the man, and if Gerard hadn't pulled him off him, he would have killed him right there. He turned and mounted his horse, and then his man handed the child to Giles. "Let's get back to the lodge and get these children fed and taken care of." He looked back; he couldn't understand how people could let children starve, but maybe he could—he hadn't been paying attention to William's care till Cat called him out on it.

When they got back to the lodge, Gerard and Giles took the children inside. Catherine looked up at them and said, "Put them down at the table. Let's get them fed. Where did you find them?"

"In the village, in a barn a man was trying to kill them. I am afraid I beat him rather badly."

"Did you kill him?"

"I don't think so."

"Too bad. Do they have names?"

"The little boy says no. I think they get called something else."

"I can imagine. Well, let's get them fed, then bathed and go from there."

"Is it all right that I brought them here?"

She just turned around and kissed him. "I think it is the most all right thing you have ever done."

As she looked at them, she knew they were Raiders children: blond hair, not as blond as Beth's, and blue eyes, but still very pretty children.

"How in the world did they survive this long? They can only be about four or five years old, so they must be from a raid before the one I was taken in."

"Apparently, their mothers put them out when they were barely able to feed themselves, and the village elder and his wife have tried to keep them alive. They slept in the barn. There were three of them. The third one didn't survive last winter."

Catherine was furious. "How do you let a child just starve? Are they brother and sister?" She watched them at the table; they were eating like they couldn't get enough.

"I don't think so, but he won't let her out of his sight, so I don't think they can be separated."

"They won't be. I will figure out something if I have to raise them myself."

The whole room heard that, and it didn't even surprise him; he had already figured that out when he brought them home, and that was all right too. She sat down in front of them and said,

"Hello, my name is Catherine, and I guess we are going to have to figure out some names for you two."

The little girl started to cry and grabbed the little boy's arm, and then he said, "Where are you sending us now?"

Catherine got back up, picked up the little girl, took her over to the rocker, and just started rocking her as she told the boy, "You are not going anywhere but here. You are mine now."

The little boy looked up at the big man, and he just shook his head yes. "She is the lady of this land. If she says you are hers, then that is the way it is going to be."

Tears started to fall down the boy's face, and he said, "Nobody ever wanted us before, not even our own mothers. Our fathers were Raiders." He stated it as if nobody knew.

At about that time, Beth came into the room, and Catherine said, "This is my daughter, Beth. Her father was a Raider as well."

The little boy looked over at Giles and then back at Beth, and Cat explained, "Giles is to be my husband, but Beth's father is a Raider."

"And you didn't leave her to starve?"

"No, I would never have done that to my child, and I won't do that to you."

"I will work and do anything you want. Just don't put us out again. We can sleep in the barn." The little girl was already asleep in her lap, so Giles came over and picked her up. Cat took the little boy's hand, and they headed down the hall to the room beside Beth's. Giles opened the door, and Jennie has already made a bed for them and set a fire. Giles laid the little girl down, and the boy covered her up. Cat just watched.

"Do you want us to put a separate bed in here for you, or do you want it left like this for now?"

She squatted down so she was at the same level as he was, and he turned and said, "Let's leave it like this for a while so she won't be afraid. Is that all right?" Catherine smiled and nodded her head, but before she could stand, he asked, "May I give you a hug and him?" Then he pointed up at Giles.

She shook her head yes, and he put his arms around her and about squeezed the life out of her, and she hugged back. Then he looked up at Giles. He reached down, picked him up, and received the same hug. The boy also a whispered, "Thank you for bringing us to her."

"You are very welcome." Then Giles put the boy in bed and covered him up, and they had hardly left the room before he was asleep as well.

"I wonder how long it has been since they had a full belly and a warm bed."

"Do you really think they ever did?"

"I didn't ask how you felt about this. I just did it, and now my family is three instead of one. You can change your mind, or I can see about other arrangements."

"Would you really want to do that? Besides, that keep is big enough for a lot of children, and I dare anyone to comment on who their fathers are."

"Besides, you have gained a hard worker in that child." He just smiled at her. "I bet that child has worked as hard as most men just to stay alive and to keep that little girl alive. But we really need to give them some names. We can't keep calling them the boy and the girl."

"First thing tomorrow, Daddy, you can name your new babies. You did a good thing today, Giles. I am proud of you." She couldn't have said anything to make him feel any better than that.

Catherine had barely got her gown on when Beth came to her room and said, "Mama, that little girl is in the kitchen, and she is crying. I think she is hurt."

With that, she started pulling her toward the kitchen; and sure enough, the girl was hidden in a corner with a part of a loaf of bread clutched in her arms and crying. Giles was there by then, and Cat told both of them to just stay put at the door. She walked over and sat down on the floor in front of the girl and asked her, "Are you still hungry?" The child shook her head no.

"This is for tomorrow for Jacob and me." This was the first time this child had said a word since Giles had picked her up out of the barn.

"You won't need to hide any more food because tomorrow there will be food for you in the morning and at lunch and at supper. You won't go hungry again, I promise." As she reached for the bread, she pushed back the girl's sleeve, and she could see the burns on the little girl's arms. She figured there was worse elsewhere.

"Jacob and I can stay?"

"Yes, but do you have a name as well?" She couldn't meet her eyes.

"Jacob calls me Ann."

"Well, Ann it is then. Would you like to go back to bed?"

"You promise you won't take me back to my mother? She says if she ever sees me again, she will kill me. You promise? You don't know how much she hurts me." She turned around to Giles and motioned with her head to get Beth out of the room; he just nodded. She loosened the ties at the top of her gown and let it slip a little; then she turned around. When she felt the little hand on her back, she turned back around, and Ann just looked at her.

"Yes, I do." That was all it took; she crawled up in her lap, and Cat sat and rocked a quietly crying child who finally had found a mother. The next thing she knew, Jacob, Beth, and Giles were in the kitchen, watching.

"Well, where does everybody want to sleep tonight?"

Everybody said, "With you!"

"I don't think my bed is that big?"

Then Giles piped up. "Mine is."

"You know we are going to have to change the sheets in the morning? These children need a bath."

He just grinned at her.

"And you, sir, are going to help. Then we are going to the village."

"Why, are we looking for more children?"

"No, but I will not see any more starved to death or killed. I won't help them. They will have to fend for themselves if they can't at least feed a child."

As everyone crawled into Giles's bed, he had three little blond children and one brown-haired lady, and they all belonged to him.

He couldn't have been happier. Ann was on Catherine's arm, Beth was lying across her stomach, and Jacob was lying in front of both girls; he seemed to have taken both of them on as protector. Giles looked down at the group and said, "I will sleep on the floor."

She just gave him that look and patted the bed, and he snuggled in beside her; as he kissed her shoulder, she put her hand on his face and said, "You aren't the same man I met at court. I like this one better."

So did Giles. She was packed in so tight she couldn't move—her child, the man she loved, and now two more children who had already started working their way into her heart. That was all right; she had a big-enough heart for a lot more. Giles just covered everyone up, and they went to sleep.

The next morning, as everyone woke, Jennie had already started heating water for baths. Cat dressed and took the children to breakfast. Ann would hardly leave her or Beth's side, but Jacob and William were becoming fast friends. Both children were surprised that there was a morning meal as promised, but Ann still looked over her shoulder every time the door opened, something Cat didn't miss. The boys bathed first; after, Cat cut Jacob's hair and then washed it; he was a handsome boy, but it was going to take a while to untangle Ann's hair. So they sat on her bedroom floor and started to brush it out.

Jennie was changing the water and had walked past the bedroom when she looked at Cat and nodded toward Ann. Cat turned her around, and she was crying

"What is wrong? Am I hurting you? I was trying to be careful." Ann pointed to a spot on her head, and as Cat put her hand on it, she felt a large lump; the child had been hit with something.

"Why didn't you tell me I was hurting you? I would have been more careful."

"I was afraid I would make you mad." What was she going to do to win this child's trust? The only thing she could think of was to keep doing what she was doing.

"Look at me. I won't hurt you on purpose, and if I am, tell me. I will stop I will be more careful, all right?"

Ann nodded. She gestured to Jennie to come to her, then whispered in her ear, "Have Beth come in here with her dolls and play with Ann. Watch her face and tell me if I am hurting her. I don't think she will tell me. Tell her it is a game." Jennie just nodded and went to get Beth.

"All right, let's start again. You have such pretty hair. We are going to get it clean, and then we will braid it and put ribbons in it." It took another hour of careful combing to get her hair detangled and get all the hay out of it. Then Catherine trimmed it to one length, and they were finally ready to bathe her.

When they went to take off her clothes, it was just Jennie and Cat in the room because she was afraid of what she was going to find on this little girl's body. She didn't want Beth to see, and she was right. Ann had fresh bruises from whoever had hit her on the head. Jacob had said she wasn't as fast as he was, and he had several marks; she also had old burn marks and cuts. No wonder she was so scared of her mother. She knew Raiders children weren't treated well, but this was unforgivable; she had found out the other child was a girl. So what had she gone through before she died?

They scrubbed Ann gently and then washed her hair; at least she had no open wounds when they got her out of the tub. Then they rubbed her down with some cream Cat used on her hands because her skin was so dry; this child was skin and bones. They didn't have a dress that would fit her. So they found a shirt from one of the smaller men, cut it down, and made a belt until they could get her a dress; at least it was clean. They combed her hair with Beth giving directions, and then she darted off and came back with a blue ribbon, one of her favorites, for her sister's hair.

Ann just looked at Catherine. "Is she my sister?"

"That is the plan, if it is all right with you."

"And Jacob, will he still be my brother?"

"Yes, and Beth's brother too. Is that all right?"

"You will be my mama and the big man my Daddy?"

"Yes."

"What if my mother comes for me? The man she lives with said he would sell me to some man. He was mad when I ran away. They will come for me." That's why she watched the door, and nobody knew her name; they were hunting for her. Well, they could rot in hell before they got her.

"Nobody's going to get you from me, but you can't go outside. Do you understand? And you don't go anywhere alone. Do you understand? You and Beth go play in her room. I need to talk to Daddy."

She looked at Jennie and said, "How about we fix it for the boys to sleep in one room and one for the girls; if that is all right with you? We will have to watch her till we leave. I will not let her mother get her back." Jennie just nodded and started down the hall to make the arrangements.

She went down the hallway outside and found Giles; she was almost running when she got to him, and he could tell something was wrong.

"Was it as bad as you thought when you bathed her?"

"Worse, but we have a bigger problem than that." He just looked at her. What could be worse than a child beaten half to death? He had already heard about her head and regretted not killing the man in the barn.

"She was not thrown out. She was running from her mother and her friend who was going to sell her for God knows what or to whom. That's why she watches the door."

"What did you tell her?"

"That I wouldn't let her mother take her, that I am her mother now and you are her daddy. Beth has already claimed both of them, so if you want to run, you better do it now before the wedding."

"I am not going anywhere, and neither is my daughter. But we better put some guards on the house till we leave. After that, she should be safe at the keep. No one will challenge us there. Do you think we should change her name? She could become the little girl that died last winter."

"I thought the same thing. I don't think anyone bothered to learn their names, and if they don't see her, I don't think they would know her. I am not sure you will. She is beautiful."

"Do we have time to go to the village today? I need some clothes for her."

"Did I ever tell you that you are the most loving person I know and the best thing that ever happened to me?"

"Not today you haven't, but I always like hearing it."

"Let's go find our daughter some clothes after I post some more guards."

"I knew there was a reason I loved you."

They rode to the village while Jennie kept Ann and the boys occupied in the house; she needed clothes for Ann, and she wanted to see if anyone was looking for her. When she got there, she called a meeting in the center of town; she had brought Beth with her. She was asleep under her cape, and nobody could see her yet. It was going to be a surprise.

Once they were assembled, she could see the man Giles had beaten; he could barely walk. He came up to her and started complaining. "Your man here beat me yesterday over a couple of Raiders brats I was going to dispose of, and he wouldn't let me. What are you going to do about it?"

"My name is Catherine Demarco, and I own this land. The man beside me is going to be my husband, and he is responsible for the improvements on your land. But he has been doing them for my daughter, who will inherit this land and be the owner when she is of age. I would like you to meet her."

She moved her cape to show Beth, and the sigh that went through the crowd was audible—she was a Raiders child. Catherine looked down at the man who had tried to kill the children and told him, "You are lucky he only beat you. If I had been here, you would be hanging from a tree." His skin turned so white he looked like a piece of bread.

"I understand a child died last winter. That won't happen again, or I will cut off all help to this village and let you starve like those children. If you find a child, bring it to the lodge. I have people who will see to their care. Am I understood?"

Giles was getting off his horse and taking Beth from her, and the beaten man had disappeared. She turned to Brian and asked, "I need some clothes for the little girl."

"What are you going to do with her?"

"I am taking her and the boy home with me. They are mine now."

All he could say was, "Oh." They weren't saying the children's names around anyone; they didn't want any parents coming for them. After finding dresses, they thanked Brian for trying to take care of the children. Cat thought he could have done more, but Giles told her the village didn't like what he did. So she made him her representative in the town; now they would leave him alone. She didn't see anyone looking for Ann or asking about her, so they began to leave. She turned her horse and said one more thing. "I better not find out another child starved or froze in this village because they were Raider born, or you won't like what happens." Then she turned and left.

Now that they had seen the woman who had run the keep for all those years without a man and had made it a thriving land, they didn't want to be on the wrong side of her.

They hadn't slept with each other until they were married except last night; that was the way that Cat wanted it. She didn't want to take the chance of anything else happening to embarrass her in front of people. Giles wasn't particularly happy with this idea; he couldn't understand what difference it made now. She would soon be his wife, but he let her have her way. He didn't know that Cat regretted that decision; she thought she was sick at the time, but she couldn't take it back.

She had never been so pampered; she had always been the responsible one, and now someone else was in charge. Giles had taken care of her and everything else, and she was quite pleased with the results. He really acted as if he cared for her, but until she was legally married and she knew for sure that Jane was out of her home, she wouldn't be completely satisfied. She wanted to make sure he kept his promise to keep this land for Beth. She liked that idea more and more because this time, she actually had time to be a real mother.

Ann and Jacob wouldn't let her out of their sight; they were afraid this would all disappear. But the boys played together, and Beth was little by little pulling Ann out of her shell; she even gave her one of her precious dolls. This was going to be a full-time job; it was a good thing Giles was going to be around to run the keep.

Catherine expected to be married at the keep, but Giles didn't think he could wait that long to have her again. So he sent men out to see if there was a priest anywhere close to the old castle. Two days later, one of his men came back with the news that he had found a priest about twenty miles away at a small monastery. Giles was thrilled, but he needed to talk to Cat about it before he sent for him to come here; he didn't want to antagonize her about this wedding if she had other ideas. He started to realize that a month ago, he wouldn't have given a damn about what a woman thought; he would have just done what he wanted. Cat, Ann, and Beth came out of the small area they had set up for the cow to be penned in and walked toward him.

"I need to talk to you for a minute. I would like to ask you a question."

"All right. Do I need to take the girls inside, or can they walk with us? We can't go far from the house."

"That will be just fine."

He reached down to pick up Beth and took Catherine's hand. Ann had her hand, and they started walking down the path to the lodge. He and his men were repairing the end of the lodge, and it was much easier to keep it warm, and everyone seemed to be content with the new surroundings.

"I have found a priest within a couple of days' ride and wondered if you would consider marrying me before we left here. I know women want to make a big deal out of a wedding and all the trimmings, but would you think about it? I can see about having a dress made in the town if you agree."

"That won't be necessary."

His heart just fell; she wasn't going to let him do this, but he had misunderstood what she was trying to tell him.

"I have a wedding dress. It was made for me before I went to court, and after, I put it away. But Jane threw it down the stairs with everything else. I don't know if it was damaged, but we can see if it is usable. If it isn't, we will do something else. Send for your priest, and we will do this."

He didn't realize how much she wanted him almost as much as he wanted her. She had never felt as safe or loved as she had in his arms, and she wanted that again; she just couldn't ask. She was afraid he would think less of her, but that bedroom seemed so empty without him.

He turned to look at her; then he reached down, pulled her to him, and kissed her soundly on the lips. She didn't struggle; instead, she kissed him back with great enthusiasm.

"Well, little girls, your mama is going to marry me. We'd better get things ready for the big day."

As they walked into the lodge, Jennie turned to say something but stopped in her tracks; she had never seen Cat look this happy since the day Beth was born. Beth was laughing, and Ann was smiling.

"What is going on here? Everyone looks happy this morning."

"Do you know where my wedding dress is and if it is in good-enough shape to be used in a few days? It looks like we are going to have a wedding here."

"I know where it is, but I haven't looked to see if it was damaged when we left."

"Well, I guess we had better see what it looks like and if we can repair any damage done to it."

Cat started to walk to her room to find the dress, and Jennie just looked at Giles and thought he may be the right man for her lady after all. Giles just looked at her and smiled as he held a sleepy Beth in his arms.

"Go help your lady. I will take care of the girls."

"William is asleep on my bed. Put her in there with him."

"Ann, you want to come with Mama?" She just shook her head yes; she still didn't talk much, but some was more than none.

Then he walked down the hall to take Beth to the room to lay her down in bed like any good daddy would do; this didn't go unnoticed by either Cat or Jennie.

He placed the little girl in the bed and watched her as she fell asleep; he didn't realize how much he wanted to be a daddy until right now. William seemed to be thriving under Jennie's care; he was a lucky little boy as he lay next to Beth. This little girl trusted Giles with all the innocence of a child. After all the things he had said about her to her mother, would she ever forgive him when she was older? He knew that one day, someone would tell her about it because secrets never stay secrets. They were going to have such a good life together that she would never doubt that she was loved by him. Maybe if they were lucky, she would have some more siblings to love and play with; at least that is what he hoped for, that they had a good start.

Jennie was pulling out the dress she and Cat had made in what seemed like such a long time ago; it was in better shape than they had expected. It was a little dirty from being thrown on the floor but didn't have but one small hole in the hem, which could be easily repaired. It was a lovely dress made of the finest velvet. It was the very palest green color that they had been able to find. It made her green eyes look even greener when she wore the dress. Cat didn't want white because she wasn't a virgin, but she still wanted a beautiful dress. It was fitted at the bodice with ties in the back and front; she had a lace chemise that went under it and showed prettily at the top of the bodice. She still had her mother's wedding ring in her possession and supposed she needed to ask Giles about a ring even though she didn't know how to broach the subject.

Giles knocked on the door and waited until Cat came to open it, and then he asked if the dress was presentable or if they needed to see about having one made.

"The dress is in very good condition and will be ready by tomorrow."

She smiled and shut the door, then returned to cleaning the dress. Giles turned and proceeded to send his man after the priest, but if this place was to be a wedding chapel, there were still things that needed to be done before the priest got here. He didn't want Catherine to be disappointed in the event.

Jennie kept looking at her as they cleaned the dress until Cat said, "What is wrong?"

"Nothing, I guess I am envious of you and your happiness."

"Robert and you sleep in the same room, and it seems that William is devoted to both of you. Do want me to talk to Robert?" Jennie looked pleadingly at her and just nodded.

"Done, I will talk to him today. Maybe we should see if we have two dresses just in case."

"I have a pretty one I have been saving for some time."

"Good, I will be back in a while." She looked back at Ann to see if she wanted to come with her, only to see her sound asleep on the bed. She gently covered her up, kissed her forehead, and walked out the door. She went to find Robert. When she got to the stables, he was hauling stones to the back of the house. She walked up to him, took his hand, and walked away with him to the little stream bordering the property; she then turned and stood in front of him. "I want to talk to you."

"What is the problem? Are you all right?"

"Jennie wants to marry you while the priest is here, and I want to see if you will."

"I am not talking to you about this. I will talk to Jennie."

"Then talk to her! What are you waiting for? I am not a child who still needs your protection. Now it is time for you to have a life with her and that little boy."

Robert just stood there for a minute and then asked, "So you really think she would have me?"

"Why do you think I am out here? She loves you! Surely you are not that blind, and she has for some time. I think you feel the same for her even though you won't admit that even to yourself. I am going to be all right. Now it's your turn."

"You know I will always be there if you need me." Then he kissed her cheek and started inside to talk to Jennie.

Giles walked past him after watching this conversation and took Cat's hand in his. "Is everything all right?"

"Yes. I think we are going to have two wedding ceremonies. We will find out in a little while. Would you care to go for a walk with me?"

"I would love to accompany you wherever you want to go." They began to walk toward the stream, and when they reached it, he discovered there was a place to cross without getting wet. She held up her skirts and lithely crossed the water with him close behind. They came to a wooded area with shrubs surrounding it, and much to his surprise; she parted them and entered a small clearing. There was moss on the ground, and the shrubs were dense enough to cut out most of the wind.

"This is my secret place where I can come and be alone. I found it a couple of days ago." Then she turned, put her arms around his neck, and kissed him.

"I know I told you I didn't want you sleeping with me until we were married, but this is neutral territory and just ours, away from prying eyes." She didn't know how else to say what she was feeling, but she didn't have to; he took her in his arms and almost crushed her to him. He took off his cloak, spread it out on the ground, and laid her down on it. He lay next to her and continued to hold her; this was wonderful. She took off her cloak and covered them both with it.

"It is probably too cold to try this, but I wanted to at least be near you for a while." He pulled his shirt off over his head; he didn't seem to even feel the cold, and then he helped her remove her outer dress, just leaving her sheath underneath. He unlaced the top and worked the skirt up so he could touch her. She pulled him to her so she could feel his warmth against her, and he took it from there. How he got out of his britches she didn't know or care, but he was soon inside her, and his mouth was everywhere else. Once again, she just held on and waited for the explosion that she knew was coming from this man she loved. Her hands held his head as she kissed him, and he moved with a gentle motion at first, then faster as he took both of them over the top. He lay beside her as she snuggled up beside him and rubbed her face on his chest, her body warm against his side.

"I guess I am still banned from your bedroom until the marriage?"

"Just until we are married. I think my people would respect me more, but there is still this little hollow, unless it rains."

"I may wind up freezing to death holding you. That wouldn't be such a bad way to go. Let's get dressed. Someone will start looking for us soon, and I have a wedding to get planned. I don't intend to wait any longer than necessary."

He looked to be a very determined man going back to the lodge, holding his woman's arm next to his side. During the walk back, all he could think was, *please don't rain.*

CHAPTER 6

Everything seemed to be going as Giles had expected it to, and it was beginning to look like a chapel for a wedding. The chambers had all been cleaned, and fires were set and ready to go when their guests arrived. They didn't know how many would arrive with the priest, but they were sure he wouldn't be alone. It wasn't safe for even a priest to travel alone around here. Giles had already made some inquiries about hiring some men to guard this place and keep it for Beth; he was trying to find local men who would want to start families here and maybe bring this village back to life. There weren't many people left after all the raids the Raiders had made on this land. If there were a constant number of men stationed here, the Raiders descendents of the Vikings would think twice before raiding here anymore.

The old castle was almost completely demolished, and the stones were being set aside to add on to the existing lodge. After taking down several layers, the old castle collapsed in on itself, saving them a great deal of time. The stones were being put to use on the end of the lodge, but only Giles was seeing to this construction; he didn't want Cat to see what he was doing. Several extra workers were around, and Giles was having certain things renovated without her knowledge.

Cat had already drawn out plans for the new kitchen; she had a good eye when it came to buildings and stables. They were well laid out and workable; even his men commented on how nice they would be when they were finished. Giles's men had come to like Cat very much; she took care of their wounds and their animals. She knew each of them and called them by their given names. Even Giles wasn't sure he knew them all. Everyone seemed to be excited about the wedding because they saw both of their masters happy and relaxed, and this was a new side of Giles nobody had seen for a very long time.

Three days later, Father Marques arrived with three guards and Giles's men as escort. He was at least fifty years old, but still very spry for his age. When he came into the lodge, he was very surprised at how good things looked. Several years ago, when he saw this place, he didn't think there was any saving this village or this land. So he was most impressed. When Giles walked toward him, the small man was awed by his size and obvious wealth and wondered why this wedding wasn't taking place somewhere more lavish.

"Father, it is good of you to come this far. We do appreciate it and hope you will be comfortable while you are with us."

Giles led the old man to a chair by the fireplace.

"My lady will be here in a few moments. She is taking care of the children."

Farther Marques looked a little taken aback but was reluctant to say anything, but his curiosity was getting the better of him. He had come through town and been told that the lady of the town had taken two Raiders children from them as her own; they figured she had killed them. Some of the people didn't trust her, and some couldn't say enough good things about her and this man; he would judge for himself.

He wondered if the lady was not so pretty and if that was the reason for this out-of-the-way wedding. It wasn't long before that idea was put to rest because the lady in question came into the room, carrying a beautiful little girl. He looked from Giles to Catherine to the little girl and knew she wasn't this man's child; he had seen too many children born in this country after raids not to know a Raiders child when he saw one. This man seemed to accept this child, and that was more than what most men would have done. Right behind her came two more children, both of whom were Raiders born.

Giles said, "This is Jacob and Ann. We adopted them recently from the village. They are also our children." So much for killing them; this woman had taken them as her own. He liked her already. Whatever was going on here, it seemed like a good thing, and that made him feel much easier about it.

They sat down for supper because the priest was tired and asked if the ceremony could be postponed until tomorrow. Giles said that things would be ready whenever he was and that there were beds for him and all his men to rest. They enjoyed a most pleasant evening and meal. Father Marques enjoyed talking to both of these people. Giles made it clear that he really loved this woman, and she seemed to love him. Catherine was more reserved than Giles, and the Father Marques was curious about that but wasn't going to ask. He was asked to perform two ceremonies, and some of his people wished to be married as well. He finally told his hosts that he was ready to retire and was led to a bed chamber; it was warm and comfortable, better than what he generally was used to because this was a poor country.

Giles had said, "I am leaving men to watch and protect this place after we leave, so maybe it will be a safer place to live. Some of the people may come back if they feel like they are protected."

Father Marques was glad to hear this because his flock was getting smaller each year, and the coast was wide open to raiders. It was easy to see that this man was intent on protecting this land if for no other reason than to please this woman, and he wondered why the lady was still hesitant about this union. They had planned on having two ceremonies on two different days so that each bride could have her own day.

The next morning, everything was ready, and Giles sent Jennie to tell Cat everything was on schedule. Cat was dressed when Jennie came into the room, carrying something over her arm. It was a veil made of white silk with a lace headband made of the same lace as her chemise. Jennie had made it for her last night because she thought every woman should have at least a veil even though she wouldn't wear a white dress. Catherine just looked at the veil and started to cry.

"Do you really think I am doing the right thing? I still don't know if I can trust him."

Jennie just looked at her and said, "He treats you better than your own father did, and he loves your daughter as well as two orphan children. What else could you want? I think you are a very lucky woman, and I know he is the luckiest man in this country because he will have you."

Catherine just smiled at her and said, "I love you too."

When she walked into the room with Robert escorting her as her father would have, Giles was amazed; she was even more beautiful in her wedding dress. The girls were standing on one side with white lace ribbons in their hair, and the boys were on the other side with dark little tunics on. Giles hadn't been too sure about it when Jennie had told him the dress was green, but Jennie was right, and they both were beautiful. He didn't know where the veil had come from because Cat had told him there wasn't one. She walked toward him and the priest, and he was very proud. Catherine walked up to both men, and then Robert put her hand in Giles's. He took her hand in his and turned toward the Father Marques, and they both knelt before him. She hadn't had time to talk to him about the ring, but Jennie had told her it was taken care of; she assumed he would use her mother's.

Father Marques began the ceremony with the usual words, and all went well; then he got to the part about anyone objecting, and Giles looked around the room as if he would kill anyone who dared say a word. The priest finally asked Giles, "Do you take this woman to be your bride?"

Giles looked at Cat and said, "For all time and as long as I shall live."

Father Marques asked Catherine the same question, and Giles held his breath until she finally agreed to take him as her husband.

The father then said, "Please give her the ring."

Catherine looked down to see not her mother's ring but a gold ring set with a large emerald surrounded by diamonds. She looked up at him and realized he had either brought the ring with him or had it made since he got here. It was the most beautiful thing she had ever seen, and she could see Jennie crying. So she had known about this all along.

Robert then touched her shoulder, and when she turned, he handed her a band for Giles hand. The band matched her ring without the stones; it was equally as beautiful. She turned and slipped it on his hand. She looked up at him, confused. He whispered, "Marie."

She looked up at him, touched his face, and said, "All my love for as long as we both shall live."

That was all she had time to say before he took her in his arms and kissed her for the first time as his wife. The children were on either side of them, and they were clapping; they weren't quite sure what was going on, but it was fun.

They all celebrated at supper with roasted quail and vegetables. Catherine wasn't paying attention to anything but her new husband. He was talking to everyone as if they were all old friends even though she knew that he had only met some of these people in the last few days. People from the nearby farms and his men had been invited to the wedding as well as the priests, so there were a lot of people in this little house.

Catherine took Robert aside to talk to him. "Well, are you ready to do this again tomorrow with Jennie as your bride? Giles is going to walk her down the aisle at my request. Is that satisfactory?"

"Thank you, Catherine. You are the best daughter anyone could have had, and your mother would have been so proud of you."

She pulled Jennie aside. "Where did you get the lace? It is a beautiful veil, and the ribbons for the girls' hair was a wonderful idea!"

"I had hidden the lace for a long time, and at least that woman didn't ruin it because I had already packed it. The girls loved dressing up. I don't think Ann ever had a nice dress or her hair done. She is in heaven. I may not get her out of the dress tonight."

"Just tell her she can wear it again tomorrow, and she will be fine. Do you need help getting her to bed?"

"No, as long as her sister is there, we are good."

"Good. I will see you tomorrow."

After a while, Giles looked at her and motioned to the door; he was ready to leave for their wedding night. She stood up from the chair and said, "I thank everyone who helped put this wedding together. It could not have been any finer if it had been in the king's own court. Thank you! We are going to take our leave now."

Everyone stood as Giles rose and took her hand to lead her out of the main room. They walked to the door, and Cat started to turn toward Giles's room at the end of the hall, but he guided her down another corridor to the opposite end of the building. She looked up at him and said, "Where are we going? This is the wrong way."

He just smiled and kept leading her down the hall. When they got to the end of the hall, there was a new door there. She hadn't noticed being installed with everything else that was going on around here lately.

She had noticed the men working on the end of the lodge, but she assumed they were still repairing the hole in the end, and the entrance was always blocked. When she got close to looking at it, someone always scurried her away.

Giles opened the door, picked her up, and carried her inside; he then closed the door with his foot, and she looked around at the room. How had he done this? He set her down so she could better view the room.

"Do you like it?" he asked hesitantly.

She just looked at the room, turning slowly around. There were tapestries on the wall and floors that she had not brought with her. There was a huge bed made out of the most beautiful wood she had ever seen. The bed covers were a soft burgundy velvet, and the mattress looked to be feathers of down.

"How did you do all of this, and where did it come from?"

"Do you approve?"

"It is the most beautiful room I have ever seen."

"Some I sent for and the rest came from local artisans and markets."

"This must have cost a fortune."

"I was not exactly destitute even before I came to your land. Besides, I wanted this to be perfect for you, something you would always remember. Oh, there is a letter for you." He handed her a jewelry box, obviously the one the rings had come in, and she opened it; inside was a letter to her.

Dearest Catherine,

At least he has good taste. He came to me to help him pick out the rings. I hope you are pleased. I am sorry about Jane. If I had known she would go to him when I got her banished, I would have waited. Be happy, my little sister. And if you ever need my help, you know where I am. You have to come see my new horse. You will love him.

Love, MARIE

"So you enlisted Marie's help with the rings and what else?"

"Oh, just a few things a woman would know more about. Your friend the queen loved spending my money on you."

She walked over to him and put her arms around his neck, and then she said, "You didn't have to do all this. Make love to me, and I will always remember how you made my wedding night something special just for us."

"Look on the bed. There is another surprise for you over there."

She walked to the bed and put her hands on the softest gown she had ever seen; it was white silk and light as a feather. She picked it up as if it were glass and turned to look at him with tears in her eyes. "Why?"

"You deserve to have someone do things for you, and as I am now your husband, that someone is me. Besides, I have only seen you in the blue gown. I wasn't sure if you had another."

He walked toward her, and she didn't even move this time; she wasn't afraid of him anymore. She just knew she wanted him. He picked her up again and laid her on the bed; he leaned down and kissed her. She kissed back and soon was pulling at his shirt; she was working at the laces until he pulled it over his head and smiled.

"What are you thinking?"

"That the best thing I ever did was offer that contract to you even though it didn't work out quite like I had planned."

He rolled her over and unlaced the dress she was wearing and peeled it off her; when it was gone and she was nude in his arms, he said, "Contract or not, you are the best thing that has ever happened to me." He then started to put little kisses down her neck until she couldn't stand any more. She took her hands and brought his face to hers; she wanted to feel all of him next to her. She kissed him like she had never done before with wild abandon; he was so surprised he didn't know how to react.

He raised himself above her and gently entered her, and this time, she moved back against him. They rocked in a gentle motion for a while, then became faster until they were both spent. He rolled to the side of her and closed his eyes for a moment; he just wanted to enjoy the moment. When he again opened his eyes, he saw she was looking at him. She was leaning on her arm, watching him.

"What are you thinking? I didn't hurt you, did I?"

"No, I was wondering."

"Wondering what?"

She began to move her hands on his chest, touching the hair as it curled down the center; she then put her face against him and rubbed her face against him. This was almost his undoing, but he keep perfectly still. She could feel the muscles underneath the skin on his ribs and hear his heart beating. She rolled over on to him and took his face in her hands, then ran her fingers through his hair.

"You are mine now, and I love you. Never forget that and remember I won't share you with another woman—ever!"

He couldn't believe what she had just said; he never expected to hear those words come from her mouth, and he couldn't believe how much it pleased him to hear them.

She lay down on his chest, and he held her to him like she would disappear if he didn't; then he rubbed his hand down her back and felt the scars. She started to move away, but he wouldn't let her go. "Don't. They are a part of you, and I love all of you, scars and all." He still reminded himself if he ever found the man who hurt her; he would pay dearly for it.

He then decided to teach her a new way to make love, and as she sat up, she was surprised when he lifted her and had her sit her on his manhood. There was this surprised look on her face he would remember till the day he died. Cat got that funny grin she always got when she was enjoying their lovemaking; he didn't even think she knew she was doing it. After a moment or two, she got the rhythm, and he leaned up to bury his head in her breasts. She put her hands to the sides of his head and leaned down to kiss him; long gone was the girl afraid to be touched at least by him. This woman wanted all of him and made sure he knew it. She loved making love to him; it was like he was inside her skin, and she couldn't get enough of him. When he was finally spent, he just wanted to hold her, and she clung to him. She hoped in their time together, he had given her a child; she would love to have his baby.

They slept late the next morning because it had been a long night. They had made love several times and fell asleep in each other's arms. Giles had come to realize this was the best way this union could have happened. Cat would have been terrified if they had wed so soon after meeting her; now she liked him as well as loved him. Things couldn't be better.

At about that time, Beth came running down the hall, calling for her mama. Cat rose from the bed to go open the door, but Giles got up instead. He grabbed his fur robe and put it on; then he opened the door. In came Beth; not far behind was Ann, though she just stood at the door with Jennie in hot pursuit. She looked up at him and apologized. "Sorry, sir, she was just too quick."

"It is all right."

He watched as those little legs tried to climb up the bed, and he just smiled.

"Well, looks like our day is starting early."

"Sorry, do you want me to take them back in their room?"

"No, they are just fine here." Beth snuggled down beside her and promptly went back to sleep. Cat motioned for Ann to come in too; she came running and jumped up on the bed and pulled the covers over her head. Cat looked up at Giles and noticed he was smiling.

"Want to come back to bed and snuggle with us?"

"No, if I do, we won't get out of bed at all today. And I still have some things to take care of."

"I will get dressed and help you."

"No, go back to sleep. It is probably going to be a long night again tonight."

"Really? Promises, promises. Are you sure you aren't too tired?"

"I'll show you tired," Giles said as he grabbed her and kissed her soundly on the lips. Then he turned to go bathe and dress. She pulled the girls to her side and started to drift off again; she really was still tired. Giles peeked back in before he left the house and saw that Beth was snuggled up as close to her mother as she could get and still breathe, and Ann was as close to Beth as she could get. Those two were already sisters. Cat's arm was over both of them. He just kept smiling; he couldn't believe how lucky he was and how he had almost ruined this.

He had ordered Jane out of his home, and she had better be gone when he got home, or Cat would be furious. He still had to make some arrangements for men and arms before he could leave, so some of his men went into town with him to take care of it. Giles wanted to go back to what was now home. Jacob and William were in the barn looking at a new calf; they had become fast friends. It seemed like this was working out like someone planned it to.

Robert came up to him soon after and thanked him for wanting to walk Jennie down the aisle. Giles was thrilled; this finally meant that Robert was leaving Cat's protection to him.

Later that afternoon, Robert married Jennie, and Giles formally gave custody of William to them. Things couldn't have been going better.

He asked the old priest to stay a few more days while things were settled. He came to find out there were several couples in the village who wanted to take advantage of a priest; things around were starting to come back to life. He really liked this old priest a lot, more than the one in the village at home; he might have to see about a change. He asked him if he would consider moving, and Father Marques said he would think about it. Giles said he would see to it he was moved in the utmost comfort and had a very cozy church to live in. Father Marques said, "I would need a replacement."

"I have a priest in mind that doesn't like my lady and is very disrespectful, and I would like to replace him. Cat likes you. Please consider coming with us. We will leave soon, and I can see to it that you are moved with us."

The whole village now knew who he was and that he was trying to leave men to protect the village. It seemed more people began to return every day, and Giles was very pleased. There would have to be some towers built to keep an eye on the ocean to watch for raiders. The fields were still barren of any life, but the seed he had provided will take care of that problem soon. When the harvest came in, the people would be able to take care of themselves; but until then, he needed to provide, or they would starve.

Brian had agreed to be Giles's man in the village and see to it that everything was done the way he had laid it out. He had already sent men out to buy a few animals to help these people get started again. He seemed happy with the way things were going, so they began to head back to the lodge and his family; he really liked knowing Cat would be waiting for him, and the children would sit in his lap and eat supper.

The land was so barren with no crops or animals, and he wondered how long it would take to make this a livable place again. Some of his men had already asked to stay because they had met single women here. There seemed to be a shortage of men, and his had been well received, but the men that had come with Cat were going back to the keep with them. He still didn't understand why they were tied to her forever. No one had told him the whole story of their trip here; when he finally heard it, he would never wonder about their allegiance again.

They arrived back at the lodge, and Giles could smell supper cooking, and he didn't realize how hungry he was. He stepped into the kitchen to find Jennie cooking chicken. They had bought about twenty to start a coop, and they weren't to be butchered, but he guessed one less would be all right. Jennie turned and said, "This old bird had a terrible accident this afternoon and broke her neck."

Giles just smiled and nodded because it smelled too good to argue with her about it. He started down the hallway and heard Cat trying to get Beth and Ann bathed with very little luck; at about this time, a naked little girl came running down the hall, squealing with delight about escaping from her mother. Cat rounded the corner just in time to see Giles scoop her up in his arms. She came to a screeching halt in front of him and said, "I may have to tie her up before I can get her bathed. I seem to be losing my edge."

"What edge? She is always one step in front of both of us."

Beth hung on to his neck, dripping wet, and giggled. So he walked with her mother to the bath and helped her finish bathing her. When they had finished, he wrapped her in a bath sheet and dried her off, but he couldn't quite manage her clothes; his hands were too big and her clothes too small. Cat picked her up and got her dressed, and she was already getting droopy eyed, so she started to go to the rocker to rock her to sleep. Giles stopped her and said, "Let me try. I want to get used to doing this, and I haven't had much practice."

"Not 'much,' how about 'none'? Have you ever rocked a baby before?"

"No, so it is time I learned."

She handed him Beth, stood back, and watched; it took him a bit to get her arranged so they were both comfortable. But soon, he had her lying on his chest covered by her blanket, and they were rocking. He was doing very well, so she tiptoed out the door and down the hall to help Jennie with supper.

"Where is Beth?" she asked.

"Giles is rocking her to sleep." They looked at each other and smiled; neither one of them expected this to work out this well. It was a nice surprise. They continued to prepare supper.

Giles came past them, carrying Beth to her room; he looked into the kitchen and asked, "Is there anything special I need to do when I lay her down?"

"Just make sure she is covered up good so she won't get cold, but don't cover her face."

"I am not stupid," he said with some contempt and walked down the hallway.

Jennie looked at Catherine and, with a straight face, said, "Well, he isn't, you know."

"Ann is already asleep, so don't wake her." Cat just wanted to smack her, but it was just too funny. Giles came back to the kitchen, sat down, and was served the accident-prone chicken and dumplings; it was very good, but he couldn't understand why every time the women looked at him, they laughed.

Ann craved attention from a bath or rocking because she had never had either, but she still took a nap when Jacob didn't; she was still so skinny. William and Jacob were always doing something and were always under one of the men's watchful eyes. It was one thing to become a daddy once, but he had managed to become one three times in the span of a few months, and he was doing a pretty good job of it.

It was a few days later that a man and a woman showed up at the lodge and wanted to speak to Catherine. She didn't like the look of this woman, and when Ann saw her, she started to scream. Cat put her hand over the child's mouth and took her back to her bedroom; once she got her calmed down; she asked her, "Who is that woman?"

"My mother."

Cat's heart sank. Jennie was in the room by now with Robert. "She wants to talk to you."

"Don't let Ann out of this room. Robert, go get Giles. He is at the barn. Tell him to come quick. Don't let Jacob come out either. Tell him to bring Beth outside and tell her not to say a word, Mama says."

As she left the room, John came up to her. "Do you need help?"

She just shook her head. "That is Ann's mother, and I am not giving her back. That means I am going to have to lie. Are you good with that? Because if you aren't, stay in here."

"I saw what she did to that little girl. I will back you up. Lie all you want." As he went out the door, he grabbed a sword. She walked out to meet this woman whose child ran away instead of being sold after being abused by her.

The first thing the woman said was, "I hear you have my kid?" The woman was dirty and smelled; her fingernails were filthy, and the man with her was the kind you wouldn't leave a young woman alone with.

"I don't know what you are talking about. What kid?"

"A little girl, I think I named her Ann or something like that. She is half Raiders, and a man from the village says you got her. I want her back unless you want to pay me for her." So that was the reason she was here; this kind of scum would never have enough. She would always be back for more; this ends now. Dead or alive, she was leaving today.

"I have no idea what you are talking about. I took two children from town, but neither one was named Ann. There was a third, but she died last winter. She starved. Could that have been the child you cared for so much?"

"Bring her out and let me see her, and then we will know."

Giles had just walked up, and Cat turned to him and said, "Why don't you go and get our youngest daughter and show her that she isn't hers."

Giles just smiled and walked into the lodge; she hoped he understood what she was doing, and when he walked back out, he did—he was carrying Beth.

"That's her! That's my daughter. You have to give her back to me now or pay me for her, and I think you can afford a tidy sum."

"And what do you plan to do with her if I don't pay for her and just give her back to you?"

The man stepped forward and began to speak. "She is getting mighty pretty. I know a lot of men who like little girls."

She put her hand on Giles's arm so he wouldn't kill him; the negotiations weren't through yet.

"First of all, this is my daughter, Beth. She will own this land someday. You don't even know what your own daughter looks like. The name of the little girl I rescued is Gayle, and if the man in the village didn't tell you, I promised anyone abandoning a child to starve or beating them that I would hang them. Maybe the dead child is yours. Shall we go dig her up and see? Then we can hang her parents for letting her starve." The looks on their faces were priceless; they hadn't expected anyone to actually want the child, much less punish them for not taking care of her. The man in the village had sent them up here to get killed, and she knew it.

"I suspect the man who sent you up here is the one my husband beat for going after the Raiders boy. He hadn't been warned, or he would be hanging now. I only give one warning. Shall we go see if the other child is yours?"

"No, she wasn't ours. This was all a mistake. We shouldn't have come here. The girl is yours. You can have her."

"I don't ever want to see your faces again, or I will see them from the top of a tree. Get out of my sight!"

As Catherine turned around, Beth said, "Mama, her name is—"

Cat put her finger to her lips and went, "Shhh."

Beth smiled a secret smile; she liked secrets.

Catherine went back inside to the bedroom. Ann was waiting with Jacob, and she asked, "Do I have to go now?"

"No, you never have to go anywhere except back home with us to the keep."

"Is it as nice as this place? Will we have a room, or will we need to sleep in the barn?"

"No more sleeping in the barn. Everybody will have a room."

Turning to Giles, she said, "We are going to have to do some renovating when we get home."

"Don't even start. I have workers working as we speak."

"You were confident I was coming back?"

He just shook his head and shut the door but looked back to make sure Ann's parents were still running. He was pretty sure who told them about where she had been taken; he would like another shot at that man in the barn. This time, he wouldn't get up.

It was a couple of days more when they left the lodge; it would be an easier trip this time because Giles had rented a coach and horses for them to use on their return home. It was funny how easily that word came to his lips now; it was like his whole personality was changing. He was much easier with the men and joking when they were working, not so angry all the time. He rode outside for a while, then came inside the coach with the women for lunch; he told them he had made arrangements with the same inn they had stayed at when they came here for tonight. They would have to be a bit longer on the road than he wanted, but he didn't want to have to stay out tonight in the weather; it looked like rain. When lunch was over, he again got on his horse, but Cat came out to ride with him; the children were asleep, and she was tired of being inside the coach. They traveled for a while without talking.

Then Giles looked at her and asked, "Is there something troubling you?"

"No, I just hate leaving the lodge. We were so happy there, and now we go back to the real world."

"Things aren't going to change that much, you will see. We will just go back to our home, my wife, instead of being all alone. And you won't have to be responsible for everything. I can take over your duties for the upkeep of the land and tower."

She gave him a look that would have burned him if she had been a fire. He looked stunned at the look she had given him.

"I am not saying you didn't do a good job, but now it is my job to maintain and protect my family and the land we live on. It is your job to be my wife and the children's mother. You left with one and are coming home with three, and maybe if we are lucky, you will mother some more children."

She wasn't sure she hadn't just been insulted, but it wasn't worth a fight right now; besides, she liked the idea of him calling it his home and her his wife. They rode for several hours more until well after dark when they finally got to the inn. The innkeeper was waiting at the door for them and had everything ready; there was food and hot water for bathing.

Catherine sat down at the large table and fed Beth and Ann, who could hardly keep their eyes open. Jennie fed the boys on the other side of the table, and they were just as tired. Cat was so tired; she wasn't hungry, but she ate anyway so she wouldn't wake up hungry in the middle of the night. She fixed Giles a meal and some extra bread and cheese because she was sure he would be hungry. Cat headed upstairs to the room prepared for her and her husband, only to see it was the same room she had occupied the first time they were here. There was a fire and a bath, and it looked wonderful; she took her clothes off and slipped into the water. The tub was small, so she couldn't stretch out, but she lay back and relaxed; as she closed her eyes, she didn't hear Giles come in. He walked quietly into the room, leaned down next to the tub, and slipped his hand into the water. Cat didn't even open her eyes; she had heard him when he had opened the door. Then she said, "You'd better be careful, sir. My husband will be here soon."

He grabbed her and said, "You cheeky girl, aren't you getting cold? This water is cooling down."

"You had better call for some more hot water then for your bath," she said.

"I am not as fragile as you. I can bath in cool water, and it is fine."

With that, she splashed him with water and began to get out of the tub; he grabbed her and put a towel around her. "There, that was all I wanted anyway, your naked body."

"Well, you had better dry me off because now I am freezing."

"Well, let's see what we can do to remedy that." Then he lifted her out of the tub.

"Oh no you don't! You smell like our horses, and you aren't coming to bed like that."

"Well, get out of the way so I can get in the tub, if you are going to be so picky."

She walked to the fire to dry off as he bathed; then she put on her gown, her old blue one, and crawled into the bed. She pulled the covers up and snuggled down into the feather mattress, and before she knew it, she was asleep. Giles turned around to see that she was asleep and couldn't bear to wake her. He dried off in front of the fire and then put on his fur robe; he could still smell her on it from when she occasionally wore it. He would have to have her made one, but he liked it when she wore his; it was always warm when he put his arms inside to hold her to him.

There was food on a little table, and he realized he was very hungry; he sat down and began to eat. Cat had set a big plate out of meat, bread, and cheese; and he consumed it all. When he was through, Giles walked out the door and down the hall to check and see that everyone was comfortable and warm and that the children were all right. Somewhere in all this madness, he had come to think of them as his, and he was very protective of all of them. Inside the next room, they slept on two small beds with William. Jennie looked up when he opened the door and asked, "Is everything all right? Is Robert on guard?"

He just nodded and shut the door so they could go back to sleep.

He turned around and went back to his room. He closed the door, blew out the candles, and got into bed with Catherine. Giles didn't try to wake her; he gently pulled her to him, and she snuggled up without even waking. He pulled the covers over both of them and laid his head next to her. He hoped she wasn't right about things changing when they returned home; he rather liked things the way they were. If things weren't right when he got home, he would fix it. He dozed off, holding Cat in his arms.

The next morning, Cat could hear the wind and rain hitting the side of the building with considerable force; when she dressed and started to go check on the children, she could hear Beth laughing downstairs. She walked down the stairs to see several men seated at the table, eating. Giles was on the floor in front of the fireplace, feeding something to Beth; when she got closer, she could see that it was bread dipped in honey. Giles looked up and said, "Look, Beth, its Mama."

She sat down beside them on the floor and pulled Beth into her lap.

"Is this all she has had for breakfast?"

"No, she has already had eggs and some oatmeal."

"Well then, I think you should share your honey and bread with your poor starving mother."

Beth just shook her head no and giggled, so Cat bent down and kissed her neck and began to tickle her. Beth began to laugh and try to get away from her, and when she succeeded, she ran over to Giles and said, "Daddy."

Giles looked stunned, and then he looked very pleased. Catherine just watched and couldn't believe the change in his face; he really did love her child as his own, and now her child loved him too. Everybody was silent until they saw how he was going to react.

"She called me Daddy, didn't she?" He asked as he looked at Cat.

"I do believe she did. Is that all right with you?"

"Most certainly! I want all of them to think of me as their daddy."

Catherine just nodded and smiled. Giles was so pleased he couldn't seem to let the little girl go; she finally wiggled free and ran over to the table where Ann and Jacob were and climbed up on the bench with them. Giles looked at Catherine and said, "Do you think they will ever think of me as their daddy?"

"Yes, it is just going to take a little more time. They have never had one. They don't even know what to call you yet. Just give it time."

"We are going to have to stay here at least one more day. The roads are too wet and treacherous to travel on today."

"It is a good thing we went ahead and got here last night. At least we aren't on the road."

"The men are taking care of the horses and equipment, so we can leave as soon as the weather lets up."

"We will be ready to go when you are."

He helped his wife up off the floor and led her to the table where breakfast was set, and Beth was trying to get up on the table. He grabbed her and sat down, then put her on his knee as he sat beside Catherine. Ann and Jacob just watched.

They left early the next morning, and it was slow going until about lunch; then the road was drier. It was still a long way till they got home. That night was spent in a tent, and it was comfortable and warm—only one more day till they would see the old keep again.

Catherine would be glad to be home; she just wondered what Jane had done to it while she was gone. She seemed to get quieter the closer she got to the keep, and Giles wondered what was wrong. He slowed his horse to let her catch up with him and then asked her what the problem was.

"I don't know. I just feel strange coming back like this after the way I was thrown out of my own house by that woman. What are my people going to think of me?"

"They won't think anything bad. They were most anxious to tell me how Jane had treated you, and I thought Helen might kill her. Your people are always going to think the best of you. They love and respect you."

"I hope you are right. I have so missed the old place."

"In a few hours, we will be back home, and everything will go back to normal."

She looked at him and raised her eyebrow. "Was it ever normal?"

He looked at her and had to admit things around them hadn't ever been what one would call normal.

As they rode into the courtyard, a few people were outside; one or two ran inside, and within a few minutes, there were a least twenty people to greet them. Cat got off her horse and hugged Helen, who nearly knocked her down, and she was drowning her with tears.

"I didn't think you were ever getting here! That fool of a man said you would be here days ago."

"We ran into some rain, which slowed us down."

Helen looked at Giles getting Beth out of the carriage, then looked at Cat and said, "Things are well?"

"Yes, we were married, and things are very good."

Helen walked over to Giles and simply said, "Thank you for bringing her back home." Then she reached up and patted his cheek like he was ten years old. Beth jumped out of his arms into hers, and she caught her as if this was expected; it had surprised him, but not Helen. Then she turned and started into the keep.

"Helen, you'd better wait a minute. I have some more people for you to meet." And at that, he reached in and pulled out Jacob and set him on the ground. Then he grabbed Ann and held her on his hip; then Catherine introduced them to the people standing around her.

"We adopted two children when we were gone. This is Ann and Jacob, our new additions to the family."

Helen didn't even skip a beat; she grabbed Jacob's hand, started toward the keep, and said, "Well, let's go. These children look hungry. Let's get them fed." And off they went.

Giles watched her go and realized Beth was as happy to be home as he was, and Jacob went with Helen like she was his grandmother; there were some women that kids just trusted.

Catherine had gotten off her horse and was stretching; she was tired and sore. It had been a long ride, and she wanted a hot bath. Giles took her arm and led her into the house with Ann on his hip, so there was no doubt that she was his, and he wanted the staff to know he had done the right thing by her. It wasn't so long ago that he wouldn't have cared what they thought of him, but now he did.

When they walked inside, Giles could see the damage Jane had caused had been taken care of, and the keep was back in order. Catherine stopped and addressed her people. "Lord Giles and I have been married, and we appreciate your welcome home. It is good to be here."

Giles took Ann over to a waiting Helen so she could feed her too, and when she picked her up, she looked up at him. "I will tell you later." He could tell she wondered at how skinny this child was.

Most of her people were there, and they began to clap and hug her; they were as glad she was back as she was.

"Thank you for our welcome, but your mistress is tired, and I am going to see her upstairs."

They walked upstairs, and Cat was indeed tired; but when she turned to open the bedroom door, Giles stopped and picked her up in his arms to carry her across the threshold.

"What are you doing? This isn't necessary. We have been married for weeks."

"Well, this is home, and I want to carry you into our room."

They walked inside as she leaned up to kiss him; then she looked around, and she saw there was a new bed and new bedding.

"I wanted to bring the bed from the lodge, but it was built in the room, and we couldn't get it out. But I wanted something new for us here, a fresh start."

He must have sent someone ahead to have it ready when they got home; it was such a sweet thing to do. She kissed him again.

"If you don't stop that, your bathwater is going to be cold."

"Well, you could warm me up." And there was that crooked smile again.

He set her on the ground and swatted her behind, then said, "Get in your bath, madam, while I get us something to eat and check on the kids." He really did like that smile, and he stopped outside the door, but he could wait till later. He was pleased that she liked what he had done; he wanted a fresh start, and that included a new bed.

As he walked down the stairs, he could see some dings in the wall, so he asked Helen what had happened to the wall.

"The lady that was here before broke some of my lady's furniture against the wall before throwing it down the stairs."

"Was it replaced before we got back?"

"Yes, the best we could manage. Some of the pieces weren't repairable."

"It is a good thing Jane is gone. I might have had to wring her neck."

She looked at him with some surprise and said, "She isn't gone, sir. She is living in town with that soldier that helped ruin my lady's things and wouldn't let someone go find you."

Great, Catherine was going to have a fit; he would have to tell her later if he couldn't get Jane to leave for good. Maybe if he offered her money? That would wait till later; he was anxious to get back upstairs, so he asked Helen if she would fix a plate of food to take back with him and asked where the kids were. Helen looked around and pointed to the table where Beth was all but asleep in Jennie's arms, but William and Jacob were still eating.

"Where is Ann? Is she all right?"

"She is fine. My cat had kittens, and she found them, and she is playing with them in the pantry. Come look." He found her in a pantry closet playing with a little gold kitten, holding it like it was made of precious fabric. She held it up to her face, and when she turned and looked at him, he had never seen such a look of happiness on this little girl's face.

"Look, Daddy. Isn't she the most beautiful kitten in the world? May I have her?"

He looked at Helen with tears in his eyes; she didn't know why, but this was the first time she had ever called him Daddy.

"Can she, when they are old enough?" Helen just shook her head; she didn't quite know what was happening, but she figured it had to be good, especially when Catherine came up behind her and squeezed her arm. She too had tears in her eyes; there was a story here, and she couldn't wait to hear it.

He just stood there and watched as Cat pulled Helen away and told her. "Giles found them in a barn, starving and beaten, with a man trying to kill them. They have always called me Mama, but that is the first time she has called him Daddy."

Helen turned around and looked at him, and he looked back at her and just smiled; then she went up to him and kissed him on the cheek.

"Ann sweetie, we need to let her go back to her mama for tonight, but you can see her tomorrow. Are you still hungry, or do you want your Daddy to take you upstairs?"

She gently put the kitten down next to her mother, stood up, and put her arms up for Giles to pick her up; then she laid her head on his shoulder. Catherine had Beth and said, "Let's take them upstairs and put both the children to bed, if that is all right?"

"Yes, of course, and the rest of the unloading we will do tomorrow." Jennie had already taken Jacob and William upstairs and put them down; the girls would sleep in the room across the hall. Giles had started renovations on several rooms before he had left, and it was a good thing he had because they were going to need them.

They put both girls down and covered them up, and Cat looked around the room; he had extensive renovations done. It was warm and dry in here; the girls were going to love it. He also had beds made; he must have sent word ahead because there were two. They went ahead and put them in one bed because they would be in the same bed before the night was over anyway.

"There is bread and meat and some of the winter fruit from the cellar." He nodded to her and started to return to their room.

"I need that tub worse than you do. I can't go to bed with such a lovely lady in this condition."

"Well, if the lady doesn't mind, you can."

"Get into the bed. I will be there shortly."

She watched as he took a rather cool bath and then started to dry himself; then he just wrapped the bath sheet around him and headed to bed. Catherine had pulled on her night gown because the room was still chilly even though the fire was burning; it had not been going long enough to heat the room entirely. She snuggled down into the warm covers, and he soon joined her. He put his arm out, and she snuggled into him and pulled the covers over them both.

"I never imagined things could be this good and I would be so happy."

"Are they truly the way you wanted?" Giles asked as he laid his head on hers and felt her hair next to his skin. "Is there anything else in this fantasy that I can provide?" he asked with amusement.

She looked up at him seriously and said, "A baby."

"That, madam, I would be most pleased to do. But don't you have enough for right now?"

"You're just glowing because Ann called you Daddy. I saw you downstairs. You could light up a room with that smile."

"Did you see her face with that kitten? I didn't think I have ever seen a child so happy, really happy."

"Was it worth it?" The smile he gave her said it all—it was worth it

Soon, the gown was gone, and she pulled him on top of her. Soon, the room was more than warm enough.

He was already talking to Robert about expanding his room upstairs to accommodate his growing family. These and other repairs were some things Catherine couldn't afford before. They were opening up the old west wing; several of the rooms were going to be used for bedrooms, and one big room was going to be used for the children's playroom. Cat realized she didn't have anything for the children to play with or, for that matter, to teach them with; she wanted all of them to know how to read and write. Giles asked her to accompany him to the west wing, and the boys wanted to come with him. She turned and picked up Beth, and to her surprise and Giles's, Ann reached up for him to carry her. Jacob had been watching and was finally letting go of her and trusting her to someone else; he was finally acting like a kid instead of her guard. He and William were at the top of the stairs when he yelled down, "Mama, Daddy, hurry up! You are so slow today!"

Giles just looked at Cat and smiled, and they moved a little faster. "We are getting older by the minute." She didn't even answer him; she just smiled.

When they got to the rooms, they were dusty, and the old tapestries were falling off the walls; they put the girls down and pulled some of them down.

"We are going to have to have new rugs and tapestries after these rooms are cleaned and the windows scrubbed. There are a few windows broken in the other rooms. I will have someone come in to repair them this week and a chimney sweep clean the chimneys. You, my dear, are going to have to find rugs and tapestries for this room. I know a man who can make new the furniture for these rooms."

"There are some in the other rooms."

"I have looked at them, and they are rotting too. We will have to replace most of them. You can go through and see what is still usable, but the rugs are rotted. I am having them removed. They are filthy."

"There is a fair coming in about a week not to far from here. They will have some of what we need, and I also need cloth for clothes for the children."

"And for you and Jennie. I never see the two of you in anything but the same two dresses, and we will need drapes in here as well."

"That is a lot of money to spend."

"As I told you, I wasn't exactly destitute when I came here, and you made me an even richer man. This place needs repairs. I won't have our children living like your father thought you should live on nothing while your people live better than you do. We have plenty, and I am going to see this place repaired and our children taken care of."

"Yes, sir, I will start making a list."

The next few days went smoothly enough, but Giles seemed preoccupied with something. She still didn't know that Jane was in town living with the soldier who had helped to humiliate her. Later that evening, she was called to town to deliver a baby and left without telling Giles; when he returned from checking the borders, he panicked. He went to see Helen when he couldn't find Jennie.

"Where is she?"

"My lady is in town delivering a baby. She should be back soon."

"Where in the village is she?"

"Robert will know where she is. He knows all the people in the village, and I am sure he can lead you to her."

He turned and sprinted toward the big room, shouting for Robert. Robert knew where she was and how to get there, although he didn't understand why his master was so upset. Catherine was fine; she had a guard with her, but Giles was in a big hurry to find her. As they rode into town, Robert's curiosity got the better of him, and he asked, "Is there a problem I should be aware of? Is Catherine in danger?"

"No, she isn't in danger, but Jane is still in the village. I should have told her before she runs into her."

"She is going to be furious. Is that soldier with her?"

"Yes, and that makes it even worse. I should have attended to this problem before now. Maybe I can take care of this before she finds out."

Robert just looked at him like "Are you stupid? Nothing ever works out that well."

They continued to ride toward town without saying anything else. When they got to the small cottage, Giles burst in, scaring Cat and the new child she was holding in her arms; the baby began to cry, and she began rocking back and forth. How do all women know how to rock a baby like that? She cradled the baby, and she began to quiet down as Cat gave her to her mother. The woman in the bed looked exhausted but was smiling at the new baby. Giles hadn't ever seen a smile that beautiful. He had spent his whole life in the job of killing, and he was finally beginning to get a family back.

Cat turned, looked at him, and asked, "Is there a problem at the keep?"

"No, but I need to talk to you when you are finished."

"All right, but I will be a while longer. You can sit by the fire."

Giles sat down as Robert walked outside. He just watched as she wrapped the baby and took care of the mother; she was quite skilled at what she did, and he was very proud of her. When finished, she left instruction on any problems that might arise and to call her if any appeared. They started to walk out of the house, and she mounted her horse with his help; and when they began to ride, Robert fell back a little out of earshot because he didn't want any part of this conversation. Cat turned to see Robert falling behind and turned to Giles and asked, "What is going on that is so important?"

"Jane is still here!"

"Are you serious?"

"No, apparently, she stayed here with that soldier that helped her at the keep."

"Why are you just telling me about this now?"

"I was afraid you might run into her before I could tell you."

"What are you planning to do about this?"

"I was thinking I could offer her money to leave?"

"No! I am not letting that woman get away with slapping me, ruining my furniture, and then offering her money. And I am not about to run from her either."

"You knew about the furniture?"

"Of course I did. This has been my home since I was born. I knew every piece of furniture in the house. It just wasn't something to fight about because it was ruined."

"How do you want me to handle this situation?"

"She was banished from court?"

"You were right. Marie had her banished so she can't go back." Catherine just smiled. Giles looked at her. "How good of friends are you and the queen?"

She just looked at him and smiled again. "Good enough to get someone banished from court."

He looked at her; what was he missing? The two of them had a secret, and he wasn't sure he wanted to know what it was.

"Leave it alone. It is not worth the fight unless you still fancy her, but I don't want that man anywhere near my family."

"I will see to that, and the only woman I fancy is sitting on the horse next to me."

"Then it is settled. Let's go home. I am tired and hungry."

"I was very proud of you tonight. Your people are very lucky to have you around."

"Thank you. Is there anything else I should know about?"

"No, right now, I can't think of anything."

"Good. I am too tired tonight for any more surprises."

As they rode, the sun was beginning to light up the sky, and Giles still couldn't believe how lucky he was to have stumbled so badly into such a good situation.

Several days later, Jennie, Catherine, and all the children went to the fair with six guards: John, James, and four others. They had taken a large wagon for their purchases and a cart for the children and the women. When they got there, it was a lively affair. Jennie and John took the boys, and they went to look for toys for them and household items in one direction, and she went the other; they decided to meet in the middle for lunch. As she took the girls down the booths, she found writing tablets and some bolts of material, which she bought and had set aside to pick up later. But she also noticed a man watching her and the girls. He was tall and dark blond, and he was trying not to be noticed, but she saw him watching her and especially the girls three times. She made sure the girls didn't get far away from her; she was afraid it was someone looking for Ann, but then she kept getting a bad feeling they were looking at her.

Catherine wasn't paying attention when Beth said, "Mama, look at the dolls. That one is so pretty." She looked up at the stall to see it was filled with dolls.

"Do you want one, baby? Just pick the one you want. Ann, do you want one too?" As she looked for Ann, she was a few steps away at another stall. Cat quickly went, picked her up, and brought her back.

"What is wrong, Mama?" She looked around for the man, and sure enough, there he was, watching her again. She called her guards over closer to her and had them stand by the girls and told them she thought she was being watched and to stay close.

"Beth, what doll do you want?" Beth picked one; then Cat paid for it, then turned to Ann, "What were you looking at, baby, at the other stall?" They walked over to it, and there were stuffed animals of all kinds. Ann pointed to a stuffed lamb.

"We would like to see the stuffed lamb please."

The man was rather rude and said, "I don't let the kids touch the merchandise."

"You will this time." And then the man turned around and looked at who was asking; he didn't have many ladies ask for his wares, and now he had just insulted one.

"Yes, ma'am. Right away, ma'am." He took the lamb down and handed it to her, and she handed it to Ann. She loved it; she cuddled it like her cat.

"Is that what you want?" She just nodded yes. So she turned around, paid for it, and walked away with the girls and her guards to meet Jennie; it was time to go home.

They met Jennie at the center of the fair; they got some meat pies to feed the children and started loading what they had bought. She told Jennie about the man that had been watching them, and Jennie was worried as well. They collected their parcels and bolts of cloth and were starting to leave when a ruckus started at the end of the market. Catherine turned to see a squire using a whip on a very large stallion who was fighting with another horse.

"Cat, don't." Jennie tried to stop her, but somebody was going to get killed; the squire didn't know what he was doing. He was making it worse.

"Watch the children. Don't let them out of your sight. I will be right back." She started down the center of the fair, with John right behind her. She got behind the squire, took the whip out of his hand, and then took the reins away from him; he turned and was going to hit her. No way was John going to let that happen. He grabbed the squire and pulled him away from Cat and the horses and let her handle the problem. The knight that owned the horse was running down the street as fast as he could as well as the owner of the other horse when they stopped dead in their tracks. They figured they were going to watch this woman be killed; instead, she took the whip, dropped it to the ground, and stood there. The horse started to rear and stopped as well as the other horse; she just stood there a minute, very still, and then she walked up to them and stroked them till they both calmed down. Both men walked up to her, and she handed each man his horse's reins; she patted each horse's head and walked away. When the horses were separated and Cat had left with her guards, one of the men finally asked who she was.

"That is Lady Catherine Broussard, Lord Giles's wife."

"I wondered what she looked like. She really is as good with horses as they say."

"Well, now you know."

There were other eyes watching and listening as well; he hadn't been sure, but he was now. Another man was watching her little girl and smiling.

When she got back home, she had another surprise waiting for her. Father Marques was in the great hall, talking to Giles; she couldn't wait to hug him.

"What are you doing here? I am so glad to see you!"

"Your husband asked me to come and replace your current priest. He said you and he don't get along, so I thought about it. And after what you did for those two children, I decided I wanted to be here."

She smiled at him and thanked the Lord for small miracles and for her husband.

"Well, is Helen getting you fed? Then we will get you a warm bed for tonight, and we will take care of the rest tomorrow." She handed him over to Helen and took Giles aside and said, "I need to talk to you in a little while. It is important."

He looked at her funny. "Is everything all right?"

She shook her head no. "Put extra guards out tonight and for the next few nights."

Now he was worried; they were bringing in carpets, tapestries, and the children. Cat was talking to Father Marques, but Jennie had all the children where she could see each of them, and Beth and Ann came to sit by him at the table like they were scared something had happened today. They all sat at the table to eat. Beth had a new doll, and Ann had a stuffed sheep. After supper, she didn't even go see her kitten. The boys had new toys, and they were in front of the fireplace playing with them. Jennie and Cat wouldn't let any of them out of their sight for one minute, and the girls wouldn't leave Giles's side.

After supper, the children were tired, so they got everyone to bed. But the girls wanted their door left cracked, which was strange. Cat left a candle burning.

When they got to their room, Giles shut the door, he turned to Cat, and said, "What the hell is going on? The girls are scared to death, and so are you. What happened at the fair today?"

"Someone was watching us. At first, I thought they might be watching Ann. But later, I realized it was me and Beth they were watching, and I don't know why. I saw the same man several times today, and he was definitely watching us. So I had the guards stay close, and we got finished and got out of there."

"Did they know your name?"

"I don't think so, but I don't know who does and who doesn't know me."

"You won't go back. I will send somebody if we need anything else. I still have enemies out there, and you and the children would be great hostages."

"I will keep all us close to the keep or inside."

"That means you don't travel to the village, you or Jennie—she is just as much at risk as you are now. If they need you, they are going to have to come here. I won't lose another family, understand?"

"What about Father Thomas?"

"We will take care of him tomorrow, but with plenty of men."

"Crack the door. I want to be able to hear the girls if they need me."

"All right, but what if I need you?"

"You will just have to be a little quieter than usual." He climbed into bed and thought it wasn't him that was noisy.

The next morning, they escorted Father Marques to the village with six guards, and they had hardly got into town before Father Thomas met her. Giles was at the back of the carriage carrying Father Marques. "I heard you were back and with two more Raider brats. Wasn't one enough? Are you collecting them from around the country? Did Lord Giles take pity on you and let you come back to scrub his floors or be his mistress? You're good for nothing else."

That was as far as he got. Giles walked out from behind the carriage and said, "I told you to never insult my lady again, and now she is my wife. Pack your bags. You are being replaced today."

"You can't do that."

"I already have. These men are here to help you pack and then put you in this carriage and take you to your new church. This is Father Marques, and he married us. My wife likes him, and she doesn't like you. So you are leaving. I warned you, and you didn't listen. So now you are gone. Men, help him pack."

Giles helped Father Marques down out of the carriage as the townspeople came to see Catherine; the guards went to help Father Thomas pack. Cat introduced the new father to the villagers, and two hours later, Father Thomas was packed and loaded inside the carriage. He didn't say a word; he just looked at Cat, and she smiled; all he had to do was be nice to her, and he couldn't even do that. Giles was good to his word, and now he was gone. She walked over, slammed the door, and waved goodbye. If looks could kill, he would have melted to the seat of that carriage.

Giles just stood back and watched; he had wondered how she would handle that, and it was perfect. They turned around and helped Father Marques settle into his new church. Giles had some ideas for some renovations to this place; the old priest was going to be quite comfortable here.

He also told the village elder that Cat wasn't going to be wandering outside the keep for a while, so if anyone needed attention, they should come to the keep. The elder wondered what was going on, and Giles said he was worried about her safety. Then the elder told him that people had been asking about Catherine and Beth while they were gone. Giles wanted to know who, and the man said he didn't know, but he would try to find out. Giles thanked him and then gathered Cat up, and they headed home; he didn't plan on telling her about this new information. She was scared enough as it was; he would wait till he found out more. That wasn't going to be long.

The next day, as the wagon was being unloaded, Cat and Jennie were busy in the big room upstairs; the new rugs were on the floor, and the children's toys were being brought in. Cat had bought a rocking horse and some more stuffed animals as well as building blocks for the boys to play with. Right now, one of the men had got them a board and two small hammers and some nails, and they were driving nails in them. There was no particular reason for the nails, just something to bang on, and they were having a good time. She had asked the workman about it, and he had said his children started out that way; they put them in, then took them out; that was how they learned. She just backed off and watched. Sure enough, they put them in and then took them out and then did it again. They were having a wonderful time, and each time, they got them in straighter.

The girls were playing with their dolls in the corner, and Cat had a box built for the mother cat and her kittens, and they were up here as well;

neither girl had ever had a pet, so she wanted to watch them as they played with them to make sure they didn't get too rough.

She and Jennie were telling the workmen where the new tapestries were to be hung when she noticed a new girl she hadn't seen before dusting some of the new furniture. She turned and asked Jennie, "Do you know that girl over there? I don't remember ever having seen her before today."

Jennie just shook her head no, and they both started walking over to where the girl was working; they didn't notice, but James was following them as well. When she got to the girl, she touched her on the shoulder and asked her name. "I don't think I know you, and I know most of the girls that work for me in this keep?"

The girl looked surprised and looked over Cat's shoulder to James, and then she turned around to look at James and said, "Is there something I should know? James, who is this young lady?"

James began to blush, and Cat looked at Jennie, and they both smiled. Well, well, James had found himself someone, and they were just now finding out about it.

"My lady, this is Caroline Adams, and she is from the next village. Her father died a few weeks ago, and I got her a position with Helen downstairs, but she sent her up here today to help you."

Helen wanted Cat to see James's lady, the sneaky old woman. They would all have to have a chat later and compare notes. She was very pretty, slender, with long brown hair. She was a little younger than James, but the way he smiled at her, he was totally smitten.

"Well, young lady, where are you living now that your father is gone?"

She finally looked up at her and said, "The rent is up in a week on our cottage, so I am trying to find another place in town to stay. There is a lady that says she has an extra room for rent. I was going to check on it tonight."

"And the name of this woman? I know most of the town."

"I believe it is Jane." Both James and Cat went into a fit of coughing.

"No, my dear, there has got to be a room in this keep where you can stay. I will personally find one. James, remind me if I get lost in today's work." He nodded his head.

"Thank you, my lady." She grabbed her rag, and they started back to work. Then Jennie motioned for her to come over to the window, and when she got there, she pointed down to two men talking in the trees at the edge of the corrals.

"Look at those men. Doesn't one of them look like the man at the fair?"

"Now you are getting paranoid." But as she watched, he looked up, and he noticed them watching him. So he moved himself back into the woods; it was the same man. By the time James and some men got down there, he was gone; he had a horse tied up, and he and the man with him were far from the keep. She just wondered who was watching her. She didn't find a separate room for Caroline. She asked her if she would mind sleeping in the girls' room and explained what was going on. The boys were next to Robert and Jennie's room with a connecting door, and now it was kept ajar. Someone was keeping tabs on them, and she wanted the children watched at all times.

CHAPTER 7

Catherine was beginning to be sick in the mornings and had all the other signs of pregnancy, but she still hadn't told Giles; she was waiting for the perfect time, and it hadn't happened yet. When they got back home, she discovered that her clothes were beginning to get tight, so she started having some new clothes made. She had assumed Giles would notice and comment about the changes in her, but as of yet, he hadn't.

Giles had been downstairs most of the morning with some of his men; there had been a letter sent to him from the king, and he was talking to them about it. When he came back upstairs, he looked like a thundercloud and stomped into the room; she decided this wasn't a good time to talk babies.

"What is the problem? I heard you yelling downstairs."

"I need to go to court. I have a problem that the king and I need to discuss. Will you be all right for a few days? I will leave plenty of men to protect you."

"What do we need protection from?"

"Beth's Raider father wants her and you as payment on some kind of truce with the king, and he thought since I was so reluctant to marry you in the first place, I would agree."

Catherine was stunned; now he showed up. Well, at least she knew why she was being watched; he wanted to know about his daughter.

"What are you going to tell him? This could be an important truce for the king."

"I don't care if the whole Raiders army invades. You and the children aren't going anywhere with anyone but me. The men and I are going to the king today, but I am still leaving a sizable army here to protect you. Now we know who was watching you and Beth. You have got to stay close to the keep."

"Yes, I won't make the same mistake twice."

"I love you, and I will straighten this out. If not, we will just take the children and leave."

She went over to him and put her arms around him; everything had been so good, she knew it couldn't last.

"Just come back to me, please."

"Nothing on this earth could keep me from you. I will be back."

He leaned her head back and kissed her softly on the lips.

"Help me put some clothes together. The sooner I leave, the sooner I can be back."

They spent the next hour in the room talking and preparing for him to leave. She wondered if she should tell him about the baby and decided he had enough to deal with right now. One of his men came, knocked on the door, and told him everything was ready to go when he was. He kissed her again and held her tightly for another moment before he went out the door. She ran up the stairs as quickly as she could to see him ride away; she hated this, but once more, her past was coming back to haunt her. She watched him all the way out of sight; it always seemed the people she loved left through these same gates and never returned.

Giles's hands were clenched in front of him on the table as he looked across at the man who was Beth's father. Lars Sorenson was just as mad as he was, and it was all King Charles could do to keep them from killing each other. Lars had simply stated that he should be allowed to have his daughter, and the whole meeting had gone to hell. Charles was glad now that he had taken his wife's advice and brought extra men into the castle before this meeting, or he wouldn't have anything under control.

"She is my wife, and Beth is her child. She wouldn't give her up to marry me, and now I won't give either one of them up to you." Then he slammed his hand on the table. The king had thought that a threat to take his land might improve the communication; instead, Giles said, "Take it. I will take Catherine, Beth, and my other two children and go to my estates in France. I am sure my men will follow me."

Charles couldn't understand what had happened; a few short months ago, this man wouldn't even talk to this woman. Now he would give up everything to keep her as well as two more Raiders children. This Raiders was willing to trade with them to get her and his child.

"Calm down. We will work this out without you shedding blood on either side."

He might as well have been talking to himself for all the good it was doing.

"Can I at least see the child? I would like to know for sure that she is mine."

Giles began to come over the table at him, and the king's men had to restrain him. Charles stood up and motioned Giles over to him.

"At least let him see the child. Maybe he will disavow her as his, and this problem will go away for all of us."

Giles knew that this was just a ploy to get close to his family, but there was little he could do about it here; besides, out of this castle, he had more maneuvering room. In this room, he was under too much scrutiny from the king, and he could decide to have him jailed if this went badly. That would leave his family alone with not enough men to protect them; besides, he knew from looking at this man that Beth was his child.

"All right, that is acceptable, but he can't take her anywhere. He can just see her, and only he is allowed into my keep."

"That is satisfactory, but I wish to take my men. They can camp outside the wall of the keep."

Giles wasn't happy about that at all, but the king seemed to think this was a good decision. Giles said, "You may look at your daughter, but she isn't going anywhere—ever."

"What if I ask your wife to come with me?"

"She won't. I would bet my life on it."

"It seems we are betting both our lives and futures on her decision."

Lars stood up and shook the king's hand, then turned to go. Charles didn't like this; he had the feeling that he had just seen the start of a very nasty war—this one over a woman. It hadn't been that long ago that Giles had wanted to be rid of this woman. He should have listened to his wife when she said Giles should meet Catherine and that he should have insisted on it. God, he hated it when she was right.

There was something Giles had to do before he left, and he asked the king if he could speak to the queen. He was given permission and called for his wife.

He met the queen in her garden, and he knelt in front of her and kissed her ring; then he stood in front of her and said, "My lady sends her apologies for not coming, but this is not the time. Your Majesty, I wish to give you my deepest apologies for my actions on our first meeting. I was a bastard."

She just smiled. Then she had him rise, took his arm, and led him to the pond; she shooed her ladies away for the conversation she wanted to have with him. She wanted to have it in private.

"There are too many ears around, so we will walk out here. So you found Lady Catherine to be a good match after all?"

He just nodded his head and blushed.

"I probably need to be going before Lars can get to the keep."

"Don't worry, you have several hours before he can leave. His horses have gotten loose and mixed with mine. I wanted to talk to you, so he will be delayed." She looked up at him with a wicked little smile. He bet the king didn't get away with much with this lady.

"I won a very nice bet with the king because of you—a very nice stallion. He bet me you wouldn't marry her. That is why I had him put in that clause that Catherine had to stay until you got there, and she had to show you the land."

"That was your doing?"

"Yes, and it worked. Once you met her, you realized what you were giving up, didn't you?"

He just nodded.

"May I ask what the king lost in his part of the bet?"

"There is a duke here with a very pretty daughter. Charles was making eyes at her. My youngest son is looking at the girl too, and I didn't want her ruined. I wanted the family gone from court. Now they are back at their estates, and my husband's eyes are back on me."

The queen was a woman you don't cross, he thought.

"Did Catherine like the ring I chose for your wedding?"

"Yes, she was very pleased with it, and I thank you for picking out all the other rugs and tapestries. They are wonderful."

She nodded. "I like to spend other people's money. Catherine still has a way with horses?"

"Yes, she is unlike anyone I have ever seen with them."

"I would like to see more of that. She may have to help me with my new stallion, but what about Jane? She left the same day you sent for the contract, and my spies said you told her not to come. I am sorry. I think I sent her to you, and I did not mean to do that."

"I told her not to come, but she came anyway. She slapped Catherine, who ran away from me, and I had to hunt her down to get her back."

"Where is Jane now?"

"She is still in the village by the keep living with another man."

"Are you crazy? You have to get her away from your family, even if you have to buy her a house somewhere else!"

"Catherine says she won't pay her to leave."

"Well, that is the first dumb thing that girl has done, and you can tell I said so. By the way, it seems you have picked up two more Raiders children along the way. That keep too big?"

"It was that or leave them to die, and that old keep had plenty of room, and so did we."

"I am sorry, I have offended you. Just two more to love?"

When he smiled, she knew she was right.

"Good man. I knew there was one in there somewhere, and Catherine was the woman to find him." One of her men motioned to her, and she turned to him and said, "Time to leave. The Raiders are getting organized, but you will still beat them home by several hours. Tell Catherine I want to see all of you when this is over. Please be careful and don't get killed. I am sending several of my men with you." She pulled him down to her and kissed him on the cheek.

"Be careful. You might get me in trouble."

"If I was trying to get you in trouble, it wouldn't be in my garden in front of everybody." He was right; this lady could be trouble if she wanted to be.

"Why are you sending men with me?"

"Because I want to know what is happening, and they will tell me before it gets out of hand, if Catherine can't handle it."

He didn't know it, but one of her men had a letter for Catherine's eyes only, and he would see she got it.

"What about me handling it?"

"Men start the wars. Women have to stop them, or there wouldn't be anybody left."

She should have sobered Giles up and boxed his ears until he met Catherine like she wanted to, but her husband didn't want to interfere; next time, she would know better. She also should have gotten rid of Jane sooner, but she thought maybe her dear husband might have had a fling with her before, but she got her banished anyway; she was gone now.

She wasn't about to let Charles forget this one, and he was going to hate that. She was right about this match; she just hoped it wasn't going to start a war.

Giles gathered his men and headed to the stables when Gerard asked, "Is it as bad as we thought?"

"Yes, we need to leave." They mounted their horses and started the long road home.

As they left, Lars's men were still trying to catch the Raiders horses and get their wagons loaded; whatever Queen Marie's men had done had delayed them nicely. Giles smiled; he would have to remember not to anger that lady.

Lars walked outside to talk to his men to get them ready to travel, but he looked at one of the men whom wished he had not allowed to come on this trip. Vatic was the man who had dragged Catherine into camp that day and he suspected he was the one who beat her so badly; if Giles ever found out, he suspected he would kill him. There had been times he had wanted to do the same. He couldn't leave him at home; he didn't trust him. Maybe that was why he had brought him, or maybe it was because he couldn't kill him for hurting her without losing the trust of his men, but Giles could. It had been said that she wasn't the only woman he had beaten, and he was sure he had killed one of the village women but he couldn't prove it.

Giles and his men were already on their way home as fast as they could; he had to talk to Catherine before these men reached the keep and if necessary get her and the children ready to run if this turned out the way he thought it was going to. He was sure she would pick him over Lars, but he had to know. After everything that had happened, he wouldn't give her up, and he suspected Lars had the same thought.

Catherine had heard the men arriving in the middle of the night; she had hardly slept since Giles had left, so she went running down to meet him. He came into the great hall, and she about knocked him down.

"You came back to me!"

"Of course I did! I told you I would. You are my wife." It sounded so simple to him; he didn't understand that no one else had ever returned. She looked so tired; there were bags under her eyes. He asked, "Are you all right? Haven't you slept since I left, or are you ill?"

"I am fine. I just missed you so much. I didn't rest well. How did it go at court? Is it all settled?"

"It didn't go as well as I planned. The king has said the Raiders can come to the keep to see if Beth is really his and to see if you wish to go with him."

"I don't wish to see the man or for him see Beth. But if that is the only way to get rid of him, fine. When will he be here?"

"He is right on my heels. He will be out there in the morning, but only he and a few of his men are allowed into the keep."

"This isn't going to end well, is it?"

"It ends any way we let it, even if you and children have to leave."

"*No*, not without you!"

"It will only be until everything can be settled."

She just looked at him. Did he think she was stupid? The only way this was going to end was with one of them dead, so she walked to the door and left.

She went to the kitchen to check on tomorrow's bread; it seemed like this house was again becoming a prison. She heard the horses rustling in the corral close to the barn, so she grabbed a cape and snuck outside. Giles had told her not to stray far from the keep. There was another foal due soon, so she went outside to check on her mare. Most of the men were scurrying around, following Giles's orders to fortify the keep, so she stayed out of their way. She walked down to the end of the barn to the last stall, where she stopped. The mare was unsettled in the stall, so she grabbed a handful of grain to feed her; as she leaned over the gate, she realized someone was watching her.

"I kept wondering if the image I carry in my mind was right, or I had just imagined how beautiful you are. You are still as beautiful as I remember, even more so."

She didn't have to ask who it was; she still heard him talking to her in her dreams.

"I don't know how anyone could think I was anything but a bloody mess, Lars."

"I should have told you then what I thought. Maybe you wouldn't have run. Why did you leave? I told you I wanted you to come with me. You would have been treated with every respect due my wife."

"I didn't run. One of my men came and took me away back to the keep. There were times I wondered if I wouldn't have been better off with you, especially when I discovered I was pregnant. But it seems I had very little choice either way."

"You have a choice now. I can see to that."

"It's too late. The matter was settled months ago when I fell in love with Giles. I won't dishonor him, and I won't leave."

She turned around and saw him deep in the shadows; he was as tall and handsome as she remembered. Then Lars walked toward her. Beth was going to be a very pretty woman when she grew up with those same blue eyes and blond hair; nobody was ever going to think she was anybody's child but his.

"Please stay there. If you come any closer and one of my husband's men sees you, there will be trouble."

"I know. We have already been at each other's throats over this, and he has already threatened my life. I wanted to speak to you alone to see if you were really all right, or he was just telling the king that. He even told the king he would give up all this land and the keep just to keep you and our child. Would you really have come with me?"

"I don't know. I was so alone and unhappy with my life. I am not sure what I would have done, even if I had been in my right mind. From what I hear, you aren't sure my child is yours. Isn't that why you are here to make sure?"

"I never had any doubts that baby was mine from the first time I heard you had a child. I was there that night. I know you were a virgin. There are two little girls. I have seen them from a distance. She is the smaller one?"

"Yes, the other one is Ann. After all these years, I don't remember much of that night. Maybe I was just another conquest and nothing more. You seemed to be just a shadow face in my dreams. Sometimes I didn't think you were real. I always hoped you would come back, if for nothing more than to see your child. I waited for a long time, but you never came back."

"Your man almost killed me. When he took you, he hit me over the head with a large metal pot. If it hadn't been for my thick head, I would be dead, and then I wouldn't be here at all. My men loaded me up, and we headed home, only to lose two boats to high seas. And the weather has not been accommodating to get back here. After inquiring about you, I found out about the baby you had delivered and that you were truly the lady to this land. We have been trying to make a treaty with your king for some time, so I thought maybe this would be the way to get back to you and our child."

"Nothing is going to change. I made my decision when I married Giles. He loves Beth as if she were his own. I wish you would just leave it alone and go. I don't want anyone's blood on my hands over this."

"You still wear the cross I gave you. If you are so content with him, why not take it off?"

Her hand went to her neck and the cross as it had so many times, and she didn't know. Had she told Giles about the cross when she was sick? If she did, he had never said anything. Lars was right; she should have taken it off before now.

"What is our daughter's name?"

"Elizabeth, and she is beautiful child, but you have already seen her," Cat said with pride.

"Catherine, I still think about touching you and how soft your skin felt when I held you in my arms. I am not sure I can leave things the way they are, and I won't leave without seeing her!"

"I get to choose this time. Isn't this how this is supposed to work? How did you find out my name? I don't remember telling you."

"The same way I found out about the baby. My men were looking for you. It took them longer than I expected because they weren't looking for the mistress of this keep. Then at the fair, I saw you and two little girls, and then I watched you walk up to two rearing horses like they were nothing. Then I found out about your reputation with horses, Lady Catherine Broussard."

"That's why I have felt like I was being watched. I thought it was my imagination."

"I have had men watching for some time to make sure you were all right. Then I went to the king with my proposition. Who are the other children?"

"The other little girl and boy I adopted. They are my children as well. I am staying here, and so is Beth. But I would suggest that you get out of here before one of my men see you."

She didn't ever want him or anyone else to know just how much of those days she did remember or to know she would have gone home with him; it was too late now to even admit that to herself. Giles had never repeated what she had said when she had fever; she didn't know how much he knew.

"I am not afraid of your men or your husband."

"My lady, are you all right? You were supposed to stay inside."

It was Robert calling and walking down to the stall where she was standing; she turned and looked back into the shadows, only to see blackness. Cat started to walk toward him, but before she got too far away, she heard Lars say, "This isn't over, Catherine."

When he called her by name, it was almost a caress; she hesitated for just a second. Then she whispered quietly, "It is going to have to be. I don't want to have to bury either one of you. Go home. You came back too late."

As she walked back into the keep, Giles was heading out to the stalls; he started to say something, then just shut up. Cat walked past him and up the stairs. He told Robert to make sure everything was closed and that a guard was at each door; then he turned to follow her up the stairs. He wanted to see what was wrong; the look on her face told him she was not in the mood to be berated by him. She walked into their room and sat down by the window. He didn't have time to talk as one of his men came into the room to have him try on some of his armor. She watched as the campfires began to light up all around the castle, and she knew this was going to turn into a bloody siege before it was through.

Catherine turned to Giles and said, "I want to meet with him and let him see his daughter. Then maybe I can talk him into leaving."

"He is not coming into my home!"

"I believe it was my home first, and maybe this way, I won't have to watch you die."

He looked at her, and the truth was he didn't want the Raiders to see her or the baby; he was afraid she might change her mind and go back with him. They had never talked about when she was sick and the things she had said during her fever, but he knew she had been attracted to this man.

"Will you arrange this meeting for me?"

"Yes, but only a few men can come into our home, and then he can see Beth. I have to know, do you want to go with Lars?"

"No, I just don't want this to turn into a war."

She hadn't told him about the meeting in the stables. That would ruin everything; and truth be known, a few months ago, she would have gone home with him. She still remembered what it was like to have Lars hold her; it was the first time she had ever felt someone had wanted her. Giles came back and said, "He wants to have this meeting tonight, if it isn't too late."

The sun wouldn't set for a little while yet, and it was still light, so Cat said, "That will be fine. I'll get the baby dressed and meet you downstairs."

She started to dress and decided to wear her blue dress; she looked good in it, and she wanted Giles to be proud of the way she looked. Elizabeth was still wide awake; there was way too much activity going on to get her to sleep. Cat dressed her in a pale pink dress; it made her skin glow and her blue eyes even bluer. She dressed Ann and Jacob; she wanted Lars to see her life was here now and that she wasn't going to leave for anyone. Giles came back up the stairs saw Cat and smiled.

"Are you ready to do this?"

"Let's be done with this and get our life back."

As they walked down the stairs, Giles held Ann. Jacob walked between them as Cat held Beth. She felt like if Giles was close, nothing could touch her or their lives.

Lars watched her come down the stairs with the prettiest little girl in her arm; he had three sons by other women, but none of them had he ever taken to be his wife. He would have proudly wed this woman, and this child would be under his care. Giles walked toward them, holding Ann, and Lars stood up. Catherine walked across the hall of her home and couldn't have been prouder; this was her world and her children, and she wanted these men to know it.

"This is your daughter, Lars, unless you would like to disclaim her now. And all of this could be done."

"I would never say this child was not mine. She looks like my sisters. I wish they were here as well to see her. My offer is still open to you and our daughter. Will you come back with me?"

"I already told you no—my place is here with my husband and my other children."

"You seem to have a liking for Raiders children?"

"I don't like watching them starve after your men leave the women behind to have their children and then throw them away like trash." The look she gave him and his men was scalding, for they all knew what she was talking about.

Giles looked at her with a look that said, "When did you see him?"

He didn't have time to say much else because at about that time, Cat saw someone in the small group of men, and all of the color drained out of her face. If Giles hadn't been holding her arm, she might have fallen. He looked into the group of men and saw one leering at her with a cruel smile on his face; then he looked back at Cat. She was terrified and trying to pull away from him. He looked down at her and asked, "Is that the man who hurt you?"

She nodded yes.

"Robert, help your mistress."

Robert moved her back away from the table, but she would go no further. Jennie was at the foot of the stairs, and Cat handed Beth to her and told her, "Get the children out of here now."

Lars saw the look on Giles's face as he drew his sword, and then he heard one of his men pull out his sword; as he turned, he saw Vatic stepping out of the crowd. Giles kept coming forward until Lars asked, "What is going on here?"

"As if you didn't know; that man is the one who beat my wife and left her back forever scarred. I promised myself if I ever found out who it was, I would kill him, and that is what I intend to do."

Lars had not paid attention to who was in the group with him, and he should have. Vatic walked forward; he had never been challenged by anyone for beating or killing a woman before. After all, they were just women. He was sure this man would be no problem to kill; then they could go home, but the look on Lars's face told him that might not be the case.

By the time Giles reached him, he was in a killing rage; all he could think about was every mark this man had left on her back, and he would make him pay for every one of them. Lars started to stop them, but that wasn't going to happen; besides, he was furious as well, and he couldn't very well kill one of his own men. But the look on Catherine's face told him if Giles didn't kill him, he wouldn't return home alive.

Vatic took the first stroke but wasn't even close, nor was his second. Giles was on the defense and was looking for an opening. They backed toward the door, and all the men got out of their way. Thrusting back and forth out into the front of the hall, Vatic still thought he might have a chance if he got outside to where the Raiders men were, but they looked to their master and backed away. Robert held on to Catherine's arm as they followed the fighting men outside. Lars watched both men and soon realized there was no way that Vatic was going to best Giles even though it would make all of this work out in his favor. But every time he looked over at Catherine's face, he knew Vatic deserved this, and it should have been him that had done it. Vatic took a swing at Giles, and he swerved to the side slightly. Vatic never realized till the pain hit him like a boulder that Giles's sword was up to the hilt in him. He looked up at Giles and said, "All of this over that bitch?"

Giles didn't think twice; he pulled out his sword and, with one stroke, cleaved Vatic's head from his body. Giles turned and said, "My wife, my child, if you think you will ever have either, it will be over my dead body!"

"So be it." Lars turned and left with his men following close behind.

Neither man noticed Catherine sliding down the door in a dead faint; Robert reached out to catch her. She came to with Giles holding her and saying, "Breathe, Cat, breathe."

She looked at him as though he was stupid until she realized she wasn't breathing. She exhaled and began to feel better; looking to her side, they were carrying off the man who had terrorized her dreams for years now. From what Lars and Giles had said to each other, this was going to be a disaster. She began to sit up.

Giles said, "Let's go up to our room. I need to talk to you."

She already knew what he wanted to know, so they might as well get this over with. Beth was running toward them, and Giles didn't want her seeing anything outside, so he ordered the doors shut; then he picked her up, and they headed to the stairs. Giles held on to her arm a little too hard as they climbed, and she yanked it away from him and walked the rest of the way by herself. He walked into the nursery to put Beth and Ann down, not noticing that Cat just kept on going up the stairs to the roof of the keep. She pulled the door open and left it that way because she knew he would follow her. He walked up beside her and didn't say a word, and they stood watching all the campfires light up around the keep. He came up behind her and wrapped his arms around her, and then she said, "I talked to him in the stable earlier this evening. He wanted to know about his daughter and to talk to me to see if I was really happy, not that it seems to make much difference to him, or he wouldn't be doing this."

"Why didn't you say something earlier?"

"You were too busy getting fitted with your armor to even notice I was in the room."

"What did you tell him that you can't tell me? And by the way, when you were so sick, you told Jennie and me more than probably anyone knows, even Lars."

She turned, looked at him, and reached up to cradle his face in her hands. "I don't know for sure how much I told you, but at that point in my life, I would have gone home with him just because he wanted me. I had been ignored all my life. I wanted to be loved. I know you don't understand, but I am very glad things went differently. I love you and only you. I would never betray you, but I don't wish to bury you either. We have got to stop this somehow. I don't want anyone to die over what should be just between the three of us."

He put his arms around her and kissed her; then he just held her for a long time as they stood and looked out over the campfires.

They didn't realize, but down below, another pair of eyes watched both of them. Lars wanted something Giles had, and he intended to get it one way or another.

"Catherine, I just don't know what else to do without spilling blood over this. He doesn't plan to leave without you."

He put his arm around her, and they walked down the stairs to their bedroom, which was full of people waiting to talk to him; then he walked downstairs and told her he would return soon.

There was a knock on her door, and when she opened it, there was a Queen's guard standing there. "Her Majesty sent this note to you and only you." He placed the note in her hand and said, "If there is a reply, just give it to me, and I will see it gets back to her. I will be close." He bowed and then went back down the hall.

My dearest Catherine,

I can see this is going to turn into something bad, and you and your children are right in the middle of it. You would be proud of Giles. He offered to give up all the land and titles and take you away when my husband thought that might be what it would take to stop a fight. I told you he was a good man, and now he is going to prove it. If you need a place to hide to stop this, go to my man, and he will take you to one of my properties and hide you from both of them if need be. No one will look for you on the queen's estates. I will take care of the king. He won't take your land. See if you can stop them from killing each other down there. I have faith in you. We are smart women. We will get this figured out. I trust my man. Use him if you need help. He will keep you safe.
When this is all over, come see me and bring all your children. Have I got a horse for you to see!

Love, Marie

Catherine stoked the fire until the room was quite warm; she had plans for tonight, and she didn't want it cold in here. She crossed the room to where her clothes were and took down his fur robe after taking off her clothes; she just put on the fur robe and nothing else and stood by the window, waiting for him. Giles came into the room with two other men and was barking out orders; then he saw Catherine. She had that funny little smile on her face, and he sent the men away, just telling them to make things secure. Giles followed them to the door and bolted it; then he turned back to his wife, who was walking toward him. He began to take off his shirt, and she said, "No, let me."

She walked up to him and began unlacing his shirt, all the time pressing up against him and stroking everything she could reach. She walked behind him and pulled the shirt over his head and almost all the way down, so now his arms were tangled in it, and then she walked back in front of him and dropped the robe.

To say the least, he was shocked; this woman was so shy. She never started their sexual games, but his hands were tangled, and she took full advantage of the situation. Cat pushed him back on the bed and began to torture him, for there was no other description of what she was doing to him. She dragged her breasts and hair up and down his chest, all the while leaving little kisses in their wake; she straddled him, and he still couldn't get his hands loose, so he kind of bucked her off to the side so he could free his hands. He reached for her, and this time, there was no hesitation on her part; she was hungry for him to touch all of her, and he did. Giles fingers stroked her rhythmically and each movement the anticipation heightened until the pleasure became almost unbearable. She felt as if she might shatter into a million pieces, she might come out of her skin and mingle with the night. It was the best lovemaking he had ever had with any woman, and then she curled up as close to him as possible and said, "We will take care of this tomorrow." She had a plan to keep this from turning into a war.

Giles got up early, rinsed off in the tub, and started to dress. Then he put on his armor. Catherine watched quietly from the fireplace, waiting for him to leave; then she would put her plan into place. She had James downstairs and John in the barn, and they were both busy doing what she had ordered. The queen's guard had met with her in the big room where the children played, and they had talked for some time; then she had written a note. He took the note and joined John in the barn, and they continued bringing boxes down from the house. Everybody was so busy watching out front at the gathering soldiers that nobody noticed what was going on out back. There was a wagon being loaded and a carriage waiting; if things didn't work out as she wanted, she was going to one of the queen's properties. The queen's man had already decided on which one. She had had enough of this; she would see if her plan would work or not.

The smaller children—Ann, Jacob, and William—were in their playroom under guard; nobody was to go in there except her people. When James was through, he would be up there; if they needed to leave, he would load the children. Jennie was dressing Beth as Cat put on her green wedding dress; it was her prettiest dress, and she wanted to stand out in a crowd today. She looked out the window at probably at least five hundred men who were lining up on opposite sides, ready to start this little war over a woman and a little girl. Giles and Lars were the last to arrive, and they were arguing in front of their band of troops. They didn't notice for a bit that the rest of the men had suddenly become very quiet until they looked at the door to the keep. Catherine was walking toward them in what looked like the dress she married him in, holding Beth in her arms.

As she walked toward them, Lars was afraid one of the horses might trample her. Giles knew that would not happen; there was no horse on this field that would ever hurt her. He wasn't so sure about the men. She walked toward them, and both men looked at each other.

Finally, Lars said, "Are you not going to stop her? It is dangerous out here."

"She is well aware of that, but I think she has something to say to us. That didn't work out too well yesterday."

"She and the child could be trampled."

"You have never seen her around horses, have you? I think you will be surprised how they react to her, and as long as she is holding Beth, nothing will happen."

She walked up between the two men astride their horses, turned to one, then the other, and said, "Get off your horses and come here."

Giles noticed before Lars did that she no longer wore the cross; he was hoping that was a good sign. Lars noticed too and already knew he had lost her.

Giles wasn't even surprised when his horse walked toward her, but Lars was; she petted them both on the nose, pushed them back, and told them to stay.

"I am sick to death of this game you two are playing. You are ready to kill each other over me, and it doesn't seem to matter what I have to say in the matter." They both started to say something when she said, "Both of you hush and listen to me because I will only say this once."

She reached out to hand Beth to Lars, and he took her. "This is your daughter. Do you agree?"

"Yes, this is my child."

"Your child has land kept in her name to the north so she never has to be put in this situation. If you were to do the improvements it needs and keep it protected for her, I might consider letting her come visit you in the summer with an appropriate guard."

Giles started to say something, but that wasn't happening

"Now this is the way this is going to work. You two are going to sit down and settle this like gentlemen without bloodshed, or the children and I will disappear, and neither one of you will ever see us again. I will not tell Beth the man she thinks of as her daddy killed her papa, and I will not tell this baby I am carrying that Beth's papa killed his daddy. So settle it now. I am sick to death of burying the people I love, and I am not going to do it anymore. I raised one child alone. I can just as easily raise four. So decide. Oh, and by the way, the queen is on my side. So you two had better resolve this, or I will let her loose on you two. You think the king is bad? You don't know *bad*."

She reached around and took Beth from Lars and started to walk back to the keep.

"Would she really do it?"

"She already has. My mistress showed up and slapped her. It took me more than a week to find her, and she wasn't hiding. Did she just say she was pregnant?"

Lars just turned and started to follow her. Giles walked up beside him. "We don't seem to have any other choice than to settle this."

"Not if we want to see our children grow up. You know I want her, and I asked her to come with me. I should have returned sooner."

"Cat told me she talked to you in the barn and that she refused your offer, so why did you bring that man to my home after what he did to her?"

"The way things happened after she escaped, I never really thought about who had hurt her. Her man banged my head pretty hard. I don't think I was supposed to wake up at all. It was stupid on my part, but if you hadn't killed him, he would not have lived to go back home. Several people in my village suspect he beat a young woman to death, and I didn't pursue the matter. Now I know I should have. Thank you for doing what I should have done. Is she badly scarred?"

"Yes, she will wear those marks always."

"Do you really think the queen would help her?"

"She already has, and between the two of them, we are already beat. Ever wonder how your horses got mixed up at the castle when we were there? That was the queen's doing. She wanted to talk to me, so she distracted you for a while."

"That was her? It took us hours to sort out our horses, and then she said she couldn't understand how that could have happened to my face!"

"They are very good friends, and we are not going to win this game. If I am right, she is already packed and ready to leave."

Lars just looked at him in wonder.

They both followed Cat to the keep, leaving their men wondering what was going on. Cat was still so furious at both of them; she didn't realize how tight she was holding on to Beth until she said, "Mama, too tight."

"I am so sorry, baby. Mama isn't paying attention to what she is doing." She didn't slow her pace as she headed to the keep.

Farther back, Giles and Lars followed behind her. Finally, Lars asked, "How did you know that she wouldn't be trampled when she walked up?"

"I have never seen anyone who can work with horses like she can. They act like puppies that just want to be petted. As long as she was holding Beth, there was little fear of her being hurt either."

"Is that what I saw at the fair when she stopped those horses?"

"Is that how you found out who Beth was?"

"Yes. You love my daughter as she says you do?"

"Yes, and I love Catherine even though we didn't start out very well. I think she would have gone with you if you had gotten here sooner. But she swears she loves me now, and I don't intend to give any of them up."

"Well, we better come up with something, or she may strangle us both. The other two children, you love them as well even though they are Raiders born?"

"Yes, she took them in, and she ran off the little girl's mother. There is not much she can't do when she sets her mind to it. She is kind of scary sometimes. You add the queen, and we are in deep trouble."

They looked at each other and smiled; this woman was driving them both crazy, and there wasn't a thing they could do about it, even with two armies standing behind them.

Catherine walked into the great hall and saw Jennie and Robert standing next to the stairway; she had told both of them what she was going to do, and if things didn't go as planned, they also knew what had to be done. As she walked into the hall, there was a table set up in the center of the room; she signaled for the maids to set out two cups of wine, and there was vellum and ink to write with. Giles walked through the door, went to Cat, and took her by the arm; she just looked at him and motioned him to sit as she did when Lars followed.

Cat sat at the end of the table so as not to have either man have an advantage as master of the house. She sat and then began to speak. "Now both of you gentlemen have a decision to make. We can either work this out to both of your satisfaction or you can kill each other while I leave. Lars, this is Elizabeth. Would you like to hold her?"

"Very much."

Cat handed her to Lars and marveled at the likeness in the two of them.

"As I said before, there is land set aside for her use when she is older, but the land needs repair and a stable guard for the people there against invaders. Also, any Raiders-born children are to be brought there to be cared for instead of being thrown out to starve. If that is a problem, tell me now."

"Is that where those two children came from?"

"Yes, and there were three. They buried the other one." Lars just looked at her.

Then Giles said, "Isn't that like giving the keys of the henhouse to the fox?"

"Let me finish. I want all of this written down and signed by the two of you as a legal document to be honored by both of you. If everything is done to Giles's satisfaction, I will let Beth come in the summer to visit, along with a guard. You have to promise me to my face that you won't take my daughter away with you, or I will hunt you down. This is your chance to get your truce with the king, if that is still what you want, and that will stop the raiding."

She had Robert bring her the piece of parchment in his hands. Giles recognized it as their marriage papers and started to object.

"This is my marriage papers signed by me, Giles, and the king. And as long as we both live, I will honor them unless you two can't come to an understanding. Giles, is this to your liking?"

"We will work this out so it is fair to everyone. If that is what you wish as long as you don't walk out into an arena of men on the verge of killing one another and that is something I won't take a no on. Do you understand?"

"Agreed," Catherine said. "Beth is getting tired. She is rubbing her eyes. I am going to take her upstairs, and the two of you can get started. There is a scribe waiting to write it for you."

She stood up and reached down to pick up Beth.

Lars said, "She is beautiful. Is there a chance I can see her again before I leave to this new land of hers?"

"Get this done, and we can all have a meal together, if that is all right with my husband?" Then she looked at Giles.

He was rather puzzled; he hadn't been asked permission before now. "Yes, that will be fine." Then he turned to look at Cat and said, "We will talk later."

She wasn't sure if that was bad or good, and she was too mad and tired to care. Robert would oversee the negotiations because he knew what she wanted; they had already talked about it. Cat just nodded and headed up the stairs; by the time she reached the bedrooms, Beth was already sleeping. She put her in her bed with Ann, and Jennie was close behind to watch over her and the boys; while all these people were in the house, she also had a guard stationed outside both doors. She went to her own room, removed her good dress, and hung it up; she just left her shift on and climbed into bed. After all, she hadn't slept for two days now.

The room was dark when she awoke, and the sun had set already. The fire was burning brightly, and she could see Giles sitting in the chair across the room.

"How long have you been watching me?"

"For a while now, you were sleeping hard. When did you last sleep?"

"It has been a couple of days since you two started this little war."

"Is it settled to your satisfaction?"

"It is done just as you wished, so you can unpack your wagon and the coach."

"You saw them?"

"Yes, I went to the barn and found John and one of the queen's guards waiting. You really would have gone."

"If that is what it took to get your attention, yes, I would have gone."

"Where to if I may ask?"

"The queen had arranged for us to go to one of her properties and hide."

Well, he thought to himself, *the queen had all but told me she was going to help her.* He hadn't listened; the queen and his lady were double trouble.

"The queen's guard brought a letter to you from her, didn't he?"

"Yes, he did, only for my eyes."

"She is some friend. I found the letter."

"You will never know how good a friend she really is."

He got up from the chair and came across the room to sit on the bed; he picked her up and set her in his lap. She laid her head on his shoulder and just waited; he had something on his mind.

"When were you going to tell me about the baby?"

"If you had been paying attention to me instead of this feud, you would have already figured it out. I am several months pregnant. My breasts are tender, and I have a tummy, but you haven't noticed. I throw up most mornings lately, and you haven't been around to see that because you were too busy getting your armor ready. You and Lars were so determined to carve each other up so one or the other could claim me and Beth, but neither asked me what I wanted to do."

"You made that pretty clear today. Are you sure this is how you want this done? Do you trust him to honor his part of the bargain?"

She began to get off his lap, and he just held on to her. She turned around and said, "Are all men this dumb, or is it just you two? Let me go, and I will punch you in the head. Will that prove the point? I am having your child and trying to raise his child, but you are the one I married and the one I love. What will I have to do to prove this to you?"

As he laid her back on the bed, he said, "Just show me that funny smile and let me feel this tummy that carries my baby inside."

She pulled him across her as she tried to take off his tunic; then he finally did it for her. Her shift fell beside the tunic, and she could feel him against her, and it was wonderful. He put his hand on her stomach as he nuzzled her breasts, and he realized they were fuller and softer, and she was rounder; how had he missed this. He wanted to pull her inside him so she could never leave; he couldn't touch enough of her at one time, so he pulled her under him and entered her. Then he rose up on his elbows and looked down at her.

"What is wrong? Don't stop."

"You are mine—only mine—forever. Is the cross gone now?"

"I wasn't sure you had noticed. It is put up for Beth someday and for as long as we both shall live. Isn't that what the priest said?"

He began a slow rocking motion, and she met his every stroke with one of her own; in his own mind, this was the first time she was all his with no fear, and he couldn't seem to get enough of her. When he finally rolled off her, they were both exhausted; he just pulled up a cover over them, pulled her close to him, and fell asleep. This time, they didn't need any words.

The next day, they had lunch with Lars and all the children; he held Beth through the entire meal. When it was over, he prepared to leave. He looked again at Catherine as if to say, "Are you sure?" She just held on to Giles's arm till he rode away. Giles watched her; he realized then she would never be entirely his. She would always belong to Lars somehow and he couldn't change that, so he was going to ignore it. She was his wife, and he would take whatever she would give him.

Two days later, after the grounds were clear of all the Raiders, they went with the coach and headed to see Queen Marie and King Charles; as requested, they were meet at the back of the palace as Marie knew Catherine didn't like crowds. So she had them brought to her private chambers and settled there. Marie was acting like a kid; she was so excited to show Cat her new horse and worried at the same time, so after everyone was fed and the children were put down for naps, they went to the stables.

When they got there, Cat saw why she was so excited, as did Giles. There was an Arab stallion in the corrals, and he had never seen one outside the Holy Land. This one was beautiful and acting crazy. Catherine looked at Marie. "How?" Marie just looked at her sideways as if to say, "You know how I had him stolen."

"How did they get him here Marie on a boat, in a box? He is terrified, and I see rope marks all over him. Did they drag him?"

Marie hadn't really looked that close at him; he had been so upset all this time. She hadn't been able to get too close; no one had. So she called over one of her men and asked. When she came back, she said, "They chased him most of the way, and then they caught him and dragged him to a boat and got him aboard. Then they got him to this dock and put him in this corral, and he has been here ever since. No one can touch him."

Giles looked at Catherine. "Cat, he is out of his mind with fear. You can't go in there. He will kill you. This one isn't like the rest of them."

She watched for a minute and then opened the gate. Giles tried to stop her, but she went in anyway. "If I don't do something, they are going to have to kill him, or he is going to kill himself. Get me some apples and his bridle and a saddle and put them on the rail."

Then she walked into the corral. She walked out to the middle and stood there as the horse came charging up to her, and then he came to a dead stop in front of her. She waited for a minute until he calmed down; his eyes were as big as saucers, and he was shaking so bad she didn't know how he was standing. She finally put her hands up and put them on either side of his neck. She laid her head against his neck. He put his head down on her shoulder and began to calm down.

"There, baby, it is going to be all right now. Mama is going to make it better." She just stood there and stroked his neck as he stopped shaking. She stood there for a long time as the men in the barn watched, and some of them came toward her.

She told them, "Get out, all of you! Nobody comes in here but the groom and me. The rest of you, go away. Marie, come here and bring the apples with you and a knife and do it slowly."

Marie started into the corral with the apples. Giles opened the gate for her and stood back as she entered. She walked slowly over to the white horse, and Catherine told her to cut one of the apples in half then quarter it, and feed it to him. Marie did as she was told, and it was the first time she had ever touched this wonderful horse. Cat moved to the side and told Marie, "Just pet him as you feed him and talk to him. You are going to have to earn his trust. He is scared of everyone around here. You are going to have to be the one who he depends on." Cat walked over to the fence, got the bridle, took it to the horse, and put it on; then she called the groom over. He was reluctant to come. "He won't hurt you."

As Giles watched, he wouldn't have wanted to go over there either, and he knew what she could do with horses. The man came closer, and she said, "Bring the saddle with you. We are going for a ride."

Marie just looked at her. "Are you are nuts? He won't let us ride him."

Cat just looked at her. "What were you planning on doing with him? Keeping him for a doorstop? He is a horse. He should be ridden, especially him! He was bred for running, not to be a centerpiece in a corral."

They stood back as she let the groom put a saddle on him; then she got up on him and she said, "Open the gate. We are going to have some fun."

Giles opened it, and they were off into the open field behind the castle. They were flying; that little horse could move! The men who had chased the horse, dragged it, and fought it were watching as she rode it like no one had; they were amazed. It wasn't the same animal. Catherine stretched out over his back, and they were just having fun. Giles watched, and Marie looked up at him. "Lord, can she ride."

"Yes, Your Grace, she can."

As she watched his face, she had never seen someone so much in love; she wished her husband still looked at her like that.

By now, Catherine had attracted attention from the castle, and she had watchers from windows there too. But she was coming back; she had to teach Marie how to handle her horse so she could ride it as well. As she came into the corral, she told her, "Come on get up here with me so he knows you. We will ride, and then you will ride by yourself."

"Do you really think he will let me ride him by myself?"

"Of course by the time I am through he will."

Marie got up behind her, and they rode some more. It was going well as Giles watched. King Charles walked up beside him and stood watching both women on the horse. He commented, "I had heard from my wife yours was quite good with horses. Until now, I had no idea how good. Maybe you should consider bringing your family here to court and staying for a while. We haven't had such entertainment like this in a long time, and my wife could use the lessons."

Giles didn't say a word. The king had just asked him for his wife as a mistress, and he was just supposed to comply. Well, that was not going to happen in this lifetime. When the women got back, Cat got Marie on the horse by herself, and she was doing very well. Giles took her aside and told her what had been said. She was livid.

"Get the children. We are leaving, but I have to tell Marie why. Can you get another coach for us?"

He just nodded his head yes and started to leave. "I will meet you out back in an hour." Then he reached down and kissed her.

Marie saw what was going on, and she dismounted. She was holding the reins of her horse as she walked toward Catherine. "What is wrong?"

"The king just asked Giles to move our family to court."

Marie's face fell; all the joy of the day disappeared, and you could see she understood what he wanted as well.

"What are you going to do?"

She took Marie's face in her hands and said, "Giles nearly went to war to keep me from another man, and you helped me. I am not about to betray that trust, even with a king. So we are leaving. I love my husband, and you love yours. You, my lady, are welcome at my home anytime. But I will never come here again. Do you understand why?"

Marie shook her head yes. She hugged her, kissed her cheek, and told her, "Anytime you need me, you know where I am little one."

"Oh, and I think you should name that horse Khan. He deserves a noble name and a noble lady to own him. If you ever need anything you need taken care of and I can be any help, just write. Or better yet, come to me. We can have some fun."

Then Cat turned and left; she met Giles behind the castle, and they went home.

Michel was born about five months later, and a more proud daddy you have never seen. It was at about that time that he was to take Beth to Lars, and he went with the guards to make sure everything went well. Lars had been making the repairs, and things were well under way, and the raids had been stopped. He talked to Brian in the village and was pleased with the way it was improving. He set up rents and set about putting away moneys for the coming years for Beth and grain for the village. He didn't tell Lars about any of this yet until he knew this arrangement was going to work. They only let Beth stay for three weeks this time because she was so little, and Giles didn't want to stay away too long because of his new son.

Lars was happy he was getting the time he got; he just wished he could have seen Catherine even for a day. By the time they left, he was already counting the days till next year.

Every summer was better. Giles and Lars were becoming at least friendlier; they both knew that they both loved the same woman and always would. Lars had sons by other women but would never marry any of them. By now, Giles and Catherine had another son, David. Lars was happy for them. One day, when they were watching Beth play, she was seven or eight; Giles asked him, "You still love my Catherine, don't you?"

Lars looked at him and said, "Until the day I die, she is the only woman I have ever truly loved."

Giles turned back around and stared at Beth and then looked at him. "If something ever happened to me, would you take care of her and all of my children as well as yours like they were all yours?"

Lars looked at him for just a second and then said, "Yes, without a second thought. Would you do the same if something happened to me?"

"I already am and have been for some time. I just hope if something happened to me, she would come to you. She would need someone, and she still loves you."

That was all they ever said about that; it was all they ever needed to say. They both knew what the other was thinking and always had.

The next summer, he was late. Lars was about to start to go to him for Beth, but he sent some guards with Beth, Ann, and Jacob; it seemed they wanted to learn about their Raiders heritage. He learned from the children that Catherine had been very ill, and Giles hadn't wanted to leave her alone, and Lars was worried about her. Giles sent word a week later that she was better because he knew Lars would worry when the children told him she was sick.

The next year, Giles went to France; it seemed he had found some of his relatives still alive, and he went to find them. He did, and when he did, Giles found out about how his mother and sister had died; the food and supplies he had sent them had never arrived because they had been diverted because of the king. When the king's own supplies were not available, he took Giles's supplies and left his family to starve. When Giles found out about this, he was ready to go to war again against his own king. Catherine stopped him, but in only a few days, it wasn't going to matter anymore; her world was going to change and not for the better.

Giles needed to go check the borders, and he was going tomorrow. Catherine had everything ready as usual, but when they went to bed, he was acting different; she found him in his old fur robe by the window, looking out at their land.

"What are you doing? The air is cold. It will be snowing soon. Come away from there."

"Do you remember the night I first made love to you, and I found you here soaking wet, looking out this window? Were you looking for Lars?"

"Yes, I remember. It was a long time ago. Why do you ask now?"

"Do you know how much I love you and our children, Catherine? I really love you. I didn't remember how lost I was until I found you and then our children. You gave me back a life—even that tiny baby boy buried in the cemetery. Catherine, you have to be careful. I know you and Marie are together in something, and you won't tell me about it. The king is mean and petty. You two need to be careful. He will come after you if he finds out."

She went over to him, and he wrapped her in his robe and held her while they watched the horses and looked at the land. She took his hand and led him to bed; then he gently made love to her like it was the first time. Gently and softly, he entered her like the first time when she was so scared, then with a rocking motion, which took them both over the top and left them both breathless. Then she curled up beside him, and he pulled her to him so tightly she could barely breathe. But she didn't move away, and she didn't say anything. It was like he was going somewhere she couldn't follow, and it scared her. He left the next morning with his men while she watched from the tower.

CHAPTER 8

He had been gone two days, and she was outside with the children in the front of the keep.

After ten years, the grounds had finally healed from the battle that had almost taken place there. The horses' hooves no longer showed in the grass, and the campfire pits were long gone. She watched as her children played in the grass on this spring day with her three sons and two daughters. Jacob was seventeen. Ann was sixteen. Beth was almost fifteen. Michel was nine, and David was six. She wanted more children, but Giles had been so spooked after David when she had a miscarriage; she was so ill that she had almost bled to death. He had been careful not to get her pregnant again. After the other night, she intended to talk to him about that very thing when he got back from this trip because enough was enough. Jennie and Robert had a new baby, and with William, that made four. It was time to add to her family as well.

Two riders were coming toward them at a run, and Cat called the children to her; she was going to give these men a piece of her mind when they got here, and then she recognized Robert and James. They would never ride a horse like that unless there was trouble. She sent the children to the door where Helen was standing and waited for the men to get to her.

Robert rode up to her and handed his reins to James, and James headed to the stables in a big hurry, barely even stopping to acknowledge her. Robert grabbed both her arms and said, "Giles is hurt bad and wants to see you."

"I will get my herbs and be right back."

"Catherine you won't need them. You can't fix this, and if you don't hurry, he won't be alive to say goodbye. Do you understand?"

She just nodded; she didn't know if she understood or not but there was no time to argue. James came back with fresh horses, and Helen ran out with her cloak. She wrapped it around Cat. Cat looked at her, and Helen said, "Go to him. I will take care of the children."

Catherine mounted her horse, and they began to run and continued to run. She had never used an animal like this before; just when she didn't think they could go any more Robert pulled up and got off his horse. He helped her down, and when she turned, she could see her men standing and just looking at her. Then she saw Giles's horse struggling in the ditch; two men were trying to keep him down because he was trying to rise, but she could see from here that his front legs were broken. John was standing in front of him with a sword, preparing to finish him off as she walked over. Catherine leaned down, took his head, and just cooed to him like you would a baby and he settled down. She took off her scarf from her neck, laid it over his eyes, stroked his neck, and then nodded to John. He took the sword and plunged it into the horse's chest, and the big horse was still; she laid the horses head down and followed Robert to the barn behind her as the men just watched in silence.

Cat understood why she didn't need her bag; she could see bones sticking out of Giles's side and his leg. How they got him inside was a miracle. She sat down beside him, gently picked up his head and laid it in her lap, much like she did the big horse. He opened his eyes looked at her and said, "Did you take care of my horse? I could hear him screaming out there."

"Yes, love, he is taken care of. Now my concern is for you."

Everyone backed away; this was a conversation for the two of them, and it would be the last. None of them knew what was keeping him alive; just moving him in here was more agony than any of them wanted to ever experience. It was like he was waiting for her before he could go and they respected that, for they all knew there wasn't much time left.

"I had to see you to tell you how good my life has been since you and our children came into it—all our children. You gave me back the family I thought I would never have again and you have to know I would not leave you in any way but death. You will tell the children how much I love them and don't let them forget me."

"I don't think any of the children are going to forget you. Your sons are going to look just like you. And Beth, Ann, and Jacob think the sun rises with you."

"I love you, Catherine. Never forget that. Catherine, go to Lars he knows what to do. I love you, Catherine. Always."

"Giles my love."

But the eyes that looked back at her were now blank; he was gone. He had lasted long enough to say goodbye, and for the first time since she had walked into this barn, she noticed how quiet it was. There were men all around, but nobody spoke and they began to leave quietly out into the dark night and leave her alone with him. She gently closed his eyes and brought his head closer to her chest as if to cradle it. She brushed the hair and blood from his face and quietly said, "You rest now. There will be no more pain. It is all right."

As Robert watched, she began to gently rock and hum to him as if nothing was wrong; she leaned over and kissed his lips one last time, and it was right then that Robert began to worry. She wasn't even crying and seemed to be in some kind of trance and not a single tear fell. He watched for over an hour; then he reached down gently touched her arm and said, "Catherine, we need to get Giles back home, don't you think? The men are waiting outside with the wagon to take him home. Let me help you up."

She gently put Giles's head back on the blanket. Then she took the offered hand and stood up. She watched as the men carefully loaded him into the back of a wagon, and they started out of the barn. As she started to get up in the wagon, she saw the dead horse still lying in the culvert and

John's sword still buried in his side. They watched as she walked over to the dead animal, took her scarf off his face, and then pulled the sword out of his side, never saying a word to any of the men standing around. As she turned to face John, she said, "Please see that your master's horse is buried. He carried him for many years and he would not have wanted to have seen him wind up on a butcher's table. Will you take care of that for me, please, John?"

"Yes, my lady, whatever you want done. I will see to it personally."

"Thank you." Then she handed him his sword; then she walked to the wagon, climbed into the back and sat down next to Giles's body. Then they began the journey home.

As they made their way home, it began to snow; it was if even the weather was mourning Giles's loss. It was many hours until they arrived at the keep and many people were waiting for them at the side entrance to take his body and prepare it for his funeral. When they stopped, Robert helped the men get Giles out of the wagon and then reached for Catherine, only to discover she was covered with snow; she must be freezing. She tried to stand but was too cold; he finally had to reach over the wagon, lift her out, and set her on the ground. She brushed off the snow and slowly walked to the open door of the keep, went inside and started up the stairs. She managed to get to her room and shut the door; the snow had melted, and now she was soaking wet. She stood in front of the fireplace like a statue and didn't make a sound. Jennie walked in to find her standing, and then like a paper doll, she just crumbled to the ground. She caught Catherine's head before it hit the floor, but not by much and then Jennie realized she was blue she was so cold.

Jennie screamed for a maid as Robert ran in the door.

"She is freezing and soaking wet. Didn't anyone cover her as you were coming back?"

"It was dark, and I just did not pay attention."

A maid came running into the room to help, and Jennie said to Robert, "Get out."

Then the two women striped off Cat's clothes but Jennie was worried about Catherine's hands; her fingers were almost black—they were so cold. She had the maid go get some bowls so they could warm some water to put her hands in. Jennie rubbed her skin till she was dry then put on a gown; then she called for Robert. She was going to need some help lifting her onto the bed.

When he got into the room he picked her up and finally saw her hands; he could feel the cold coming from her body and asked his wife, "Have I let her die?"

"Not yet, but I am worried about her fingers. Didn't she say anything to you on the way back?"

"She hasn't said a word since she got into the wagon."

"And you didn't find that strange? You know her better than that. You know how much she loved him. We are going to have to watch her carefully or she will be next."

They put her hands in warm water and she moaned. Jennie knew they had to hurt, but she was glad there was still feeling in them. They stoked the fire till the room was steaming and she began to come around. When she finally woke, she just looked at Jennie and said, "How am I going to tell the children?"

"We will worry about the children later. Can you feel you fingers?"

"Yes, they hurt. I need to take care of Giles's body. Have they brought it home?"

"Catherine, you rode home with him in the back of the wagon. He is here and being taken care of. Now you lie there and sleep while I take care of your hands."

Cat just looked at her as if she hadn't heard a word she had said and then closed her eyes; it was just too hard to keep them open. Sometimes Jennie stopped what she was doing and listened to her breath; it was so quiet she could barely hear her.

The sun began to come up and fill the room with light, and the children quietly opened the door. Jennie was going to send them away, but Cat heard them and called them to her. All five of them climbed into bed with her, and they all began to quietly cry; there didn't seem to be anything else to do. Jennie left the room and let them grieve.

After about an hour Catherine called Jennie from the next room and they began to get the children dressed. She needed help because her hands were a mess. Jennie found some gloves for them because they were still black and stiff; she would surely lose the outer layer of skin, but hopefully not any fingers. It was still too soon to tell.

"Can you take the children downstairs? I will be there in a minute."

Before her youngest son left, he turned and ran to her, then looked up at her and said, "Why didn't you help him?" Then he turned around and ran out the door.

She just stood there. How do you answer that question to your little boy? Her head pounded. The only thing she could think of was Giles liked to have the bed made in the morning and his clothes laid out. If she stood here much longer and thought about this, she was going to be sick. They were waiting for her downstairs; she might as well go. She couldn't change anything now. The last thing she could do for Giles was see him buried properly.

There were people standing everywhere downstairs; the keep was full of the townspeople and Giles's soldiers. She took Robert's arm as she reached the bottom of the stairs even though she could hardly bear to touch him because her hands hurt so badly. She stood there until the men carried Giles's body up from the downstairs room where he had been prepared, and put in a coffin; her children gathered around her except her youngest son, who went to Jennie and held her hand. Cat noticed but was so distracted; it still didn't quite register David was avoiding her.

After the coffin passed, she followed, with everyone else trailing behind them. They all walked in silence across the front of the keep up the hill to the old cemetery. She walked past her mother's and grandmother's headstones and one small cross; then she saw the place prepared for Giles and she just stopped. Robert had to pull on her arm to get her to move. When they were finally in front of the spot, they lowered him down, and the Father Marques said some words; she had long since stopped hearing anything. She stood there, and Robert began to pull her away. She turned and yanked her arm out of his; then she turned to see everyone had gone. She didn't know how long they had been standing here, but it had to have been a while.

"Everyone is gone?"

"For some time now, Catherine. We have been standing here, and you watched them bury him, and then you wouldn't leave. So I sent the children back with Jennie and Caroline, but we need to go back now. It is snowing."

"I will stay a little longer."

"No, Catherine. If I have to pick you up and carry you, we are going back. I won't make the same mistake twice."

She felt her hands ache and knew he was right.

"Let's go." As they walked away, she turned back and said, "You will get the stonecutter here soon?"

"Yes," Robert replied as he guided her back home; he was already worried.

As they walked, she could see the hall was full of people, and she said to Robert, "Please stay close to me. I don't know how I am going to handle all of this."

"You will do just fine. Listen to what they have to say about Giles, and it will be all right."

As they walked into the room, all she could smell was fresh bread. Helen must have cooked all night to have put out this much food for all these people. Catherine was surprised she didn't notice it earlier, but she hadn't noticed anything until now.

She did her duty and tried to shake every hand with her gloves on even though her hands were screaming; she took every condolence until everyone was gone, and then she finally sat down in the big chair by the fireplace. Ann and Jacob were helping Helen in the kitchen; there were too many people around, and they went to Helen when they had enough. Elizabeth came and sat by her feet, as did Michel. But David stood by the fire.

"Come sit in my lap, David."

"No, I am fine right here."

"David, what is wrong? Tell me."

"You help everyone else, but not my daddy." He said it with such anger, and then he just ran up the stairs.

Cat looked at Jennie, who looked back and said, "He is too little to understand that there was nothing that could be done. I will try to explain."

Catherine and the children sat in silence for a while, and then she said, "I think it is time to call it a day. I know you have to be as tired as I am."

Michel turned around and asked, "What did happen to him? They won't tell us."

By then, Ann and Jacob were in the room as well, so she would only have to do this once.

"His horse slipped in the mud and fell on him. It crushed him. I got there in time to see him before he died, and he wanted me to tell you how much he loved his children—all his children."

All the children hugged her; there were no tears left. They walked up the stairs, and she followed. She looked in on David, and Jennie had him asleep and in bed.

As she went to open the door, she remembered her hands and realized the gloves were going to have to be removed; as she looked at them, she wondered for the first time if she was going to lose her fingers. She was smiling as Jennie came into the room, and she wondered why. Then Cat said, "Wonder what I will look like with no fingers."

Jennie was really beginning to fear for her sanity. "I brought some warm water, and we are going to soak them and then try to pull off the gloves."

After a few minutes of soaking, Jennie gently started to pull the gloves off; it was sheer agony because the dead skin was coming off with the gloves. The skin underneath was pink; this was a good sign. As soon as they got the gloves off, Jennie gently applied some of Catherine's salve for burns and loosely wrapped her hands; there was nothing else to do. If they didn't get infected, she would heal. After some tea generously laced with painkiller, Jennie got Catherine in bed and left; but before she went to bed, she found a guard and placed him across from Catherine's door with instructions to come get her if anything strange happened.

When she got to her room, Elizabeth and Ann were there waiting with Robert; they had been talking, and she came in on the middle of the conversation.

"You should send a rider and tell him what has happened. He needs to know."

"You mother gives orders like that. I don't go to Lars and tell him anything unless she tells me to, girls."

Robert looked to his wife for agreement, and she said, "They may be right. I don't think Cat is in her right mind, and if you had seen what I just saw, you would agree with me. I placed a guard on her door because I am afraid she might do something to herself."

"She wouldn't do that to the children, never! You must be mistaken."

"When she sleepwalks, she doesn't know what she is doing, but she is all right tonight. So let's go to bed. We will talk about this tomorrow."

Jennie had barely got everyone settled when she heard the door down the hall open because the hinge creaked, so she headed for her door. The guard was asleep, and Catherine was halfway up the stairs to the tower. Robert was pulling back on his pants as she screamed, "The tower!"

Robert was running and snatched up the waking guard along the way as Jennie went to get more help; as he reached the top, Catherine was climbing onto the edge of the outer wall. One step and she would drop eighty feet. Robert could hear Jennie calling for more help downstairs, but if he wasn't quick, there would be no need for them. He thought of ways he talked to her when she was little; maybe it would work now.

"Catherine, what are you doing up here?" he said in a soft voice so as not to scare her.

"Giles is calling to me. Can't you hear him? I think he is hurt. I need to go to him."

At least he had her attention, and she was looking at him and not into space. He slowly walked toward her as he talked, trying to get close enough to grab her; she was so tired, and her balance was precarious at best.

"He needs me. Can't you hear him calling me? I need to go now."

Then she turned and stepped into thin air. Robert grabbed her by her arm barely and was desperately trying to hold on; the guard with him finally got her other arm before she took them both over the top. Several other men and Jennie were there by now and helped them get her up and over the top of the parapet. James was with them; he picked her up from Robert and started down the stairs, back to her room.

Jennie just looked at Robert and said, "I told you. Now she hears him calling her."

"Now I believe."

Beth and Ann were in Jennie's room when they got back. They were no longer the little girls, but the masters of the house, and Jacob was coming in the door to help.

Beth said, "Tomorrow we fill a carriage with mama and the boys, and we go to Lars. We will not bury our mother too, and that is the only way I see to save her. Maybe my papa can snap her out of this before she goes completely insane."

"What if she won't go to Lars?"

"Then I will take her to that inn by my land and get her away from here. Maybe Papa can come and convince her. At least it will get her away from here for a while."

Jennie agreed.

"If we don't do something fast, it will be too late."

Robert didn't know if Lars could fix this, but he knew he couldn't, not here anyway.

"Giles told her to go to Lars that he would know what to do."

They all turned and looked at him. Jennie just said, "You are just telling us this now? When did he say this?"

"When he was dying it was one of the last things he said to her."

The girls looked at each other.

"It is settled. We go. Even daddy knew she would fall apart. It is settled. We leave tomorrow."

The next morning, as she awoke and started to get out of bed, there was a maid who immediately went out of the room; she didn't know where yet, but she was fixing to find out. Cat climbed out of bed only to see that she had bruises on her arms and up and down her legs as well as a huge scrape on her hip.

When Jennie came in, Cat looked at her and asked, "What in the hell did I do, and did I hurt anyone else?"

"You said you heard Giles calling and stepped off the tower. If Robert hadn't caught you and dragged you back up, well, you can guess the rest. He almost went over with you."

She just looked at her and sat back down on the bed. Jennie was angry with her, and she had every right to be; she had almost killed her husband as well as herself.

"I think I am losing my mind. What if I hurt one of the children?"

"That is not going to happen. You are leaving with me and the other children today."

Elizabeth had just walked into the room, and she was dressed, with Michel behind her.

"Jennie, please leave us for a bit. We need to talk to our mother."

"Mama, get your clothes on. I will help you. We are leaving today, and we are going to my land. If you don't want to see Papa, you can stay at that little inn you like. But we are leaving if I have to have Robert carry you out of this room."

Michel had been quiet up to this point, but it seemed it was his turn to talk. "You scared us to death last night, and we have decided no more. We know you are grieving, but we can't lose you too, so get ready to go."

It would have been funny to watch this little girl taking over her mother's chores if it wasn't so sad, so Beth and Ann helped her dress and rewrapped her hands to protect them from any more damage. After the chests were filled with clothes, they were loaded on wagons, and they got into the carriage. This ride to Beth's land was going to be more comfortable than the first one.

Catherine didn't look back; she didn't tell anyone, but she was still hearing Giles call to her. She just watched the hills in front of her as she left and wondered if she would ever return or if she would wind up in an asylum. At least Beth would be safe with her papa, and he would take care of Ann and Jacob as well; they had been going with Beth the last two summers to see the Raiders boats. It was their heritage too, after all. If worse came to worst, Robert would watch over her sons till they came of age. There seemed to be some sort of fog settling down on her mind, and she couldn't stop it.

Robert and James were riding with them; and James's wife, Caroline, was in the coach with her. She said to help her, but she knew it was to keep an eye on her. They were afraid she might hurt someone or herself, so she needed to be watched; she hated this. Robert had a new baby at home; he needed to be there with Jennie.

There were more places along the way to stay than there used to be since the Raiders had stopped raiding; the farms and towns had grown everywhere. They had a comfortable place to stay every night for the four days until they got to the inn that Cat liked, and she was going to stay there with the boys while Robert took Beth to her papa.

She had done pretty well the first two days, but then she had begun to stare off into space again and talk to herself. Again, Robert was worried. He told the little old lady who owned the inn what was going on and that he and Beth and Ann were going to leave and go to her papa's land. James and Caroline were left behind to keep an eye on Catherine and the boys, and Robert told James they would hurry. They loaded the coach and, with fresh horses, hurried off to find Lars. Robert just hoped he was home and not out on the boats.

He watched as Beth and Ann slept on the seat in the coach; they were worn-out, but they still kept going just as fast as they could. Beth was hoping her papa could bring her mother around when no one else could, but it was so early in the season that he might not be at the lodge. She was hoping he had stayed the winter this year.

Robert reached over, woke them, and said, "We are almost there. I can see the lodge from here." She stuck her head out the coach, looking for her papa but couldn't see his blond head anywhere. Her heart began to sink. What were they going to do now?

As they pulled up in front of the lodge, Lars came walking around the side of the lodge and caught his daughter as she jumped out of the coach at him. He had to calm her enough so he could understand what she was saying to him; she was babbling. It was comical; then Robert got out of the carriage, and the look on his face sent a chill down his spine. All he could say was, "What has happened?"

"Giles is dead, and Catherine is all but out of her mind."

He just looked at him for a second, not quite understanding what he was saying, and he looked at Beth. Then Ann came out of the coach, and the fear in her eyes told him this wasn't a joke.

"Go inside, girls, while I talk to Robert."

"No, Papa, we want to hear it all. It was my idea to come to you. Maybe you can fix this. No one else can get through to her, and she is going to kill herself if someone doesn't help her."

Robert hadn't known if she fully understood all about what was going on with her mother, but she understood all too well. Now she was asking her papa for help. Lars didn't skip a beat; he turned and told one of his men to saddle a horse for him. Then Robert told him to saddle two.

"You can barely stand, much less ride. How are you going to stay in the saddle?"

"I will sleep in it if I have to. I am going."

"Elizabeth, you two are not going. You go inside and get some sleep. Then prepare some rooms for your mother and brothers."

"Do you think you can get her to come?"

"Yes, darling, if I have to carry her. She will be coming."

That seemed to be what Beth wanted to hear because she turned, went into the house, and started to get some food ready for them to take with them. Ann wasn't far behind.

"Is it as bad as she thinks?"

"Worse than they know. They haven't been told everything. They were scared enough. I will tell you on the way. We have got to go."

As Lars's man brought the horses around to them, Beth was bringing out a bag of food.

Lars said, "You know almost everyone here, and Greta will watch out for you."

"We don't need anyone to watch out for us. We will be fine," Beth replied.

"You listen to me, young lady. There are too many men around here who don't know who you two are. You stay close to Greta."

"So this was Beth's idea to come get me? She thinks I can help. Well, at this point, I can't do much worse."

"What exactly did you expect us to do? I am not well versed in women losing their minds. You were our last resort. I was just trying to keep her from jumping from the top of the tower."

Lars looked blankly at him, and then said, "I am sorry. All I can see is her crumpled at the bottom of the keep, and Beth telling me she is dead too. And you are the only one I can take it out on at the moment. What am I supposed to do when I get there?"

"Make her realize he is dead and not calling her."

"What do you mean 'calling her'?"

"I forgot to tell you. That is why she was walking off the tower. She hears him calling her. That is why we left the keep. She is trying to go to him. You need to convince her he is really gone."

"Oh, is that all?"

He looked at Robert in amazement. Well, he didn't plan on letting her go again; this was his chance to have the woman he had wanted all these years—if he could just keep her alive.

"She may not come."

"Giles and I made a deal a long time ago. If one of us died, the other would see that the other's children were taken care of, and I think that this is that time. Don't you?"

"That's what he was talking about."

"What do you mean?"

"When he was dying, he told her to come to you because you would take care of her and the children."

Lars just nodded his head.

"I am coming with you. I can sleep in the saddle. Will the girls be safe here alone?"

"Greta, will you please come here? I need to talk to you."

"Yes, master. How can I help you?"

"I am going to get Beth's mother and brothers, and I will be gone a couple of days. Will you see to the girls' comfort and safety while I am gone?"

"Of course I will, sir."

Beth came running in and said, "Papa, will you bring her back home with you?"

"Yes, little one, we are going to ride hard. And we are going to bring your mother back. The coach will follow us tomorrow, and then we will come back with your mother and brothers, all right? Both of you give me a hug, and then we are going to leave. Greta will take care of you till I get back."

"I love you, Papa."

They both mounted their horses and set off at a fast clip. Lars didn't know how Robert was going to stay in the saddle since he was so tired. He knew how much the older man loved Catherine; if he had ever wondered, he knew now.

They traveled hard, and a few times, he had to keep Robert from falling off the saddle; he knew ships, not so much horses. But they kept going. They stopped at sunrise and changed horses at a farm, paying a surprised farmer an exorbitant price for two older horses.

They would run them into the ground if they had to. Fortunately, they turned out to be stronger than they looked; and by nightfall, they had arrived at the inn.

Both men were worn-out. When they arrived, Lars looked up and saw Catherine sitting by a window on the second floor, just staring out into the night. It was if all the years fell away. Robert looked at Lars, and he knew if anyone could save her, it would be him; this was his chance to have a life with Catherine, and Robert was going to give it to him rather than lose her.

They entered the inn, and Robert led him up the stairs to her room. They entered quietly; she didn't even turn until Robert said, "Catherine, I am back."

Then she turned and looked at him, but when she saw Lars, she came to her feet; she rushed over to him and said, "What is Lars doing here? Giles will be furious. You have to get him out of here now."

Robert turned and looked at Lars; then he told him, "Go and close the door behind you. I will take care of this now and keep the boys out of here until I say it is all right."

Catherine looked like a fox caught by hounds with nowhere to run, and Lars wasn't quite sure how to start, but he didn't have to.

"Leave. You have to leave now before he gets here. He will be so mad. Go now."

She held up her hands and pushed his chest, and for the first time, he saw her hands. Good lord, how long had she been in the cold before anyone realized she was freezing. He took hold of her wrists, careful not to touch her hands, and pushed her back until she had no choice but to sit down on the window seat. She searched the room for him until Lars held up her hands and made her look at them. Then he asked her, "What happened to your hands, Cat? This is a bad frostbite. How did you get it?"

"I was in the wagon, and it was so cold."

"Where was Giles, Catherine?"

"I don't know." And then she began to struggle to get away from him, and it was all he could do not to hurt her hands to keep her still, but he had to make her say the words.

"Catherine, tell me where Giles is. You know, and you just won't admit it—even to yourself. It is time. Your children need their mother back."

She finally looked at him, and he could see her behind those eyes he had dreamed about for so many years. Tears began to trickle down her face, and she whispered, "I don't know where he is, but he will be back soon, so you must go."

"Catherine, you know that is a lie. Tell me where is Giles."

"He was in the wagon with me, but he was gone, and I couldn't fix him." She had said it so quietly that he hardly heard. "He still talks to me, you know, calling to me in the mist. He tells me to come to him, but I can't find him."

"Robert told me, but maybe it is just you trying to say goodbye. But it is time to do that before you lose yourself and your mind."

"You are wrong. He is there, I know. I just can't find him."

"Is that why you walked off the tower, Cat? Do you think he wants you dead?"

"I didn't do that. You are mistaken."

"No, I am not. Do you really think Giles wants you to leave the children to be with him? I don't think so, do you?"

She just looked at him as if he was insane, and it seemed as though some memories were beginning to seep back into her brain, and she was afraid.

"Did I hurt the children?"

"No, you only hurt yourself, but that in a way is hurting the children."

"What am I going to do?"

"You and the children are coming home with me, and we will figure it out. Beth and Ann are already at the lodge. They came to get me. They are afraid for you."

"Our little girl is very smart. I am so tired, but I am afraid to sleep."

"I will stay, and you can sleep. Nothing will happen while I am here."

He sat down beside her, and she curled up beside him; he reached over her, grabbed a blanket, and pulled it over her. She laid her head on his chest.

"I will just rest for a while. Maybe with you here, I won't hear him."

He didn't know how long it was before Robert opened the door and looked in, but Lars was still holding the sleeping woman. Robert motioned that he could put her in the bed, but Lars shook his head; he had waited years for a moment just like this, and he didn't know if he would get another one. So he was going to enjoy this one as long as he could. Robert put more wood on the fire and left them alone; this had to be better than it was, or at least he hoped so.

Lars gently laid her in his lap and got her more comfortable and so he could see her better. He pushed her hair away from her face, and he just watched her. Catherine was a little older with a few gray hairs, but still the woman he dreamed of at night ever since the day he had met her. He didn't know how long he sat like this; but sometime later, he dozed off himself, just leaning his head against the windowsill.

She awoke to find herself being held in someone's arms, and for a split second, she thought it was Giles. Then she looked up at Lars's blond face and remembered, but this time, it wasn't such a defining pain as it had been before. She lifted her hand and gently touched his face, and his eyes flew open, but he didn't move.

Then Catherine said, "I was trying to make sure you were real and not my imagination. I am never quite sure anymore."

"And what have you decided?"

"That you need a shave and probably a good night's rest. You look tired. Robert and you must have ridden nonstop to get here in as short a time as you said you did."

"I am just fine sitting here, holding you. It is something I have wanted to do for many years. You seem better, but you will probably rest better in the bed."

"Yes it will be more comfortable, so we better find you a room."

"I am not going anywhere, Catherine. I will sleep on the floor by the door, but you will not be left alone until I am sure you are all right."

He helped her rise off the window seat, and he didn't realize how stiff he was until he got up. Two days of riding was catching up with him. She walked to the bed, took off her robe, threw it across the end of the bed, and then crawled in. He pulled up the covers over her and told her good night; he wanted so badly to kiss her good night, but not yet. He grabbed a blanket off the bed and the one off the window seat and lay down in front of the door so she couldn't open it without waking him.

It was quiet, and the fire was crackling. He was beginning to doze off again when he heard her quietly say, "Thank you for coming." She didn't say anything else, and he prayed she was talking to him.

Hours later, she awoke and saw him at the door and wondered why he was here and then wondered where here was. She stopped to clear her mind and began to remember certain things and decided to find Robert; he could tell her what she needed to know. Lars was in front of the door, but for some reason, that seemed to be all right; she needed to get past him, so she tried to open the door slightly and squeeze out when she found herself on the floor, with him on top of her. He looked panicked, and she didn't know why. So she said, "You are squashing me. What is the problem?"

He just looked at her; she didn't remember why he was here, but he sure liked this position; at about that time, Robert made an entrance. He looked down to see Lars on top of Cat and her grinning for a change instead of looking like a lost lamb. Then he stated the obvious. "Do you need some help?"

Catherine looked over Lars's shoulder and asked, "What is going on?"

Robert looked at Lars, and Lars said, "Get out of here. We will be down in a minute." Then he pulled Cat up and slammed the door shut with his foot.

She just said, "Well."

"Do you remember any of last night?"

"It is coming back to me, and you can stop screaming at me. I am neither stupid nor deaf." Finally, some of her old fire was coming back; anything was better than that fog she had been in. When she spoke again, she was white as a sheet.

"The children, where are my children? Something has happened. Are they all right? I can't seem to remember. Where is Giles?"

"Think, Catherine, just stop and think. Calm down. It is not the children."

As he watched, he could see her collecting her thoughts and putting everything together again.

"Beth sent for you, and we are going to the lodge for a while because I am crazy." She stated it so plainly that it was scary, and he hated to agree with her. So he said, "You are not crazy. You are just tired and confused, and you are coming with me so you can rest and the children can heal away from the keep. There are too many memories right in front of you there. The carriage won't be back until tomorrow. They had to travel slower than we did, so we will all rest today and then leave tomorrow."

"Good, maybe somebody can explain all these cuts, scrapes, and bruises all over me. What exactly did I do, and can we get something to eat? I am starving."

Well, it was a start.

Robert was waiting outside the door when Lars came out, and all Lars said was, "She is starving."

"Thank God! Is that all?"

"That is all for now, but it is a start. Anything is better than yesterday." He had to admit he was right at this point; he would take any kind of response over silence or indifference.

The day went as a day should go, packing bags, getting the children ready, and preparing food for the rest of the journey. They kept an eye on Cat at all times because it seemed her mind would wander off, and she would just stare into space. Someone would have to get her attention again, but it was happening less and less. They still couldn't figure out why David wouldn't talk to her; he had always been her closest child since he had been born. Robert was determined to find out what was going on, but things had been so hectic that he hadn't yet. But he would. There was still a ways to go before they got to the lodge.

In the afternoon, the boys went down for a nap, and they lost track of Cat. Both Robert and Lars panicked until Robert thought to check the barn, and sure enough, there she was with the horses. Lars just watched; he had never seen her around the big animals except that one time at the fair. When one began to get too close, he went to help. Robert grabbed his arm, stopped him, and said, "Just watch. They won't hurt her. She has an amazing way with animals. If anything can bring her back to this world, it is them."

And that is what they did for over an hour; they watched her feed and talk to horses that could have stomped her into dust—most of them taller at the shoulder than her head and acting like puppies. She stroked each horse's nose and brushed manes back as she talked to them; it was the first time Robert had seen her act like her old self, and he was quite enjoying it. When she left, every one of them came to the rail to see her leave. Lars had never seen anything like it before.

They didn't realize it, but they weren't the only ones watching. The old man who owned the inn had also watched and said, "I have never seen a woman work with horses like that. She has no fear."

"She has always had a way with them since she was a little girl. You should see her ride." Lars looked at him then because he had never seen her on a horse.

Robert just smiled to himself and thought, *Raider you are in for a surprise.*

Catherine wasn't paying attention when she walked toward them and almost walked into them; when she looked up, they were all staring at her. She just stared at them and said, "What?"

They all began to laugh; she didn't realize even after all these years that what she did with the horses wasn't natural in anybody's eyes but hers. So she just kept on walking, and they followed her inside, each with a smile on his face. Robert realized it was the first normal thing she had done on her own in days, and that pleased him more than even he even understood.

When they loaded up the carriage the next day, everything seemed fine. But David sat in James's wife's lap and still won't talk to his mother. She was beginning to notice. She looked at Robert, and he said, "We will talk about it at lunch."

She just nodded, and they started off on their journey at a much slower pace than the ride here. Several hours later, they stopped to have some lunch and stretch their legs. Catherine placed a blanket on the ground and set out some meat and bread that the lady at the inn had packed for them. She started to feed the children while the men watered the horses at a nearby stream. Robert came over to sit by her, and she asked, "Why is David avoiding me?"

"I don't know. But ever since the night we brought Giles home, something is bothering him, and he won't talk to anyone about it."

"It has something to do with me?"

"Yes, but I don't know what."

They both looked at each other and thought it was still a long trip. Maybe before it was over, he would come around, and one of them would figure out what was bothering him.

It was time to pack up and get moving again, so with everything loaded, Catherine again climbed into the coach with a child who obviously didn't want to be anywhere near her, and she couldn't figure out why.

She just watched David; he was hurting about something, but he wouldn't even look at her even in these close quarters, and that was quite a chore. They stopped again, and Cat had finally had enough of this coach. So she got out as the men stretched and watered the horses. She walked over to James and asked quietly, "Ride in the coach with your wife for a while. I need to ride, or I am going to suffocate in there."

He looked at her and handed over the reins of his horse; what else was he supposed to do? She was his mistress after all. He cupped his hands and got her in the saddle; she smiled at him, turned the horse sharply away from the coach, and headed out in a dead run.

Robert looked at James, and he said, "She wanted to ride."

"Well hell, she is doing that, and I don't know how with those hands."

Lars couldn't believe what he was seeing. Robert was right—she could ride better than any of his men and most Englishmen he had ever seen; she was like part of the horse.

She hadn't felt this good in some time with the wind on her face and a good horse under her. She jumped several small logs, but when she came to a small stone fence, she didn't stop for it either; it was a good thing her horse didn't balk at jumping it, or she would have been on the ground. She stopped when she realized she was in someone's field, but then they hadn't plowed yet, so she wasn't tearing anything up. After jumping off the horse, she realized she was walking in wild sage and flowers of all kinds left over from the last of the freeze and still blowing in the breeze.

Long ago, she had walked a field like this on a day when Giles came for the first time, and she thought maybe this was his way of saying to go on without him. Then for some reason, she thought of Beth walking down an aisle getting married and then a grandbaby. Think of that, her, a grandmother and her sons growing into men. All right, she got it. *Enough feeling sorry for myself. I still have children to raise and grandchildren.* Then she turned to see Robert and Lars staring at her.

Robert had taken off after her in a dead run, knowing he would never catch up to her if she didn't want him to. But he found her after about twenty minutes not too far away in a field of flowers, just walking around. Lars wasn't too far behind; he could ride, but not like either of them. When he got to Robert, she was still walking in the field, looking at nothing special with tears in her eyes; it looked like she was remembering something.

Lars asked, "Is everything all right? Has she done this before?"

"A long time ago, I watched a girl do the same thing, and now I watch the grown woman do what I think is a good thing."

She was just smiling when she turned and said, "Everything is going to be all right now. How much farther to the lodge? Can we make it today if we hurry?"

"Yes, we aren't that far away. I will tell the coach to hurry up a bit. Beth will be waiting on us."

They helped her mount so she didn't use her hands too much, and Robert rode back to the others. Lars stayed with her, and they rode at a much slower pace, for she could see he wasn't as comfortable with a horse as she was. They rode in silence for some time until Lars said, "Catherine, are you all right? Your hand is bleeding again." She hadn't even noticed; she must have opened it up when she grabbed the saddle horn, and it was bleeding through the cotton glove.

"It will be fine. I will take care of it when we get home."

She didn't realize she had said it, but he wanted to shout to the world, "Yes, yes! She is coming home! She is coming home with me, hopefully to stay!"

They rode in the quiet for a while; he just watched how her horses gave her some kind of peace, and she looked happy. It wasn't very long until riders were approaching them at a steady clip, and Cat watched as Lars put his hand on his sword, and she knew he would protect her if need be; somehow that made her feel better.

As the riders approached, she recognized Beth at the front and the men trying to keep up with her. A smile came to her lips as she turned to Lars and said, "Our daughter can already outride most men. Have you noticed?" He had noticed how good a rider she was when she was with him in the summer, but he hadn't realized until now. He was watching a smaller version of her mother on a horse; that is why she rode so well. He could also see that as much as she looked like his side of the family, she was Catherine made over. He hadn't lost Cat all those years ago; she had been given back to him in a smaller version to raise, and then a couple of years ago, she had sent him two more children to love as well—he just didn't know it.

"Yes, but until a few days ago, I didn't realize where the girls had gotten that talent from. I have never seen anyone handle horses the way you do. Robert says it has always been like that, but other people don't understand how you do it, and I think maybe it frightens them."

"Why?"

"Because you frighten them."

She looked at him strangely because Giles had said much the same thing to her once. She didn't say any more and just waited for Beth and Ann to meet up with them. When they did, Beth stopped and looked at her mother for a minute. She had a big grin on her face and said, "You are better." She rode up next to the horse of her mother, the mother she remembered from before Giles death.

"Yes, baby, I am much better. You were right to come and get your papa."

They all turned their horses and started toward the carriage, and as Lars watched them go, he knew this is what he had always wanted. He never kept a woman very long because he always compared them to Catherine, and now she was here; if he had to tie her up, put her on a boat, and take her back up north to his home, he wasn't giving her up again. So he had two daughters and three more sons, and by all the gods, they were his now.

Catherine, Ann, and Beth talked to one another while Lars stayed beside them. Beth knew her papa was not as good on a horse as they were, but she was anxious to see her brothers. They got to the carriage, and the boys were just waking and wanted to get out. Cat said, "Just wait a little bit more. We are almost there."

David turned from the window and didn't say a word. Beth said, "Is he still not talking to you?"

Jacob shook his head no to his two sisters.

Cat said, "Not a word. Do you know what is going on? He hasn't said two words to me."

"I don't know for sure, but something happened the night you brought Daddy back home, and he won't tell us what. But he blames you for it, and no, I don't know what it is. He won't talk to us either."

"Well, I guess it is about time that we find out, don't you? I have had enough of this silent treatment." They looked at one another and nodded and then rode on.

With no one to slow them down, their ride became increasingly faster, and they reached the lodge much quicker than the coach, much to the surprise of several of Lars's guards who weren't expecting three women charging up to the house. One of the guards soon recognized Beth and Ann and began to help them down from their horses; neither knew who the other woman was until Lars arrived and brushed them aside to help her down, and they got the feeling they had better not get any closer. He then introduced her.

"This is Lady Catherine, and she is the girl's mother. She and her sons are going to be staying with us for a while. I expect her to be treated with all due respect of Beth's and Ann's mother as well as her sons."

So this was the woman they had heard about; she was after all flesh and blood, and she was his even if she didn't know it yet. Now they knew why he had waited all these years for her, and she was a widow now. Even Cat realized how possessive he was acting, but she would have to deal with that later.

Her son needed her now, and he didn't need the crazy lady who lived at the keep. So they would stay, and she would get her mind back in order and see how things worked out, just one thing at a time. Cat knew how Lars felt about her; he had never made it a secret even to Giles, but she didn't know what she wanted right now. So this was going to be either a very interesting summer or a short one. She was older now. Maybe he would see that, and he would decide that there were younger and prettier women besides her around, and it wouldn't be a problem. She was the only one who thought that might happen after he had waited all of these years. Well, one problem at a time.

When they got into the lodge, all the memories came back and hit her like a sack of grain; she began to back out the door. Then she just stood there while Lars and Beth showed the boys the house. No one noticed except one of Lars's men, and he thought she was just a little odd as she started to walk toward the sea; after all, she seemed to know where she was going. Lars turned around and didn't see her, so he ran out of the house. Turning to Ann, he told her to stay. He looked at his man, and he pointed down the road. Lars was running and out of breath when he got to her, and they were almost to the cliffs; he grabbed her arm and turned her around.

She just said, "I couldn't breathe in there. It was like he was still there. I had to get out. Give me a few minutes, and I will try again."

"It is different inside now. The girls have been changing things around the past few summers. They say it needed a woman's touch, which I don't have." He talked to her as they walked away from the edge of the cliff, and then he had her sit down in the grass; when she started to breathe slower again, he asked her, "How long were you here?"

"I don't remember exactly. I just ran here to get away from him before we were married, and then we were married here before we went back to the keep."

So he had married her here.

"So the bed in the master bedroom was yours?"

"Yes, he had it built in there and then couldn't get it out. Have you enjoyed it all these years?" She actually smiled at that thought.

"Very much." But he was thinking, *I would have enjoyed it more if you had been in it*. But she was again looking away, thinking about another time. That was all right; this was his time, and he was going to make good use of it.

"It is getting cold. Do you want to try this again?"

"I guess we better, or I need to find a warm place in the barn."

Well, he didn't plan on letting her sleep in the barn; he wanted her as close as possible.

When they walked back into the house, there had indeed been many changes; extra rooms had been added, and bigger tapestries on the walls made it more cheerful and much warmer. The kitchen had been expanded, and a large room had been added to the back of the lodge for large groups of people. It was indeed a different place from what she remembered, and she began to feel easier about being here.

As soon as they entered, Beth grabbed her arm, being careful of her hands, and started to pull her around to every room; she was proud of the furniture and the way everything was arranged. She wanted her mother to see everything. Lars just stood back a little and watched as she took it all in; she didn't tell her daughter she had helped with most of the original design of this building when she was barely old enough to walk.

Soon, they were being called to the kitchen for supper; and as they came back down the hall, they passed the master bedroom. Beth and Ann pulled their mother into the room. Lars was too late to stop her, so he just followed them in. Beth pointed out the beautiful bed and the size of the room; she told her mother they had just had new bedspreads made because the old one was falling apart, and she didn't know why her papa had kept it for so long. She turned and looked at Lars, and she knew exactly why. He finally rescued her and told Beth supper was ready, and then he took her trembling arm and got her out of that room; any more time in there and she would have surely come apart. She didn't say anything, but he knew that was one step too far; he was going to have to talk to the girls.

When they were alone, she turned and asked, "Where is the bedspread?"

"It is in a cedar chest at the back of the room. I just couldn't throw it away."

"Why?"

"You know perfectly well why, even if they don't." The look in his eyes said it all; even after all these years, they weren't done—not yet.

After supper, everybody was made comfortable in a room, but Lars insisted on Cat staying in the room next to him; when she objected, he just said, "Next to me or with me. I won't have you accidentally falling off something." So she agreed.

A couple of hours later, he heard the door open quietly, and she left. He quietly followed her; she was in her robe, and she went to the cliffs again. He caught up to her before she got there and grabbed her; she was startled and turned to say, "Will you please stop grabbing me! You scare me to death when you do that."

"Then stop coming out to the edge of the cliff in the middle of the night and scaring me to death."

"I can't sleep, so I toss and turn in there, and I thought it would be better out here. At least I would have a better view, and it is one hell of a view. There is a place under the cliff, or there used to be a small cave where Giles and would go and make love when there was nobody around. I don't know if it is still there or if the tide has washed it out after all of these years."

"You have got to stop this. He is gone, and you can't bring him back and if you haven't noticed, your children need you. Then if there is a little room left over in there, you might squeeze me in as well."

"Why do you even want me after all this time? I would have assumed you would have found someone else by now and forgotten me. I am not all that special."

"I told you that night in the barn it wasn't over, and it never has been. I have compared every woman since to you, and they have all come up lacking in some way."

"I really don't understand why anyone would want me, much less two men. Maybe if I stay around, you will see I am not that special, and this obsession will leave you."

"And what if it doesn't? What if it just increases and I can't let you go this time? What then?"

"Then we might have a problem if I don't feel the same way. Let's just take this one day at a time and go with that."

"All right, but for now, we need to get back. You are as cold as ice, and you need some sleep. So no more midnight walks, all right?"

She just nodded her head because she was getting really tired.

They walked into the lodge, and he took her to her room. Then he did something unexpected; he turned her around, took her in his arms, and kissed her. To her surprise, for just a second, she kissed back; then she broke it off when she realized what was happening. She then turned and went into her room. She shut the door and leaned against it as she heard him say, "Night, little love."

She realized she was in trouble, so why was she smiling like an idiot? Why had Giles sent her here?

She walked to the bed, lay down, pulled the covers up over her, and fell into the first deep sleep she had had in a long time, at least for a little while. Lars stood outside her door, and now it was him who couldn't sleep; she had kissed him back even if she didn't mean to, and for just a second, she was his again. So he walked down the hall and checked the children.

The boys were in the first room, and he could see they were both going to be mirror images of Giles, though David didn't look like he was going to be as big a man as his dad. He closed the door quietly and went down the hall a little farther to Beth and Ann's room and peeked in. Beth was sprawled out on her bed as usual, with her blonde hair everywhere; she looked so much like his sisters. He wished they could see her. Well, maybe if things changed, they could. Ann was going to be a beautiful woman as well. Jacob had his own room down the hall; whoever his father had been, he was going to be a big man. He was already tall for a boy his age. How anyone could have killed these children, he couldn't understand. Several children had been brought to him in the years since he took over this land, and he had found homes for each and every one of them in his village up north; nobody had ever hurt another child after Cat had put her foot down on the subject of Raiders-born children. He had made sure not another one died.

Lars headed back down to his room, and as he got to Cat's room, he could smell something strange; it smelled like, well, there was no other way to describe it—a man, leather, and armor. So he quietly opened her door; there was nobody there except Catherine. He stood there a moment looking at her and started to shut the door; when he saw her hand, it was clenched so tight on the blanket that he could see blood on the bandage. He started to wake her, and then he could swear he heard something. So he stood very still and listened again, and this time, he heard, "Goodbye, my love."

There was no mistaking who was talking; he had heard that voice too many times over the years. It was Giles. So she hadn't been imagining him all this time; maybe he had tried to take her with him. He watched her hand relax, and she went back to sleep, and he finally knew the nightmares were over for her; maybe her life could start again. He walked to her bedside and pulled up her covers; then he walked out of the room, shut the door, then looked up and said into thin air, "I will take care of them now, Giles. Rest in peace."

Catherine slept the whole night and well into the next day; the children had been shuttled outside by Lars and occupied elsewhere. When she did wake up, she was startled for a moment by the lateness of the day but soon calmed down. In fact, she seemed calmer than she had been in a long time; and she didn't know exactly why, but that was all right too. She called Caroline and had her help her dress, for her hands were hurting; she was going to have to see to them soon. They walked to the kitchen to look for the children, for they were uncommonly quiet; they found the cook. When she asked where the children were, she told Cat they were with the master looking at the boats. The cook was pulling fresh bread from the oven, and it smelled delicious.

"That smells wonderful."

"The master told me to have you eat something before you came looking for them, or you couldn't come outside." The cook looked at her with some fear as though she didn't know how she was supposed to keep the lady inside if she didn't want to stay.

So Catherine made it easy for her; with a little smile, she said, "How about some of that bread buttered and some milk?"

The cook turned, looking very relieved, and said, "Maybe some eggs as well?"

Cat just nodded.

Catherine ate her breakfast and headed outside; she was walking down the road to the boats when the children came running up to her, with Lars not far behind. Michel almost knocked her down, hugging her and telling her about the boats. Of course, Beth and Ann had seen them for many summers. But when she asked David, he turned and said to Lars, "They are very big."

Jacob said, "You have to be on one when it is sailing. It is like flying. It is wonderful!"

Cat looked at Lars, and she could almost see him saying, "That boy is a Raider."

Cat looked over her son's head at Lars as if to say, "What is going on with David?" But he just shrugged his shoulders; he hadn't been able to find anything out.

"How do you feel this morning?" Lars asked as he got closer. The children ran ahead; the girls wanted to show their brothers the barns. There were some new calves, so they went on ahead. Jacob wanted to help with the boats, so he stayed with the men.

"Much better you let me sleep too long the day has gotten away from me."

"Was there something you needed to do?"

"No, I guess not. It just seems like I always need to be doing something."

"Well, not today. There is something we have to do before bed tonight, and it is not going to be pleasant."

She looked at him rather oddly and thought, *now what?*

"Look at your hands. Those gloves and that dead skin have got to come off, and your hands have to be redressed. You and I know it has to be done. So after the children are asleep?" She just nodded. "In my room, I will have your salves and dressing brought in there and bowls of warm water." He didn't know she had already had Caroline help her put some drops in her milk for the pain so she could get through the afternoon.

The rest of the day went well; the children explored the lodge and every nook and cranny of the barns and outbuilding. Lars introduced them and Cat to every one of his people and told them about the boats that would be coming soon. The more the day dragged on, the more Catherine dreaded what was coming; the feeling was coming back into her hands, and she had been taking small amounts of painkiller to ward it off. But tonight was going to be tough; pulling off the gloves and the old skin was going to be very painful, so she took a small vial of her painkiller and put it in her gown. Caroline helped her change into a clean gown and robe because she was sure after this procedure, she wouldn't want to do anything but go to bed. She told Caroline to go to bed; she didn't want anyone else watching this. She didn't like people watching her in pain; she wished Jennie was here.

She walked into Lars's room, and indeed, everything was waiting—bowls, clean towels, and a very sharp knife. Lars opened the door the rest of the way and helped her to sit down on a pillow in front of the fireplace.

"Would you like something to drink?"

"Yes please."

He handed her a glass with something in it; she took out the vial and started to empty it into the glass, but her damaged hands couldn't open it. He reached down, gently took it out of her hands, and asked her, "What is it?"

"Laudanum."

"Is this what you have been taking for the pain?"

She just nodded.

"Tell me how much."

"Just two or three drops, should be plenty. But it will take a few minutes to go to work."

He put three drops into the glass and handed it to her to drink, and then he poured the bowls half full of water and tested them to see if they were too hot.

"Put your hand in and let them soak. We can just sit here and talk. When it is time, I will try to cut off as much of the glove as possible. I will try not to hurt you as much as I can. How did they manage to ride next to you in the snow with no one noticing that you were freezing to death?"

"It was a long, dark night. Nobody was to blame but me."

"You said nothing all those long hours?"

She just shook her head no.

"Nobody noticed until you got back to the keep?"

"I collapsed in my bedroom, and then Jennie figured it out. By then, my hands were black."

"It's a wonder you didn't lose them. Shall we get started?"

She just nodded. He gently picked up her right hand, turned it over, and, with the knife, slit the glove down the center of her palm. After setting down the knife, he started gently pulling the glove away; the dead tissue came with it. It wasn't too horrible until he got to the fingertips; then it was bad. Tears were streaming down her face, and he stopped, but she shook her head. "Finish it." He quickly, but carefully finished pulling off each fingertip. Her hand looked like a raw piece of meat; he quickly covered it with salve and lightly bandaged it.

She leaned her head against his shoulder and cried; he just held her. There was nothing else to do, and they still had one more hand to do. After a few minutes, she was ready, and they started again. This time was better, and the painkiller was working; the glove came off easier because this hand was much more healed. Lars was pleased. After putting on salve and wrapping this hand, Catherine was done. She could barely keep her head up. The painkiller had all but knocked her out; she was dead to the world. So he picked her up and carried her to his bed. He laid her on the bed and lay next to her; he knew she would wake up in a little while, and he would have to move her to her room before then. But for right now, he wanted to hold her and have her be his, even if for just a few minutes.

He would never have told Beth, but the reason he would not give up the old bedspread was because Catherine had slept under it; now he could smell her on this one, and she had slept under it. She was beginning to get restless. So he opened the door, picked her up, and took her back to her room. Then he covered her up and left the room, but when he got back to bed, he could still smell her all over his room. That was good enough for the time being; he was just sorry he had to cause her pain to get her in here.

She slept for some time, but she awoke to her right hand screaming for attention; she got out of bed. Thankfully, the candle was still lit so she could see. She went to get a drink of water, but she couldn't find her bottle of painkiller. Where was it? She started to search the table, but only her left hand would work, and she kept knocking things over.

Lars was standing in front of the fireplace when he heard her rustling around, and he headed to her room; when he opened the door, she was holding her right hand up and crying. When she turned, all she said was, "Where is my laudanum?" He had forgotten it was in his pocket.

"You have to sit down on the bed. Is two drops enough?"

She nodded yes. He poured a glass of water and added the drops. He realized she couldn't do this by herself; she could barely hold the glass with her hands. She shook so badly.

"You are either going to have to stay in my room so I can help you, or one of the women is going to have to stay in here with you till your hands are better. How did you get through last night?"

"Caroline poured me a glass and added the drops before she put the children to bed. The pain wasn't as bad because we hadn't cut away the dead flesh. I can't stay in your room, so I will make arrangements for someone to stay with me at night."

He just nodded and turned to help her back in bed, then covered her up.

"From now till your hands are better, you will meet me in my room every night, and we will do this process again. But in the morning, I am telling the servants you are not to pick up anything, including your children, or get on a horse until your hands are healed. I will not see you in that kind of agony again, if I can prevent it. Do you understand me? Catherine, I have seen very few people not lose their fingers to the damage your fingers survived. And if I had known they were that bad, we would have started this the first night you arrived. I will not be that stupid again."

"I understand, but you are being kind of bossy, aren't you? I am not your responsibility, and this was my own fault. Besides, I have endured a lot more pain than this giving birth to my children and survived."

"Well, one thing at a time and you are my responsibility now." *Besides*, he thought, *if you give birth to another child, I will be there, and it will be mine.*

The painkiller was going to work, and she was going to sleep; he wished she would stay in his room so he could help her, but she wasn't having any of that. He didn't want to push her away, so he would do as she requested for now, but he was not going to let her damage those fingers any more than they already were. He left her door open a crack so if she needed him, he could hear her until he could get someone to stay the night with her. He then went to bed. At least he would get to have her all to himself for a little while each night; he just wished it was under better circumstances.

He woke early and had Caroline waiting to help Cat when she woke, with the instructions he had told her about last night. Caroline was glad someone was taking over; she couldn't give her orders, but when she wasn't paying attention, she was hurting her hands without realizing it. Lars took the boys, and they went down to the boats, they were building a new one and he wanted to see how it was coming along. Catherine called for Caroline; and she came into the room to help her dress, only to find her on the bed, holding her right hand up.

"Please get me something to drink and add a couple of drops to it now."

Caroline understood and quickly went back to the kitchen. She found some water from the well and added two drops to it, stirred it up, and headed back.

Catherine was waiting on the bed, shaking; she took the glass and drank it down in two gulps, then just sat there for a few minutes. When the pain backed down, she had Caroline help her dress. Nobody knew, but that was how most mornings had been since they left the keep; she was just barely keeping the pain under control, and her right hand was the worst. She got dressed and went to breakfast.

Beth was waiting for her; she was so excited. "Mama, we have got to go to the village and buy supplies this morning. Would you like to go with me and meet the villagers? I think they would like to meet you."

She just looked at Caroline; what she was supposed to say? *I feel like hell, and my hands hurt.* Beth was so excited, so she said, "Of course, darling, I would love to go. But I can't ride. We have to take a wagon, and someone else will have to drive, all right?"

Beth was so pleased, so she left to take care of the wagon, guards, and a driver.

Caroline looked at her as if she had finally lost what was left of her mind.

"What about your hands? The wind is cold."

"I am not putting on another pair of gloves. They hurt coming off. Maybe I can cover them with a blanket."

"Mittens, large woolen mittens. The men wear them when they are fishing to protect their hands, and they don't fit so tight. They would come off easy," said Greta.

"It is worth a try." All the ladies nodded to one another as Greta went to find some mittens.

"Lars isn't going to like this."

"I am not a prisoner, and I will be with Beth and Ann. I know a lot of those people in the village. We will be fine."

Greta came back in with a pair of mittens, and Catherine carefully put them on. They felt comfortable and warm, and they weren't horrible looking, not any worse than bandages. When Beth came back, Greta had a cape wrapped around Cat. Caroline was ready to help her get in the wagon, which wasn't necessary because when they got to the wagon, a man almost as big as Lars picked her up by the waist and literally sat her in the seat like she weighed nothing. Cat looked at Greta and Caroline and then at Beth and asked, "Where did you find him?"

"Oh, he is Eric. He was in the barn, and I asked him if he would help me today." From the way the young man was looking at Beth and Ann, she suspected there wasn't much this young man wouldn't do for her daughters, especially Ann; she had seen that look before in her life in two different men's faces. She would have to keep her eyes on this young man because he wanted one of her daughters, and Lars didn't know.

Cat just smiled to herself and then at Eric. He just smiled back then said, "It is very nice to finally meet Elizabeth and Ann's mother. I am Eric Strandhom." And then he bowed to her most formally, and she had the weirdest feeling she was meeting someone special in her daughter's life, so she smiled back.

"I was told not to let you use your hands. I didn't hurt you, did I?"

"No, you were very gentle. Thank you." And then she smiled again, and as she turned around, she saw Ann wink at Eric. So her little girl wasn't so little after all, and she was trying to impress Mama.

The young man mounted his horse, and they proceeded to town. Cat asked Beth about the people living there, and Beth said they were doing well. But when they went to town, they weren't well received. Cat wondered about this. Giles had always had good relations with the village, especially since Giles had taken it upon himself to buy livestock and seed to get them going the first year after she came here.

When they entered town, she could see they weren't well received; there were a few shops open, but some were already starting to close as Beth tried to buy vegetables. She saw a man she knew; and as soon as

Eric set her on the ground, she started toward him, telling everyone else to stay behind by the wagon for a few minutes till she came back.

"Brian Tucker, are you going to close your shop to me after all these years? Is that the homecoming I have to expect from all my people?"

He turned and looked at her for a moment, and then tears came to his eyes. Then he lowered himself to one knee and said, "My lady Catherine, I did not know it was you. Please forgive an old man. You and your husband saved this village, and these people shall always have your respect and honor. Where is Lord Giles?"

"My lord husband is dead. He was killed in an accident. That is why my daughters and I have come here to her land for a while." She gestured to Beth and Ann to come to her, and she was going to introduce them to this man. The villagers were coming out to see why the village elder was making such a fuss over this lady, and then some of them began to realize who she was and started to come forward. Then the Raider showed up; he came thundering into the village. He jumped off his horse and came running up to her and asked if she was all right. She turned and said with a smile, "I am fine, and I would like to introduce you to some people."

She was smiling, but the look she was giving him could have melted steel, and he knew he had better shut up and follow her lead, or he was going to catch hell.

"This Lars Sorenson, he is the Raider who watches over this land until my Beth comes of age. This is her land. She is my daughter, and Lars is her papa."

Then Brian remembered she had a daughter when she married Giles; things were beginning to fall into place. This child they had been ignoring was to be their new master when she came of age. "We came to town to buy supplies. If there are any to be sold, we will pay a good price. I will see you are treated fairly."

"My lady, can we get you a seat?" Then Brian started to reach for her hand, and both Beth and Lars yelled, "No!"

She turned to the startled man and said, "My hands got badly frostbitten on the night Giles died and are still a mess, so I am wearing these lovely mittens to keep them warm."

"I am so sorry, my lady. Let me get you a chair. Is there anything else you need?"

"I seem to remember your wife, Sara, always had the best buttermilk. Do you suppose she might have some today?"

He just nodded. Within a few minutes, the whole town was crowded around, and people she remembered and some she didn't were all around her. Beth heard stories about how she had delivered their babies, saw to the buying of livestock when this village was starving, and made sure there was enough grain to get through the winter and plant the next spring. Lars was watching Cat's hands shake more and more and he knew she was beginning to hurt again. Brian's wife brought a pitcher of buttermilk, and he understood the odd request. By then, there was also a small table she was resting her hands on.

"Thank you for the cup. It is hard to hold a glass." And then she looked up at Lars, and he just nodded yes. She slid the cup back a little after Sara had poured the milk, and he dropped the drops in. She drank the whole glass and sat there while people talked to her; he had never had this kind of reception in all of his years here, but they loved her. Now that they knew Beth was hers, she would always be welcome here.

Brian had disappeared but was now coming back down the side of building, holding something in his hands. Cat saw him first and told Lars, "He is the best saddle maker around. Giles always had him make his saddles and gloves. He said they were the best."

In his hand was a pair of gloves; they looked like cream-colored velvet, and when he got to her, he put them on the table in front of her. She just looked up at him, and he said, "I made them for a knight to wear under his gloves so they wouldn't rub after one of his hands was burned in a fire. They are lambskin. I want you to try them. They will be too big, but I think that is a good thing."

"Help me, Lars."

Lars came around, got on one knee, gently untied the mitten on the left hand, and removed it. When Brian saw her hand, it was all he could do not to react, but Lars so very gently put the glove on her hand. It was large enough that it slid on easily, and it did feel better. But when it came to the right one, Lars started to say something, but Catherine looked up to Brian and said, "The right is going to have to wait a couple more days. It is worse than the left, but thank you so much for them. Can I pay you for them?"

"No, my lady they are a gift."

So she turned and nodded at Sara as if asking permission, and when Sara nodded yes, she reached over and kissed Brian on the cheek. He blushed from ear to ear.

"Since you are the elder, I was wondering if maybe we could start having a farmers' market like we used to do, perhaps on Saturdays. We are going to need some chickens and pigs. If anyone is interested in selling any fresh vegetables, we are in need of those too." She was asking him; he looked at Sara, and she was so proud.

"Yes, my lady that would be wonderful. What about this Saturday? Is that acceptable?"

"Oh, I think that would give us time to get some pens built and everything ready. Don't you, Lars?" She was including him into the conversation with a smile, so he had better be nice, or she was going to strangle him.

"I think we can have anything built that you need by then. It was a pleasure to meet you. Next time, you will have to show me some of your saddles even though Catherine and my daughter Beth can outride me any day of the week."

Now there was no doubt who Beth's papa was and that he wanted her mother to stay, and he thought they did as well; they felt safe with her around.

"My lady, the other girl with you, is she the one you took with you as a child?"

"Yes, she is, and the blond boy is with me as well. Giles and I took both of them as our children, and we never regretted it."

He looked at her and the people around her and remembered those small children; she had taken them as her own, and still, she kept his people from starving. He hoped she would stay. This Raiders had been here for so many years, and nobody knew why he had protected them and helped with their land. Giles had come and taken care of the rents and properties and said Lars was the guardian, but he had never told them the whole story, if they had known things would have been different. He had better make this right, or his lady would leave again, and he didn't want that. He owed Giles more much more.

CHAPTER 9

This time, Lars put Cat in the wagon, and the girls rode with Eric. Ann and Beth didn't think that would bother their mother too much; besides, they could see their mother was about to explode, and this was going to be fun to watch. They had two guards who were Catherine's men behind them so she wouldn't embarrass him in front of his men. About halfway to the lodge, she had him stop, then she jumped out of the wagon and walked into a field; she told Beth she wanted to talk to her too, so she came as well. She turned around and let them have it.

"What were you thinking, Beth? Why didn't you tell them that you were my daughter? You wouldn't have had to put up with this all these years!"

"I didn't know they thought you were the Virgin Mother, or I would have. It would have made it a lot easier. Why didn't you tell me about all the things you did for those people? I might have had some idea what I was doing. Then they could have lined the streets in gold for me to walk on." Cat looked up to see her daughter all but laughing at her, the little brat. She thought this was funny—well, it kind of was.

"Those people would put you up for sainthood, and all I can see is my mother when you fell in the lake and came out looking like the mud monster. We laughed for two days. It was all Ann and I could do to keep a straight face back there."

"Well, I can understand you didn't know any better. Giles should have set Brian straight about what was going on." Then she turned to Lars, "These people are afraid of you and your people. You have to try and make friends if we are going to live here. I am not made of crystal, and I don't need babysitters. I just need a little help getting things in order around here. Don't yell at everybody who gets within ten feet of me. We need to get pens built for animals, and I need to get staff ready for the coming boats. The lodge has to presentable for your friends, and things have to be ready. We need those people to like you because we need supplies. We can't grow everything."

Catherine turned and started walking away toward the lodge, talking; they could hear measurements and counting of chickens. Lars turned to Beth, who had a huge grin on face, and looked at her strangely. Ann was running toward them with an equally big grin on her face.

"Don't you understand? She said 'we,' Papa, and she is measuring pens for chickens and pigs. Her mind is working. She's not lost in grieving anymore. She has started living and building a world again, and it is here," Beth explained.

Ann chimed in, "When she is aggravated, she starts working on something. She always has, and now she is doing it here. It means we are staying. She is back." She was right; the visit to the village was just what she needed. Well, they had better hurry up, or she was going to beat them home.

He climbed into the wagon and told Beth to ride his horse and stay with Ann. He then told Eric and the guards to watch the girls so he could be alone with Cat for a little while and maybe talk to her. The wagon pulled up beside Cat, and she barely glanced at him.

"Do you plan to walk all the way back just to spite me?"

"Maybe, but it probably wouldn't do any good because I didn't dress warm enough for this little walk." He stopped the wagon, got down, went around, and stopped her. Then he picked her up in both arms, carried her back to the wagon, and put her down on the ground. Then he picked her up around the waist like she weighed nothing and sat her in the seat.

"I am beginning to feel like a sack of grain. Pretty soon, someone is going to start throwing me over their shoulder to put me in this wagon. I will be so glad when my hands are well, and I can do this for myself."

"I won't. I like doing this even if you don't. I get a chance to hold you even if it is just for a few minutes."

She just looked at him and shook her head lightly. "You just don't give up, do you?" Lars just shook his head no.

When they got back to the lodge, the evening meal was almost ready, and now so many men were joining them at supper; they ate in the big hall. Cat wasn't surprised; they all wanted to see her. Lars had talked about her for so many years that they wanted to see what Beth's mother looked like; she was sure they were disappointed. Nobody could live up to those expectations. She was treated with every respect as they knew this land was Beth's through her, so she was a lady of property; she just wanted Beth to be treated well.

The day had been long, so it wasn't long till she snuck away to her room, and Caroline followed close behind. Caroline helped Cat out of her dress and into a gown, and then she braided her hair. It wasn't long till there was a knock on the door, and Lars was standing there. She turned and asked, "Where are the children?"

"They are still in the hall playing with the other children. I will get them to bed in a little while, if that is all right, mistress?"

Catherine just nodded. She walked into the master bedroom, and everything was ready, including a jug of wine.

"Are you trying to get me drunk?"

"No, I don't think laudanum and wine are good for you, so I got you buttermilk. It seems to be your preference as of late." He helped her down on a pillow, and she drank the glass dry quickly, and then he gently took the glass out of her hand.

"Tonight we wait a while for it to work better. Then we go to work on your hands. While we wait, tell me about your plans for the livestock you seem to have ordered for this weekend."

"Are you mad about that?"

He just shook his head no as he reached for her left hand.

"I thought you said we should wait?"

"I am just going to gently pull off this glove your friend gave you. If it hurts, tell me, and I will stop." He gently pulled on each finger, and it slid off with little effort and no pain; it had protected her hand with no further damage.

"I shall have to thank your friend Brian. This was exactly what you needed. How do you know this man?"

"When I first got here, the village was in ruins because of Raiders raids. I had very little money to keep myself and my men in food, and the lodge was in shambles. I took what money I had and found enough supplies to feed all of us and the villagers until Giles got here. I don't know what I was going to do if he hadn't showed up, but they didn't know that. Giles came to get me, and I told him to go away. This was my land, and these people needed me. His mistress had thrown me out and slapped me. He said he was staying, so I put him to work, helping these people rebuild and restock. They always thought it was me, and really it was him trying to impress me."

"Somebody slapped you?"

"Really, that's all you got out of that story?" She hadn't realized, but while she was talking, he had carefully been unwrapping the bandages on her hand. Now he was done with the left until he looked down, and she followed his eyes, and her hand almost looked normal.

"It is finally beginning to look better. Did I hurt you?"

She shook her head no; her right hand was still in the bowl, and he gently took it and set it on his other hand, looked at her, and said, "Now let's try this one again."

The right one wasn't as easy; there was still too much raw flesh, but it wasn't as bad as last night. After it was cleaned and salve was applied, he rewrapped it. She just sat for a bit in front of the fire, and then she told him, "Giles found Ann and Jacob in a barn one day. A man was trying to kill them, and he brought them home to me after he nearly beat the man to death. The next day, I told the villagers if any more children died, I would let them starve. Brian was the only one trying to help those children. That was when I told them to bring them to the lodge, and they would be taken care of. Another little girl had already died."

"And they have been taken care of."

"Would you sit in the window seat with me? I want to talk to you about something."

His heart fell. *Is she leaving? What am I going to do now? Had the girls been wrong?*

He sat down in the window seat, and to his surprise, she sat right in front of him, almost in his lap; then she pointed to the big barn and started to explain how she thought the pens for the pigs and the chickens should be laid out.

She turned, looked up at him, and then said, "Well, is that all right? I didn't want to have this conversation in front of your men. They would think I am giving you orders, so I wanted to talk about this in here when we were alone."

She was asking permission where to put the stupid chickens when he put both arms around her and pulled her to him. He kissed her neck and down her throat like he was drawing life from her; it was all he could do not to hurt her. He wanted her so badly, and then her hands were ever so gently on his face. He was afraid she was going to tell him to stop, but she didn't; she pulled his face down to hers and found his lips.

Her eyes were closed as she kissed him gently at first and then with a hunger she hadn't felt for anyone but Giles. Then she leaned back and let him take over with kisses on her face and neck, then lower to the tops of her breasts; she was so twisted in his lap she felt like a rag doll. That was when he started to pick her up, and this time, she didn't object. At about that time, someone started pounding on the door. Cat opened her eyes and looked at Lars as he sat her down, and all she could say was, "Really? Not now."

Lars was furious and a few other things when he reached the door to find two of his men telling him that some of the men got drunk, which had ended in a fight.

"Are the children all right?" The man in front of him shook his head yes, and Lars turned around. He turned to see Cat gathering up her glove and leaving, past the drunken men; if he had been anywhere else, he would have killed both of them right there. She couldn't look at him for fear the other men would see what was in her eyes. She wanted him; even she couldn't deny it anymore.

She went to her room, and Caroline helped her dress and get in bed as she all but threw her clothes at the wall. Caroline smiled but didn't say a word; she was just plain mad at not getting something she wanted, and Caroline was pretty sure what that was by the way Lars was yelling at the men outside the door. This was getting good and she was going to enjoy watching. She figured she would be sleeping next to her husband James very soon because Cat wouldn't need her help dressing or undressing anymore. She had to make her calm down before she messed up the bandages on her hands and they had to do them all over again.

When Cat looked at her smiling face, she asked, "What is so funny?"

Caroline just shrugged her shoulder, and Cat just kicked her robe out of the way. Caroline had to turn around so she couldn't see her face, but she couldn't wait to tell James; she might have to sneak out in a little while and go to their room. He was going to love this. From what the girls had told her this afternoon, things were beginning to fall into place. Giles had known Cat needed someone to help her, and he had sent her here; sometimes she thought she felt his presence watching over them.

Lars was in a murderous mood when he got to the men in the large hall; they were lucky not to have gotten killed. They were going to have to stand watch for at least a month waiting for the boats, and then he shut down the lodge and sent everyone to bed. He walked back to his room and stopped by Catherine's room and cracked open the door; she was fast asleep, which he was not going to be able to do anytime soon. So he shut the door again.

Caroline watched, smiled again, and thought to herself, *Yes, I will be sleeping with James very soon.* Then she went to sleep herself.

The next morning, Cat was up early and waiting in the kitchen when Lars got there; he was later than usual. He hadn't slept well. She was packing food in a large cloth laid out on the table; his curiosity finally got the better of him, and he asked, "Are you going somewhere?"

"Yes, I am taking the children to a place Giles, Beth, and I used to go if it is still there across the stream. And I am going to find out what is wrong with David. Would you like to come with us?"

"Yes, very much," he replied even though he wished it was just them.

"Good, we may need some help," Cat said as she put two very sharp knives in the basket.

"What are you planning on doing exactly?"

"It is a small hedged-in space, and it may be overgrown, and I may need someone to help me do some pruning to get in."

"Really, how were you going to prune with those hands Divine intervention?"

"I really was hoping you would come." She gave him a look that would have melted butter. Good God, how was he going to make it through the day and not touch her? He was never going to make till tonight. He leaned over and kissed her neck. She trembled, and he smiled.

"What are you doing?"

"Kissing your neck I may have to do it some more."

"Not today, there will be five little guardians. And you won't get away with that, sir." As she looked up over her shoulder with a grin on her face that said, "Just try it."

"What about tonight?"

They couldn't talk here; there were people everywhere. He was just going to have to wait. As the children came in for breakfast, she explained they were going for a walk to a place she used to go with their daddy, and she got a resounding response.

They headed out after everyone was dressed and walked for about an hour until Cat found the small hedged-in area; sure enough, it was covered up with new growth. When Catherine found the old opening,

Michel, Jacob, and Lars went to pruning and made a decent-size opening for them to get into. It needed some work inside, but as the boys worked, Ann and Beth used a rake they had brought with them. David stood by Cat and seemed to be having fun but was still barely talking to her.

After it was partly cleaned and pruned, it was deemed worthy to at least eat in for today, with further work to be done later. This was now their private getaway. They all laughed at the silliness of a hedged-in hideaway when their sister owned this land and their brother was heir to another.

Catherine spread out the blanket on the ground and set out the food, then sat the children down. It was simple fare: just cheese, fresh bread, some sliced meats wrapped in a goatskin, with jugs of milk and a jug of fresh water. They were all having a good time until Lars reached across Cat's lap to cut a branch that was caught on her dress, and the knife slipped, and he cut across the arm that was holding the branch.

She grabbed a towel out of the basket and started wrapping his arm; he was dripping blood on her dress. He wasn't cut badly, but she didn't expect what happened next. David was screaming at her, "Don't touch him! You will let him die like Daddy!" He had his arm raised; he was going to hit her. Michel grabbed his brother.

"What are you talking about, David? I didn't let your daddy die."

"You did! I went downstairs, and he was bleeding. His eyes were open, and nobody was helping him. They put a blanket on him because he was cold, but you didn't help him."

"David, your daddy's horse fell on him and crushed him. When I got to him, he was barely alive. He said he loved you children more than life, but he had to go. I couldn't save him. He died in my arms, and then I brought him home. I can help Lars, though. But we have to get back to the lodge. Can you help me hold the towel on his arm while we gather up everything?"

David nodded yes.

Beth said, "Mom, you go. Michel and Jacob can stay with us. We can take care of this. We will be right behind you."

"I will send Eric back to make sure you are all right and help you."

Fortunately, Eric never let the girls get too far out of his sight; and when he saw Lars and Catherine almost running down the hill, he came to their aid. Cat quickly told him what had happened and sent him for a wagon, and when he returned, she pointed to where Beth was now appearing from the woods and asked him to escort her children home.

With Lars and David now in the wagon, she quickly headed back to the lodge. Greta met her at the door, and Cat ordered fresh water and bandages brought to Lars's room. Lars looked at her and then asked, "How are you going to take care of this with your hands?"

"If I can't, the girls can."

"Really?"

She shook her head yes. David was still scared, so Cat put him to work.

"David, come over here. You are going to help me fix Lars's arm. Do you think you can do that?"

He walked over to her and said, "Tell me what to do."

"First, we have to take this towel off and clean the wound, and then we may have to stitch it closed and then bandage it."

"Won't that hurt?"

"Yes, so we are going to give him something so it won't hurt so much."

He just looked at her and nodded. Lars watched and smiled; she was a good teacher. She looked up at him as she handed him a glass with laudanum in it, and he shook his head no.

"I won't let your daughter stitch your arm if you don't. It will scare her to death. Now drink."

"I had other plans for tonight than this, and laudanum will interfere with those plans."

"It will for a while, but there is always later, and we may not have to stitch it."

And then there was that look again, the one that turned his bones to jelly. There was no way to talk with David in here, and then in walked the children. So he just shut up, sat back, and watched her work—of all the days to get careless. It wasn't as bad as they thought; when they got it to stop bleeding, it didn't need stitches—just cleaning, salve, and wrapping. She sent the boys out to take care of the wagon and the horses, and the girls took care of Lars's arm while she gave instructions; she didn't have to give many. They had watched her long enough; they knew what to do. Ann finally said, "I think we are done. Beth, we just need to get the bloody towels out of here, and I think we are through."

"How do you feel, Papa? Is it too tight?" He shook his head no and looked at each girl with admiration; they weren't little girls anymore.

"Thank you, ladies. That is a fine job."

They walked out of the room with the bloody rags, and David went with them. "I am right behind you."

Catherine got Lars to bed, and he was falling asleep; it was late afternoon. She kissed him on the forehead, but he reached up and pulled her down and kissed her soundly on the lips. "Will you come back tonight?"

"You will just have to wait and see. Now go to sleep. I have to go talk to my son."

She went to the boys' room, and all three of them were there; she went in. Beth and Ann followed her in, and when Cat sat on the side of the boy's bed and patted it, David came and sat beside her. Then she asked him, "Why wouldn't you talk to me about this before now? Why did you wait so long?"

"Nobody would tell me what was going on, and then we left and came here, and you were acting so strange. People said you were crazy, and then I didn't want to make Lars mad because I like him, and I was afraid you might scare him."

Well, the child was right; she was acting strange, and he didn't know what was going on, and nobody had bothered to tell him. He was the only one who didn't hear the explanation of what happened to Giles that night at the keep, and no one had told him since.

"Honey, Lars would like us to stay." A knowing look passed between Ann and Beth; they both had seen how Lars looked at their mother. Michel started to say something, and Catherine gave him a look that said, "He is not old enough, so shut up." He and his sisters did just that and then smiled at one another.

"Really, he might let us stay for a while?"

Catherine looked at the children and said, "I can ask if all of us would be able to stay for a while longer."

Michel was the first to say, "Beth, Ann, and Jacob have been getting to see the ships come in for the last couple of years. We would like to see them this year as well."

Then David said, "I don't understand. Is Lars really Beth's dad, or was Daddy? And was he Ann and Jacob's dad? They all look alike."

She just looked at Michel as if to say, "Really?"

"How about we discuss that tomorrow? I will explain all of that to you then."

He nodded his head yes; she was hoping he would forget about that for a while longer. Michel just grinned at her; this was going to be great. He was too much like his daddy; he liked to watch her squirm.

"All right everybody get a bath and then to bed. I will get the fire going higher. It is getting colder at night."

As she turned, Michel had already grabbed the wood and headed to the fireplace. "Mother we can handle this. You need to change. You have blood all over you, and you don't need to be picking up wood. We are not babies."

No, they were not babies anymore; her babies were gone. Why did she feel so old all of a sudden? She checked in on the girls, and Beth was bathing, and she realized what a beautiful woman she was going to be; she wondered again what Lars's sisters looked like; she would have to ask him tonight.

She headed to her room and began to dig in her chest for something; she didn't even know if it got packed. It was a nightgown she had bought for a surprise for Giles, but he never saw it. Sure enough,

Jennie had packed it. It was made of black silk; she had found it when she had gone to court at a shop of a seamstress who worked for Queen Marie. It had been made for a lady at court. Well, not a lady—a mistress who had fallen out of favor. Catherine had bought it at an inflated price, but she wanted it. She had never worn it, but she planned to tonight; it was now or never. She would see if there was something between Lars and her before she asked him about staying. She put the gown on and then looked at herself in the small mirror; then she put her old robe over it just in case she didn't have enough nerve to do this. Her children were braver than she was.

As she knocked on Lars's door, she was trembling. *You are such a coward*, she thought to herself. But when he opened the door, all she could see was her daughter, and she smiled.

"What are you smiling about? This generally isn't the most pleasant experience."

"I just was watching Beth bathing and wondered what your sisters looked like, if they were as pretty as she is going to be." He looked at her strangely because he had wished his sisters could see his daughter so many times; in fact, he had thought about just taking her home with him last year. Now he was so glad he hadn't. Catherine would have never forgiven him for that.

"They are beautiful. In fact, my youngest sister looks like an older version of her. We are going to have to start keeping an eye on her. The young men will be noticing too."

Without even thinking about it, Catherine said, "My darling, she is already being paid attention to. Eric has eyes for one of the girls. I am not sure which one yet. Why do you think he was so close today? He always knows where they are, and he makes sure they are safe."

He just looked like she slapped him first because of the endearment that he didn't miss and then because he hadn't noticed his daughters had an admirer. He was quickly coming to think of both girls as his. In fact, he had for some time; and if he really was truthful to himself, he had already taken the boys as his own.

"I will kill him."

"No, you will not. He watches over them, and he knows I am watching him. He protects them. Leave him alone for now. Your daughters know he is there as well. I don't think they have decided yet if he is more than a friend. One of them will tell me when she does."

He motioned her inside and started to sit down on the pillows; but before she could, he turned her around, took her in his arms, and kissed her. She kissed back. She reached up to touch his face and the bandages got in the way. She said, "Let's try and take as much of this stuff off as possible. I want to be able to feel your skin with my hands, not through gloves."

He didn't care; he just wanted her, but he would do as she said. They took all the wrapping off the left hand and left it uncovered; as they worked, he asked her how it went with the children, and she told him most of it up to the end. She was saving that for later. When the bandages came off the right hand, it was still a mess, but she put salve and a light glove on it. Then while he cleaned up, she stood up and walked to the door.

"Catherine, I was hoping you would stay." Just at about that time, he heard the bolt on the door shoved closed; the door was locked.

"I planned to." Then she walked toward him; she took off the robe and dropped it in the chair beside the door, but she was still in the shadows as she walked farther forward. The light from the candles and the fireplace began to light up what she was wearing. He didn't know what it was; the gown looked like spun cobwebs, and she looked beautiful in it. As she walked toward him, he felt like all the years were gone, and she was that girl he was holding all those years ago. He reached for her.

She walked up to him and said, "Don't. I have waited a long time to touch, and this time, I get to go first."

And then he realized why she wanted her hands unwrapped as she ran her left hand through the blond hair on his chest and up the side of his face; then she fingered a long scar on his shoulder. This was no scared girl; she was a woman who knew what she wanted. Then she brushed her hands across his nipples; he jumped, and she just smiled.

Then he said, "Enough, Catherine. This is driving me crazy." Then he put his arms around her and kissed her like a man drowning, and then he felt the scars, he had forgotten; she hadn't. She was waiting to see what he would do, and he looked down at her. "Giles said you would wear them forever. I guess I thought he was wrong."

She just looked up at him, wondering how he would react. Then he said, "I should have killed him myself."

She didn't say a word; that was what she had been waiting to hear for so many years.

"You should have killed him that night." The look in her eyes, he would never forget as long as he lived; there were tears forming, but they would never fall.

"He deserved to die, and it should have been you." He looked down at her, and she didn't say another word.

"I will never let anyone hurt you again."

"Giles made the same promise and neither one of you can promise forever. So just give me now." That was all he needed; now was enough.

He took her to the bed; the delicate gown slid off like slippery skin, and then he laid her on the bed while he got rid of the rest of his clothes. She reached out to touch him as he climbed into bed and pulled herself up on his chest. She liked touching him and kissing him with her hair dangling across him; she was driving him mad with desire when he finally rolled her over and entered her. She raised her hips up to meet him and pulled his head down to her breasts.

He couldn't get enough, and she met him stroke for stroke; he took her mouth in his and wouldn't let go. The little sounds she made were for him, and she was his now. He had waited so long, but he took her all the way over the edge; and when she was finally shuddering, he came too and left his seed inside this woman he had wanted for so long. He lay there; he didn't want to leave her body. They were one now, and he wished he could keep it that way. She looked up at him, and she didn't say anything. Her leg rubbed up beside his hip and down again. She was trying to entice him again. Well, it was too soon. Then she was kissing his neck and shoulder, and there was that leg again. Well, maybe it wasn't too soon.

She rolled him over this time with him still inside her and presented her breasts to him, and the little minx had him feeling twenty years old again. She moved her hips and started a new rhythm as he suckled her breasts, and she watched him with a smile on her face like a cat that had just got the cream. She sat up and threw her head back; she still hadn't said a word as he grabbed her hips and again pulled her underneath him. Then he held her so tight she could barely breathe. But breathing wasn't really on her mind as she climaxed, and then he came again. When he finally started to breathe normally again, she looked up at him and said, "Oh, by the way, my—your, *the* children have asked if we can stay a while longer to see the ships come in, if that is all right with you?"

Her hair was tousled, and sheets were on the floor. He was still inside her, and she was asking if she could stay. He got up on his elbows to look down at her smiling face and said,

"Oh, I think that can be arranged."

"Good, I was worried for a minute."

He rolled off her and then pulled her next to him. When she started to get out of bed, he said, "Where do you think you are going?"

"Back to my room I figured you were through with me for the night."

"I am just getting started loving you, and I don't plan to ever stop. Get back in bed, Catherine. I have waited for this too many years. You are mine now."

"You have to ask me if that is what I want. I am after all a free woman," she said as she stood there naked with one glove on after loving him with abandon twice.

"I love you and always have, and what if you are pregnant by me? Would that mean nothing?"

"I have feelings for you, deep ones. But I can't commit to anything yet till I know I won't hurt anyone and I am not crazy. As for a child, I may never carry another child. Things went badly after I had David."

"Why didn't you tell me that? I would have been much more careful not to get you pregnant."

"Like Giles was doing?"

Oh, what had he done? Giles hadn't wanted her to have another baby because of complications; he would be much more careful in the future. She climbed back in bed, and he covered her up.

"I am tired. You are tired. We will sort this out in the morning. Just get me up before the children wake up." She snuggled up to him and put her leg in between his, and she had her arm around his chest and went to sleep; he was holding her so close he could feel her heart beat. Never had he felt so content. He wouldn't let her go ever again, her or the children.

He had asked Giles once when he brought Beth for her summer visit how Catherine was, and he told him, "I thank Robert every day for taking her from you and for letting me have her. But if anything ever happens to me, I hope it is you she chooses to watch over her and our children because it will be one hell of a ride."

And then he just smiled, and now he knew why. He looked up to the ceiling and thought, *Thank you, Giles.*

He couldn't sleep, so he just held her; when she rolled off his arm, he got up carefully and put on his robe. He picked up her gown; he had never felt anything so soft. It felt like water spilling through his fingers. He sat down in the chair across the room and just looked at her back; even from here, he could see the scars. He watched as she reached out, and he wasn't there; she panicked for a minute in a strange room. Then he said, "I am here."

She turned over and found him in the dark, and that was when he asked her, "Why didn't you wait for me to come get you?"

She walked over to the chair, put on her robe, sat back down on the bed, and then said, "I did. I waited almost three years and never heard a word from you."

"There was a raiding party the next year. They couldn't find you, but they weren't looking in the castle."

She just looked at him strangely.

"You didn't even come yourself?"

"I broke my leg and couldn't come, but I sent men to look for you."

"Even if they had found me, it would have taken an army to take me back. And by then, it was too late. I looked for you every night for all those years, and you never came for us. So I finally gave up. What was I supposed to do? You left me with no other choice. The first time Giles made love to me, he found me looking out to the sea and crying, and he told me you weren't coming back. If you were, you would already have been there. He told me I had built a wall around myself to protect Beth and me, and he started tearing it down, brick by brick. I had decided when I came here the first time I was going to try and find you and at least tell you about your daughter, but I didn't know how. I felt so betrayed by Giles, but he repaired that, and we were finally married. I needed someone, and it was Giles. When you finally did come, you were too late. He had finally torn down the wall."

She sat there for a minute and then started to the door; he stopped her before she got there. He took her in his arms as she cried, and he just held her; he pushed the robe off her shoulders and led her back to the bed. She lay down; and he joined her, covered them both up, and held her.

"No more tears. We will waste no more years waiting and wondering what is left of our life that I would like to spend with you. So go to sleep. We start again tomorrow."

Cat awoke to him kissing her shoulder and caressing her hip. "I would have thought you would have had enough of me for one night. Go back to sleep." But when he cupped her breast, pushed her over, and continued, she opened her eyes and said, "Maybe not."

"Why did Giles not want you to have another baby?" Well, that came out of the blue and really great timing because that wasn't what she wanted to talk about now; he was starting a fire she wanted put out.

"We can talk about that later." Conversation was no longer on either of their minds as she pulled him up to her; they were tangled in the sheets, and he had to get on his knees to get them off the bed, and then he just looked at her a moment, but a moment was all he got when she said, "You are wasting time."

He eased back down and entered her, and she said "That's it."

Lars stroked and stroked until she was clawing at his back; then he asked her again, "Why?"

She looked up at him as he stopped, and when he didn't continue, she said, "I lost a child after David, and I almost bleed to death. It scared Giles, and he said no more chances. I may be too old, and it may not make a difference anyway. Now can we continue?"

"It makes a difference to me for you to have another child of mine, a great deal of difference."

"Well, then shut up and finish putting out the fire you started. We have a long day in front of us, unless you are too tired, old man."

That got her a swat on the bottom, but he finished putting out the fire. When they were both breathing normally again, she leaned over and said, "You keep saying you want me to stay, so we will have to discuss this later." With that, Lars kissed her again. She looked out the window and saw the sun was coming up, so she started to wiggle out from under him.

"Where are you going?"

"I have to get bathed and dressed. You are all over me, and it is Saturday. We have to go to market."

"What, you don't want everyone to think you spent the whole night making love to me? Would that be so bad?"

"No, it would be too soon. Remember, I am a widow and crazy. Not everyone knows of our past, and I would like the children's opinion on this as well."

"Do you think they will disapprove? They have asked to stay."

"I don't think they exactly had this in mind, do you?"

After he looked at the bed and Cat, he had to admit if he were the children, he might not be too pleased.

"You are right. Go, I will see you in a bit after I have a bath."

Catherine threw him his robe as she grabbed hers. "Where is my gown?"

He picked it up and handed it to her. "Wear it tonight." And then he kissed her as she snuck out the door, but she had a smile on her face. The way the bed looked; this wasn't going to be a secret long.

Lars entered the kitchen, and the children were already at the table eating. They all turned to look at him at once, and Beth said, "Well, can we stay till the boats come?"

Ambushed and not able to run off, he panicked. "Ask your mother," he replied as he sat down to eat.

Catherine was in her room bathing with Caroline, and Caroline was having a grand time trying not to laugh till Cat finally splashed her with water and told her she wouldn't need her services anymore at night. That was when they both broke down laughing.

"You come sneaking in here looking like something the cat dragged in half dressed, and you have to tell me I am not needed at night anymore—how dumb do I look?" That got her splashed again.

"Just help me get dressed. Everyone is waiting for me. We go to market today, and I need to be presentable."

"Yes, my lady," Caroline said, and then she curtsied.

"Really, I may have to strangle you before the morning is done." Cat threw a wet washcloth at her. Caroline dodged it and grabbed her dress before they got it wet. Cat got out of the tub and started drying off as Caroline noticed a couple of bruises on her arms; their lovemaking had gotten serious. From what she had heard, she hoped Cat was up for another relationship so soon after Giles. After Cat was dressed, she reached into her jewelry box, grabbed something, and put it on while she walked to the kitchen, where she walked into five sets of eyes waiting for her. She stopped dead in her tracks.

"What is wrong?"

Michel and David said in unison, "Lars said we had to ask you if we could stay to see the boats. Can we, Mama, please?"

She just looked at him like "You made them wait for me?"

But all Beth and Lars were looking at was the small filigree gold cross around her neck. He looked at her, and he knew she was his again. As she looked at him, she said, "Yes, we can stay."

Beth looked back and forth from one parent to the other, and she knew something had changed dramatically, and she just smiled at her mother. As Catherine had walked in, there was a change; no longer was she the wild lover from last night, but Lady Catherine in every sense of the word. She had on her dark gray dress with gold thread at the neck and sleeves; nobody would mistake her for anything but nobility. When Beth stood up, he realized she was dressed and looked the part as well. These were his ladies of court now, his to protect and serve, because his daughter outranked him here. It was after all her land till she was of age. Ann was wearing a dress as fine as both of the other women, and all the boys had on very expensive clothes; he didn't know if he was dressed well enough to be seen with them.

He walked over to Cat and asked, "Am I dressed well enough, or do I need to change?"

"You are very presentable."

"Well, shall we head to town and see what we can find? Maybe we will be better received this time. They like your mother."

Lars put Cat in the wagon and then sat beside her; the boys sat in the back. Beth and Ann rode their horses beside Eric and Jacob, whom Lars was beginning to pay quite a bit more attention to.

Lars and Cat talked about nothing special going to town, especially with little ears just behind them. The trip didn't seem that long, with the boys asking questions about the boats that were coming. They heard the town miles before they got there; the people were waiting for them. The Raiders guards in front of them and the ones in back waited for Catherine to enter first; she told them to enter behind them so she could introduce them. The Raiders thought this was stupid, but Cat convinced Lars it would be better. Brian, the saddler maker and his wife were the first to the wagon; and Lars and his men couldn't believe the difference in the town. There were tables set up down the center of town, livestock tied to posts or in cages, fresh vegetables everywhere. Never had they been so welcomed in all the years they had been here.

Brian gently helped Cat down and stood her beside his wife; then he held out his hands for hers, and she put them in his hands. He gently took off the left glove and approved and then looked at the right, and she shook her head no. "But the glove is helping. It will be better soon. Thank you so much." He helped her get the left one back on, and then they headed to the market; this time, Lars just stood back and watched. Then he walked behind her and her friends.

There was so much to see. Catherine was treated like she had never left, and this time, Lars was included as her escort. He was told stories of how she had made this land come alive when she came to the lodge all those years ago. He watched Beth, and they loved her as well; they had learned she would be the new mistress, and she was acquainting herself with everyone. She was buying vegetables, and the boys were carrying them to the wagon, and they had found several new boys to play with. Ann and Jacob were included as well, with Cat watching; she didn't want them excluded, and she would see to it that they weren't. Brian couldn't believe they were the same children. Cat took him aside and asked him about Ann's mother, if anyone had ever heard from her again. Brian told her that her husband had killed her about a year later in a fight over another daughter. When she asked what happened to her other children, he told her the woman's sister took them to Scotland, and they hadn't been heard from since. Things were going well, and everyone was having a good time.

The Raiders men weren't stupid either; this was good land, and there were quite a few available women around. Lars had told them to behave themselves, or they would answer to him. Before the day was over, Brian had chairs set in front of his store. Cat, his wife, and several other women were talking while the townsmen were talking inside the store about grain planting and livestock, both here and going back north when the Raiders boats went back. Lars was excited that some of the men were willing to sell stock, some even land. Brian's wife leaned over and asked, "Mistress, are you and the children going to stay?"

She looked at Lars and said, "For a while at least."

Catherine leaned on Lars as they walked around town and talked to the people; they heard what needed to be done or repaired. Then they went back to Brian's shop, and they sat down at the table in a small office. Brian sat, counting out the rents due to Catherine. Lars knew nothing of this, so he just sat and watched; there was a tidy sum, and Cat wanted Beth to be present, so they called for her. When she arrived, she sat beside Cat, who explained it all to Beth; then Brian explained the books to Lars.

"I generally like a portion of the rents to be put back into the lands so that new stock and seed can be purchased each year. The rest is put up for Beth when she needs it later in life or for her family. At least that is how Giles and I had it set up. Is that satisfactory with you?"

Cat looked at Lars; he looked at the totals and was amazed to see his daughter was a wealthy woman already. He looked at Cat and just nodded. When Giles had been coming with Beth, he must have been taking care of all of this without Lars even knowing about it; he had made his daughter a wealthy woman right under his nose. There were also moneys set aside for Ann as a large dowry. For Jacob, he would be able to buy a sizable parcel of land when he came of age. Both children were taken care of; they would never have to ask anyone for help or ask for a husband to support Ann. She could decide. Giles and Catherine had made sure their daughters would never be put in the same situation as her.

"Brian, is everything ready for winter? Is there enough food supplies put up and wood? Do we need to be doing anything about housing, or is everyone taken care of?"

"The only problem we have is with the village priest. He seems to complain about everything, and now it is about the church. He says it is not big enough to suit him."

"Is it big enough? As I remember, he had a problem filling the church at the keep because he was such a . . . how shall I say? . . . not such a nice man."

"Still isn't."

Cat had to smile. Giles had replaced the old priest who had married them with the nasty one from the keep when he insulted her one too many times and sent him out here; she would bet he had no love for her still. She was fixing to find out. Into town walked Father Thomas, still acting like he owned the world.

Catherine just stood at Brian's door and watched the man as he walked through the crowd. These people didn't like him, and he knew it. Brian got up from the table, put away the books, and walked outside with Beth and Lars. They walked to the center of town. Cat stayed inside of the shop and watched; she wanted to see how he acted around Beth before she stepped out.

He was nice enough to Brian at first and then started to ask about improvements on the church; when he was told he would have to deal with Beth because of Giles's death, you could see his face light up. Then he started on her. "My lady, I need to talk to you. These heathen, they don't understand that the house of the Lord needs to be a special place and needs all of their attention."

Beth answered, "What exactly do you want? I thought the church was large enough and well maintained?"

That's my girl, Cat thought to herself as he continued getting more flustered that a little girl would contradict him, not noticing that Lars was getting even more aggravated.

"A church needs to be the center of the town and should have everybody's prayers daily as well as attention to their priest's needs."

Cat couldn't just let that one go by; she started to walk to the center of the square, and as he turned, he saw her coming. He got that same cruel smile he always had on his face; he was going to go after her again, and that was going to get him killed. So she hurriedly shut him up. "Maybe they would be more attentive to the priest if he was more likable and nice to his people. You beg favor from a girl who, you told me, I should give to the nuns when she was born because she made me a fallen woman. You, sir, should watch your words very carefully because the man standing next to my daughter is her papa." She walked across the courtyard and stood in front of the man who had insulted her in every way he could for so many years, and now it was her turn.

"Is there something else you wish to say to me there always was?"

"This is my daughter's papa, Lars, and Beth is the heir to this land. If you can't treat these people any better than you treated the people at the keep, I personally will find somewhere far away from here where I will never see you again. If I ever have to say this to you again, it will be while they put you on a horse to somewhere else. Am I understood?"

The priest just nodded and started to walk away, but Cat said, "I think you should join us and mix with your people, don't you?" It was an order he couldn't very well disobey; the look Lars was giving him was not one to be disobeyed. This Raider was not Giles; he was not even Christian.

He made himself available to the villagers, and he was at his most pleasant as Catherine watched; he thought he was finally free of her influence when he came here, but it was not as nice a position as the keep. But he had insulted her one too many times, and Lord Giles replaced him with and old priest from here who had married them. He really should have learned his lesson and kept his mouth shut.

"Catherine, don't you think it is time we started home? It is getting late." Darkness was beginning to fall, and they still had a ways to go before they got home. The men had already started back with the livestock and grain hours ago, so she nodded her head yes and started to say goodbye.

When she turned to Brian, he gently took her hands in his and said, "We will be seeing you soon, my lady?" Then he gently kissed her hand and helped her get in the wagon. Lars had already loaded Michel and David, who had lay down on some sacks of grain and had fallen asleep, so he just covered them with a blanket and climbed up beside Cat.

They had gone several miles without saying anything until he finally asked her, "Giles made my daughter a wealthy woman and didn't say a word about it to me. Why?"

"He didn't do it for you. He did it for me. Giles always treated all the children as his and treated them the same. Beth was as much his daughter as she was yours and always has been. As you saw, Ann and Jacob are taken care of as well."

"What about the boys and their future?"

"Michel will be the new lord when he comes of age. I will be lady until then, and there is a small fortune for David's use when he comes of age for him to purchase land or whatever he wishes to use it for, which I will add to as they grow. They will all be well provided for."

"What if you don't come back for a while and decide to stay with me? Will your estates be safe?"

She looked at him and looked back at her sons. "Robert will watch my interests for me until I am in control again and it is safe for me to take the children home."

He was going to tell her about what he had heard that night in her room so she wouldn't feel like she was crazy, but now he thought he would just keep his mouth shut because he didn't want her to leave.

"I enjoyed today. Those people love you."

"All accept the priest. He despises me and always has."

"He told you to give our daughter away when she was born?"

"Insisted on it, and I told him to go to hell, and he hasn't liked me since. Wonder why?" She just grinned at him.

"He picked on the wrong woman. Did you ever think that was the right thing to do?"

"No, not even when Giles wanted me to do the same thing before he would marry me, and I refused."

That caused the wagon to stop, and he looked at her in the waning light, and he was angry.

"I thought you were just telling me about how he loved my daughter as much as his own children, but he asked you to give her up before he would marry you? I should have killed him!"

"His mistress talked him into that little clause in the wedding contract, which I refused. Upon seeing your daughter, he fell in love with her on first sight, so get off your high horse and calm down. He made his mistakes, and you made yours. And Beth and I got to pay for both of them."

Not much more was said as they rode to the lodge; when they got there, Lars carried David into his bedroom, with Michel close behind. Cat was seeing to the grain being stored so it wouldn't get wet while Lars took care of the wagons. When she got back inside, she called for some water to her room, and she started to take care of her hands herself; she had had enough arguing for one day. She was tired, and she just wanted to be done and go to bed.

The more she thought about it, the more she came to realize how much she owed Giles; he had always thought of her and the children first, and she was feeling guilty about how easily she had let Lars into her life. She had always had a spot in her heart for Lars that she couldn't admit to anyone, even to herself. But it seemed like she was letting go of Giles to easily. She reached up to feel the cross around her neck and instantly regretted putting it back on. So when Caroline came into the room, she had her unclasp it, and she put it in the jewelry box again. She had Caroline help her with her hands and then told her to go to her own room; she was again dressed in her old gown. Caroline could tell something was wrong because when Cat was upset, she just stopped talking, and she hadn't said ten words since she came back.

When Lars came in, there was no light in Catherine's room, and he assumed she was in his room; but when he didn't find her in there, he went to Caroline's room. He knocked, and James answered the door. Caroline was in bed with their child next to their bed, and he could tell he had awakened them.

"Where is Catherine?"

"She was in her room the last time I saw her and that was about an hour ago."

Lars closed the door and started back down the hall, checking on the children as he went. He found her sitting in the dark in a chair by the fireplace; if he hadn't stopped and really looked, he wouldn't have seen her because she didn't say a word. He walked in, closed the door, and sat on the bed; when it became obvious she wasn't going to say anything, he finally asked, "I thought you were coming to my room tonight. What has changed? Did I do something wrong in the village today?"

"No, I think it is I who has done something wrong. I think Giles knew for all these years that there was a part of me that would always be yours, and still, he did everything in his power to make my life wonderful. He left me wealthy and independent. All the children are taken care of, and still, I come to you and fall in bed with you like he never existed. What kind of person does that make me?"

Lars noticed for the first time since he entered the room that she had taken the cross back off; he was losing her again, and he had to make this right now or risk losing her forever. He walked over to the door and opened it and the one to his room. Then he went over to her; she started to protest when he went to pick her up, but he just said, "No, Catherine, hush." They walked into his room, and he sat her down on his bed; then he moved across the room to the fireplace, and then he turned.

"Giles and I talked years ago about this, and he said much the same thing as you just said. But he said it didn't matter. He would take whatever you would give him. You were his. We made a deal that if anything ever happened to either one of us, the other one would see to taking care of you and the children—all of the children. You see, he loved you no matter if it was all of you or just a piece. Catherine, you are not crazy about hearing him. The night before we worked on your hands and they were so bad, you had gone to sleep. I walked by your door, and I heard Giles talking to you."

She stopped him right there and said, "He told me, 'Goodbye, my love.'"

"That is exactly what he said, and you haven't heard him since, have you?"

"No, so I guess he is finally at rest."

"I hope so. I told him outside of the door I would take care of you now if you will let me. Will you let me? I promise no more nightmares."

She stood up and took off her robe, and he came over to her. "I am so tired. Let's go to bed." He pulled back the covers, and they both lay down. He covered them as he cradled her in his arms; he could have sworn he heard a gentle sigh in the room.

CHAPTER 10

The next morning, Beth awoke before Catherine did. She entered her papa's room and found both her mother and papa in bed. Lars woke up to see his daughter staring at him and her mother and shooed her out of the bedroom; then he quickly grabbed his robe and followed her. She was in the hall, looking kind of stunned, but with a smile on her face. When he came out, she turned and said, "You and Mama, I knew it! She had on the cross."

"And now she has taken it off again."

"Why?"

"She thought she was betraying Giles."

"No, Giles wouldn't think that. He would want her to be happy. He would never want her to be like she was."

"I know, but I am trying to convince her of that. But you have to be quiet about this till she tells you. She thinks it is too soon for you children to know."

"All right, it is our secret."

"Now go. I will see you at breakfast."

He turned and went back into the bedroom, but Beth went into her mother's room and shut the door. She went over to her dressing table, opened her jewelry box, and carefully pulled out a silk bag; then she sat down on the bed and just held it in her hand.

Lars walked into his bedroom, and Catherine was getting out of bed, and she said, "Good morning. Why are you looking at me so strange?"

He just shook his head, hugged her, and said, "I missed you last night."

"What do you mean? I was right here,"

As he started to undress her, she said, "Oh that kind of 'missed.' Well, you are just going to have to wait until tonight, sir. I have a busy day, as do you."

Then she scooted away, and he swatted her bottom. She turned, smiled, and quickly shut the door. When she opened up her door to her room, she found Beth sitting on her bed, holding something in her hand and crying; she sat down beside her, took the small bag, and emptied it out into her hand. It was her wedding ring. It had been cut at the bottom and stretched out, and she looked at Beth to explain.

"When they brought you home, they couldn't get it off your hand. So Robert cut it off, and I put it in this bag."

"Where is your daddy's ring?"

"Robert took it off his hand." Then she walked over to the jewelry box and took out another small bag and handed it to her. She poured it out into Catherine's hand, and there was Giles's ring; he had never taken it off since she had put it on his hand at their wedding.

"Mama, I miss him so much, and I know he wasn't my real daddy."

"No, don't ever say that. He was as much a daddy to you as Lars ever was. He loved you from the first time he ever saw you, and he has made sure you are a wealthy woman with land and property so that no man will ever have power over your life. He couldn't have loved you any more if you were born to him. Don't ever forget that."

"I don't have anything of him. I don't even carry his name, and I wouldn't want Papa to think I don't love him, but Giles was always Daddy to me."

"We are trying to make two worlds into one and still pay honor to the old one, aren't we? How about this? We put these rings up, and when it is time for you to marry, I will have my ring repaired and sized for you."

"What about Ann? She loved Giles as much as I did, and he was hers as well?"

"We will take your daddy's ring, and I will have it redesigned to match mine, and you girls will have rings that match from your daddy because he and Queen Marie designed them. You can pass them down to your daughters how about that?"

"You would let us have them?"

"Of course, you are his daughters."

"You aren't crazy, you know. I heard daddy one night too. He said goodbye."

She just held her daughter and didn't say anything; there wasn't anything else to say. "We'd better start getting ready. Your brothers will be up soon and hungry. I think Jacob is already in the kitchen."

Cat jumped up, kissed Beth on the cheek, and started down the hall to her room to dress. God, she was getting old; she was talking about Beth getting married and about grandchildren, and the sad part was she still wanted another child of her own. Oh well, she would probably have to settle for grandchildren.

The days passed quickly for Cat as the buildings were readied for the boats to arrive, and the villagers got ready for winter. New roofs were put on and buildings repaired; several of the Raiders men even came to Cat with cuts and ailments that they wouldn't normally have let an Englishwoman touch. The village people called on her often as a midwife and a doctor, but she was beginning to think it was about time to head back home. She had promised the children they would stay until the boats came, and they hadn't come yet, so they were still here. She was spending every night with Lars, and it was an open secret that they were living together. That might have become a problem because for all her protests that she couldn't get pregnant, she was afraid she might be.

Lars had mentioned marriage at first, but not since, and she didn't quite know how to handle this; maybe she was wrong. He would want her to go home with him, and she couldn't do that; she had a son who was heir to the keep and all that it entailed. She had already sent Robert home to watch over things till she could get home again. They would have to go back, and she didn't think Lars would like being just a stepfather to a small boy who was going to be the lord of the land he would be living on.

She had been called to town to deliver a baby, so she left the children with Caroline and took James and two Raider guards and headed to town. It took all night, and as they were coming back, they could see the sails of the boats coming toward the beach. One of the Raiders said, "They are coming, and I wanted to see them land."

They looked at her rather sullenly, and she looked at James and said, "What are you waiting for?"

"We were told to guard you, madam."

"Then guard." Then she turned her horse and took off like a bat out of hell.

James just looked at the Raider guards and said, "Well, guard if you think you can keep up with her." And then he took off because he knew he could barely keep up with her, and he left the Raiders men staring after them.

Catherine saw James behind her, and she was smiling at him; she was having a ball. She could see the other two were still standing still, just looking at them. When she came to the first log, she suddenly realized she didn't know if her horse was a jumper or not. Well, she was about to find out; she put her hand on his shoulder, and they glided over. James was frantic now in trying to catch up to her because his wife was her confidant, and she also suspected she was pregnant, and she didn't need to be jumping logs. She also had an audience; her sons and Lars were watching from the dock.

David said, "Here comes Mama."

Several men turned to watch as she jumped yet another log and rode toward them, with James fast on her heals.

One of the men standing next to Lars asked him, "Is this Beth's mother, the Englishwoman you have turned down so many Raider women for?"

"Yes."

Catherine was riding a dapple-gray stallion she had purchased and had on a gray dress; the two of them seemed to be one creature as she rode with her skirts flying.

"Why didn't you tell us she was a Valkyrie?"

Lars thought they were making fun of her, but when he turned around, he saw that the men were looking at her the way he did, and he didn't like that at all. When she stopped her horse, she waved up at the boys and smiled at Lars, but he seemed angry. She started to dismount when James got there and said, "What do you think you are doing, jumping logs? Are you nuts! What if he threw you? And you shouldn't ride like that in your condition."

That got her attention.

"What do you mean?"

"You know exactly what I mean. Caroline isn't stupid."

Lars had heard just enough of this conversation to get very curious; and by the time he got to the horses, Catherine was ready to go back to the lodge, pack her bags, and leave.

"Caroline isn't stupid about what?"

He didn't get an answer because several men descended upon Cat and her horse to introduce themselves; one even reached up and tried to take her off the horse. She panicked; she backed up her horse and galloped away. One of the men laughed and said, "What is her problem? She not like men?"

"Not really, not after a Raiders man beat her half to death years ago. So don't touch her again. She is mine and only mine."

Lars gathered up the boys and headed to the lodge to find Cat; something was wrong, and he was going to find out what. Beth met him halfway to the lodge, and he had her take the boys inside; he asked if she had seen her mother, and she pointed to the barn. When he walked into the barn, he saw her putting her horse in his stall, and James was again talking to her. "You aren't even going to tell him? We are just going to leave. Do you think he will let you go?"

"Where are you going, Catherine, and why now? And why is James so afraid for you?"

James backed away; this was a conversation he wanted no part of. She wouldn't look at him until he turned her around, and then he put it together. "I have never seen James afraid for you to ride a horse until today, so why is today . . . ?" Then he stopped. "You're pregnant. Look at me and tell me I am wrong."

She couldn't.

"You were going to leave me and not tell me about another child? You would do that to me again? How could you even think it?"

"I am not sure, and I don't know if I can stay pregnant. I have miscarried before, so I didn't tell anyone. And you hadn't said anything about marriage, so I didn't know how you would feel about it."

"The same way I felt the first night I found you in my camp all those years ago. I love you, and I always will. And baby or no baby, you are mine. James is right. Till we know for sure you stay off the horse because they have more sense than you do. We will talk some more tonight, and if I see you pack a single item of clothing, I will lock you in the bedroom. Are you sure you are all right?"

When she wouldn't turn around and look at him he just stood there and watched her take care of her horse; that always calmed her more than anything else did.

"They scared you, didn't they? Giles told me when he first met you that nobody touched you, and it took him a long time before he could."

"Yes, I don't like to be touched by most people, especially men if I don't know them." She finished with her horse, turned around, and looked at him. Lars took her hand, and they started to walk to the lodge.

"I am sorry. Your men probably think I am some sort of coward for not wanting to be around them."

"No, you are no coward, and no man but me will touch you again. I will see to that. Besides, they think you are kin to the Valkyrie women."

"What is that?"

"They take the dead from the battlefield to Valhalla."

"So that is a good thing?"

He just nodded. When he got to the lodge, they went past the kitchen and went straight to his bedroom; and after they were inside, he shut the door.

"Start talking. What is going on that you won't tell me? Am I that scary all of the sudden? You never did tell me why Giles didn't want you to not get pregnant again. Now I think I should have been more insistent."

She sat down on the bed and just sighed, and then she looked up at him

"I am not absolutely sure I am pregnant. Caroline thinks so, but I am not sure, and I won't be for another few weeks. So I haven't said anything. Giles and I wanted more children, but Giles said enough. We weren't taking any more chances."

"What do you mean any more chances?"

The look on her face said it all—she had almost died. He got down on his knees and put his head in her lap. "How could you let me be so stupid when you knew how dangerous this was for you? And then you try to leave me? What were you thinking?" As he looked up at her, all he could see was how upset he was making her.

"Stop, Catherine, I am sorry. Is this what you want, another child?"

She just shook her head; she couldn't speak, and there were tears beginning to form in her eyes.

"All right, but no more riding across meadows like the devil is chasing you. In fact no more riding at all. We could sail to my home in the north to my family where you could be taken care of. Would you like that?"

"We can't. I have to get Michel back soon. He is the heir to his daddy's land, and he has to be there to inherit, and I have to be there to watch over him until he is of age."

"Can you have a husband by your side while you do this, even if he is a Raider?"

"Yes, but you realize you will have no power there except as my husband. It is Michel's land and titles. Can you live with that?"

"I can live with anything as long as I have you and the children. Will you marry me?"

"Yes, but I think you need to ask for permission first."

"From who exactly?" And then it hit him "The children."

She just nodded yes.

"All right, but they are a tough group. It may take some convincing. I will talk to them later tonight after we get everyone settled, all right?" He took her hand, and they headed out the door and down the hall; they could hear the voices in the main hall, and she held his hand tighter.

"Just hold on. I won't let anyone hurt you, my love. By the way, do you wish to get married here? It seems this is the place you get married at. If it would please you, I know a great bedroom for a honeymoon."

She finally smiled at him and said, "That is a wonderful idea! How did you come up with it?"

"I knew this man who had a bed built for his lady in a room, and it was so big they couldn't get it out afterward. So it is still there. It is a wonderful love story I will have to tell you sometime. He was a very good man. You would have liked him. I did."

She just smiled, but he could see there was still something wrong.

They entered the main room to everyone yelling his name and men pounding him on the back; he hurried her away and sat her down at the big table along the wall beside Beth. He sat down beside her as supper was served, and everyone began to regale him with tales of home and the trip over. But as he watched Cat, she neither ate nor drank anything. She kept a smile on her face, but he could tell she was uncomfortable. Several of his men came up to meet her, and she said hello, but they didn't speak English. So he had to translate, but one of his men came to the table, and she wouldn't even talk to him.

He finally said to her, "Catherine, could you at least be nice to these people? I was polite to yours."

And then he handed her a glass of ale, and when she took her hands out of her lap, it took both of them to hold it because they were shaking so bad. She just took the glass from him and sat it down on the table and said, "I am sorry, I am embarrassing you. May I leave now?"

Then she stood up and almost ran from the room. Before he could follow, two of his friends grabbed his arm, and he wouldn't let Beth leave without a guard. James saw what was happening, but before he could get across the room, she was gone. James grabbed Beth and took her and Ann out and was soon followed by Lars. Then he said, "Girls, let's get you to your room where I know you will be safe for the night." He passed Eric and Jacob along the way, grabbed Jacob's arm, and said, "Come with me."

Once the girls were at their door, he put Eric outside of it and told him to guard them and not to let anyone else enter; then he put Jacob outside the boys' room. Then James and Lars started to look for Cat.

They couldn't find her in her room or his, and then he really began to panic.

"What is scaring her so much?"

"She spent years after the raid where nobody touched her except Robert—nobody. She didn't go into crowds, and she didn't have people around. She didn't go anywhere without a guard, and there were only four of us she trusted. She had nightmares where she roamed the keep in the dark. Giles said she was running from whoever beat her. She even fell a couple of times. It got better after he killed that man of yours. She never went to court except to see Queen Marie, and that was a private audience. You put her in a room of strange men. Some of them look like the man in her nightmares, and she came apart. What did you expect?"

"I didn't know all of this. I never did."

"She didn't tell you? Giles didn't tell you?"

"It seems she doesn't tell me a lot lately. You seem to know more than I do. Where could she be? She is not in this lodge anywhere."

Then they both looked at each other at the same time. "The horses."

They both started running; there were too many men around here for her to be out there alone, and they were right. When they got to the side of the building, they saw two men skulking around the stables, but they ran as soon as they saw Lars. When they got inside the barn, sure enough, she was sitting at the back of her stallion's stall, feeding him grain. Anybody would have had to go through him to get to her, and that would have been difficult. She was just sitting on a pile of hay in the dark with a horse that could have killed her at any time. She was just petting his muzzle, content as could be. The mares in the next stall were nuzzling their heads through to be touched as well.

"Is it always like this?"

"Always, she does better with them than people, maybe because they have always treated her better than most people have."

"I asked her to marry me."

"She won't go back with you."

"How do you know?"

"I've known her for a long time. She only feels safe at the keep. If you won't go home with Cat, don't marry her because she won't be happy anywhere else."

Lars was coming to the same conclusion rather quickly himself. Now it was his turn to decide; if he wanted her as a wife and the children as his, he was going to have to follow Cat into her world to keep her, and that meant giving up a lot of control to a woman and a little boy.

"James, I want guards on your wife, Cat, and all the children all the time. They don't go anywhere alone until we head back to the keep. Do you understand?" James nodded. Yes, it seemed Lars had made the decision of where he was going to live with Catherine.

They both walked into the barn, and she saw that it was Lars. He came over to the rail and leaned up against it. "Are you ready to come in? You won't have to deal with any more people tonight or any more crowds, I promise. We will talk in the room. Come on, Catherine. We will protect you."

She stood up, and the stallion blocked her way; he seemed to understand she was upset. The horse was better at this than he was. She made him move, and they opened the gate, and she walked up to the house. But both men noticed they still were not alone; there were two shadows watching them.

When they got back inside, James went to his room and made sure the children were all right. Eric said he would take first guard on the girls' door, and James made arrangements for another guard for the rest of the night. Jacob said he would just sleep in the boys' room in front of the door. James said he would explain everything in the morning.

Lars got Catherine to their bedroom and told her to get ready for bed; he had her lock the door while he closed the house and made sure everyone was settled. The main room was still going with quite a party, and Lars told them to have a good time, but he was going to bed and told them where their beds were when they wanted them.

She heard knocking at the door and assumed it was Lars; it wasn't. It was a very large man with long dark hair and a beard, and once she saw him, she didn't open the door any further.

"What do you want?"

He looked at her and started to push open the door until he had pushed her back. "I am looking at what I want. So you are Lars's woman? There are men that rank higher than him, and I am one of them. Maybe you should reconsider."

"Get out now."

She had hardly got the words out before Lars had his hands on the dark man's collar and had thrown him out of the room; the man was furious. "How dare you touch me?"

"This is my land, and tomorrow you will be off it."

"No, it is your daughter's land. Maybe I should take her and take the land?"

"No, it is my land, and Beth will inherit through me. I am marrying Lars. And tomorrow you will do as he says because he told you to."

At that, Catherine slammed the door. "I think we need some guards at Beth's door tonight."

"Already done. Someone has been watching you. We saw them when we came to get you at the barn. None of you go anywhere without guards anymore until we go back to the keep after the wedding."

"Does that mean you will come home to the keep with me and the children?"

"I will go anywhere as long as it is with you."

"Who is he, and why is he watching me and Beth? It isn't just the land. He hates me."

When he looked at her, he knew this wasn't the time for any more lies. "He is Vatic's cousin, and he has wanted vengeance since Giles killed him."

Catherine looked at him and then said, "We leave tomorrow. I will not let him near my children. If I had known who he was, I would not have been here tonight." She turned and started to dress as he grabbed her arm and pulled her to him.

"Where do you think you are going in the middle of the night?"

"I will stay with the children so they are safe. Horic can't get to them."

"He won't touch them. I'm having Horic escorted out to the boats. He can sleep out there, and all the children are guarded as well as Caroline. Horic will be gone in the morning. One of my boats will escort him back home. I am sending for my oldest son to come back here. I have some things that he needs to take over for me."

"What things?"

"My sons are going to have to take over control of my lands and run them for me in the North Country if I am going with you. I will take care of these lands for Beth and help you with the keep until Michel takes over—if that is what you want. It is obvious you are not ready to meet my people, so my family will have to come here to meet you. I will ask the boys' and Ann's permission tomorrow for your hand in marriage. Beth has already said yes. Then we will go about doing this, but I would like to wait for my son to come back if we could."

"As long as that man is gone, I will wait for a while longer."

He looked out the window to watch the men taking Horic to his boat with the men he had brought with him; at least he thought it was all the men he had brought. He hadn't told Catherine that the message he was sending with the men on his boat had also requested his sisters to come here to his wedding if they wanted to. Lars had also explained the circumstances and invited his other two sons as well. He didn't know if any of them would come, but he had invited them anyway. His sisters had wanted to see Beth since he had told them about her, and now he might have another child on the way; he hadn't said anything about that. He was afraid to even admit to himself how much he wanted another child.

He turned to see Catherine taking off her robe, and he was amazed that she still took his breath away every time; as she turned, she looked at him, smiled, and said, "What are you looking at? I am an old lady who made a fool of herself in front of your people tonight and feels very foolish?" Then she grabbed her hair and pulled it all around to her back, and he walked over to her and started undoing the laces of her gown till it slid off her shoulders and landed in a puddle on the floor. He pulled his shirt over his head and then pulled her to him, and then he ran his fingers lightly up and down her neck and face.

"I don't see an old lady. I just see the lady I love and the only one I have loved for so many wasted years." And then he ran his hand down her belly, which wasn't so flat anymore, and they both knew she was carrying a child, and he just hoped he hadn't killed her. He laid his forehead against hers, and neither said a word as she put her arms around his neck; then they just walked to the bed, got in, and covered up. He pulled her to him, and she went to sleep.

It wasn't very long before she woke again. Lars was holding her too tightly; she rolled over, looked up at him, and asked, "What is bothering you? You should be sleeping. You are getting as bad as the children. Do I need to tuck you in? Or maybe something else will help you sleep."

She brushed her hand down the side of his chest, touching his nipple, and he jumped. But as he looked down at her, he could see that funny smile she got when they were making love, and he frowned at her. She stopped what she was doing and said, "What is it now?"

He pulled away from her and said, "I don't know what you are talking about."

"Yes, you do. Sometimes you look at me and wonder, 'Did she do this with Giles or just with me?' You do it all the time. What is it this time?"

He didn't know exactly how to say, "You have a funny smile when we make love. I just wondered if it was for me."

"No, it isn't. I had the same stupid smile for Giles and probably a lot of other things. You have got to stop comparing the two of you. It isn't fair. I loved him. I love you, and I won't spend the rest of my life apologizing for that. If you can't accept that, then this won't work. I don't know what you expect from me—to just forget that part of my life like it never happened? I can't."

"I want you to be happy," Lars said as he squeezed her so tightly she could barely breathe.

Then she said, "Breathing, breathing would be good." He quickly loosened his hold on her, and she let out a long breath.

"Sorry."

"Stop worrying about everything else and pay attention to the stupid smile. I need a little attention." With that, she got a smile from him as he rolled her under him and entered her gently with a soft rocking motion; he got her arching her back into him for more of his attention. When he was still being too gentle, she looked up at him. "What are you waiting for? I am not made of glass, and I am already pregnant. Or are you not up to this?"

"You little devil!"

As she wrapped her legs around him, he pulled her up to him, and she looked at him. "Much better Raider, now finish it."

And he did. They both slept very well after that, wrapped in each other's arms.

The next morning, Lars was gone when she awoke, and she started to dress. She looked out the window and could see two boats already well out to sea. Good, they were gone, but Lars was talking to several women, and one of the women looked familiar, and she wasn't quite sure why. She and Beth needed to go to the village this morning to pick up more supplies; there were still so many people here, and it would give her some time away. When she got to the kitchen, Helga asked her if she wanted anything for breakfast; and before she could say anything, her stomach told her no. She put her hand on her mouth, shook her head no to the cook, and headed outside before she had to smell any more of the food; the girls looked at her funny and then finally realized what was going on.

They ran outside in a near panic, and as they caught up with their mother, all Ann could say was, "Please tell me it is not true you are pregnant."

When her mother nodded, she thought Beth was going to cry.

"You know how dangerous this is. You know what happened last time."

"Yes, dear, I was there, remember? That was a long time ago, and there were other problems. It won't happen again."

But Beth wasn't convinced; she had been old enough to remember the last time, and now she was terrified. Ann was just as scared.

"This will be all right. We are going back to the keep, and I will be taken care of there, and I won't take any chances."

"Papa is going back with us. Are you going to be married?"

"Yes, we will all talk about it in a little while." That seemed to satisfy her, for the time being anyway.

As she walked, she noticed she had a guard following her, and Lars was coming toward her with the women he had been talking to earlier. He stopped in front of her, and the women stood back a little, except the one she seemed to recognize; then it hit her. "Claire, you were with us the day we were captured. The Raiders took you with them."

"Yes, my lady, they did. I was already on the boat when Robert came for you, and I was taken to the North Country as a slave."

"You don't look like a slave now."

"No, my lady, the man who took me married me. I have had a very good life, better than I could ever have had here. My husband is over there, but the master wasn't sure you would want him near you."

Great, now they were afraid of her; this had to be put to right now if even in a little way. "Please have your husband come over. I would like to meet him." Then she looked at Lars so all right, a little at a time.

The man came over; he was huge, with red hair and a long beard. He made Claire look tiny, but Cat could tell she loved him. Claire had taught him English, and he spoke it fairly well with a strong accent; he said he was pleased to meet her again. He had remembered her from long ago, and Lars had talked of her often; she smiled at Claire. She had done better than she would have ever done here.

"These men are trying to purchase land to homestead for their families. That is what I have been trying to broker between the village and the king, to stop the raiding and start settlements between the English and us."

"What do you need me to help you to do?"

"I think a marriage between Lars and you is a good start, and if we can start a settlement, it would be even better."

"Well, the wedding part is already in the works. We will have to work on the rest."

Claire looked at her and asked, "We know you have a problem with crowds and with Raiders, but we would like to help with the wedding. I remember from long ago, and I told them it wasn't just Raiders. It is a lot of people in general. Could we maybe do this in smaller groups?"

Cat smiled at her; they had to think she was strange.

"Yes, please. Once I know people, it is not so bad. If you would like, I have to go to the village to buy supplies. Would some of you ladies like to go with me?"

Several of them volunteered. Claire would translate, so they all rode in the wagon with three guards. By now, everyone knew Horic had threatened Catherine.

Ann looked at her mother and at Lars and then said, "Wedding? What wedding?"

Beth smiled at her and said, "Come with me. Papa wants to talk to us."

As they left, Lars was headed back into the lodge to talk to the boys about their mother. The girls were now following, with Beth filling Ann in on what was going on, and behind them were Eric and Jacob.

Lars had already sent a messenger to the keep asking Father Marques if he felt up to making the trip to the lodge to marry him and Catherine; if he didn't, he wouldn't tell Cat. If the old priest was up to it, the messengers were to see to his comfort all the way back here. He would have the best coaches and inns; he was to be well taken care of. Lars wanted the best for Cat, and that wasn't that priest in the village. That is why they weren't getting married in the church—that and he wasn't Christian. He was sure the king wouldn't mind, for he had been trying to set this up for several years with other women as bribes, but he couldn't give him the one he wanted until now. Queen Marie was going to love this; he wouldn't be surprised if she didn't win another bet or show up at the wedding.

He found the boys in the main hall; they had found several boys their own age and were talking to them about boats. Michel was interested, but David couldn't get enough; he knew he wouldn't be tied to the keep as Michel was going to be. He could do something different. He watched them for a minute; they were already becoming men their daddy could be proud of. Jacob was already talking of going north one day, and he could see he would be a Raider in every way; that is why Cat had been sending him to Lars in the summers with the girls. This was going to be his world.

"Boys, could I talk to you for a minute? I need to ask both of you a question. You know, your mother and I have become close since she came here, and I want to know if it would be all right with you boys if I marry your mother."

By this time, the girls and Jacob had arrived in the hall as well. They both looked at him as if he were kind of stupid, and then Michel said, "Daddy always said if something happened to him, we were to come to you. He said you loved our mother before he did and that you were Beth's papa. He told me you would take care of Mother and us. We just assumed that is what was supposed to happen. Were we wrong?"

Giles had told them everything. Had he known something was going to happen, or did he just want to make sure their sisters and Jacob never took any abuse from anyone? And they didn't know why.

"No, you weren't wrong. We are going to get married, and then we are going back to the keep. It now belongs to you, and we have to keep it safe for you till you are old enough to watch over it yourself."

"What about this land? It is Beth's. Who will watch over it?"

"I will have men watch it and protect it till she is old enough, and we will come back in the summer to check on it. If you boys wish to come with me, I would be honored. I would be proud to call all of you children mine as well, if that is all right with you?"

"It seems daddy had this planned. Were the two of you always this close?"

"No, but I will tell you that story another time. You children have to start helping me get ready for a wedding because it is going to be here."

"Here in the lodge, not the church?"

"Yes."

"Good, Mother hates that priest, and he treats her like dirt. But who are you going to have perform the ceremony?"

"I have sent for the priest at the keep if he will come."

"He will come for Mama, unless he is on his deathbed and probably still then."

"Well then, children, we are going to have another wedding here."

"Another?" Michel seemed surprised by that statement.

"Your daddy married your mother here, and Father Marques did the original ceremony."

"Oh, then he will come—even on his deathbed. He won't let anyone else marry Mama but him, and I bet Robert and Jennie will be coming too."

"There is one other thing, and I am not sure your mama wants you to know. But I am going to tell you anyway. We think your mama is going to have a baby."

David said, "Great, another baby! I am tired of being the baby."

Michel didn't say anything; he just looked at Lars, shook his head no, turned, and walked outside. He took the girls aside and talked to them for a while, and then he went to his room. When Lars pulled Beth aside, he asked her, "What did he say?"

"He is afraid for Mama."

"Was it that bad?"

She just nodded yes. "Mama had gone to the village to help with a fever outbreak, and then they came and got Daddy she had lost the baby. She was sick a long time."

He started to think there were women that could get rid of a baby; he had heard of them. Maybe it would be better than taking a chance of losing her, but then he thought if he did that, he would lose her for sure. His sister was coming, he hoped, and she was one of the best midwives he knew; maybe he could talk her into staying and helping Cat. He just couldn't lose her now, and to tell the truth, he very much wanted this child; it seemed like it would make this family whole. It was that day he started watching the water for the boats and started praying to his gods that his sisters came to see his bride and his new children; he needed his family now like never before.

Cat and the Raiders women went into town and bought supplies for the extra people at the lodge, and it was a wonderful day; the village people were beginning to accept them instead of being afraid of them. Cat had asked Brian if anyone was interested in selling land in the area, and he said several older couples who were childless were interested. Claire had heard the conversation and was thrilled. She said, "I have so wanted to come back home with my children and live. I have talked to my husband for years about it, but until Lars started to take care of this land for his daughter, we didn't see a way."

"Well, it looks like a way is coming true after all. What happened to the other woman who was taken with you? I don't remember her name. She was a maid."

Claire looked down at the ground and didn't say anything for a minute, then looked up at Cat and said, "She didn't survive the first winter. Vatic took her after Lars took you and wouldn't let him have you back. He was so mad, and he took it out on her every day. He finally beat her so badly that she killed herself."

"And Lars's didn't do anything about it? He just let him get away with it?"

"He had broken a leg trying to build a new boat to get back to you and was very sick with fever. He didn't even know what was going on.
We tried to protect her, but we couldn't. When Vatic didn't come back and we heard your husband had killed him, we were so glad that you had found a man who would protect you. Lars has done nothing but talk about you for all the years since and turned down every woman offered to him by your king. Did you know that?"

"That is why nobody had bought land or settled because they were waiting for a marriage contract to make a permanent settlement."

"Yes, my lady, that's what we have been waiting for." She didn't say any more; she felt sorry for her lady. She had to lose one husband to marry another to make her life possible here, and it didn't seem right somehow.

After they had gathered everything they needed, they got back in the wagon and headed back to the lodge; all the women were talking mostly in the Raiders tongue, and that was fine. Cat was thinking. James was riding next to her and was just watching her; he had heard most of the conversation and was going to tell Lars about it when he got back. It was almost like they wanted her to feel guilty for not having Lars put this together for them earlier by marrying some other woman.

When they got to the lodge, Lars was waiting for her at the door, and he came and helped her down out of the wagon. He took her to one side and said, "You need to go talk to Michel. I may have said something wrong and scared him."

"What did you say?"

"I asked about the marriage, and they were all excited about that. Apparently, Giles had told them that if anything ever happened to him, they were all mine."

"Really, Giles said that to the children?"

"Yes, but I also told them we were going to have a baby."

"Oh, you shouldn't have done that! Michel will panic."

He looked at her. "That is exactly what he did. The girls were talking to him, but he went to his room. Jacob is in there, and he hasn't come out since."

Catherine started walking into the lodge. "Help them unload and leave this to me." She walked in the kitchen, and Ann just pointed to Michel's room; when she got there, Jacob was sitting on the bed with Michel and David. "Jacob, will you take your brother out to your sister for me?" Jacob picked David up, and as he passed her, she winked at him.

"It is going to be all right, isn't it, Mama?"

She kissed him on the cheek and said, "Yes, baby, it is." She hadn't called him baby in years; he was taller than she was, but he smiled back at her with that precious smile from that beaten little boy from years ago.

She sat down next to Michel and asked, "What is wrong?"

"You already know what is wrong. That is why you got everybody out of here—so you could tell me you are going to die. This baby will kill you."

"Is that what you think?"

"You almost died. Daddy wouldn't even let us see you when he brought you home. We thought you were dead."

When she looked at his face, she realized he was telling her the truth. Lord, what had she done? She should have explained this to him years ago, and she should have never gotten pregnant again if he felt this way. All she could do was try to explain it to him now and hope for the best.

"Honey, look at me. That baby was born early, after I got hurt badly in the village. I was so very tired and weak. It took me a long time to get well after he was born. That won't happen this time. It was just a onetime thing. We are not even sure I am going to have a baby yet. Why don't we just get through the wedding first and get everybody home?"

"I love you, Mama. Don't leave me too."

He hugged her so tight she could hardly breathe; that night, Giles had to drag the midwife out of bed, drunk. She had almost killed her. It had been Jennie who had followed him and finally taken charge and saved Cat. If she hadn't, she would have died. She didn't realize how terrified her other son had been, and now he was again; she had to reassure him, and they had to go home.

She walked back through the kitchen, saw Jacob, and caught him in an unguarded moment; he was looking at someone with a look of a man looking at a woman he loved. She smiled to herself; her little boy was growing up. She looked past him to see which girl he was looking at and realized it was Ann, and she was standing by Eric. When he turned, the mask on his face was again in place, and she walked up to him. She just looked at him and then at Ann, and he knew that she knew; they didn't say anything to each other. She pointed to the side of the building, and they started to walk.

"I don't know what to do. Every time he gets close to her, I want to kill him, but she is my sister." She could see this was tearing him up inside, and she didn't quite know how to handle this.

"She isn't your sister. That is what you are thinking, but you have always been her protector. Then when we took you in, you both became our children, but she is not your sister by blood. You have lived such a sheltered life. You have never been around many other girls. Maybe if you had more choices, it would be different."

"What if it is not? What if she is the only one I want?"

"She still has to want you. Have you talked to her? You talk about everything else since you were children. If it is a problem after you talk, I can see about you staying here in the village with Brian if you don't want to come back with us for a while till you two can sort this out?"

He just nodded.

"Talk to her and see how she feels about this. You are both so young. Maybe time will sort this out for both of you. She may just think of you as a brother, so be prepared."

They walked back to the lodge, and Ann was still talking to Eric. But as soon as Jacob came into view, she ran to him and left Eric with Beth. It wouldn't surprise her if Jacob went home with them; those two were meant for each other since the day he found her hiding in the woods under a log. Some things are just meant to be.

Michel met her at the door and took her arm. "We need your assistance on some things inside, wedding things." She followed him in.

Days went by with getting rooms ready, beds made, more beds brought in, and extra firewood cut and stacked. Then one morning, a carriage arrived, and out stepped Robert and Jennie and their new son. After they got down, Robert helped Father Marques out of the carriage, and Catherine rushed over to give him a big hug; then she turned to Robert and said, "How did you know?"

He just turned and looked at Lars. "He sent a message you were going to marry him and that if we wanted to attend, we'd better get here and to please bring Father Marques if he was up to it. The good father said he was coming if he had to crawl, but we didn't make him crawl."

"My lady is not going to get married without me doing the ceremony. It is my rule and in the lodge again seems most appropriate. Sir Giles would have approved, and where are my children?" With that, they all came out to greet him; they loved him as much as Cat did. She was already feeling better about this union. She introduced Lars to the priest, and as Father Marques pulled him aside, he told him, "You will take care of my lady and her children. They are special to me, and I won't be around much longer to take care of them."

"I will look after them. We are going to back to the keep after this. I am taking her home, and that is where we will stay." He just nodded; he approved. Giles had told him that Lars was a good man, even if he was a Raider.

As they started inside, the men started yelling. The boats were coming in, and Lars and the boys turned to see. When the boys started to run to the dock, Lars stopped them.

"Wait till I see whose ships they are and who is on them, then come up." He went down to the docks. Jacob, Eric, and some of the other guards started to unload as they kept one eye on the boats. They kept the women close until Lars started coming back with three women right behind him. It wasn't a question of who these women were; they were his sisters—they had to be. One of the ones following was an older version of Beth—almost identical, but twenty years older. The other sister looked like her too, but redheaded. The oldest sister was older than Lars and almost white-haired like Beth, with the same blue eyes as both of them and a smile that had to have broken at least one man's heart because Lars said she had seven children and was a midwife. Behind him were three of the best-looking young men she had ever seen; the youngest was about sixteen, and the oldest maybe twenty-five. These had to be Lars's sons; this is what he had been waiting on, her family and his.

The woman holding his arm didn't even wait for introductions. Cat got the feeling she didn't wait for anybody or anything.

"So this is the woman you waited so long for and my niece? Come here, little one." She pointed to Beth; she knew exactly who she was.

"Well, little girl, it was worth the wait. You are beautiful, and as for your mama, she will do." Then she nodded her head. "My little brother seems to know what he wants and is willing to wait for it. Hello, my name is Gretel, and I am the oldest of this group. Now he is all shy. He is afraid I am going to spook you, but I am not, am I?" She held her arms out, and Cat came to her and gave her a big hug like she had known her forever. Gretel whispered in her ear, "It is going to be all right now, Catherine." And she kissed her on the top of her head. Cat felt like her mother had just come home.

"Now that redhead is sister number 2. She is Sasha, and the one that looks like Beth is Breanna. My dear, we have waited years to meet you and that little one, but it seems you have more children for us to meet? I think Lars would like for you to meet his sons, if it is not too much at once."

"How did you know about me and my not liking crowds of people?"

"He sent it in his letter to me and the boys, and by the way, I had men posted to watch over Horic and his men to protect your people here. They shouldn't be a problem." She just looked at Lars.

His son finally said, "When we want anyone really scared, we send her after them. She is the scary one." His sons just nodded their heads.

Gretel started to walk away with all the children, and Lars's son said to Cat, "She knows where the bodies are buried literally." Then he just raised an eyebrow and began to introduce himself. "I am Doeri, and I am the oldest at twenty-five. Latt is twenty, and Victor is sixteen. We all decided to come. We hope you don't mind. He has never gotten married before, and we wanted to meet our first sister."

Cat looked at Lars and the boats; there were people still coming off them.

"That is why you have been in such a hurry to get everything done. You knew all these people were coming?"

"Actually, I didn't. I invited only my sisters and my sons. The rest are a surprise, with the exception of Queen Marie. I also sent her an invitation when I sent the king the papers for the land titles."

"I wouldn't expect her. She has been very ill, but thank you for inviting her. Now let's go see your sisters. I already want to take Gretel home with me."

"Good, she is a great midwife, and I asked her if she would come home with us for a while."

"What if I hadn't liked her?"

"My sister handles people like you handle horses. There was little worry about that." She looked at him for a moment; then she smiled. He was right—that woman walked into her life like a whirlwind and just landed like she belonged, and now she did.

When she walked into the lodge, Gretel had already introduced herself to the children and knew each one's name and age, including Eric's. They were all calling her Nana; it was like she had always been in their life. Catherine thought she knew how to run a village; these women ran countries when the men were gone and fought when they had to.

Supper was wonderful. Gretel sat beside her, close to the corner and the door, and told her, "It always made it easier for me to have my back to a wall and a door close in case I had to get out in a hurry. So if we need to get you out, we can." She hadn't realized it, but all of the sisters were close and watchful of who got too close to her. Gretel sat next to her, and Sasha and Breanna introduced people and translated, but they didn't let people overwhelm her. This time, she enjoyed the banquet. When it quieted down, Gretel turned to her and said, "Lars says you had a difficult time your last pregnancy, and he wants me to come back with you to the keep when you leave. Your son is worried as well. I wanted to ask permission from you instead of having my brother just force me down your throat, so I wanted to talk to you privately."

"It is a problem that I don't think will repeat itself, but I would love for you to come with us if you can spare the time."

"My children are grown, but my sisters will be returning. Besides, I have five new grandchildren to get to know. Several children were brought to the North Country from here with Lars after you threatened to kill anyone who hurt Raider-born children, and I assume Ann and Jacob were such children. Why didn't you send them?"

"They were already mine, so they went with me."

Catherine nodded her head.

"Ann and Jacob aren't blood sister and brother, are they?"

She just shook her head no.

"Good, you know that he loves her, don't you?"

"Yes, I am just waiting to see if it is more than jealousy over Eric."

"I don't think it is. I am just glad they are not blood."

"He has watched over her since he found her as a small child, and I think he had always loved her. I just don't know if Ann feels the same way."

Things were moving along at the lodge; it was becoming a chapel. When a carriage arrived two mornings later, it had the queen's crest on it. Cat came rushing out; two men came out of the carriage. She knew Queen Marie was too sick to travel, but she was disappointed anyway.

"How can I help you gentlemen this morning?" She recognized one of the men as the queen's personal secretary, and the other gentleman she didn't know

"I have a message for you, Lady Catherine, and some paperwork for your husband-to-be, Lars Sorenson. May I see him?"

She started to walk back in, but the man stopped her and gave her an envelope with Marie's personal seal on it, and then he continued on. The letter said "PERSONAL" on it, so she turned around and walked to the barn, with James following her. She walked into the stall with the big stallion and sat down in the back on a pile of hay and carefully opened the envelope.

Dear Catherine

I am so sorry to hear about Giles. I know how much you loved him and how much he loved you. I am glad you have found Lars again and the children are happy. I have seen to it that the Raiders will have everything the king promised all those years ago when he offered the land for your hand and then some. It is a good deal. They should be pleased by my last deal for a friend. Now I have a favor to ask of you. My stallion, Khan, has never been handled by anyone but me and you. In fact, you taught me how. When I am gone, they will have to kill him. No one will be able to handle him, so I am giving him to you. He is old, but you know what his bloodlines are. He can still make you a rich woman. I am sending his papers to you with this letter. I will send a special knight with him soon. Please take care of them, but if you can't, you finish him. I have seen how you are with horses. Please make this my last wish between us. I also sent a wedding gift. I hope you like it. I helped Giles with the last ones. Maybe you will like these as well.

Love, Marie

She just sat there and cried for a while; then she looked at the papers. They were the breeding papers for Khan; he was the Arab stallion Marie had won on a bet she had with Charles about them getting married. He had paid an exorbitant price for him because he came from Arabic bloodlines, and there weren't any anywhere outside of the Holy Land, and he was Queen Marie's favorite. Cat had taught her how to calm him and ride him, and only she and Cat could do it. So now that the queen was ill, he was coming to her. She got back up, brushed off her dress, dried her eyes, and started back to the lodge, where inside the other man she didn't know stood standing, waiting for her.

"My lady, my name is Sean Deter, and Queen Marie sent me with a gift. Is there somewhere private we could talk?"

She led him down the hall to her private office, and they walked inside, with James and Caroline not far behind; they didn't really need a guard inside. Caroline was just really curious. The man had Catherine sit down, and then he opened a bag; inside was a box he had been carrying since he got off the coach, which he opened on the table beside her.

"I helped Lord Giles and Queen Marie design, and then I made your wedding rings. So the queen and I have been working on a new set for this wedding, so she sent me to bring them for your approval and to size them. We had an old ring the first time and the groom, but we didn't this time. So I came. I hope that is satisfactory?"

She just looked at him, kind of stunned, as Gretel came in and heard most of the conversation; then the man pulled out a tray with two rings on it, wide matching gold bands. But hers was set with a large round diamond with smaller ones on the side. She turned to James and said, "You had better go and find Lars and tell him to come to my office."

Gretel was stunned.

"Your lady queen did this for you?"

"Yes, we have been friends for a long time."

When Lars entered the room, he looked at her and then at the rings, which were worth a small kings' ransom. He just said, "Marie?"

She just nodded.

"She had the king sign over almost twice the land he originally agreed to, almost a thousand acres. Most of this coastline is now Raiders land because of our union. My people will have farms and good land to come to because of you and our daughter."

They all just looked at her, and all she could think about was Marie alone and if she was being taken care of. She was quiet, and then she asked him, "Do you approve of the ring? Marie designed them and sent a jeweler to size them if you like it."

He looked at her kind of funny; something was wrong, but this wasn't the time or place.

"Yes, they are beautiful as long as you like them."

"Good, we will get you sized later. Now I would like to talk to you about doing some work for me while you are here if you would. Come with me down the hall."

Lars followed her down the hall as she called for Ann and Beth to follow her; by now she also had Lars's attention as they went to her room. The girls followed her in as she went to the jewelry box and pulled out two velvet bags, and then she sat the girls on the bed with her.

"Ann, Beth and I have already talked about this, but she would like to have my wedding ring to wear to remind her of her daddy, Giles, and I said yes. But since they are identical, except his doesn't have a stone, would you like me to have a stone put in his and you can have his to wear for your wedding ring? I can have them sized and a stone put in them while I have a jeweler here, then I will put them up for later."

"I would like that very much. Do they have to be the same stones?"

"No, you can have whatever you want."

"You have a ring with a pale blue stone in it. May I have one like that?" She figured if the jeweler didn't have one, they could take the one out of her ring.

"Yes, my love. If that is what you want, that is what you will have. Then you both will have something from your daddy."

Lars just stood there, listened, and looked at his sister. Giles had loved his daughter enough that she wanted to remember him forever, and his bride had a friend who had given his people a place to live without having to die for it. Gretel just looked at him and then whispered in his ear, "She was worth waiting for, I was wrong."

The wedding was two days away, and things were coming together beautifully; the three sisters had taken over in a nice way. They had become her sisters. Well, not Gretel—she was more like her mother. They organized, put things in order, and made sure she didn't get overwhelmed by too many people she didn't know wanting everything at once; they made sure all these new people went through them or Lars before they saw her. They still weren't too sure Horic wouldn't make a run at her now more than ever.

They had to build a new corral for the new stallion coming; having two stallions in the same barn was never going to work. She hadn't heard any more from Marie; maybe she was better—she hoped so anyway.

There was a banquet tonight; the wedding had better be soon. They were running out of space to put people. Everybody was laughing, talking, and eating, of course. It was a nice evening. But Cat had a bad feeling, and every once in a while, she thought she heard something. The crowd quieted down for a toast. As one of Lars's men started, she heard her stallion scream, and so did James. Before Lars could stop her, she was gone; she had grabbed a lance, with James close behind, and they were out the door.

As soon as they were outside, she could hear her stallion, Cloud; she was running faster, and James couldn't catch her, and he was sure she was running headlong into something bad. He could see Lars behind him with his sister. When he got to the barn, there was a man in her stallion's stall, and he was pretty sure he was dead. The stallion had trampled him, but there was another man still in the stall at the back. When he got there, there were two men with crossbows aimed at her horse, ready to kill it. Catherine was getting in front of them; he wasn't worried about the horse hurting her. He was worried about the men.

"James, call them off!"

"The horse killed a man. He needs to be put down!"

"They put one arrow in my horse and I will kill them! Get them away from him!"

"Cloud, come here to Mama, come here."

The horse walked over to her as she opened the gate, and she put her arm around his neck; there were men with lanterns coming in then, and as she turned, she had blood all over her. Lars started to come to her, and she said, "Stay where you are. It is Cloud's blood, not mine. Someone has cut him to pieces. That is why he killed that man, but there is still someone in here. Stand up. I can see you in the back."

A man started forward, but Cloud wouldn't let him get too close to Catherine.

"Just stay right there. Why did you do this to my horse?"

He scooted farther away from the big horse and closer to the fence, as though to jump and run. But two of her men put that thought right out of his mind. As the big horse came close to her and put his neck over her shoulder, she just petted his nose carefully, not taking her eyes off the man in front of her and still holding the lance in her other hand.

"I will ask again. Why did you cut up my horse?"

"We just came out here to look at him, and he attacked us, and we protected ourselves. Then he killed my friend. He should be killed."

"You are a liar. You had to sneak around the back of the pens to even get in his stall, and then you had to use a lance to even get close to him. So who ordered this? Tell me, or I am going to let him finish the job!"

At about that time, the man on the ground moaned, and Cat looked down at him. The other man said, "He is still alive. You have got to help him."

"I can't help him. His head is smashed. His body just doesn't know he is dead yet."

"Isn't there anything you can do?"

She turned back and looked at Lars, and he shook his head yes, and he was going to do it. But she walked forward, took the lance, and ended this man's misery the only way she could—by putting the lance in the middle of the man's back. Then she looked back at the other man and said, "Who ordered this?"

The man stepped back. "Horic, he said you and Lars would never share the land and that your husband had killed Vatic for no good reason except he slapped you around a little."

"This stops now." She walked forward to Lars and turned around. "Unlace them." She pulled her hair to the front of her dress.

"Are you sure you want them to see?"

She nodded her head yes, and he unlaced her dress halfway down; it was enough—even Gretel gasped. Lars had told her some of it, but not all.

"Hold the light up and let everyone see what Vatic did to me. He beat the girl he took back with him, and nobody helped her till she killed herself. I hear there were others. The only reason I am alive is because Lars took me off a post, or he would have come back and finished the job. Lars is trying to make a place for you here for everyone, but I will not put my children in danger for people who don't appreciate what is being done for them. I am through for tonight. Do what you want with him."

She walked out, and her horse followed her—no reins or rope, just her hand under his chin.

Gretel came up beside her and asked, "What do we need to do to fix him? I am not so good with horses."

She just smiled at her and said, "I will show you."

Then she stopped when Gretel grabbed her arm and tied her dress back up. "We don't want to scare the children or have they seen it?"

"Just the girls the boys haven't. Not very pretty, is it?"

"Lars said you were good with horses, better with them sometimes than people. I can see now why people are a problem. Do you think he will let us fix him? He is cut pretty bad."

"He is as gentle as a kitten."

Gretel remembered the man on the stall floor stomped to death, but she also remembered the woman who put a lance in his back to put him out of his misery; she had a feeling you really didn't want to see the dark side of this lady.

They worked on her horse for the next few hours in a stall at the end of the barn, and Cat was right—as long as she was there, he never moved. She stitched and cleaned. Gretel washed and handed her salves, and they talked. When they were done, the big horse would let Gretel touch him and get close, and Cat said that was the start of his liking her.

"How do you get along with them so well? I have a problem even riding, but you, they like."

"It has always been that way ever since I was little. I walked into a corral when I was two, and nobody saw me. When they found me, they couldn't figure out why they hadn't trampled me. I was sitting on a pile of hay, feeding the horses. It has been like that ever since. They just seem to trust me."

"Lars says you ride like no woman he has ever seen. Will you teach me?"

"Certainly, but he has banned me until the baby comes."

"Why?"

"He thinks it is too risky. Truth be told, the day I made the promise, I was jumping logs."

"Really, I can't understand why he would think that was too risky."

"Maybe we can change his mind if you don't jump logs."

"Let's get through here. I don't know about you, but I am getting tired, and we still have a couple of long days ahead of us."

They finished with the stallion and headed inside; she left a guard on the horses' stalls. Now it seemed even her animals were in danger. She stopped inside; and Gretel turned to her, gave her a hug, and said, "Go now and get some sleep. You and that baby have got to get some rest. I will take over the morning drama."

She just nodded. Good, she could sleep a little later. Wrong. When she got to the room, there was a bath steaming; and Lars and Jacob were sitting on the bed, waiting on her. Jacob had come to the barn while she was working on Cloud, but he didn't say anything, and then he had walked away; she figured she would see him sometime soon. She just didn't figure this soon. She walked into the room covered in blood, and her son looked at her; he had something to say.

"Out with it. What is wrong? Something is bothering you. Tell me. Your mother desperately needs a bath."

"Why didn't you tell me about what the Raiders did to you? Those people out there know more than I did until tonight. Even the girls know. Why couldn't you tell me?"

"It was something I didn't really want you to ever have to know, and the girls know because they have seen me without clothes when I have had children or most recently when I was hurt. It was a hard secret to hide from them."

"I want to see them."

"No, you don't. They are not pretty."

"If they know, I want to as well."

She just breathed deeply and turned around; when Lars stepped over, she whispered, "As little as possible to satisfy him." He just nodded his head. He loosened the knot Gretel had tied hours ago and started to untie them, and she turned toward the fireplace. She could hear Jacob inhale, and she told Lars, "Enough. He has seen all he needs to see." Then she felt smaller hands on her back, softly touching the scars.

Then Jacob asked, "How far do they go?"

As Lars gently pushed his hand away and pulled up the dress, he said, "All the way down her back."

Jacob stood staring at her, and when she turned around, he looked at her and asked, "Why did you take us in when the Raiders had done that to you?"

Lars had wondered the same thing a hundred times and had never had the courage to ask her.

"You were children hurt, alone, and starving. And you had no more control over what was happening to you than I had over what happened to me, and I fell in love with both of you the instant I saw you. You were fighters like me, so you belonged with me. Have you for one instant in your life not felt loved by me or your daddy?"

"No, never. We were always part of your family like we were born to it since the moment he picked us up and put us on his horse."

"And you always will be. As long as I draw breath, you are my children no matter who gave birth to you. Does that satisfy your questions?"

Jacob nodded yes and went to give her a hug. Then Catherine said, "I will get you all bloody."

"I don't care, Mama."

She smiled at him. "Now get to bed. You have to walk me down the aisle, remember? If you still want to. You are my best man, after all."

The grin she got as he walked out the door was priceless.

"Now please, Lars, help me out of this dress for the last time today. And after my bath, maybe you can remind me why I decided to marry a certain blond-haired Raider who half my children look like."

"You decided to marry me because you have so many blond-headed children, and you needed a papa to match up with them. You know I had wondered why you took those children in and was too afraid to ask.
Jacob is going to be quite a man, and he is going to be a Raider. You know that, don't you?"

"Yes, I know, and it wouldn't surprise me if Ann doesn't follow him as well."

Cat then sank down in the tub to wash off all the blood she had on her. Lars was helping her bath. Well, helping may not have been the right word; there was water going everywhere, even some on Cat. Lars's fingers were working magic on her and not in just a soothing manner as he said, "We can find a good Raider husband for Ann, and she will have a large dowry and land. She can pick whoever she wants."

"My dear, I think Jacob and Ann have already chosen, if I am not mistaken. I am hoping they will wait a couple more years and make sure. Then we will see."

"Who? I have seen no one that they are around except each other." And then the light came to his eyes. "Oh . . ."

"They are not blood. They have just been together since they were little, and she seems to feel the same about him. So let's give it some time and see what happens."

"What about Eric? I thought he had eyes for Ann?"

"I may have been wrong about that. He may have been watching out for the other daughter."

"Beth? I will kill him."

"You can't kill every man who looks at our daughters—only if they touch them. Now let's get back to this bath. No, let's get out of this bath and get in the bed. I have some ideas for an old blond Raider because your sister said I could sleep late in the morning."

"Did she now Odin blesses my sister?"

CHAPTER 11

The next morning, she slept a little late till David came screaming into her room and said, "They are going to cut off his head!"

She didn't even stop to ask; these people were driving her crazy. She grabbed a dress. Caroline was tying it up in the back as fast as she could as she explained that a boat had come in this morning and some elder was about to behead the man from last night; they couldn't find Lars, and they thought her horse needed to be killed as well.

"Find Gretel!"

She started running; she grabbed her staff beside the door, with John and James beside her and David not far behind. She headed to the meadow, where she saw men with ropes around Cloud's neck. They were opening the gate to his stall, and he was fighting; all she could think of was all those stitches she had put in him last night.

"James, just cut him loose. He will come to me. John, come with me. Somebody find Lars."

And she kept running; then Cloud was beside her. She didn't think as John cupped his hands. She grabbed a handful of mane and jumped on his back, and away she went toward the men in the meadow. When she got there, sure enough, they were fixing to execute the man from last night

"Stop this right now!"

An old man with a beard lowered his hand, and the man with the sword started to deliver the blow, so she ran him over with Cloud and then slid off him.

"I said stop this and I don't generally have to repeat myself." The man on the ground came toward her and started to grab her; she warned him, "I don't like strange men touching me." When he tried to grab her again, she took the staff, put it behind his knees, knocked him on the ground, and then popped him in the chest; he wasn't going anywhere now. He was too busy trying to breathe. She leaned down and said, "Next time you try that, I will put it through your chest, and you won't ever get up again. Don't touch me."

"This man attacked the lady of this land last night and has to be punished, and the animal that killed the other man has to be killed. That is our law, and you have no right to go against me."

She just nodded her head, then said, "I don't know who you are, but I am the lady of this land, and you can go straight to hell!" She went over, grabbed the man from last night, and picked him up by the scruff of the neck. Then she grabbed the knife she carried in her boot and cut his bindings; the Raider that was getting up off the ground started to object, but James and John were there by then with swords drawn.

"What is your name?"

"Bruno, my lady."

"From the wounds I repaired on my horse last night, all of the wounds came from the front, and that would have been from the man who was killed."

"That is why the animal is going to be destroyed."

"Shut the hell up! No one is talking to you. He was doing the most damage to him. That is why he killed him. He just backed you up in a corner."

"My lady, I cut him once, but I didn't understand why we were hurting such a beautiful animal. So I was trying to stop him." She had seen the one cut; she didn't know if he would admit to it or not, and sure enough, he did. Well, how was she going to fix this?

"Get on your knees."

"Yes, my lady, whatever you want."

James and John just watched. Lars was coming, but he was still too far away; she was on her own.

"Bruno, do you swear your allegiance to me for the rest of your life for whatever I ask you to do?"

John and James were both smiling; she had saved him and given him a better life, and he didn't even know it yet. He was a lucky man.

"You can't do that. I am the elder."

"He is mine now, my man, and you can't touch him."

The man on the ground was trying to get up; she just raised an eyebrow and shook her head no, and he stayed down. John and James were enjoying this to no end; they hadn't seen Cat give anybody this much grief in a long time, and now they were going after her horse. This was just getting good.

"That animal is dangerous and should be put down. He could kill someone else."

As he put his head over her shoulder, she leaned down and told Bruno, "Don't move a muscle." Then she looked at the men beside her and smiled, they knew something was coming. She lifted her hand up and said, "Up, Cloud."

And Cloud reared both legs above her head and pawed the air, the Raiders moved back. Lars and Gretel stopped and held their breath. If he came down wrong, he would crush her; then she moved her hand down, and he landed with both legs on either side of her and again laid his head on her shoulder and put his muzzle in her hand.

"My horse doesn't hurt anyone who isn't hurting him, and I will not allow anyone to hurt him. Is that clear? I don't know who you are, but I don't take orders from you or anyone." Then she turned and walked with her horse and her men past Lars and Gretel, whom she winked at, and went back to the lodge.

"I don't know who he is, but I think I made him mad."

Lars stopped James and asked him, "Do you know how dangerous that was?"

"With the horse, they would never touch her. I have seen her do that too many times. It used to drive us crazy, so she stopped. Her father threatened to beat her the first time we saw it, and the horse almost ran him down because he was yelling at her. How do you think we learned what they would do for her?"

"Her father knew."

James nodded, and then he wouldn't say any more

"You are one of the men who came here with her, weren't you? And I think John."

"Yes, John came with Giles, injured, to the keep. But when we left, John and two other injured men went with her, and we are still her men and always will be. She gets undying respect from her men with very little effort and keeps it forever. She protected and cared for us just like that man today and she doesn't even know him. So let me be very clear. We will protect her against anyone until our dying day."

There, it had been said—what all these men had wanted to say to him since they got here: she came first, above anything. Lars was going to have to prove himself, protector of Catherine and her children.

He went down to the men shouting by the boats. Sure enough, it was the village elder from the North Country, and he was fuming. He figured he could calm him down and settle this easily, but he walked into a hornet's nest.

"I want that woman disciplined. She should be banished from this place, and her husband should beat her. No woman has the right to speak to me in such a manner. I will be the leader of these people. She should bow down to me and give me that man to execute as I see fit. I am thinking I will have my men drag him out here and do as I will."

By the time he had finished his speech, Lars was furious. How dare he threaten Catherine on her own land? She was right; these people had no respect for anything he had worked for all these years. She, all the children, and all her friends had to be guarded on her own land because she wasn't safe here except in the village—and only there because Giles and Cat had made those people love them because they kept them alive all those years ago. He was beginning to see how this was going to go.

His people were going to take over, expecting this land that was being given to them as theirs alone; and then if anybody disagreed, they would kill them.

"The woman you were talking to owns this land, and she had every right to decide what happens here. You will show her the respect she deserves. You will not kill that man. He is hers now, and no one touches her horses—ever. You come here and expect to run this land she worked to get for you and treat her like this?"

"The king made this contract possible."

"Is that what you think? I live on land that is hers that my daughter will inherit, and the contract you talk of was forged by Queen Marie, her friend, to help Catherine because she is marrying me—if she still will have me after today. You come and insult a woman who has done nothing but try to help her people and ours and proceed to take over land that is not even ours yet!"

The man in front of him looked stunned; he didn't realize he was not going to be in control here, and that didn't sit well with him, and neither did this woman having all the power.

"I am sorry. I have overstepped my bounds. Of course, you must marry first. Then you will have control, and then we can talk again. But you must let me wed you in the old Raiders ways."

"No, most certainly not. She will have none of that, not after today. And as for having control, my lady is just that, a lady of the English court and her son is a lord. So she will always have control. Her family has owned this land for two centuries. When I leave this land to go back to her keep with her, my son Doeri will take control for me here on my daughter's land. And if it is not what you want, I suggest you get back on that boat because I won't have my wife threatened again."

This was not what he wanted; he wanted it all. Lars had just decided that he should leave more men who were loyal to him here. Maybe Victor, his youngest son, would like to stay as well; he could bring messages to the keep on a regular basis.

"We will see to your comfort, for the wedding is tomorrow. But keep your men under control."

When he was escorted into the lodge, he was properly introduced to Catherine.

"Lady Catherine, this is Seaue Valantri, the elder from the North Country."

That was all he said; he let her take it from there. She put out her hand for him to shake; she wasn't going to curtsy to him, not after the way he had treated her. He took her hand and kissed it, and then he looked at her and said, "Now I know why my men think you are a Valkyrie. I should have never threatened your horse. I never will again. Forgive me."

Well, she wasn't expecting that; she looked at him for a minute. She knew he was trying to make her think he was some kindly old man trying to gain her favor; they both knew how to play this game.

"Valkyrie women escort the dead from the battlefield to Odin's table, right?"

"That's close enough. I will have to explain the legend to you sometime."

She leaned down, smiled, and whispered in his ear, "You touch my family or my horses, and you can find out if it is true or not for yourself."

And then they just smiled at each other; the battle lines had been drawn, and they both knew where the other stood.

"Would you like supper? We are just about to sit down."

Most of the people in the room thought the argument had been settled, but the people who knew each of them knew better. It wasn't long till she came into their room. There was a hot bath waiting for her; she quickly climbed in and was soaking when Lars came into the room.

"Seaue says he needs to be the one to marry us tomorrow in a Raiders wedding."

She was already coming out of the tub; now she had to fight another war. He put his hands on her shoulders, pushed her back in the tub, took a rag, and started to bathe her.

"I have already told him it was not going to be allowed. Your priest was going to do the ceremony."

"You mean there is something today I don't have to fight for? How nice, and that man does not like me even with all the pretty words he says."

"I know you have been right all along. If I don't leave enough protection for the village people, men like him will massacre them in a month, and it will be war. I am going to pick and choose who stays with your men to help here, and I would like Victor to stay as well to help his brother and keep us updated at the keep."

"That sounds like a good idea. I would like to keep this together, but I want the village safe too, and I am not too sure all your people have the same thing in mind."

He rubbed her belly, which was expanding rapidly. Well, she had three other children, but there was a chance that this child could be Giles's—a slight one, but a chance still. They had talked about it, but there was nothing to done about it now. She had even given him the choice to call off the wedding; there was no way he was doing that. He had waited too long.

He helped her out of the tub and rubbed her dry; this would be the last night she wouldn't be his wife, and he smiled. There had been women before her and after her, but since the night he had found her on that post, there had only been her. When they were in bed, she pulled him to her, brushed her fingers through his hair, and rubbed her face on his.

"You always do that before you make love to me. Why?"

"It is what I remember most in my dreams of you. I could almost feel your skin. And when I put my fingers through Beth's hair after she was born, sometimes I would rock her, and I would see your face."

She kissed his eyes, his cheeks, and his mouth ever so gently like little whispers as he moved over her and entered her; there were tears in her eyes.

"God, forgive me. You were always there, and I think Giles knew that. But you were always there."

He didn't tell her, but Giles knew—he had always known. He loved her in a gentle rocking motion like lovers who have known each other forever do till it became fierce and wonderful, like a thousand exploding stars. Then he collapsed on her, sweating and breathing hard. He put his hand on her hard little tummy, and he didn't care whose baby it was; it was his now as she curled up next to him and put her hand back in his hair like he was going to disappear.

He laid there for a while till he was sure she was asleep, and then he climbed out of bed and pulled on his robe; the night was still young, and he wanted some answers. He walked down the hall and knocked lightly on Robert's door, and when he answered, he just said, "Come with me."

The same with James, and then they went to the empty kitchen; it didn't stay empty long. Two blond heads poked around the corner and said, "What is going on?"

"Go back to bed. I want some information about your mother, and you are too young."

"Wrong, we do too, and we probably know more than you do. So we are staying. By the way, where is she?"

"She is still in bed."

As they sat down the hall, in came John, Michel, and Jacob; they had been talking so they came to see what was going on. When they found out, they sat down as well.

"You might as well do this all at once so we don't have to do it again. She doesn't tell anyone anything unless you back her in a corner."

James laughed in a funny kind of way and Robert gave him a dirty look.

"Just start. We have all night, but I am marrying her in the morning. I saw a horse protect her this afternoon, and there are things about her I don't understand and I think it is about time I do so I know how to protect her before I walk her into something else she is terrified of."

Robert didn't know if he was doing the right thing or not, but he had done the same thing for Giles, and it had seemed to help him understand her.

"When Cat's mother married her father, it was to get her title and land. It was all hers."

"You mean this land?"

"No, I mean all of it—the keep and this land and all the money and the title. She was the wealthy one. The marriage was arranged by his mother. He never liked her much. He just wanted an heir, and their first child was Catherine, and he told Cat's mother how worthless she was in those words on the day she was born. Catherine's mother told me to watch out for her daughter because she was afraid her husband wouldn't, and he didn't. Cat's father, Silas, had no use for the child even though she followed him everywhere. And I followed her. Evelyn had three more pregnancies and died after the third, delivering a stillborn boy. It was then he decided to pay some attention to Catherine.

"When she was two, we found her in with the horses, and we discovered they wouldn't hurt her. So we would put her up on them, and before she was four, she was riding by herself. Her father made her work like a boy for years until her grandmother told him he might make a match and find a husband for her if she didn't look so much like a boy, maybe even bring in a title or more land. He let her hair grow, and she was beginning to look like a girl. But she wouldn't give up her horses, and that infuriated him until she started treating them. Then everybody started to bring their sick animals to her.

"One day, a small group of men and a woman came to her with a horse with a badly infected leg, and no one could touch him. The lady said they were going to have to put him down if she couldn't help, but when she saw the girl, she didn't realize how young she was. Catherine walked up to the sick animal, and you have seen how they react to her. She took him in the barn, put him in a stall, looked him over, and told the woman she would have to cut open the leg and drain it. The woman started to cry, saying, 'You might as well kill him. He won't let you do that.'

"'Yes, he will.' As we watched, he lay down for her. She put hot rags on the leg, and then she carefully cut open his leg and let it drain. She worked on that horse all night long as the woman sat beside her, holding that horse's head. He was better in the morning, but she told the lady she needed to keep him a few more days, and then she could send her men back for him. Her father came in about this time and started screaming at her to get to work. She didn't have time to be messing with some nobody's horse and started to kick at the horse. He was on his knees before he could move, and the woman was in front of him, and one of the men holding him said, 'This is Her Majesty, Queen Henrietta Marie.'

"'That is enough. We don't need the whole list, but the only reason you still have a head is your sweet daughter saved my horse, and he is going to stay here until he is well, and she is going to be well paid, isn't she?' Her father just nodded.

"'Sweet girl, you need me, you send word to me at the castle. You understand? My men will be back for him. You have the touch, little one. We will meet again.'

"After that, I think he hated her. One night, he threw a party with a bunch of old men and I think the idea was to sell off Cat to one of them for a good marriage. She wasn't but fifteen at the time. By now, her grandmother could see what was going on, and she told me to watch her as well. I think he thought one of them might get drunk enough to hurt or rape her and be obligated to marry her, so he left her in a crowded room of men she didn't know."

Well, one more question answered; little by little, it was beginning to fall into place

"I found her with some old man ripping her clothes off and hitting her. After I took care of him, I took her out to the barn. I knew she would be safe out there and I had James watch over her while I went to talk to her grandmother.

"Silas was furious. The man complained he wouldn't have his daughter under any conditions, and all the other men agreed. Then they left, and he went looking for her. He found her in the barn and dragged her into the corral. Her grandmother and I were coming, but not quickly enough. But he had left the gate open to the stall. Her horse and James were not far behind, and he picked up a rod to hit her with, and the horse came running up behind her. She looked back and told James to move out of the way, and then she did what she did today. We all froze, but after the shock wore off, he came at her again. And this time, her horse ran him down. She walked over to him, took the stick and threw it away. Then she leaned down and said, 'That is the last time you will use me, hit me, or treat me like a whore. Or I will go to the queen.'

"That was the day our Catherine was born. Three weeks later, her father was called to lead a troop for the crusades, and I think it was Cat's grandmother that sent the letter to Queen Marie on her own son before Silas killed Catherine. We asked her about the horse and what he had done, and she told us he had saved her from a boar in the woods the same way, and then trampled the boar. She had finished him with her spear, then dragged him to town for the people to eat. When asked who killed it, she had told them one of her men."

"What about Queen Marie? They seem to be good friends, but she can't handle crowds."

"When she went to see Queen Marie, we were met outside and escorted into the queen's private chambers. They visited and ate. They had very little interaction with anyone except the king and a few ladies-in-waiting, even when the children were with her. They have their own time, and then she leaves. Now she comes to the keep and stays for a few days, and no one knows that the pretty older lady buying vegetables at the village market is Queen Marie, and that is how she wants it."

He looked at the faces around the table and realized all these people had been privy to royalty in their home, and it was nothing because their mother was a special lady to a queen.

"Keep going. That's not all of it. Men touching her what about that?"

"That one you have to take responsibility for. After the attack, she couldn't stand to be touched except by a few of us, and we kept our distance. Your man broke her pretty good and when we finally got her back it took weeks of putting her back together."

"What do you mean 'putting her back together'?"

"She had a broken wrist and then her back and a fever, not counting the scrapes and bruises from being dragged."

He just looked away; he hadn't paid that much attention. All he cared about was taking her home.

"If you had put her on a boat, she probably would have died of fever before you could get her home."

When he remembered those high seas and the weather, if she was that bad, she would have died; it was a good thing Robert had found her, or he would have lost her.

"We had to watch her all the time. She had nightmares so bad she would go for days without sleep just so she wouldn't have them. When she did sleep, she walked, and sometimes she fell. She hurt herself badly several times. That is what your man left her with."

"Were they better after Giles killed him?"

Ann and Beth asked at the same time, "Daddy killed him, not you?"

He had felt guilty before when Catherine had said the same thing to him, but how do you answer these two?

"No, Giles killed him. I should have, but I didn't, and it is something I regret."

They both looked at him and shook their heads.

"What else?"

"There's more?" The girls were terrified. What else?

"The queen arranged the marriage and personally picked Giles, but when he came to the king's chamber, he ridiculed and spoke badly of your mother and told her if she didn't give up her child, he wouldn't marry her."

Beth looked like she was going to cry.

"My daddy said that about me to Mama?" She started to stand up, but a voice from the door stopped her as her mother walked into the room.

"His mistress had convinced him I only wanted him to watch over my land, and I had to be a horrible person. But when he came to the land, there was this blond-haired, blue-eyed little girl who he said had to be the prettiest little girl he had ever seen. He said he fell in love with you the instant he saw you."

Beth sat back down as Cat leaned against the doorway. "He also walked into a barn and saw two children running from a man and started to ride away, then turned around and went back and brought them home to me. He almost beat the man who was after you two to death. Then he gave me two more sons. When I got to him the night he died, he told me that I had given him back the family he had lost. He thought he would never find that again and that he loved each and every one of his children with all his heart and the only thing that would take him away from them was death, and that was the only thing that did. Whatever happened to me in my childhood is all right now, and everybody knows all the gory details. But I still have all my family and maybe one more. So if everybody is satisfied with my life story, let's get to bed so I can get married tomorrow."

"Yes, Mama."

"Kisses from everybody. Even the men, get over here."

Everybody got a kiss tonight; she had forgotten how these men had sacrificed to keep her alive when she was little and had no protection. When she kissed Robert on the cheek, she whispered in his ear, "Thank you for all you have done for me all my life and for my mother."

"It was my pleasure. Just stop with the horse thing."

She just smiled. "Which one?"

He just rolled his eyes; she was going to be the death of him.

"At this rate, the only one going to be awake for the wedding is the priest."

Lars looked at her and down the hall at all the doors closing and asked her, "When are you going to tell them about the fight between Giles and me over you and Beth?"

She started to walk to their room and then turned. "They have had enough information for one night, and so have you."

"How much did you hear?"

"Most of it I woke up when you left and wondered what you were doing, so I just listened. I didn't realize how I scared them with the horses."

"You don't see it like we do. You look like one of the old goddesses being protected by her animal. It is unreal, but your people might think you are a witch. You have to be more careful."

She nodded her head. Giles had said the same thing to her a long time ago.

"So now I am an ancient goddess? I am getting old fast."

"That's not so bad. You will be revered by the young people and songs sung about you."

She looked up at him to catch him smiling at her; he was making fun of the whole situation. She turned around and smacked him on the arm, so he just picked her up and carried her to the bedroom before she could do any permanent damage. Goddesses were strong after all.

The next morning, the house was a mass of people going everywhere at once. Cat and the girls were trying to get ready. Jennie and Caroline were trying to get the guests organized and, in some instances, separated so they didn't kill one another. Catherine heard a few conflicts, but Jennie said not to come out under any circumstances or she would never get dressed. So when she heard the knock on the door, she figured someone had been killed. It was the jeweler that Queen Marie had sent; she had invited him to stay, but it looked like he was preparing to leave. "I have to talk to my lady before I go."

"All right, please come in. Is it all right if my daughters stay?"

He nodded yes.

"I need to pay you for all the work you have done for me. The girls are most pleased with the rings you fixed for them, and mine is beautiful."

The man looked as though he was about to cry, and she said, "Is something wrong?"

"Yes, my queen is dying. They say you know things, and I think you know this true."

She just held his hand and nodded. "I have felt her life fading for days now."

"I want to be there when she is put to rest, but I promised to stay until you married because there is one more gift she wanted me to give to you on your wedding day." He reached into the bag he carried with him everywhere and pulled out a velvet case, and as soon as Cat saw it, she knew what was in it. He opened it, and there was a choker of teardrop diamonds and emeralds that went to a long V. Marie had worn them often, and Catherine had said how very beautiful they were. Marie had told her they would be hers someday; she had thought she was just kidding. Queens don't give away their jewelry, especially this piece. She knew whom it belonged to and the story behind it.

"May I put it on you?"

She just turned in the chair and let him hook the clasp, and she looked at it in the mirror; then she started to open her mouth.

"Before you say anything, I might as well tell you the queen said if you refused them, she would take back all the land."

Cat just smiled. Marie would say just such a thing and probably do it.

"All right, you have done what she asked. Go, and I hope you get there in time."

"There is one more thing. These are from me. You and the queen have made me and my family wealthy, and I appreciate it. Goodbye, my lady. If you ever need me, you know where to find me." Then he turned and left quickly out the door.

She opened her hand to find he had made matching earrings for the necklace, so she turned, put them on, and said under her breath, "Hurry, my friend, for I fear you may already be too late. And for that, I am sorry."

The girls were too stunned to even talk; they just stared until she said, "Are we ready, ladies? They will be coming to collect us soon. Have we got everything?"

As she looked at them, she smiled; they were so beautiful. She hoped Giles was watching; his daughters were lovely. He would have been so proud. There was another knock at the door, and Beth said, "You have anyone else coming to bring you jewelry?"

"Not today, except the ring at the altar, and your brother had better not have lost it because the jeweler is gone. We will have to use a piece of rolled-up straw."

"Oh, that will go well with the rest of the jewels. It will blend right in."

She swatted her velvet dress, and they started out the door, giggling.

"Girls, behave yourselves. This is a solemn occasion." The only problem was she couldn't wipe the grin off her face.

Jacob was waiting for her outside the door, and she took his arm. But first, she looked him over; he looked so grown-up. Then she kissed him on the forehead and asked, "I am so pleased you wanted to escort me down the aisle. My children are growing up so quickly. You will all be gone and have your own families soon, and I will be a grandmother."

"We can never thank you enough for the life you have given us. We love you, and if this will make you happy, then this is what we want for you." With that, he kissed her hand, and they started following the girls down the hall to the large meeting room.

Well, it was pretty much what she expected; it was split into two sides: the Raiders side and the English side. She looked at Jacob, and he said, "It was either this, or they killed each other."

"What a wonderful way to start the day! I am not going to worry about them. I am just going to enjoy this wedding. They can kill each other later. Just don't get blood on the dress." Jacob just smiled at her.

As she looked down the aisle, she saw Lars, and he was dressed as a Raider; he had on some sort of fur vest and leather pants, all white. With that blond hair, he was very handsome, and all she could do was smile at him; he looked like the day he had captured her. As she walked toward him, his smile became a frown, and she realized he had seen the necklace. When she got up to him, she could see he was angry. He leaned over to her and asked, "Did you have to wear everything Giles had given you today? I could have supplied you with more jewelry if you needed it."

"This piece was from Queen Marie with the stipulation I wear it or no land. Shall I take it off?"

"Your queen has an evil sense of humor sometimes."

"You have no idea, and this is one of those times. Just deal with it because the elder is having a fit."

As he looked over her head, he could see the elder was indeed having a fit; he wanted this land and all this property, and he thought he could weasel his way past this woman if he tried hard enough. Now he could see she was someone he was going to have a problem with. She was too rich and carried too much power with the queen; he couldn't just run over her as he could most women, and they hated each other.

As they knelt in front of Father Marques, she could feel Father Thomas's eyes on her back; he had been invited to this wedding as a formality, but he was furious he was not doing the ceremony. It was an insult to him. She knew it, but she didn't care. When their vows were said, he put on her ring, and she put on his, and the wedding was done. They turned and stood, and the whole room stood and cheered. Most of these people were happy for them; some weren't. Lars was going to have to decide who would stay and who would go, but not today. Today was a celebration, and both sides knew how to celebrate. There were tables and tables of food, both to satisfy Raiders and English alike, and there were musicians and dancing as well as guards. The children knew to stay within sight of a guard or one another at all times. The adults, Caroline and James, were watching the girls; and Robert and Jennie were watching her three boys and William.

Lars and Catherine stayed at the party for several hours and then snuck off to their room for a little privacy, for there wouldn't be much in the coming days. They walked into the room, and she realized he had the bedspread changed and the tapestries and rugs replaced; he had to have done it today because that was the only time she had been out of here. She walked around the room; it looked totally different, and then she turned around and asked, "How did you do this without me knowing, and why?"

"The children have been helping me. The girls have been getting all the rugs and tapestries and the bedspread made, and today the boys and I made a mad dash to get it all in here while you were exiled from here for one morning. I didn't think we would get it done, but they worked like demons. They even came in here after the wedding to finish."

So that was where they had disappeared to after the wedding with Caroline and Jennie; she would have to thank them tomorrow.

"I was going to say how much I liked this outfit you are wearing. I haven't seen you look like this in a long time, and it was quite a surprise. I like it."

"When did this new piece of jewelry show up? It was a surprise as well. Are there any other strings attached to it?" He was getting angry as he put his hand underneath the necklace and took a closer look, and when he did, he could see just how costly it really was.

"The jeweler wasn't supposed to give it to me until my wedding day with instructions that if I refused it, she would take back the land. I don't know if she was kidding or not—probably not. She is used to getting her way."

"How much longer do I have to be at this woman's beck and call, or do I always have to wonder if this land will ever be mine?"

She looked at him strangely, and then she backed away as she started for the door. "Not too much longer. She will be dead soon. I can feel her life waning as we speak, and all he wanted to do was get home in time to see her buried, but he stayed to carry out her instructions. But I told him to leave, and I hope he gets there in time, and then you won't have to worry anymore." Then she walked out the door and slammed it behind her, and before he got to her, she was lost in the crowd of wedding well-wishers.

She walked toward the ocean without a guard; she didn't care to have anyone with her right now and sure enough, the elder saw her leave and took it as his chance to confront her.

"You have problems on your wedding night. Do you think it will get any better? You are not Raider. He will tire of you and will want someone who is more like him. He will want his own children, not another man's castoffs. You make him less of a man by showing him your last husband's wealth and jewelry at his own wedding. Did you think he would approve? He will never approve of you. Give up this land to us and the control of your daughter, and I will find her a good match for a husband. Then you can go back to being an English lady, and we can have what we want here."

"And what exactly is it that you want here?" She turned around to look at him.

"We want to be in control, and that will mean we need this lodge and all the land and your daughter as a wife to someone I choose. He can control the way she runs this place and this land." She just looked at him; she had spent all these years taking care of this land just so her daughter didn't wind up in a situation that he was willing to put her in.

"I will never let you or anyone else use my daughter as some kind of chess piece in this little game of yours, and besides that, I am going to see you leave this land and never come back. My daughter is rich and will have her pick of men of her choosing, and she will never give up her birthright to you or anyone else. She will be master of this land that I have fought and bled for. She will have the right to do just that, and you are not going to take that away from her."

He came closer to her, and she realized she had put herself in a bad position; she was at the edge of the cliff with no one to protect her and an angry man in front of her.

"What do you plan on doing? Kill me on my wedding day? Don't you think someone might think that a little odd?" She was trying to sidestep him so she could run when the chance came when another voice came out of the darkness.

"Yes, what exactly do you plan to do with my wife? Is she going to have an accident like your other enemies have had? Because that won't go over well here. She is too well respected. Would you ruin all these people's chances at a better life here on this land just so you can be in control?"

"A Raider needs to be in control, or this won't work. These English don't know our ways, and they will not treat us right."

"If it hadn't been for Catherine and the friendship she has with Queen Marie, we wouldn't be here at all. In the morning, you will be on a boat, and you are leaving with anyone else who thinks as you do. And as for my daughter, my wife is right. She will choose—no one, but her. And this will always be her land."

The elder turned to look at Catherine again and then started down the hill to the lodge; as he went past Lars, he said, "Your people won't respect a woman. You need to let me be in control. I have earned the right."

"Not here you haven't, so prepare to go back. The only way this will work is if you are gone."

After he had disappeared into the dark, Lars went to Cat and said, "You knew better than to come up here by yourself. That man has been known to kill people who disagree with him and make it seem like accidents. What were you planning if he came at you?"

When she raised her hand, she was holding a short sword about a foot and a half long, hiding in her skirt. "I didn't exactly come unarmed, just alone. I wanted to know what he wanted, and now I know."

"What were you prepared to do if he attacked you?" At the look in her eyes, he knew.

"Kill him, and if he comes for me or the children again, I will do exactly that."

"He will go in the morning, and that will take care of that."

"No, it won't. He wants something he can't have. He will find men who agree with him, and he will be back. You'd better start preparing, or you are going to get caught by surprise, and you will lose it all."

She was right, and he knew it; he needed to start getting more soldiers and protecting these people.

"May I have one night with my wife before I have to leave and take care of everyone else?"

She smiled at him; they were married now, and they should get at least one night together after the last few days. "That, sir, would be nice. Could you escort me home?"

They walked back to the lodge and through the hall, and Lars stopped for a few minutes to talk to some of his men and some of Catherine's. He told them what had happened on the hill. He ordered a watch set on the elder and his men and all the children as well; when he was sure they understood how dangerous the situation was, he finally went back to Cat. She had been watching the elder talking to certain men before he saw her, and she wanted anybody he had been talking with to leave with him tomorrow. When he saw her, he quickly stood apart from the men, but it was too late; she had already seen who he had planned to leave, and now they would be going too. Lars came to her side and took her down the hall. Then he asked, "Did you see who he was talking to?"

She just nodded.

"Good, you can point them out to me in the morning, and we will rid ourselves of a few more."

As they passed the elder, she just smiled, and then she stopped and handed the sword she still had in her hand from inside the fold in her skirt to one of her guards and thanked him for its use. Then she looked back at the elder, and he knew he wasn't the only one with murder on his mind out there on that hill tonight. He had picked on the wrong woman, and now he knew she would fight too.

They went to their room and went back in, and he locked the door; before she could get very far, he turned her around, kissed her, and started undoing her dress. If she was nude, she couldn't run, and he was done chasing her for tonight. The dress slipped to the floor, and her chemise was of the finest lawn; it was so soft. It was like a second skin. He started to slip it off when she stopped him.

"What is wrong?"

"Nothing I just want to see this outfit you have on, and I want to take it off. So come over here by the fireplace."

She started with the vest; it was some kind of fur, and it was white and so very soft. She slowly unlaced it, running her fingers over every piece of skin she could touch in the process, and then there was the belt. She seemed to be having trouble with that, so she leaned in and had to rub her head and ear up and down his chest before she got that undone.

"God, woman, I can do this faster." Then he heard her giggle; she was driving him crazy just because she knew she could, and she was enjoying it.

"Why are you doing this?"

"Because I knew it would keep you occupied, and I wouldn't get the lecture on going out there alone. Now wasn't that more fun than the lecture?"

He picked her up and carried her to the bed, stood her up, and took off the chemise; then he looked at her and asked, "You were going to kill him, weren't you? You knew he would follow you, and he would threaten you."

"Yes, and the next time he comes after me or Beth, I will. So you are warned. This isn't over. He will be back. You should have let me kill him."

He just looked at her and realized she would have done exactly what she said she would do.

They hadn't had time in days to do anything but get ready for the wedding, so it was nice not to be in a rush. He pulled her under him and kissed her, and she kissed back; then he sent little nibbles down her neck, and she arched up to meet him and gave him her breasts. Warm and soft, he could bury his face in them as his hands explored the rest of her chest and hips. She wasn't exactly idle; she loved to run her fingers through his hair and down his back. The muscles rippled with soft fine hair on them, but she had enough just touching; she wanted all of him.

As she pulled his head up to hers, Catherine said, "I have waited a long time to say these words. Make love to me, Lars. You finally are mine."

He looked at her, and suddenly, it was all there; she had been waiting all those years, and she couldn't say those words even to herself. Now, at long last, she could. He entered her slowly as the tears came to her face; she had kept so many secrets even from herself, and now she was finally free. He was hers.

He started a rhythm and slowly increased the speed until she thought she would shatter if she didn't come soon, but he wanted this to be like no other. So he kept her soaring. After all these years and children, he wanted something to be just theirs; she was clawing his back and begging please until he finally pulled her up off the bed and had her hips in his hands. With two final hard thrusts, he took her over the edge like never before. She just lay there, looking at him. It felt like she had shattered, and she was shaking as he lay down on top of her, still inside of her.

"Is that what you have been wanting from me?"

She didn't say anything; she just looked at him with tears still in her eyes.

"I loved Giles, I really did. But there was always you somewhere buried deep in my heart, and now I can let that part out. Thank you for waiting for me. I waited so long to say that."

"You were always mine, and I knew it the moment I set eyes on you. That baby in your belly is mine, no matter who the father is. So stop worrying about that." He kissed her again, and then she shivered;

he rolled to the side and pulled up the covers. "Let me take care of this situation. Then we will go to the keep, and you will be taken care of until this baby comes. And then no more babies, all right? Giles always knew that you loved me, and he accepted it. He knew you loved him as well, and he said he would take whatever you would let him have of you. So we will take the rest of what is left of our life as a gift from him, and I will take you home."

She shook her head; home was sounding better every day, but she was sure they weren't going home anytime soon. There was too much left to do here. She hadn't seen the queen's horse yet, and she couldn't leave until it came, or she heard otherwise.

CHAPTER 12

The next few days were a jumble of duties. Lars got the elder sent off on one of the boats after Cat had pointed out as many of the men as she could remember she had seen him with that night. They thought this was going to displease many of the people there, but they came to find out they were glad he was gone; they were afraid of him. After he was gone, Lars and the people started making plans to go north and start the settlements. Claire and her husband were given a tract of land close to the lodge so Cat could see her when she came back, and it was a good tract of land. Wagons were loaded, and today they were going to head out. Lars had split the guards, taking half with him and leaving half with Cat.

"That should be enough. The townspeople will help if there is trouble, and I shouldn't be gone long, about four days. I am leaving all of your men with you, so no strangers. But I do want you to stay close to the lodge or the village. Do you understand? You won't wander off?"

"I have nowhere to be except here, so I will be fine. Go get your people settled. Just watch your back and watch the water. I made that old man mad, and he won't forget it, and he may come after you."

"I am more afraid he will come after you or Beth. Stay close promise?"

"Yes, I promise. Now go so you can get back quicker."

He kissed her soundly on the lips and then on the neck, and she said, "If you continue this, you are going to have to explain to these men why you are starting late."

"No, I won't. They already understand. Shall we go inside?"

She just looked at him, then at his smiling men; then she turned him around, pushed him to his horse, and waved goodbye as his men just grinned at her. Then she shooed all of them. "Go and be careful, all of you, and come back safe!"

Then she started to walk away as she could hear all of them laughing. She started back inside when Gretel met her halfway there.

"We need to make a trip to the village. It is Saturday, and we are out of supplies. Isn't this the day they have the market?"

"Yes, it is. We will need a wagon. See if any of the children want to come."

"The girls want to, but the boys have other activities they are training with the men today."

"Even David? He is too little to train."

"There is a boy about his age, one of the soldier's children. They have become fast friends, and he wants to stay and play with him."

"Who will be watching them?"

"Brenna will be watching over the younger children, and Doeri will be watching over the boys."

"All right, then we shouldn't be gone too long."

Robert rode with the women to the village, and when they got there, they started to fill the wagon with essentials when two knights came running through the town. They had gone through when one of them pulled up on his horse to a dead stop and turned him around. Cat recognized the tall knight; he was one of Queen Marie's. He came running back to her and jumped off the tired horse. He bowed before her as the other knight followed him and got off his horse to do the same. Robert was behind her with his hand on his sword when Catherine said, "What is wrong?"

The knight on the ground could barely breathe. So she put her hand on his shoulder, got down on her knee, and again said, "What's wrong?"

The man looked into her face; a lady shouldn't have to get on the ground to talk to him, but talk to her he did. "You are Lady Catherine?" She just nodded. "We bring you the queen's horse, but we can't get him here. We are killing him. We need help."

"Where is he?" As she stood up, she motioned for drinks for the two men, and Brian saw to it they were brought to the men; as she handed them the drinks, she asked, "Where is he now?"

"Several miles from here. The first couple of days, he was fine. But the farther away we got, the more agitated he became. Now we are either dragging him, or he is fighting us all the way. He won't eat or drink. I finally tied him to a tree and came to find you. The queen said you have a way with horses. Maybe you can help us. Otherwise, we are going to kill him."

They hadn't noticed their own horses had gotten as close to her as possible while they were talking, and Brian had just gotten out of their way. As both men turned, they saw that the horses were indeed close to her, and she reached out her hand, and they came to her; she turned to Gretel and said, "I promised to stay close and not to ride, but I made this promise a long time ago, and I am going to keep it. I will need your horse so we can get there faster. Brian, I will need a bridle and a saddle for a smaller horse sent in the wagon."

"No, my lady, you won't. Marie sent you her saddles and bridles made for this horse. It is all with Khan. I don't know if you can ride this horse, ma'am. He is a little spooky."

"Don't worry about it. What is your name again? I don't remember."

"I am Bruce, and he is Peter."

"Gretel, you can go back. Lars will be mad, but this is something I have to do."

"Just go and be careful. I will be in the wagon behind you with this other knight in case you can't ride him home."

"All right, let's go."

The knight helped her into the saddle, expecting the horse to give her some grief he always did; but no, he was as gentle as a kitten with her on his back. As soon as he was rested, they were off. He went slowly at first until she said, "I thought we were in a hurry? Let's get going."

So he started a faster gait. As it seemed they were just following the road for now, she set the pace, and it was one he could hardly keep up with. He just looked at her; the queen said she was something he wouldn't believe with horses. He hoped she was right, or he was going to fail with his promise to deliver Khan to her. He didn't want to have to kill such a beautiful animal. When they were getting close to where they had tied up the horse, he got in front of her and took her down a ravine; they could hear the horse screaming from here. Cat didn't even slow down; when she got close enough, she slid off her horse's back and told two men watching the horse to get a bucket of his feed ready. They just said, "He won't eat it."

By then, Bruce was there. "Do what the lady says now."

She started walking toward the horse; he was white except where she could see blood around his neck, where he had been fighting the ropes. She walked up to the man holding the rope around his neck and said, "Give it to me. I have got him now."

"Don't let go, or we will have to chase him all the way back to the castle."

She let the rope slacken, and the horse looked at her and stopped struggling. She started walking toward him, coiling the rope in her hand as she went; he had stopped jumping and screaming. When she got to him, he had a halter on with a lead rope hanging from it, which was tangled around his feet; she took the rope, pulled it over his head, and threw it away from her. The men just watched; they figured they were going to have to chase him down again. She got down on her knees as the horse nuzzled her hair and untangled the lead rope. He was still tied to the tree. So she led him over to the tree, untied that rope, and took it off his head. Then she threw it away and then took the horse to the stream, where he took a long drink. All the time, she stroked his neck and checked his wounds; they weren't too bad, mostly rope burns. She could feel his muscles quiver underneath the skin; he was afraid. When he had had enough to drink, she took him over to a log, sat down, and started talking to him as she stroked his face.

"Well, Khan, they think you are crazy. But you and I know you are just scared. Do you remember me from the first time we met, baby boy? It has been a long time. Well, baby, you are going to have to come with me now because Marie can't take care of you anymore. She didn't want Charles getting you."

At about that time, the wagon and Robert showed up; and he helped Gretel down out of the wagon, and they watched as Cat talked to the horse. One of the men had brought the bucket of oats to her, and she was feeding them to Khan while they sat on the log. But Robert was wondering why all the men looked like they were ready for flight.

"You all look like you are ready for something. What did I miss?"

"She took off all the ropes, and she is just holding him by a lead rope. If he takes off, we will have to catch him, and he is fast."

"I don't know if you have noticed, but she isn't holding the lead rope, hasn't been since I got here. And I doubt if he would ever run from her. *To* her? Yes. *From* her? No."

They began watching, and he was right; she wasn't holding the rope. The horse was just standing for her. Suddenly, Catherine looked up at the hill, put her hands to her face, and started to cry. Then the rest of them heard. The knights crossed themselves, kneeled, and bowed their heads; all Robert heard were bells softly in the distance.

"What is it?"

"The queen is dead, and the bells are tolling."

As they watched, Cat cried, and Khan put his head over her shoulder; they couldn't hear what she was saying, but it was something.

"She is dead, Khan. I couldn't even be with her at the end. You and I will have to mourn her by ourselves, won't we, baby boy?"

"Should we go help her?"

"No, she is fine, and don't worry about the horse running. He is hers now. He will come with her, and he won't fight anymore."

They all stood and watched as she mourned a friend quietly with her friend's horse; then Robert and Bruce began to walk toward her, and the horse started to move.

"Now he will run."

"No, now he will protect her from us. Just walk slowly until she convinces him we won't hurt her, and everything will be all right. He won't go anywhere."

Cat turned her head and saw them coming. She got up from the tree stump and gathered the lead rope from the ground so the horse wouldn't get tangled in it again; then she started walking toward them. She was barely holding the rope, and the horse was right beside her; this horse that they had fought for days was calm and being led like a pack animal. He should have gone for her sooner. There had been a reason Marie had wanted him to go to this woman; they would have had to kill him otherwise. She came up next to Robert and said, "I guess we need to be heading home. It is getting late in the day."

As she turned to the men who had escorted the horse, she asked them, "What were you supposed to do when you finished delivering the horse to me? Were you to go back to the king's services?"

Bruce answered, "We were the queen's men, so we will have to go back and find employment with the king or someone willing to pay our wages. We hadn't gotten that far yet."

She looked around at six well-armed knights and thought to herself, *I might have need of you. Besides, Marie's letter said they; there is something I am missing.*

"Shall we head back to my lodge? I may have need of some more men in my service if you are interested. You might want to talk to your men on the way back and see if they would consider it."

Bruce just nodded; he was sure they would. It was a long way back, and they would have to start at the bottom of the king's guard if they pledged to him. Further, this woman was most interesting, and his lady had spoken highly of her. Besides, he couldn't go back.

She tied the horse to the back of the wagon, and Robert put her up in the seat, and they started down the road. Khan wouldn't move; they were dragging him again, so she got down and walked beside him, and everything was all right until she went back up front; then he froze again.

Bruce rode up beside her and said, "My lady, he is standing and waiting to be saddled. He wants you to ride him, and I don't think he is going to move until you do."

She had figured he was too tired from struggling all day to be ridden. Guess she was wrong.

"Do we have a saddle and bridle small enough for him?"

Bruce dismounted and started toward the wagon; he uncovered a beautiful saddle. "Yes, my lady, the queen sent all her tack that was made special for him. It is in this wagon."

She looked over the edge and saw beautiful saddles, bridles, and blankets.

"Well, saddle him, but not with a sidesaddle. And we will go home."

It only took a few minutes to saddle the beautiful horse. Bruce was the only man he would let close to him, and Cat noticed that. Then she was helped into the exquisitely tooled saddle, and as they watched, it was like the two of them were meant to be; no more kicking, he carried her as he had carried a queen, even better. They were all astonished. As Bruce looked at Robert, all he said was, "He is hers now. That is why Marie sent him to her. Catherine taught Marie how to ride him."

They all watched her ride this amazing horse; he was smaller than theirs and could run like the wind. These horses were why the knights in the crusades were left standing still in the sand. With their armors and large horses, they were outmaneuvered every time. No one had a stallion, and they wanted Marie's, but there were no mares to breed him to; it was said some people were trying to smuggle some out, but nobody had seen any yet. Now Catherine had the only Arab stallion outside the Holy Land.

He was beautiful to watch; not even the queen had been able to make him behave like this woman could. Just watching her gallop on him was a treat after days of fighting him. She stayed close to the wagons, but Bruce had the feeling that if she wanted, she could outpace them and run like the wind. He said as much to Robert.

Robert replied, "She is pregnant, and she promised her new husband she wouldn't ride. So she is being easy. Otherwise, she would be jumping logs or fences. And with that animal, she could leave us all in the dust. But she is in danger, so she is staying close. She asked you to stay for a reason. She may need your help, and that means fighting. Are your men up for that?"

"Who would hurt her?"

"Her new husband is Raider, and it is some of his countrymen who want her gone."

"Doesn't she have Raider children?"

"Yes, two of them adopted and one of her own. Does that make a difference?"

"No, not to me. I will fight for her, and I know several of my men will also. I will have an answer from the rest by the time we get to your lodge. Is she all right to be riding? He can get out of control sometimes."

"Not with her, you watch. He will be on his best behavior. They always are."

They rode for a couple more hours, and as they got to the village, several people were running out to meet her in a panic. Brian was at the front of the crowd, and he had a pitchfork in his hand; she noticed two of the knights were getting in front of her to protect her. Well, it looked like they had made up their minds who they were going to fight for. She came up to Brian and asked him, "What is wrong? Why is everyone so upset?"

"There are boats landing, and that man that Lars sent away is back. It looks like he is going to attack the lodge, and there aren't enough men to protect it. So we were arming ourselves."

She looked back at the knights around her and said, "Well, now is the time to make a decision. If you don't want a part of this fight, leave now. If you will swear to me, come on, my family needs protection."

They all nodded, and Bruno said, "Tell us what you want us to do, and you had best stay here."

Well, that wasn't happening; she wasn't leaving her family unprotected.

"Robert, you and one of the knights get to the lodge and get everybody into the main hall. Those doors and windows can be barricaded. Gretel, you go with him and watch over the children. Brian, you and some of the other men get to the barn and turn all the horses loose. They will at least cause confusion. You knights, come with me, and we will see if we can push them back until Lars arrives."

"What makes you think he will arrive?"

"Look north. That dust is his men. I hope he has figured out that he has been betrayed, and he is coming back. If he isn't, we will all get in the lodge and wait for his return. We have food and a better fighting position there."

"You will get inside as well when we get there."

"Just as soon as I see who it is that comes looking for a fight. I want to know if it is Horic or the elder."

Robert just looked at her. "You knew they would be back."

She nodded and then started ahead, and they all followed; she had been waiting for this fight. She was surprised it had taken this long. As they got closer to the lodge, she could see the sails on the boats; they were just getting landed, so her men were a little ahead of the game. By now, the horses were loose, and knights were in place.

She could see Horic walking down the road and beside him was the elder; she was still on Khan, and Cloud was headed this way. The men were trying to get her away and into the lodge; when several men caught Khan's reins and tried to unhorse her, she kicked out and caught one under the chin. She was pretty sure she broke his jaw. She got away and off to the meadow. Now she was cornered. Horic saw her get away and followed, so did two knights; they kept his men busy while he kept coming toward her. She slid off Khan, and Cloud wasn't too far away, and she had an idea of what to do.

"My cousin told me he had planned on keeping you alive for a while because you had some fight in you. He would have enjoyed killing you slowly. I guess I will have to finish the job for him. I will deliver you back to Lars in little, tiny pieces. Then I will take his daughter, and you can't stop me."

"You think if you kill me, you will get this land from Lars and you and the elder will have it all to yourselves? Do you think I will just let you kill me? I am not tied to a post now."

"How do you intend to defend yourself? Are you going to send one of your horses after me?"

"As a matter of fact, yes, I am. Cloud!" As she brushed her arm down, the big horse ran the man down and then stomped him. She backed the big horse up and looked at the man on the ground; he was trying to stand up. He had a broken arm and a nasty gash on his head.

"I gave you a chance to leave, and you didn't. You came back no more chances."

As he stood up and came at her with a knife, she stabbed him in the chest with the knife Robert had handed her before they had separated them; she looked him in the eyes as he died, and she said, "You should have stayed gone."

As she pulled the knife out of his chest two knights watched her come toward them as Lars was quickly approaching; both stallions were on either side of her, escorting her toward the elder. Horic's men stood to one side as her men took their weapons away. She walked up in front of him as Lars came to a stop beside her; he had seen what had happened from a distance, and he wasn't close enough to help. She walked up to the old man and wiped Horic's blood from the knife on his shirt.

Then the Elder asked, "What do you plan to do with me, woman?" The knife was at his throat before he even saw her lift the blade, and for the first time, she saw fear in his eyes because he knew she could kill him without a second thought. A hand closed over hers and moved the blade away.

Then Lars said, "I am giving you another chance. She will not. If we ever see you on any of this land, we will bury you in it. Am I understood? Because if I am not, I will let her finish."

He nodded and started to walk away with his men; then he turned and said, "I thought you had betrayed us by not marrying a Raiders woman. I was wrong."

He looked down at her face, and she was angry.

"You should have stayed out of it and let me kill him! He came after me and our children. He deserved to die!" She was furious, and she still had blood all over her dress; she had been close when she killed Horic, very close. When he went over to his body, he found he had a very large knife. So she had been fighting for her life. Gretel was beside him and saw the same knife, and she had watched as Horic had threatened her.

"You should have let her finish. The elder wanted her dead, and she knew it."

He just looked at her. Catherine would have cut his throat, and then the threat would be gone. Or would it? He watched his wife escorted by two stallions as well as two new knights he didn't recognize, but they had protected her. Where had they come from, and where had the new stallion come from? He couldn't leave her alone for a couple of days without something major happening. At about that time, one of the soldiers helped her into the saddle of the new horse, and she rode the rest of the way to the stables. He was giving orders as men rounded up men still fighting and separated out the men who came with Horic and the elder.

Then Gretel grabbed his arm and said, "You had better go to her. You still don't know who you can trust except those knights with her, and I have decided she is a woman you don't want to be on the wrong side of. I am not sure how she is going to handle killing another man, so you had better go take care of her."

"She doesn't seem to need my care. She seems to be able to take care of everything by herself. If I am gone, she disobeys my orders and rides. And where did the new men come from? I think I have a right to be mad."

She just smacked him on the arm and then looked at him like he was ten years old again. "Don't you remember the queen's stallion was coming? They couldn't get it here. She had to go and get it, and when we returned, we walked into this. So she hired the knights. You know she has a way with men as well as horses, so just keep being an ass and find out how long she keeps you. You weren't here to protect her and the children. You trusted the elder, and it almost cost her life. But she saw your dust, and she stalled for time until you could get here."

"I didn't want her to ride because of the baby."

"If she was going to lose a baby, she would have done it by now. And she wouldn't have done it riding, more likely fighting with Horic. He scared me more than her riding. He talked to her before she stabbed him. Ask her what he said to her. I'll bet it wasn't nice." He looked down at his sister and started to walk down to the stables.

"Go to the lodge. I will meet you inside. Have a bath drawn for her. We will be in soon."

Cat had taken the horses down to the barn, and James had taken Cloud to his stall at the end of the barn. Cat took Khan to the opposite end; when she had him in the stall, Robert asked, "Catherine, are you all right?"

She ran out of the stall to the back of the barn, threw up, and then just leaned on the corral fence. At about that time, Lars rounded the side of the barn and saw what was happening; he took her hands, which were knotted into fists, and held her against him. The blood was still wet on her dress. Her hands were crossed against her breasts, and she was shaking so bad he didn't know how she was standing up.

Then she said, "I am so tired." Her eyes rolled back in her head, and she just melted in his arms; he yelled for Robert as he held her and just sat down on the ground.

"Go get some water. She won't want the children to see her like this." He just held her as she shook in his arms with her hands in fists. She was like a child having a tantrum; it was Gretel who took care of her. She had seen what was happening and had come running while Robert went to get water.

"Just hold her and talk to her. What happened?"

He just looked at his sister and brushed the hair back out of Catherine's face. "I don't know. She came around the barn, got sick, said she was tired, and then collapsed in my arms."

"It has just been too much today with the queen dying and all of this. She just had too much. She will be all right. Give her a little while."

Robert was there by then with a bowl of clean water and cloths. Gretel started to bathe her face, neck, and anywhere else she could get to.

"What do you mean the queen dying today?"

"When we went to get the horse, we heard the bells, and the knights that had brought the horse said that meant the queen was dead."

He looked down at Cat. Her hands were beginning to relax, and she was shaking less, and her eyes were beginning to flutter open.

"She really liked that lady. They were great friends. We heard the bells, but I didn't know what they meant. It has been a long day for her."

Cat began to breathe easier, and her eyes opened; as the new knights came around the barn, they saw her on the ground and asked if Lars needed help with her. He told them no and then told them to put up their horses and come inside; they would be taken care of and tomorrow he would get acquainted with them. Robert helped Catherine stand. Lars got off the ground, picked her up, and carried her inside. She didn't even argue with him; she was just too tired.

When he got her to their room, he set her on the floor and quickly helped her bathe to get the blood off her; then he put her in a clean gown and put her to bed. He watched for a bit, then went to settle the house and make preparations to send the elder and his men away again and make sure his house was secure. He had put their lives in danger, and it wouldn't happen again; he had decided the ship carrying the elder home was not going to arrive with him alive. He hadn't protected her once, and it had cost her; he wouldn't let it happen again. When he went back to their room, he got in bed and pulled her to him. She couldn't kill the elder; his people would hate her. But the elder could have an accident, and he would never haunt her again. She reached up to touch his face and rolled over to snuggle in his arms; he would protect her this time—even if it had to be murder.

Sometime during the night, she woke; she didn't know why, but she wasn't scared. As she rolled over, she knew. She sat up and put her legs over the side of the bed and stared at the corner of the bedroom. Lars awoke and rose up on his elbow, and before he could speak, she put her hand on his arm and said, "Shhhh . . . look in the corner of the room. Don't you see her?"

He couldn't see anything except a swirl of smoke; at least he thought it was smoke, but it didn't evaporate. It just hung in the air. There was also a lovely scent of perfume he had never smelled before in the air; it was definitely not Catherine's. As if she was reading his mind, she said, "It is Marie's perfume you smell in here. I don't know why she has come. Her horse is safe."

Then the wisps of smoke—he didn't know what else to call them—came toward them and went through the window. Cat grabbed her robe and started out the door.

"Where are you going now? She is gone."

As she turned, she simply said, "To the barn. I think there is more I am supposed to know."

As if this happened every day. Well, maybe it did in her world. So he grabbed a robe and followed her. She cut through the main room and passed a guard, who was half-asleep, and Lars started to rap him on the shoulder to awaken him, and then thought better of it; maybe they didn't want an audience for this. She went to the barn where Khan was being kept, and as she entered, sure enough, there was the wisp of smoke as she calmed Khan. Then out of the corner walked in Bruce Cat looked at him, and then she realized what Marie was trying to tell her.

"It's you she is trying to tell me about. She finally took a lover, and she sent him to me with her stallion, and she is making sure you are safe and that I know about you." He just nodded, came forward, and stroked the horse's head; and Khan let him.

"Khan was the only time we could be together, and so I couldn't let him die. It would have been like losing her all over again, so I came to get you. She said you were the only one who could take care of him. I think King Charles was figuring out what was going on, and she sent me away, or I would have stayed with her till the end."

"The king could take as many lovers as he wanted, but he expected Marie to be faithful always even though it hurt her to be second. I am glad she had you, but you can never go back. He will kill you if he knows, so you are mine as well as Khan. That is why she is here. You must promise to stay with me, or she will not rest. She wants you safe from Charles's wrath, and she knows I can protect you. You must promise to stay with me."

"Yes, my lady. From now on, I am your man, whatever you need."

As she turned to the wisp in the corner still hovering, she looked up at it and said, "All right, Marie, I think everything is taken care of now. I will take it from here. Rest in peace, my friend. I will love you always. Come, Lars, let's leave them alone. If you want to come inside, there is a bed waiting for you. Good night." She took Lars's hand, and they walked away. But as she turned back, she saw the wisp of smoke leaving the barn and Bruce on his knees, crying by the white horse; he had really loved Marie. Cat was glad. Marie deserved at least that at the last of her life.

"Can you protect him from the king, or were you just trying to pacify Marie?" What was he saying? He was talking about a ghost.

"The king shouldn't come after me. Marie and I were really good friends, and he doesn't know how much she really told me about him, and I think that scares him sometimes. All the gifts were to pay wages and take care of her horse if I ever needed money, which I don't. But she was just making sure I was well taken care of. I thought there was something going on, but she couldn't put it on paper. It might have wound up in the wrong hands. That is why the horse was sent only to me with that escort.

She was protecting the people she had to get out of the king's way, and that was the only way to do it."

"And the jeweler; was the necklace a message too?"

She looked at him.

"In a way, she was telling me she was dying and to watch out for myself, and she did what she did about the land. As a last gesture, she was telling me to hurry. We were running out of time. If things had gone wrong, I could have used the necklace to buy the land. The deal was in place, and the necklace was the price, but it all worked out the way she wanted it to."

"Why didn't you tell me any of this?

"There are too many people I don't know or trust, and this was between me and Marie, and it could have been screwed up so easily. Did you know Horic wanted your position and had talked to the king about replacing you?"

He just looked at her and started to ask her how she knew, but he already knew the answer.

"When did you two start putting this in motion?"

"When I realized I wasn't crazy and I was in love with you and what needed to be done, I contacted her. She got back with me and told me she was very ill, and we went from there. Robert and James have helped me. I have always been able to trust them with my life and now with yours. Marie needed some things, but she wouldn't tell me what they were. She didn't have anyone to trust enough to send messages through till now. She wanted her lover protected, so she sent him with her beloved stallion. She knew I couldn't come to her funeral, so they would be safe here."

"Why couldn't you go to the funeral? You are a lady of the court and a friend of the queen. Why wouldn't you be welcomed at the king's court?"

"Because I might be too welcomed at the king's court. He has roving eyes, and they settled on me at one time, and Giles didn't like it at all. So Marie started coming to my keep instead of me going to the castle.

That's why all of this has been done in secret by her and me under his nose and away from his eyes until the last minute, including our marriage."

"You mean the king wanted you?"

"At one time, he thought he did. But he wouldn't have liked me, I am sure. So it is done now, and I am just a memory, an old one."

He looked at his wife and wondered if the king still thought about his wife as an old memory, or was Cat just hiding from him? Marie had been worried enough to keep her away from him. They walked back into the main room, and this time, he did thump the guard on the shoulder to wake him to stand guard as they went back to bed. Cat lay down and went back to sleep as if nothing had happened. Lars lay awake for a bit. He wondered about this woman he had married; she had negotiated a peace and a land deal right under his nose. She talked to ghosts, and she killed a man today, and now she slept in his arms like nothing had happened. Maybe she was kin to the Valkyrie, and he was lucky enough to have caught her. Anyway, she was his, and he was keeping her.

Days were dragging into weeks, and still, they weren't ready to go home. Cat was growing larger by the day; this child was going to be big. They had decided she had guessed wrong on the dates, and it was probably Giles's baby. But every time she said that, Gretel smiled at her and just walked away. She had finally told Lars she was going home before she got too big to travel and that he could follow, but he said they would leave within the next two weeks. Then he got a message from an arriving boat, and plans changed rapidly; it seemed the elder had come down with a fever and died out on the ocean and been buried at sea. Lars would have to tell his people, and they would have to elect a new one. The look on Lars's and Gretel's faces told a different story; he had been killed at Lars's order, and Cat couldn't have been happier. Finally, she didn't have to worry about that man anymore.

They started packing the next day, and it didn't take long to get things organized to leave. Gretel was going with them. Sasha was going home to her children, and Breanna was having her children brought to her to live at the lodge. Lars's sons Latt and Victor were staying here to take care of the lodge and go back and forth between the lodge and the keep. Doeri was going back north to take care of his father's land there and come back in the summertime to see the family and bring his family here.

Four of the new knights were staying here as they had found women they liked, but Bruce and Peter were going with them. Cat had insisted; she had promised to protect them, and only the four of them knew who she had promised, but they were hers now. Cat didn't know, but Lars had told Gretel and no one else about that night, and she had looked at him in disbelief; then she hugged him and said, "The gods are looking out for you in that woman. Keep her close, and she will protect you."

"Even if she is not having my child?"

"Who says that is not your child? You are both fools. Wait and see."

As she walked away, he wondered what she knew that he didn't; women, there were too many women around here, and the men were outnumbered.

It wasn't but a few more days and they were on the road to the keep, and Cat couldn't have been happier. She was getting bigger, and she was uncomfortable, and she just wanted to get home. She had things to do to get ready for this child, and she had some new rooms to open and get renovated. Lars had been watching her, and there was something wrong; she was afraid, and it wasn't about the baby. She had something else on her mind, but she wouldn't talk to him about it.

The traveling was not so bad; they had inns to stay at every night and were most comfortable all the way back to the keep. They took their time because Cat was tired easily. On the sixth day, they finally arrived; and when the doors finally opened on the carriage, the children poured out, and Helen came running out of the keep. The children looked back at Catherine, and she just waved her hand and said, "Go, you are free. We will take care of this later." She just smiled as they almost knocked Helen down.

Lars got down, then turned and helped Cat down; then Gretel looked out to see her new home and was amazed at the size of it. Lars reached to help her down, and she looked at him and said, "You never said it was so big."

"It is bigger inside."

Helen saw her mistress and came over to her and said, "My lady is everything all right?"

"Helen, this is Lars Sorenson, my new husband, and his sister. This is Beth's papa and this baby's father."

Helen had tears in her eyes, and Cat put her hand on her cheek and said, "It is going to be all right, I promise." Helen just shook her head yes and walked back to the children and took them into the house.

"She is afraid for you." Catherine just started to walk to the house; there was so much more that could go wrong right now. She wasn't worried about the baby; in fact, she was feeling pretty good about that.

When she got inside, she started to give orders about new sleeping arrangements and setting new guard posts. She had already told Bruce and the other men where to take the new stallions and how she wanted them separated. She wanted them close to the keep, where she could keep an eye on both of them, and she wanted Bruce to sleep in the keep.

Lars just listened to all of these orders until she was through, and then she said the rest was just unloading the wagons and carriages. She turned toward Helen and asked her if she would show Gretel where her new bedroom was while she showed Lars where theirs was. She took Lars's hand and started up the staircase to her room, and when she got to the door, he stopped her. "Is this your room?"

She shook her head yes. He reached in front of her and opened the door; then he turned, picked her up, carried her in, and then just stood there. It was a beautiful room, much like the room at the lodge; he had brought the lodge back with him to please her. Even here, he could almost feel Giles. He sat her down and walked around the room; it was big and beautiful. At the window, he could see land going on for miles; he could see the horses and her roses in the walled back garden. He could hear the children playing above him, and he could see the fear in her eyes.

"What am I missing? You are terrified, and it is only since Marie died. What is wrong?"

"I know some things the king may find to be a threat to him, and I don't know if he will act on them or not."

"And if he does, what will you do?"

"It will be a mistake on his part to mess with me. I know too much, but it may be messy, and I didn't want you or the children involved. But Marie left me no choice."

"We will deal with that when it comes and not before. You are tired and need to rest."

"Not yet, I would like to show you the house. It is yours now too. Come with me." They walked down the hall to where he could hear the children playing in a big room, and they found the playroom, a larger room with carpets on the floor and tapestries on the wall windows with light pouring in a lovely room for children.

"I was buying items for this room when your men found me at the fair that day."

"When you stepped in front of the two horses that were fighting?"

"Yes, and you saw Beth for the first time. I forgot you were there too."

"You scared me to death when you stepped out in front of those horses. I had never seen anyone do that before."

She took his hand, and they kept walking; there were more bedrooms on past the main room, and she showed him those rooms and explained she was having some more done so his relatives could come and visit in comfort anytime they wanted to.

They walked down a back hallway into the garden, and there was a bench. She sat down, and they just sat and looked at her roses and the flowers.

"This is my favorite place. I can see the horses and smell the flowers, and it is cool back here, and I can hear the children upstairs. I know this is all a little daunting for you. It is like I have brought you into

Giles's world, but really, it was my world first. Do you think you can handle all this change, or is this going to be too much?"

"You saw the look on my face when we got to your room. It looked like the room at the lodge, and it spooked me a little. But as you say, this was your house first, not his. And now it is our house. Why is Helen so afraid for you?"

"I have already told you, but this pregnancy is nothing like that one. So don't worry."

"I am going to worry till this baby is born and healthy, and so are you."

"Gretel isn't worried, so listen to her. Shall we go back inside the keep?"

"No, let's just sit out here for a while and look at your beautiful roses. You know, I don't think I have ever seen such pretty ones."

He put his arm around her and kissed her until Ann leaned out the window and yelled, "Mama, William's got my cat!"

She just raised her eyes up and said, "Time to be parents again."

Lars just smiled.

That night, as they again went back to their bedroom, he noticed changes. The bedding had been changed, and two chairs that hadn't been here earlier were here now, and a new rug was on the floor; it looked entirely different. Catherine came up behind him and said, "Better? Not so much Giles?"

So she had noticed earlier; that is why she had hustled him out of here so fast. "You didn't have to do that." He turned around, held her in his arms, and kissed her neck.

"Yes, I did. I saw that look on your face when we walked in here. All you saw was the lodge, and it hurt you, and I don't want you to only see Giles in here. I want you to see us."

He walked over to the window, opened it, and looked out at the land and buildings; it was a beautiful place he hadn't noticed before. She put her arms around him and looked out as well. Then he asked her, "Did you ever look for me out this window?"

She walked in front of him and stood looking out and said, "Every night until one night, Giles told me he thought the only way you wouldn't have come back for me was if you were dead."

As he slid his arms around her, he asked, "Were you afraid of him when he first came?"

As he held her, she decided no more lies. "Yes, very afraid. But he was very gentle and slow, and I finally gave into him and trusted him."

"Were you afraid of me when you were with me?"

"Yes, but the laudanum and the pain made things different. I began to want you, and then, you too, were gone. Then I didn't care if I lived or died until I found out I was going to have Beth. After Beth came, I looked for you every night, and then the nightmares started, and I didn't sleep at all."

They didn't say any more; so much time had been wasted, but he was glad it had been Giles who had been there for her and not someone else; she had needed someone like him. Tomorrow she planned to make this more of his world; she wanted him comfortable here, and that meant including him in the everyday running of the keep. As they lay down, he could almost see her planning tomorrow. She would make this their world come hell or high water. Just watch.

He kissed her neck and said, "Go to sleep, Mama. We have a long day tomorrow." He laid his hand on her rounding belly and got a sharp kick from the infant inside. All he could think was, *Be good to your mama, little one. She is tired.*

CHAPTER 13

As the weeks went on, Cat thought maybe the king had forgotten about her, and she went about her life. She was getting bigger by the day, and she suspected this child was going to be earlier than expected and big. But every time she brought it up to Gretel, she just smiled and walked away; it was infuriating. Bruce and Peter were working in nicely; she could see Bruce still dearly missed Marie, but there was nothing to do about that. He talked to her about it sometimes, but there was no one else he could confide in. Who else do you tell you had an affair with a queen?

Ann and Jacob had talked to Catherine about going with Beth this summer to the lodge after the baby was born if everything was all right and staying with Latt and Victor. They still didn't quite know what to do with the feelings they had for each other and thought maybe they could sort it out by being with other Raiders. Cat had a feeling it had been sorted out a long time ago in a barn when he had taken on the role of her protector, and it would never change; that was for them to figure out, and they would.

Catherine had been watching the children with the horses, and she had noticed Beth and David had the gift with horses, Beth especially. They followed her around like they had her as a child; she didn't even notice it yet. After the baby was born, she would start to teach them how to train the horses to behave. Even a Raiders woman could use that skill; she would be well thought of among her people, and she wanted her well thought of. Lord, she was tired of just sitting and doing nothing; it was boring. She had workmen working on the house, and they—furniture builders and guards—were everywhere.

Then what she was afraid of happened—the king made his presence known. A small group of men came to the front of the keep and asked for an audience with the lady of the keep. When told who was at the gate, she started issuing orders, and Lars started asking questions. "Who are these men, and why are you so upset?"

"They are from the king, and I am sure they want something I don't intend to give them. See that they are taken around to the back of the house, and I will see them by the corrals."

He looked at her strangely, and she just said, "It will be fine."

As soon as he left, she grabbed Robert by the arm and told him, "Get both stallions in the back corral close to the garden and get Bruce and the children in the house. Set guards on the house. I don't want anybody I don't know in this house, and tell Bruce don't show his face outside."

He just nodded and started doing what she wanted; he already had an idea what this was about. He told John and James to escort her outside, and he was sure Lars wasn't far behind.

The five men being escorted into her garden were Duke Lloyd Dunton and four of his men; as he came up to her, he asked her if he could dismount, and she said, "You may, but only you." He looked surprised that she would order him about, but he had been told she was an exceptional woman. He dismounted and walked toward her; she was very pregnant. This should be a simple-enough problem to take care of, and then it was back to the castle.

"I had heard you had remarried after Lord Giles died. I was sorry to hear of his death."

By now, Lars had joined them.

"This is my husband, Lars Sorenson. Lars, this is Duke Dunton, and he seems to want something."

The duke began to look uneasy. Most women didn't act like this; they were more, well, womanly.

"The king would like to buy back the stallion the queen gave you and have him escorted back by the man who brought him to you." He looked at her most pleased with himself; he figured this wouldn't take long, and he could be gone.

Then she just looked up at him and said, "*No*, not a chance in hell that you or the king is ever going to have the horse or the man. He just wants the horse so he can butcher him and serve him for dinner because Queen Marie liked him, and we both know why he wants the man. The king could have all the women he ever wanted, but Marie waited for what was left, and she waited till she could no longer have any more children. He told her she was of no more use to him. No, I have both, and I protect them. And if he wants them, it will take a fight."

"Do you think a horse is worth a fight?"

"Have you ever seen the horse?"

"No."

She took his arm and started to walk to the corrals, and when they got there, she opened the gate to Cloud and Khan. "These are my stallions. Aren't they beautiful?"

As he looked, he wondered why they weren't killing each other, and then he remembered he had been told she was good with horses; if he knew how good he would never had walked into this corral with her.

"By the way, tell your man with the crossbow that if he is thinking about shooting either one of my horses, he had better look up at the battlements. He lets loose an arrow or even thinks about it, he will be dead before he hits the ground."

There were at least twenty men gathered on the battlements and that many more on the ground, and they were all armed.

"You were expecting someone, weren't you? If not me, someone."

She just smiled at him.

"I knew Charles was too petty to let it go."

"What about the necklace? Where is it?"

"The one I wore at my wedding? The one the original owner knew was at my wedding?"

"He was there?"

"He was not, but one of his men was. I thought it best it was returned. Or were you planning on killing him too? I would like to know how you go about killing a czar's nephew."

He had misread this lady, and now he was in trouble. She never even blinked.

"What do you plan on doing now? Have your horses run me down?"

"Well, I have had them do it before. After that, the man still came after me, and I stabbed him with a very long knife. But he had been warned twice. You have been warned only once."

"Am I really supposed to believe you are that good with horses?"

She just breathed deeply and backed up in front of Cloud, and Robert and Lars both stopped breathing. Lars started toward her, and Robert said, "Stand still. Don't spook him. If you do, he could miss and kill her."

She raised her hand up, and Cloud was up and pawing the air; then she put her hand down, and he landed with both feet on either side of her. All she said was, "Yes, I am. Tell the king they are both mine, and I keep them, the man and the horse. And if need be, I will call Giles's family from France. We found out why his family starved all those years ago, and they will help me if I need them."

The duke didn't know what that was about, but he had a feeling the king did, and it wasn't good. A simple little errand wasn't a simple matter with this woman. He had been told Queen Marie and this woman were nothing to be messed with, so now he knew why the king had sent him. She had been right; the animal was to have been slaughtered and the man killed, and now he had to go back and tell the king. He was going to be lucky if he didn't wind up on the gallows. If his daughter wasn't carrying the king's grandchild by his youngest son, he wouldn't go back at all, but he still had her to protect.

He started to head to the horses. Cat turned to the stallions, put her hand in Cloud's mane, and held on. Now if she could just keep the two of them from killing each other till these men left. Lars saw what she did, and he walked toward the duke, but he told Robert, "Take care of Cat while I talk to that man."

Robert could see Cat was struggling with the horses, and something else was wrong, but she didn't want the duke to see. He walked up behind her, and she said, "Help me get them separated and into their paddocks like this is normal. Where is Lars going?"

As he grabbed Khan's halter and started to lead him away, he told her, "He wants to talk to the duke."

Cat just looked back and wondered at that conversation. Before the duke could remount, Lars turned him around and said, "I don't know all that my wife told you, but if she needs the men from France to protect her, she will also have all my men from the North of England and the North Country if she needs them. If your king wants a war, he can have one. She holds her allegiance dearly and her friendships even more, and he shouldn't threaten Catherine—not now, not ever. He wanted this treaty for a long time. Don't make me regret it, or the Raiders raids can start again with a vengeance."

The duke just nodded and looked back at Catherine walking the horses away. What had he walked into? He had always been a friend to Marie, and now he felt like he was betraying her.

Lars had men follow the duke and his men until they were well off their land, and then he followed Cat to the barn. "What do you want to do?"

"I was just talking to Robert, and I think we need to send for Giles's men in France. I will send money to pay them, and we will camp them outside the walls just in case."

"Cat, you know they will come just because you ask. They are as mad about what happened as you and Giles were."

She looked at him and smiled. "Everybody should be paid for a day's work. Get some men on the way there. You decide whom to trust, and make it fast. I don't know when or if he will make a move on us."

Robert turned and started down to the end of the barn, leaving the two of them alone because he knew she was going to have to start doing some explaining. Lars grabbed her shoulders to turn her around, and she winced and scooted away from him; then he realized she was hurt.

"What is it?" As Cat grabbed her shoulder, Lars gently moved her hand, pulled the dress aside, and looked; there was a large bruise already turning black.

"Is it broken? He got too close this time, didn't he?" he asked as he gently pulled the dress back up.

"Yes, I moved a little and got in his way. It was my fault."

"Why, you promised you wouldn't do it again, and the children were watching from the playroom window. They saw you do it this time. They have never seen you do it before. How are you going to explain that to them?"

"He goaded me. He asked me just how much control I thought I had over my horses, and my vanity took over from there. I just had to wipe that smirk off his face."

He put his forehead to hers and said, "My love, you are going to be the death of me."

She looked up at him and said, "Please don't say that, not that Giles said that once."

He just hugged her gently and took her arm, and they headed inside.

Once inside, they were surrounded by the children at the door, and the first question was by Beth. "Can you teach me how to do that?"

Lars looked down at Cat with that "I told you so" look, and she looked at the children and said, "No, that is very dangerous, and I was trying to make a point. We may have trouble coming, so there are a bunch of French soldiers from Giles's side of the family coming to protect us, I hope. Michel, we will need to make some space for them. Can you and Robert start planning? Jacob, will you help?"

Lars just looked at her as he was being shut out again.

"I was kind of hoping we might get some help from your men, if we needed it."

At that, he smiled; she asked, not ordered, for a change—like he was actually in charge of something.

"Yes, I think they would be pleased to help. In fact, I told the duke that the men from the English coast and the North Country would help if need be."

"Don't you think you'd better warn them in case he goes after them so they won't be surprised?"

"I already have two men picked out to go to them. You go upstairs. I will meet you up there in a little while."

She talked to the children, told them more about what was going on, and explained more about the horses; then she went upstairs. Before she got upstairs, Bruce meets her at the top of the stairs and asked to talk to her. "I will give myself up to him, and this will all go away, and you will be safe. I just wanted to tell you before I left."

She took his arm and led him into one of the side rooms. "You really think this is just about you? Once before when Marie had a favorite horse, Charles tried to ride it, it threw him. Charles was furious, and even worse, Marie laughed. A week later, at a supper, he had the horse served as steaks to Marie and his guests. It made her ill, and Charles told her he got the last laugh. I was brought a beautiful necklace of emeralds to wear on my wedding day, and I wore them for everyone to see. They were a gift from the czar's nephew to Queen Marie, but it made Charles furious. She wore them every chance she could just to make him mad. The necklace was from the king to the boy's mother when she was the king's lover, and he wanted them back and the boy dead. Marie and I hid the boy, and only I know where he is now."

"I told the duke they were returned, but I still have them. If he comes after me, I am going to use them as leverage. So you see, you aren't the only pawn in this game. But you are under my protection, and you aren't going anywhere. Charles is a bully, and Marie couldn't fight back. I can, and I will. I promised to protect you and that boy, and I intend to do just that."

"Now I know why she liked you so much. You could do and say what she couldn't, and I will stay and fight because she couldn't."

"Now you are getting the idea. Now go get some sleep and don't think about leaving again. Marie would never forgive me if something happened to you."

He reached down, took her hand, and kissed it. "She couldn't have picked a better friend."

"No, it was the other way around she saved my life once."

Then he walked out of the room, feeling lighter than he had for a while even though he was probably the start of a small war; he had to say, though, if you had to fight for something, these two women were worth fighting for.

"By the way, what happened to the boy?"

"He is safe, and the king won't find him."

Then she just smiled.

Lars came looking for her and passed Bruce, who actually had a smile on his face as he passed him in the hallway. He found Cat in one of the small rooms, and she was headed to their bedroom. She smiled up at him. "Are you mad at me? I seem to cause you a lot of trouble."

He looked down at her and smiled as they walked to the bedroom; she was making so many changes the house didn't even look the same as when they came the first day. She wanted so badly for him to feel like it was his home.

"Yes, I don't know what I am going to do with you. I am so bored. There is never anything going on around here. My pregnant sedate wife who never does anything except remodel the house to suit me, start wars to protect other people, let horses jump over her head to irritate royalty—it is just too boring around here."

He looked down at her, then picked her up, went into their room, and pushed the door shut with his foot. He stood her on the floor, started to undo her dress, and slide it off her shoulder; as he did, he saw the bruise.

Cloud didn't miss just a little—he missed a lot. Her shoulder and part of her arm were bruised; he didn't say a word. What was done was done, and right now, all he wanted was to hold her. He dropped the dress and then the chemise on the floor, and then he saw his very pregnant wife; it didn't take him long to get out of his clothes and then to make it to the bed. He threw back the covers, laid her down, and carefully lay on top of her.

She said, "I am not going to break." So being careful of her shoulder, he entered her; and sure enough, she didn't break. They made love like they hadn't had each other in years, fast and furious; and when they both reached the explosion they wanted, she still clung to his sweaty body. He rolled over and held her to him.

"Don't go."

"I wasn't going anywhere. I thought you would be more comfortable without me and the little one on top of you." She rubbed her tummy and received a sturdy kick; then she put his hand over the spot, and he got a respectable kick as well.

"I think we have disturbed him or her." As he kept rubbing her stomach, he finally put his head on her belly and said, "Hey, little girl, I am your papa. You be good in there." That was the first time he had ever acted like this child was his more than saying the words.

"What would you like if you had a choice, a boy or a girl?"

He looked at her lovingly and said, "You alive and a healthy baby. But if I had a choice maybe a little girl. I missed the first one." He just lay next to her for a long while till she fell asleep, and then he again prayed, *Please let this be all right and let them both live.* Then he covered them up, and they all rested.

Within a week, there were troops camped outside the walls and Raiders on the way. They had only a brief sighting of royal men in the vicinity, one of three occasions, and she thought maybe the king had lost interest in her. She had finally told Lars about the reason the French troops had come to her so willingly and had refused payment. When Giles's family was starving in France during the war, he had made arrangements for supplies to be sent to them on a regular basis; it wasn't until later that he had received a letter from a cousin that told them they were starving. He had headed back, only to find out he was too late; they were all dead. They had died from starvation or disease, and his supplies had been rerouted by the king to his troops instead.

Giles had lost everything—all his land, family, and titles to a king he had unwaveringly fought for; he had been furious. Catherine had convinced him there was nothing they could do about it at the time, and he had died a short time later. But he had been able to tell what was left of his family what had happened, and that is why they were here now.

Several days later, Latt arrived telling them the Raiders villages had been raided but were able to withstand the attacks because of the early warning. The king's men weren't ready for them to be armed and on the offensive, so they had been knocked back easily; it seemed Lars's warning to the king hadn't been heeded.

Since then, there had been very little activity around the keep; few men had been seen. She had a visitor she had never expected to ever see again a few days later. Caroline came to the garden one afternoon and said there were visitors who wished to see her; she was sitting with Gretel, and she had the couple escorted back when she saw who it was. She started to regret her decision to see her. The couple standing before her was Jane and Kevin; she knew they had stayed, but they had stayed out of her way all of these years. Why did they want to see her now? Then behind them came Father Marques and two children, a boy of about five and a girl about three. Jane immediately went to her knees and Kevin followed. Gretel turned and looked at her; she had never seen anyone do this in front of Catherine, and she wondered if she should leave. Cat put her hand on Gretel's leg as if to tell her to stay where she was.

"What do you want, Jane? I haven't seen you in all these years. I had figured all our business was done, especially since Giles is gone."

As Jane looked up, she looked at the Father Marques and then the children. Cat could see there was a story here, so she just waited.

"My lady, I owe you an apology long overdue for all those years ago, and now I have to pay the bill."

"Just get on with it, Jane. What do you want?"

She and Kevin were both still on the ground and Robert and Jennie were behind her by now; this confession was going to be very public.

"Those two children, Kevin and I are married we have been for ten years. Several months ago while you were gone, there was a fire in a neighboring village. Kevin helped put it out. He saved the children, but their mother was killed. We would like to adopt the children, but Father Marques said we have to apologize to you and ask your permission."

"I thought you didn't care for children. You told someone that once." She didn't use names, for they both knew who she was talking about.

"I have discovered what a fool I was, and we have tried for years with no success. We would really like a chance to have a family. We would be very good to them."

"All right, all right, get off your knees. It doesn't look good in front of the children. What do you think of this idea, Kevin?"

He rose, helped Jane up, and then held her arm. Cat noticed all of this and then motioned for the children to come over to her. After they were in front of her, she asked, "Who are these people?" She pointed to Jane and Kevin.

The little boy answered, "He is our new father, and she is our new mother."

"Are they good to you? Do they feed you and keep you warm?"

"Yes, and they hold Mary at night when she cries about the fire."

"Did she get burned?"

"A little, but she saw our other mother die when the beam fell on her, and Kevin pulled Mary out of the fire. Her dress was burning. He burned his hands."

"Kevin, let me see."

As he held out his hands, he had indeed been burned and still had some damage to his arm. She looked up at him; this obviously wasn't the same man who had held her at sword point years ago.

"You want them as well and will treat them as your own and not mistreat them?"

"Yes, my lady."

She looked at them again and then looked at Father Marques. He was smiling and shook his head yes, so she turned back and said, "All right, but I will keep an eye on both of you. And if I hear that you have mistreated these children, I will take them away from you. Are you agreeable? Kevin, before you leave, I want to give you some salve for that burn. It will help heal it better than what you are using."

He just looked at her and then said, "You would help me after what I did to you?"

"That was a long time ago, and this makes up for it. But I had better not ever find out you have beaten those children, or I will come down on you like the wrath of God."

He watched as she went to get the salve for his arm. What an idiot he had been in his youth and how many years he had lost; now he had Jane and a family.

After everybody had gone, Caroline suggested she go upstairs and rest and she would take care of the children. She looked at Gretel. "You would think I was a hundred years old, crippled."

Gretel took her arm, walked beside her, and told her, "I have been waiting to have some time to talk to you by myself. Maybe this is the right time to do it."

"Well, maybe it is. Let's go. We can go to the solar on the second floor. It will be cool up there, and we will be alone. Is that all right?"

"Sounds perfect to me."

She called back down to the kitchen for a plate of bread and cheese and some cold buttermilk and wine for Gretel. As they climbed the stairs, she felt like she weighed as much as one of her horses; she had never gotten this big with one of her pregnancies, and she wasn't eating that much. Gretel thought it was time they talked because she wasn't eating enough.

"I want to hear what happened to this pregnancy that has everybody so scared for you. This one seems to be progressing fine, but if you sneeze, they all look like you are going to die. I would like to know what happened."

"I was about five months along, and a fever broke out in the village, and I went to help. I had the keep sealed—no one in or out after I left. Everything went well for a few days. The fever was nothing like I had seen before—high fever, vomiting, and aches. I lost older people and two babies, and there was nothing to do except try and keep the fever down and give them plenty of liquids. We had a fire break out in a small barn, and there was nobody to fight it except five men. So we did the best we could to keep it from spreading and then just let it burn. As we stood to the side, it collapsed in on itself, and a corral collapsed as well. One of the top rails fell on me, and I was caught under it. The men got me out from under it and took me to the church.

"Giles was there by then. He had seen the smoke and refused to stay in the keep any longer. Father Marques brought Giles to the church. There was little they could do. It was enough to miscarry the baby. Between the fever and the blood loss, I barely survived, but I did. All the children saw was me white as a ghost and as weak as a kitten for a month. But the fever didn't come to the keep, and it was gone soon after. Now why do you smile every time I ask you about this baby and how big I am getting?"

Gretel smiled again, but this time, she said, "I have a secret, but you have to eat something while I tell it to you. And you can't tell Lars until the right time."

"When is the right time?"

"Oh, you will know."

As she began her story, Cat began to laugh, and then she stopped her and called for Jennie and Caroline. "You might as well only tell this story once because this is too good."

After she called for the women, she called down for some food—well, really lots of food—and asked Helen to join them upstairs too. They might as well make an afternoon out of it. When all the women were in attendance, the story started again with Cat telling all of them what had happened to her the last time, and they all agreed that the miscarriage couldn't have been avoided now that they knew what had happened. Now the good part started, and Gretel started to tell her story; and as they ate and laughed, several men were listening one floor below.

"What do you think is going on up there?" Lars looked at Robert, and Robert just shrugged his shoulders; by then, James had joined the group and looked up.

"Should we go check on them?"

Robert grabbed his shoulder. "Are you crazy? The children are upstairs, and our wives are all laughing, and the Frenchmen are jousting out on the field. I say we run and watch them before anyone knows we are gone."

They all looked at one another and, not running but briskly walking, left the keep before anyone could stop them to go see a bunch of Frenchmen knock one another off their horses. They were smiling too.

It was quite interesting watching them try to kill one another in a mock battle. Lars had never seen this before and didn't understand.

"They are not trying to kill each other. They are just trying to unhorse the other man. Why, what is the point? If I was doing this, I would be trying to take off the other man's head, not just knock him off the horse or kill his horse."

Robert turned to him and said, "Do not ever tell Cat that you cut up a horse in battle or otherwise. Do you understand me? She will never forgive you."

Lars looked at him as though he was kidding, but the look he got from Robert and James told him they weren't.

"But it was battle. She would understand."

They both looked at him, and James grabbed his shoulder, saying, "Not even if someone was trying to kill you would she understand. Don't ever tell her that you ever hurt horses. Promise us, or you will regret it." They were serious.

"I promise I never hurt a horse."

Then they went back to watching the jousting.

The women had moved to the garden and were watching as well except Cat; she was watching a mare in the herd of the Frenchmen when she asked Caroline, "Look at that white mare in the herd. Doesn't she look smaller than the rest of them?"

"Yes, a lot smaller. She looks like Khan."

As she looked, Catherine got up. "That's what I thought too. Let's go see."

And she started walking toward the temporary corral set up for the Frenchmen's horses. As they walked out to the corral, several men noticed her; and they went to their commanding officer, who was on the field at the time. After he got off of his horse, he was told that the women were going toward the corrals, and he noticed them too. Surely, they wouldn't get too close, but he would see that she was stopped. He could see the Raiders lord standing at the side of the arena; he could take care of the woman. There was a stallion that was wild and dangerous in there. He walked toward the Raider as he watched the women, and she wasn't slowing down; now she was at the gate.

"Stop, there is a dangerous horse in there."

She just looked at him and walked in. Was this woman stupid? He got up to the Raider and grabbed his arm.

"We have to stop the lady. My stallion will kill her to protect his mares. Who is she?"

"My wife, and I doubt he will hurt her."

He jumped over the fence, grabbed Lars's arm, and pulled him toward the corral; and as they got there, the stallion was indeed having a fit.

As Jacques started to open the gate, Lars stopped him. "Just stand here and be still. You will spook him. She will take care of this."

God, he hoped so; he was never sure. Jacques stood and watched; the stallion was running toward her, and she was standing beside a white Arab mare. When Catherine looked at him, she knew what it was.

She just smiled at him, she knew. The stallion came running up to her, and she turned and put out her hand; he came to a dead stop, stood there, and then put his muzzle in her hand. Then she walked to him and stroked his neck, and he put his head down so she could reach more of him.

"I told you he wouldn't hurt her."

There was a big stone not far away, and Cat led him to it. She stood on it and then grabbed a hunk of mane and climbed on his back; and he carried her to the gate with the little mare following them. Lars opened the gate, walked inside, helped her down, and then turned around.

Cat put her hand on Jacque's face. "You can start breathing now. He wasn't going to hurt me. They never do."

He didn't even realize that he was holding his breath. "Nobody has ever been able to even get a saddle on him, let alone get on him. How did you do that? You are Giles's woman that talks to horses?" She just nodded. When Giles had told him about his wife who talked to horses, he thought he was kidding him; now he believed.

"I am Jacques St Cloud. I am Giles's cousin. We haven't met, but he told me about you. I thought he was exaggerating your skill, but he was right—you are very good. Maybe you can help with this devil."

"I am more interested in this pretty lady. Where did you get her, or should we talk in private?"

"I think you already know where she came from. I am looking for a stallion to breed her to. Like her, all of these are too big."

By then, James was there with a halter, a small one; the Frenchman didn't know where it had come from. He had one specially made for the small horse when he got her. She put it on her and led her out, but the stallion objected. Cat just petted him and shut the gate.

"She will be with me. Come, I have something to show you."

"Cat, do you want to ride if it is all right with him."

She turned and looked at Jacques, and he nodded his head and lifted her up on the pretty mare's back. She looked like she belonged there. They walked toward her corrals, and she could hear her stallions talking to her; they could smell this new mare, but she wanted one in particular to show his head, and he did. Khan came running. Jacques's eyes bugged out of his face. Khan came running like an Arab should, and he was beautiful.

"You have got him, Queen Marie's horse! I thought the king killed him?"

"That is why I have got him so he wouldn't. He is part of this little war. I would like very much to breed her to him. I will keep her safe."

"You know that I stole her, don't you? It was the only way I could get her out of the country."

She looked at him and smiled. "That is how Marie got Khan. Didn't you know?"

"I do now."

Giles had said he would like his lady and that she was something special.

"A foal from them would be the first in this country, and it would be very special. Would you consider the idea?"

He looked at her, and he had already decided. "Anything you want to do is fine, my lady."

"My name is Catherine, and I would like to put her in this corral before your big stallion gets too friendly. I don't think she could bear one of his foals and live, if it is all right with you?"

He hadn't thought of that when he brought her with them; he just didn't want to leave her behind because he knew someone would sell her before he got back.

"Do you think I have waited too long?"

"I don't think so. She is still pretty young. But soon, if it is all right, I will put her in here. The corrals are guarded."

He looked at the stallion and knew he was not young, but he still looked like he could sire some more foals. And what choice did he have? There were no other Arab stallions on this continent.

"Please, it looks like she will be happy while we are here."

"Don't worry, I won't keep her forever. When she is pregnant, you can take her home if you want or after she delivers. She is still your horse. I am not stealing her. Don't look so lost."

"I am sorry. She has become so special to me."

"Will you join us for supper and meet the rest of my family?"

"I would be honored, madam."

She turned the mare into the corral with Khan, and they ran around the corral as the children came out. Beth stood on the fence, and on the second turn around, the new mare stopped in front of her and waited for her to pet her. When Beth starting talking to her, she came even closer and Jacques didn't miss any of this

"What is her name, Mama? She is as beautiful as Khan." The mare was taking a special liking to Beth; it was the first time Cat had seen any one horse pick her out. She was becoming more and more like her every day when it came to the horses.

"I don't know that she has one. You will have to ask her owner if she has a name."

She looked over at Jacques and Cat was going to introduce them when Beth said, "Well, does she have a name, or can I name her for you? She is too beautiful not to have a name."

The way Jacques looked at Beth, well, there wasn't any other way to put it—if she had asked for the moon, he would had figured out a way to get it. "Whatever you wish to name her is fine." He was going to say more, but Cat put her hand on his arm; she was afraid he was going to say too much.

"Good, are you coming to dinner? We can think of a name then." He nodded yes. Beth grabbed his hand and started leading him into the keep. The young man was already smitten.

Cat stood there a minute, shook her head, looked at Lars, and then said, "I think we are going to have a French son-in-law. He did say he was Giles's cousin, didn't he? Well France is not so far away."

Lars was just looking at her.

"Who was that child? I don't believe I know her. All of the sudden, she is you. The horse and she just takes over. She is a little you."

"Not so little by the look in that young man's eyes. He was ready to give her that horse, and I think she would have taken it. How are we on dowry?"

"Really, I can handle only one child at a time. That means getting that one born first before we marry any off any of them. Besides, she is too young."

"Tell them that, Papa, one thing at a time."

When they got into supper, Beth had Jacques sitting by her; all the children were asking him questions, and he was holding his own. They came to find out he was the middle child of eight, and so this wasn't at all strange to him; he was right at home, but he didn't take his eyes off Beth. She didn't seem to mind; she had already decided he was hers and told her mother so later that night. Jacques and Beth decided on a name for the mare: Queen. Somehow, Marie would probably have liked that; it would have angered Charles even more.

The next day, a courier arrived with a letter from the nephew of the Czar, and Catherine took it to her solar to read it.

Dear Catherine,

I am safe and back at home, thanks to you. I took your advice and finally talked to my aunt about my problem with the necklace and the girl that Queen Marie had helped me with. She was very sympathetic and then very angry that I didn't come to her for help in the first place. She wishes me to tell you how much she thanks you for your help in this situation and wishes she could thank Marie, but she understands that this has caused you troubles. She went to my uncle, and he sent a letter to King Charles, and your problems should be coming to a close soon. It seems Charles doesn't want Russian troops helping Raiders settlers along the coast who are being randomly attacked by bandits, so he is going to send support if needed. I hope you know what I mean and are in good health, with all your troops around you for a while longer. Please keep the necklace and wear it. My aunt says wear it proudly. You earned it, and she dares anyone to say a thing about where it came from. If you ever need anything, my aunt says call on her or my uncle. You will always be welcome in their home. By the way, I married the lady that you and Queen Marie helped to hid us from King Charles's and his men for so long, and we are very happy.

With all my love and gratitude,
Alexander

Lars came and read the letter over her shoulder. "So now we are being randomly attacked by bandits, and we are getting protection from Russian soldiers?"

"Looks that way. At least that is what he can tell people when they ask why he is going after the people he made a truce with and the Russian army starts coming down. This is turning into a political mess, and he needs to back away or look like a fool."

"Let's see what he does. He thinks he can do anything." He turned her around in the chair and asked, "I thought you sent the necklace back after the wedding?"

"I didn't know where to send it. The boy was in hiding, so I still have it. Do you want to see it again?"

He thought about it because he really hadn't paid much attention to it on the day they had married, so he shook his head yes.

"Come with me." She walked up to their bed room, went to the window, and opened the window seat. She took out the blankets there, handed them to him, and then reached down to a board; she pushed it down. It came up on the other end, and she pulled it out. Inside was a velvet box; she took it out, put it aside, went to the bed, and sat down. When she opened it, inside was that beautiful necklace as well as the matching earrings.

"It was a gift to one of Charles's mistresses who was a lady-in-waiting to the czar's wife and the boy's mother, and that is how he got it after she died. Marie found the boy and the necklace and hid them.

She got the boy out of the country and the necklace to me. If the land deal didn't work out, I was to use it to pay for the land. Charles wanted it that bad. That is why I wore it on our wedding day. It was blackmail. Marie already had the land deal in place, so I didn't know what to do with the necklace. Then Bruce and the horse came, so I kept it as leverage. It is beautiful, isn't it? And it is always good to have something Charles wants, and Charles always wants something."

"I am just glad I was never on the bad side of the two of you." Then he kissed her on the top of the head and said, "I wonder if that thing would look good on a naked pregnant lady."

"Oh, I don't know. Shall we lock the door and see if it needs a fancy dress or just skin to shine?"

He hooked it around her neck and started unhooking everything else. Emeralds and diamonds go good with everything or nothing. When she was nude, she was standing in front of him; her skin was stretched so tight on her stomach that he could see little feet moving across it. He put his head on her stomach and got a sharp kick in the head.

"That's what you get for disturbing the tumbling lesson."

He looked up at her with his hands on either side of her stomach. "Does it hurt when you get kicked?"

"Not unless those feet are under a rib and pushing, then it is a bit uncomfortable."

He put his head on her stomach again; he loved to feel that baby move, and Cat just rubbed her hand through his hair. She had married him, and he didn't know half of what he was walking into.

"Did you pay this much attention to your other women when they were pregnant with your sons?" It was an honest question, but he wasn't sure she would like the answer.

"No only the first one; Doeri's mother. I would have married her, but her father didn't think I was good enough for her, and neither did she. When he was born, she married a rich man in our village, and she died two years later of fever. Doeri has lived with me ever since. The mothers of my other two sons I never even considered marrying. They were just my children's mothers. I took care of them and the boys but never wanted to marry anyone but you."

"Why me? I am not that special, but it seems you have wanted me from the first."

He looked up at her face and smiled as he stood and pulled her robe around her shivering body. "From the first moment I saw you and you looked down at me, I knew you were the only woman I would ever really love in this life. Giles and I became friends, but every year when he left with Beth, I hated him because he was going back to you and I wasn't. And every year, when he came with her, I hoped to see your face on a horse beside Beth. But you were never there. I was going to visit a couple of weeks early this year to pick up Beth and the other children just so I could see you. That is why I was at the lodge. I hadn't figured out what the excuse would be, but I would have thought of something.

"Every time I went home, my people told me I needed to find a new woman and get on with my life. But I just couldn't give up the idea that we were meant to be together, so I stopped going back so often. Do you know I am a grandfather? Doeri has a son, and he is having him and his wife brought on the next boat to meet you. He told me you make him feel like he has a family again."

She smiled and put her arms around him, and he held her as close as his child would let him. At about that time, he got another swift kick, and he looked down. "I just wish I wasn't so worried about this child hurting you and could enjoy this more. I am so scared I will lose you after all this."

"The other afternoon, Gretel and I had a talk about the last time."

Then she explained what had happened to the other baby, and it looked like a weight had been lifted off his shoulders. "So it was just the accident, and you don't think anything will happen again with this baby?"

"Everything is going smoothly, and Gretel thinks it was just bad luck last time. So stop worrying. Soon, I won't be as big as a house, and you will have a new child, Grandpa."

"You are not going to let me live that one down, are you?"

She just grinned. "No way, we are going to have several generations of family in this house, dark and light hair. We had better start clearing out and renovating more rooms, don't you think? But didn't we start something else when we came in here?"

She wiggled her eyebrows at him, and he held her close. "I believe there was mention of something else, but I get kicked whenever I get close to you."

"Then this is really going to make your child mad."

She pulled his head down to hers and gave him a kiss. Then they tried to figure out how to do this; it was becoming quite a balancing act, but they always figured it out. After his clothes were shed, he did indeed find a way to make his child even madder in a quite interesting way, but it was quite satisfying for its mother. She now took the role of being on top, and that was one she was trying to like. But even that was getting awkward; when they were done, she lay down beside him.

He held her and said, "We are not going to be able to manage this much longer. We are just going to have to wait until after the baby is here."

"What are you saying? I am getting too big now? Are you going to find someone else to take care of you until I can again?" She was getting angry over nothing, and she was getting out of bed when he caught her and dragged her back.

"What is wrong with you? I didn't say any such thing. You know that is not what I meant. You are not enjoying this. I am hurting you, and you can't tell me I am not. Now look at me and tell me the truth."

She couldn't look at him; she knew he was right. She had never gotten this big, and she was uncomfortable, but she was afraid he would find someone else to take care of his needs if she didn't. She didn't say anything; she just lay there and held him. He pulled the covers up and held her.

"I am not going to someone else. I think I can wait until you have our baby. I won't die from neglect. You may without my godlike lovemaking."

And then she knew he was making fun of her, and she looked up and hit him square in the chest. "Godlike, really? Aren't you puffed up today? You think you were Odin himself the way you talk. Godlike? Ha!"

He started laughing at her and then kissed her head. "At least you aren't feeling sorry for yourself anymore, are you, Mama? You can make horses and most people do anything you want, but sometimes you just can't always get what you want. You won't be pregnant forever, and things will get back to normal. Maybe Doeri will come and bring his family to see us, and that will make you feel better."

"Soon, I hope. I would love to see his child. It is a little boy, isn't it?"

"Yes, and you are going to love him."

With that, she fell asleep in his arms, and he thought, *Please let this war be coming to an end so my children can come here.* He wanted all of his family together; the Christian Christmas was close, and he knew Catherine and the children made a big occasion of it, and he wanted everything to be good for her this year, and this child should be here by then.

Two weeks went by, and Doeri did indeed show up at the gates to the keep with his wife and son in tow; as the gates were opened, Lars went down to meet them. Catherine wasn't far behind; she reached the bottom steps as they got to the front doors, and she saw Doeri's wife and his son. His wife wasn't Raider; she was either a captive or the daughter of one. She would find out later. But as soon as she got closer to them, the little boy began to struggle to be let down out of his father's arms, and Doeri finally let him down. The boy ran straight to Catherine. She leaned over as he nearly knocked her down, and she scooped him up in her arms; he put his arms around her neck and hugged her.

"Well, hello, little one. And what is your name, and why are your parents looking like I am about to eat you?"

Doeri still looked stunned, as did his wife. Lars was wondering what was going on as well when Hanna said, "He doesn't let anyone touch him, and he never goes to anybody by himself ever. He never leaves our side. I am worn-out because we can't even have a nanny for a little time off."

"Well, now you can. He knows his grandmother when he sees her. So come on inside, and I will take you to you rooms."

"We have rooms?" Doeri looked at Lars.

"She opened up another wing and had it renovated for you boys and your families. You each have your own rooms and adjoining rooms for children. They are set aside permanently for your use and no one else's. She expects you to come often and stay, only if you want to, of course?"

Hanna looked at Doeri and then just followed Catherine up the stairs; when they were in the rooms, she just looked around in awe. She had never seen such beautiful rooms, and they were for her and her family. Deep lush carpets were on the floors, and fires were already being set to warm the rooms. Tapestries that cost more than she could ever afford were hanging on walls. There was a large bed and cabinets for clothes and closets for hanging dresses and a small room where she could bathe. The next room was for her children, with a smaller bed, a cradle, and toys with another rug on the floor and a window for light with drapes. These two rooms were bigger than those of most of the houses she had ever been in.

She turned around and looked at Catherine and said, "This is our room, just for us?"

Catherine looked at her. Maybe she had overdone and spooked her. "Is it not to your liking? We can change it."

Hanna began to cry, and Cat went over to her and put her arm around her. "It's all right. I get a little over-the-top sometimes trying to please." That got a snort from Lars and a look skyward from Doeri, so she put her hand under Hanna's chin and asked her, "I don't even know your name or the baby's name. Maybe somebody will tell me."

"I am Hanna, and he is Ian." She looked so tired.

Cat looked around at the boxes being brought in and asked her, "Would you like to take a hot bath before dinner and maybe a nap? I could watch the baby, and the men are going to talk war or something. You look like you could use some rest."

"That would be wonderful. Do you think you can handle Ian for a while? He may get fussy." She looked at her; there was still something wrong, but she wasn't going to talk in front of the men, so she had to get them out of here.

"I have raised five children. I think I can get through the day with one more. You two, go. Lars, send in my tub and some hot water. I will stay for a minute more and see everything gets settled before I leave."

After they left, she made sure the chests were put where Hanna wanted them, and the tub was moved into the little room; things were to Hanna's liking. When everybody left and the tub water needed to cool, she turned to Hanna. "What is wrong, Hanna? You are scared of me, and I want to know why. And it is not just this room and the way your baby has taken to me. What is it?"

Hanna wouldn't look at her for a minute; then she took a deep breath and decided this woman was to be her mother-in-law and had put a lot of effort into making this a home for her family. "They say you had your horse run over Horic, and then you stabbed him. I just can't believe the woman who holds my child could have done that."

Catherine looked at this child and decided she might as well get this out of the way one way or the other; this was going to have to be told. "They are right. I killed him, and I had my horse run over him first. But did they tell you it was the third warning I had given him? He had threatened me and my family twice, and Lars had sent him away, and he came back to kill me and take my daughter. I wasn't going to let that happen. He came after me with a knife, and I had my horse run him down. I gave him another chance to leave. He didn't, so I killed him. If someone comes after my family and now that includes all Lars's sons and their families, I will protect them with everything I have—money, men, weapons. And I won't ever apologize for that. You and your child are under that protection now and always will be. You are mine now. So am I still so scary?"

Hanna just looked at her for a minute as this woman held her son who wouldn't let anyone hold him; he trusted her. Then she realized she would never let anyone hurt him or her family as long as she lived. What else could you want? She had carved out a place in her home and her life for all of them, and she didn't have to, but she did.

"I don't care what anyone says about you. As far as I am concerned, my son knows whom to trust and whom not to, and I trust him. I thank you for all you have done for us, and the rooms are magnificent. We are most grateful. My husband said if I ever met you, I would like you. But he was wrong—I love you as he does. But I will let him tell you that if he can ever get the words out."

"What does that mean?"

"I am not supposed to tell you, but I think I owe you one. The boys all would like to call you Mother, if it is permissible with you. But none of them have enough guts to ask you. Victor was going to when he came last time and was a nervous wreck when he came back, and they all gave him hell because he didn't ask."

She looked at her funny and scrunched up her brow. "Isn't Victor's mother still alive? I know the other two aren't, but I thought his was?"

"She is, but she all but shunned him, and she is a vindictive bitch who tells him all the time she wishes him dead because Lars didn't marry her. And it has been worse since he married you. That is why he won't go home to the North Country anymore. He stays at the lodge and volunteers to come here all the time. He would live here if he was invited, but you don't know that."

"I don't care if they call me Mother. They are Lars's children and now mine, and Victor can live here if he wants. He is only sixteen. He still needs a mother. Your water is getting cold. Get in the tub. Go take your bath and I will feed your son and take care of this other problem."

Neither had noticed Ian was sound asleep on her shoulder and quite content. Well, one down, one to go. Hanna went to take a bath all by herself. What a luxury! She might stay in until she was a prune or the water was so cold she froze. Ian was draped across Catherine's shoulder, perfectly happy and asleep. Grandmothers were nice, not that Catherine looked like a grandmother. If she wasn't her mother-in-law, she would be jealous of her.

Cat walked down the hallway and saw Lars and his son at the bottom of the stairs. As he looked up, she called to him, "Come to the playroom when you are through. We will be in there."

She continued on around the hallway and met Caroline coming out of her room, and she asked for a blanket for Ian.

"Is this Doeri's son?" Cat just nodded and looked down at the sleeping child.

Caroline handed her one of her baby's blankets, and she continued on to the playroom. Over the years, this room had become stocked with every toy imaginable, including rocking horses and stuffed animals; and it was always kept clean with no rats. She kept men in her home all the time to keep vermin out, at least the four-legged kind. When she went in, Ian was waking up, and she sat him down. He started looking around, and he found the chest with the stuffed animals in it; he started to pick them up and throw them out until he found the one he wanted. She smiled at the one he chose. Then she carefully sat down on the floor near some blocks, and they started building as he held his animal. That was how Lars and Doeri found them.

Doeri couldn't believe this room, and it was just for the children to play in; he looked at his father and asked, "Is she really as rich as some of the people think?"

"I don't know what they think, but she has more than enough to live three lifetimes or more. Is that what you want to know?"

He just nodded; he didn't know what else to say. He had wanted to ask her a question, but now he was afraid to because she would think he just wanted her money. So he would keep it to himself, and he would talk to his brothers. Cat was watching, and she saw the same expression as Hanna's on his face; now she was going to have to convince him she wasn't someone to fear. They started to leave, and she told Lars, "Go find Robert and talk to him and leave Doeri with me."

He looked at her funny. "Why am I talking to Robert?"

"Because I need to talk to your son, and I don't need you around. Now go find Robert and talk about something please."

He just looked at Doeri and said, "You are on your own."

"Come, sit down and talk to me. There is something bothering you and you won't talk to me, so Hanna did. Now you are trapped, so sit."

He was going to strangle his wife; she had no right to say anything, especially since she was afraid of Catherine. She must have done some talking to have taken that fear away. "Hanna shouldn't have said anything, and it doesn't apply now."

"Why doesn't it apply because I am rich? I was rich before when you boys wanted to call me Mother, and nothing has changed. I would love to call you my sons. I have even asked Lars about it, and he said you would ask if it was all right. So whatever you say, this is my grandson, and I would like it if I could call you boys my sons. If Victor would like to live here, I would like that. All of you will be welcome here always."

"Don't you think that would be pushing it with all of us?" He smiled at her.

"Have you looked at this place, *really* looked at it? There are rooms I haven't seen in years, and there is room for many more families. Do whatever you want, but don't be afraid of me because I have money. Giles taught me how to use it to enjoy my life and make it better for my family and the people around me, and I will continue to do just that. And that includes you boys now."

Ian climbed into what was left of her lap with his lamb and sat down, and she looked down at him and said, "My first grandchild, and I think he is getting hungry. Do you know that pretty wife of yours is in the tub upstairs? She could probably use some help drying off, and then you both could use a nap before supper. Your father and I always enjoy a nap before supper." Then she smiled up at him.

"What about Ian?"

"Ian is good with me. I will feed him, and we will play if you will help your fat mother-in-law up off the floor."

A voice from the door said, "Take care of your wife, and I will take of mine, and we will take care of our grandson."

As Doeri walked past his father, he just winked at him, and Lars smiled. Then he went to help his struggling wife off the floor because her grandson was trying to help her up, and it was the cutest thing, but she wasn't laughing. As he reached down, he said, "Do you need more help, dear?"

"Oh, just shut up and help me, or I will wipe that grin off your face."

"Not in front of our grandson, dear."

She just narrowed her eyes at him, and Ian thought whatever they were doing was funny and started laughing; soon, they were all laughing.

A couple of hours later, Doeri and Hanna came downstairs, both smiling and looking for Ian. They couldn't find anybody. They found Helen in the kitchen and asked where everybody was, and she said she thought they were in the gardens. They had talked about all Catherine had said to each of them and decided she was right about everything, and they would send a message to Victor and Latt as soon as possible. They would like to become a permanent part of Catherine's and Lar's world. They could stay the summers in the North Country taking care of his father's land and the winters here.

As they walked outside, they saw Catherine in the corral with Ian. They were surrounded by several horses, smaller than the ones around here. But still Raiders weren't used to horses. Doeri started to run toward them, and Hanna was panicked. Lars stopped them before they got too close and said, "Watch. He is perfectly all right with her. They won't hurt him."

And as they watched the little boy, he touched and petted the horses, and they walked among them as the horses just followed them; soon, she had him feeding the horses oats out of his hand.

"How did you know they wouldn't hurt him?" Doeri asked his father.

"I watched her walk out on to a battlefield carrying Beth with five hundred armed men, and not a single horse moved against her. Giles knew that as long as she held Beth, she would be safe. It was the first time I ever saw her work horses. Sometimes I think if you give her enough time, she can do the same thing with men."

"Even with a king?"

"Maybe not a king, but she had a queen for a best friend. That is why we have that land, because of those two ladies and that white horse."

All of them watched as she took her grandson for his first walk among the horses she loved so much, and he was having a ball. Cat looked over her shoulder, and the sun was setting; she said to Ian, "We had better get you inside. I will bet you are as hungry as these horses, and we are probably scaring your mama. She will kill me."

They walked to the gate, and Lars opened it. They walked out and started to the house. Hanna took Ian when Robert came up and gestured to Cat, and she motioned them inside. "I will be there shortly. What is wrong?"

"I need to talk to you about the French camp. There is a fever outbreak, not a bad one, but we need to talk."

"Later, after everyone is asleep, I will meet you in the accountant's office. And you can tell me what is going on until then, nobody in or out of this keep to the camp. Is Jacques inside the keep?"

"Yes, and he has been since yesterday."

"Good, he doesn't leave. Have him there tonight." She gave Robert some instructions to look for certain things in the camp without getting too close; she wanted some information. At dinner, she watched everybody for signs of fever and saw none, so it had not spread to the keep. She told Helen, Jennie, and Caroline what was going on and what to watch for; then she got everyone to bed. When Lars was asleep, she snuck downstairs, and there were Robert and Jacques.

"Robert, what did you see when you were at the camp? Is it as I suspected?" She sat down in the accountant's chair; she figured they would be there for a while, and she was tired. It had been a long day.

"Yes, I think they have contaminated their water supply, and the water they are taking out of the river is contaminated by the runoff of the camp."

She sat there a minute, and then she talked to Jacques. "Your men are going to have to move their camp away from the keep several miles. They are contaminating the water supply and making themselves sick, and there is a fever outbreak. I have herbs for the fever that will help, and we can send fresh water from our well. But they have to start boiling the water, or this is going to get worse, and they must move the camp."

"I will go tomorrow and take care of this. Will you come with me to take care of the sick?"

"No, she most definitely will not be going. Don't even think about it, Catherine." Lars was standing at the door.

"I wasn't going to. I am not that stupid twice. I will send the herbs, and the instructions are simple. If they have fresh water and move the camp, it should be all right. But if you go to the camp, I wouldn't let you back in the keep. It is too dangerous to people inside if this fever is contagious. I am going to ask some of my single men tomorrow if they will go and supervise moving and the doctoring for extra pay. I will see if some of the village women will go also."

Jacques looked at her and then turned to go, but he looked back. "You have to understand I have to go. Your men don't speak French, and they will need my help. But you have to tell Beth goodbye for me."

"No, she doesn't. I am going with you."

"No, you are not," came out both their mouths at the same time."

Beth looked at them and said, "I am a grown woman, and I can do as I wish."

"You are not grown enough that I won't lock you in your room." Catherine stood up, and then Jacques came to stand beside Beth.

"And I will take the key with me. I will not have you with me. You could get sick, and I won't have you where you are not safe. You stay here, my love."

Well, he wasn't very old, but he wasn't stupid. Cat at least could say that about him.

"I can help. I have helped Mama."

Catherine just watched; this was his fight, and he was going to have to fight it. But if he couldn't, she would see to it her daughter didn't get anywhere close to that camp if she had to send her to the lodge. They talked, and there were tears; he finally convinced Beth that it was better that she stayed here and helped her mother put together the herbs for the fever when he sent men back for more.

"All right, everyone, to bed. We will start in the morning. I already sent men to the village to get some volunteers, and we proceed tomorrow."

She walked upstairs and left the men to get organized downstairs; as she neared her room, she decided to turn and go to the west wing. She passed Doeri and Hanna's room; she checked in with the guards and asked one of them for a torch. He looked at her funny and handed her one and asked her if she needed an escort; she just shook her head no and continued on. She looked back over her shoulder and told him, "If someone comes looking for me, I went this way." She pointed down the long dark hall. For some reason, he figured someone would come looking for her. She walked in the near dark and wondered why she was here; she couldn't get over the feeling she was going to need these rooms and soon. She pushed open one door, and inside was an old room that hadn't seen a broom in a very long time, probably since her great-grandmother had been in this place. It had stood for over two hundred years, and it hadn't been until Giles that it was being used again as a home. She would come back tomorrow and look at more rooms and see to their cleaning and open up more of this wing.

"Who do you hear talking to you, Catherine? You are smiling." She turned; she knew Lars would find her. He wasn't ever very far away.

"No one tonight I was all alone. I was just looking at all the room this old house still has to offer and that I need to be cleaning and getting these rooms ready."

"Who are you expecting to come?"

She turned and looked at him. "I don't know, but we are going to have guests and soon. We need these rooms ready for them."

He looked at her strangely, but he had learned not to mistrust her intuition; she was generally right.

"We will start having them cleaned in the morning, and I will see that they are structurally sound. All right, now can we go to bed?"

"Yes, it is cold in here. We can come back tomorrow. I think there is a broken window in here. I will need to get some new drapes made." As she turned to look once more at the room, she could have sworn she saw a puff of smoke in the corner. No just her imagination.

The next morning, she awoke to two tiny eyes staring at her at the side of her bed, and she almost jumped out of the bed until she realized it was Ian.

"Well, good morning, little one! What are you doing in here? Your mother is going to panic."

"Who are you talking to?" Two little legs climbed up on the bed and into the center of the two of them.

"Who do you think? My new lover, he is taking your place. Ha-ha!"

"How did he even find his way here, and how did he get in the door?"

At that, a guard opened the door a little and peeked in. "He was kicking on the door and banging. I figured you wouldn't mind?"

"No, but I figure his mother is going to be hunting for him any minute. You'd better go find her before she has a fit. Please tell her he is with us."

Ian was quite happily playing with his grandfather when she looked over at him and said, "Will you please get me a gown before Hanna gets here? You and I are not exactly dressed for company." As he looked down, she was right. They were both nude.

"Does this mean we are going to start wearing something to bed? Well, at least you?" That was when she threw a pillow at him. He quickly got up, grabbed his robe, and threw her a gown, which she pulled on just before Hanna knocked on the door.

"Come in. Are you looking for someone?"

"How did he find you? I didn't even know where your room was."

"We came in yesterday for a while looking for some shoes, and I guess he remembered, and he found us this morning."

"You mean he found you, my dear. He came hunting for you." Ian climbed up her chest to play with her hair; it was obvious who he wanted.

"You go with your mama while I get dressed, and I will see you downstairs in a bit." After they dressed, she headed downstairs to find several men as well as two women waiting on her. She assumed they were the men and women who were willing to go to the French camp and help for the extra pay; the only one she didn't expect was Kevin, and neither did Robert.

"Why is he here? I never thought to find him here."

"He says he wants to help, that he owes it to you."

She pulled Kevin aside, and she asked him, "Do you know what this is about? I am sending these men into a camp with fever, and once they are there, they can't go back to their families until it is over."

He nodded his head yes. She took him to the kitchen so she could talk to him in private. "What is this really about? And don't lie to me."

"We both did you wrong a long time ago, and I am trying to make it right, and we could use the extra money for the children."

She looked at him for a minute and finally made a decision. "You are not going to the camp."

He looked broken. "But they tell me you are a good carpenter and a mason, is that right?"

"Yes, and I am very good at both."

"I need both here in the keep. I am renovating several rooms, and they need to be done sooner than later. You can start today if you wish, and I will have more work after that."

"Yes, I would like that very much, and I can go home at night to my family."

"Do you need your tools?"

"Yes."

"Then you can go get them, but wait just a minute. There is something I need you to take to Jane."

She went to the kitchen and asked Helen to quickly pack a bag of food of cheese and bread, and when she had done so, she handed it to Kevin. "This is for your family. Now go get your tools and I will put you to work."

Helen saw what she did, and when he left, she told her, "They have been having a hard time. Work has been hard to find because Jane hit you."

"Well, now he works for me. They will be well taken care of from now on. You should have told me sooner."

Helen would have but she had been sneaking them food; if something hadn't happened, she would have told her. But instead Helen had him volunteer today, and things worked out just fine. Helen just walked back to the kitchen. Cat thought she didn't take long to put together a bag of food; the little minx, she had this all planned.

She went back to the men, and Robert had them organized, and they were ready to go. Jacques was there to lead them, and there were bags of the herbs they needed for fever. Beth was waiting for them, and she saw her little girl having to say goodbye for the first time. Cat thought it doesn't get any easier when you are older. They were taking containers of fresh water until they could get to a fresh well several miles away, and he was taking them to the barn Giles had died in; there were corrals already set up and fields for tents. He couldn't send them home and risk sending the fever with them, so they were setting up camp a few miles away; hopefully, with her fever medicine and fresh water, things would get better.

She couldn't get over the feeling she needed to be busy and get things in order, so she started to get her people working on the rooms upstairs. After they were stripped of all the old rugs and tapestries and thoroughly cleaned and mopped, it was better, and she put Kevin to filling cracks first. Then there were shelves and beds to be made. She would get one room started, and then she would wander to another room and decide it to needed to be done, and they would start again. But she always came back to the room Lars found her in on the first night. She was wrong about the window though; there was not a broken pane in here, but she had never gotten the cold feeling in here again. She put the most time and money in this room though as if she was decorating it for someone important; and she didn't know why.

After two weeks, the fever was breaking, and it looked like moving the camp was the right thing to do; the men were better, and no new outbreaks of fever had been reported in three days. She thought if this went on for a week, Jacques would be allowed back into the keep, just in time for Beth's birthday.

Victor showed up on that particular day, and it was excellent timing; the weather was good, and he had good news. He met his father at the door as Cat came down the stairs, and he stopped talking to his father and walked over to her and started to bow. But instead, she just grabbed him, hugged him, and whispered into his ear, "You don't bow to your mother. You hug her, silly boy!"

At that, he grabbed her and twirled her around until she was dizzy; then he sat her on the floor. "You sure it is all right if I live here?"

"I would not have sent for you if it wasn't, darling." Then she smiled, and he looked at his father.

Lars said, "This was her idea from the very start. She has said she thought of all of you as her sons."

"Thank you."

"You're welcome, but you know I am into slave labor?"

At that, Hanna started laughing, especially since Ian was climbing up the front of his grandmothers' dress at the time. He just looked around for a minute; then Lars said, "She is kidding." Victor looked at Catherine with a huge smile on her face and his nephew squirming on her shoulder.

"You were just way too serious. Come on in. This is your home now. Are you hungry?"

"Yes, actually, I am."

Lars walked around him and took Ian; he was using Catherine's tummy as a stepladder to climb on her. So he took his grandson, and they went to the dining room. As they went up to bed that night, she checked the bedroom to see if it was ready. Everything was in place: the new bed, mattress, and bedding. Kevin had repaired the walls, and it was warm and clean. She had rat catchers working constantly, making sure the vermin were under control in this wing. Lord, how she hated those things. It was fit for a queen or a lesser royalty; now she could sleep.

Later that evening, she was awakened by Caroline and asked to come downstairs. Lars was sleeping hard and didn't hear her leave, so she pulled on her robe and quietly left the room. Caroline grabbed her hand and pulled her down the stairs, and at the bottom was Jane, and she was nearly hysterical.

"What is going on? Calm down and talk to me. Is it the children?" She was afraid the fever had made its way into town, and if it had, Jane had just spread it to them.

"*No*, my lady, there is a pregnant woman at my house, and she is in labor. I think she is dying."

"Why didn't you bring her here?"

"She has been in labor most of the day and night. We can't move her. She is in too much pain, but something isn't right."

She turned, and Caroline ran up the stairs as Robert headed to the stables. "Stay here. I'll get dressed and be back down, and we will go. Calm down. Stand by the fire. I will hurry." She hurried up the stairs, quickly dressed, and went back down. Caroline was waiting, and they headed outside. Robert had the carriage waiting for them, and they were on their way.

"Tell me, what's going on with the girl? Who is she?"

Jane didn't want to talk about the girl, and Catherine was getting a bad feeling about this and was about to turn around, but they were already here. They all got out and then inside, and sure enough, there was a girl, and she was in trouble. She went to the girl first and felt the girl's stomach; then she looked at her, such a pretty girl. Then she went to work.

"Kevin, get this house warm. Get that fireplace hot."

He looked at her strangely till Jane said, "We didn't have a lot of money for extra wood."

She looked at Robert and just nodded, and he grabbed Kevin, and out the door they went. She knew in a few minutes she would have all the wood she would need.

"What is your name, little girl?" She felt around the girl's stomach.

"My name is Katie."

"Well, I am Catherine, but they call me Cat. Do you have a husband, Katie?"

"Yes, he is standing in the corner with my father." As she turned, she knew why they were standing in the shadows.

"Were you afraid I would leave if I knew it was your daughter that needed help?" The man standing in the corner was Duke Lloyd Dunton, the man who had threatened her in the first place in the king's name.

"Maybe, but I knew you would never leave Marie's grandchild."

And out walked Charles the 11, Marie's son; now she knew who the room was for at her keep and the urgency.

"Hello, Lady Catherine. Can you help my wife? We have been on the run from my father, or we would have come to your keep. My mother always said you would help me if I needed it."

At about that time, it started raining hell as the door burst open. Katie started screaming, and in came the king and two guards.

"Take them out of here, and then we will get the girl."

As the guards came toward the girl, they suddenly had two other women with short swords in their hands pointed at their bellies and drawing blood.

"Now this is the way this is going to work. Two guards, out of here now, or we are going to gut them. And if you don't know, it won't be the first time I have done that. You two get in the other room. Now James you calm your wife down. Caroline, boil water. Fix her a cup of tea with a drop of laudanum, just a little, to calm her down. I need firewood. Take those swords outside and cut wood, and if you hurt my men, I will carve you up and let you bleed to death. Understand? You two in the other room now. I don't have much time, so move!"

Then the guards were shuttled out, and the men were taken to the next room. The king started to speak. "Shut up! I don't have much time. That little girl in there is in trouble. That baby is breech, and it needs to be turned. And if I don't do it now, they are both going to die. Now you two can help me, or you can get the hell out of here."

She looked directly at the king. "But if you ever want to sleep again in this lifetime, this would be the time to make amends and help me save your grandchild."

"You know about that? Is it Marie?"

"Of course I know! And yes, it is Marie! Now let's see if we can save that baby."

As they went back in, Katie was calmer, and the small house was warmer; she had the two fathers hold Katie's hands.

"James, wipe her brow, and Caroline help me. This baby is breech, and we are going to have to turn it. So don't push until I tell you to. Just hold on to their hands. Break them if you have to. Just don't push." She kept talking to her while she did what she could to turn the baby until she had it straight, and then she said, "Push!" Sure enough, there was a little head, quickly followed by shoulders and body. She handed the tiny infant girl to Caroline to clean her up but heard no sound from her; she looked at Caroline's heartbroken face and said, "No, hand her to me. You take over on Mom."

Katie was crying, and Cat was drying off the baby as the two men were accusing each other of one thing or another. As she rubbed the infant, she held it to her ear; she could hear a heartbeat. It was faint, but it was there.

"Help me, Marie. I don't know what to do."

Then she felt warm, and she saw the puff of smoke in the corner. So did the king; he just stared at it in terror. Cat took a piece of linen and wiped off the baby's mouth; it was full of mucus. Then she breathed into it, and more mucus came out the baby's nose, and then the baby cried. Then the baby just looked at her for a second and started crying. She looked up at the smoke, and it was dissolving. She knew it would be the last time she ever saw it; Marie had done what she had come to do. As she looked at the king, he was still staring at the corner. Catherine looked at him and asked, "Charles what did you do to Marie? When we get done, I will take Katie to my house, and she can recuperate there."

"You knew we were coming?"

"Yes, someone told me to expect you." She just looked at the king, and he nodded.

"I think that would be a fine place to stay, and I think the lady has beautiful horses." Well, it was a truce—a little one, but a truce nonetheless.

Caroline cleaned the baby while Cat worked on her mother, kneading her stomach, stopping the bleeding, and getting her cleaned up. She looked up at her and told her, "You will be taken to my carriage and then to my keep. I already have a room set up for you there, and you and the baby can rest." She turned to Kevin behind her and told him, "Gather up your family and go with them and stay the night in one of the other rooms. I would like to talk to you in the morning about an idea I have."

"No, my lady, I will send my family. But I will not leave you alone here with him."

"And if you think I am going to leave you with him, you are crazy." Robert said.

The king had been silent through all of this, but now he spoke. "I would like a few minutes alone with you Catherine. I have some things to talk to you about in private."

She had some things she wanted to ask him also, so she turned and told her men, "Stay outside so we can talk alone and don't fight with the guards. I am too tired to stitch anybody else up tonight."

They both agreed, but reluctantly. After Katie was carried outside to the carriage and they had Jane and the children loaded, they were left alone. She was picking up bloody linen when he said, "Will you stop? I don't think we have much time. When your husband finds out you are here, he will be back with that carriage, won't he?"

"Yes, more than likely." She was standing by the fireplace, and he came over to her and stood behind her, too close for her comfort; but she stood still. Apparently, he had something on his mind.

"Marie told me you are scarred badly from a Raiders attack. Is that right? And you don't like to be touched or be in crowds."

She just shook her head yes.

"I want to see. I am going to move your hair and nothing else."

She froze, and he pulled her hair off the back of her dress. It was cut low enough to let him see what she kept hidden, and she heard his indrawn breath; and as soon as she did, she moved away from him. That was enough of that.

"Is it all the way down your back?" She again nodded yes. "But you married a Raider?"

"It wasn't the same Raider. Lars is Beth's papa, and Giles killed the one who did this to me."

"You know, after Giles died, I started to have you brought to court. I knew Marie was dying, and I considered you as her replacement. Now I know that would never have worked."

"What was your first clue? The fact that I can't stand crowds or that we butt heads at every turn? We would have killed each other in a week. Now I get to ask some questions. I know you don't sleep since Marie died. Is it because you see smoke in your room? I saw the look on your face tonight. You were terrified."

"And you weren't. She doesn't scare you if that is who it was."

"No, she doesn't, and that is who it was. I have seen her before. The night she died, she came to me, but I didn't treat her like you did. And we both know what I am talking about. I never cheated on her or lied to her or killed her horse and served it to her."

"Stop! Did she always know about the other women?"

Catherine just looked at him as if he was stupid. "If she knew, I knew she wrote me and told me. After you wanted us to come to court, Giles was so mad that you would try to make a pass at me. I went straight to her."

"What did you tell her?"

"Everything. She thought I might do it because you were king. I told her Giles was waiting downstairs with the children and horses, and we would not be coming back. I told her she was welcome at my home anytime, but I was never going to be yours. So she hugged me, and we were like sisters from then on. When you were gone on hunts, she came to me. The queen and I went to fairs and talked about your affairs, and she was free here like she wasn't at the castle. I took care of things she couldn't—lovers, children, even a lover and a horse you would have killed. Now I want to know—did you kill her? There is a rumor in court that you did."

"No, but I might as well have."

"What was wrong with her? No one can tell me exactly, and I want to know the truth."

"Or what you will kill me? I hear you have killed one man already. What did he do to you?"

"Actually, it's two men. They were both threatening me, one with a knife, and I killed him before he could kill me. Charles stop stalling"

He knew why Marie had always trusted her; she didn't leave her friends hanging. He wondered if she had been around, would Marie have lived longer. She had needed more friends she could trust.

"They said there was something wrong with Marie's heart, and there wasn't anything that could be done about it. I wasn't sympathetic to her. I just took another mistress, and she finally found someone else. She got weaker, and it got harder for her to go up the stairs until she couldn't anymore. So she stayed in her room. By then, I had found out she had a lover, and I began a hunt for him. I was also hunting for that necklace until I heard you wore it on your wedding day, and I screamed at her for an hour. She just smiled at me and looked out the window. And do you know what she said to me? 'I'll bet she made a beautiful bride. Giles would have been proud of her. I know I am.' And then she looked at me with tears in her eyes, and I didn't understand until this minute why. She would have given her soul to have been there, wouldn't she?"

"I kept hoping she would be right up until the last minute." Catherine had tears falling down her face; now she had known Marie was thinking about her on that day. It was like they were connected in some way and always would be.

"Keep going. You aren't finished yet."

"Several days later, I finally found out who her lover was after I went to the stable to check on her horse."

"And why were you checking on her horse? Were you going to have it killed in front of her just so you could see her reaction?" Catherine was mad again.

"Yes, I wanted to hurt her. I had found out about the land deal you two had pulled off right under my nose, and I didn't realize how really sick she was. When I saw that the horse and the knight who took care of it were gone, I finally put it together and realized who her lover was. Then they told me he was taking the horse to you, and that infuriated me even further. I had to hurt her somehow. By the time I got to her room, I was furious and screaming. They told me later they could hear me in the kitchen. She never said a word. I told her I would destroy you and the land deal, and she just smiled. She told me, 'I wrote a letter to the czar's wife and told her everything and where to find the necklace and the boy and about Catherine so she would be protected from you. And there are other letters sent to others to protect Catherine from you. So just try and hurt her and watch the wrath of God come down on you. What Catherine doesn't know, I do, and they are in letters to protect Catherine from you.'

"Marie never even raised her voice. She knew she didn't have to. She had me backed into a corner. She kept a glass of wine on her table and, beside it, a small green bottle of laudanum for the pain in her chest. And every night, she would put one drop in the wine before bed. The bottle was full when I was in there on this night. I continued to scream at her that I would get even with her for her betrayal somehow as she turned and put her laudanum in the glass. She turned back around and was drinking the wine as I screamed at her, and when I was done, she finally said, 'You can't hurt Catherine, and by now, my horse and man are with Catherine. She will take care of them. Everything else I have seen to. There is more help for her if she needs it, but you can't hurt me anymore.'

"'This isn't the last of this you are going to hear from me.'

"Marie raised her glass in the air, and she said, 'Oh yes, it is, my dear, the very last.' I stormed out the door and slammed it. The little green bottle was empty on the table, and by morning, she was dead."

He looked down at his hands, and Cat sat down. Marie had killed herself.

"*Why* did she do it?" He looked at her for answers

"It was the last thing you couldn't control, couldn't take away from her, or hurt her with. It was her decision, and you couldn't stop her. She died the way she wanted to. You left her with nothing. What did you expect? She came to me the night she died. She wanted me to know about the man she had sent to me, and she was here tonight when I needed help with the baby. But I don't think she will be back again. I think she has done all she needed to do, for me at least. I don't know about you."

"How do I get her to forgive me and stop haunting me, or is this going to go on forever?"

"You might try asking for forgiveness and stop persecuting your children, and maybe it will stop. I don't know what else to tell you."

Horses were arriving at a dead run, and carriages could be heard not far behind.

"I am going outside and talk to some very angry men. I will leave you inside. If I were you, I would talk to her if she is still here and see if she can forgive you. Maybe there is still a little love left for you somewhere. Otherwise, you may walk the halls of that castle the rest of your life. And as far as I am concerned, you deserve every sleepless night." She opened the door, went outside, and met an angry Lars and four men sitting, playing cards on the porch.

"Where did you get the cards?"

Robert pointed to one of the guards as Lars was dismounting, and he grabbed her and asked her, "Are you all right? Why didn't you wake me to come with you?"

"I thought I was just birthing a baby, and I didn't need you for that. So Caroline and I went alone." The guards started to go inside, and she told them to stay outside for a bit; he would call when he wanted them. The king was praying, and they looked at each other as she said, "For his new granddaughter's safe delivery."

Catherine turned, looked at Robert, and raised her eyebrows and shoulders; she couldn't exactly tell them about what had happened in that house tonight. A few minutes later, Charles came out of the house, and he looked like a weight had been lifted off his shoulders. He came over to Catherine; he took her hand, lifted it to his lips, and kissed it.

"I think I will sleep now. I think we are finally at peace. Thank you and please take care of my children and tell them to come home when Katie feels better." Then he looked at Lars and said, "You are a lucky man, Lars Sorenson."

As Lars looked down at his tired wife, he just said, "More than you know."

"You will have to come back and visit or hunt when you have more time." They both knew he wouldn't, but it was the proper thing to say, especially since their war was now over. After all, he was a king. The fact that Cat hated him had nothing to do with it; she would never forgive him for how he had treated Marie, and truth be known, he probably would never forgive himself.

"I would like to go home now. I am tired." Then Catherine turned and looked back. "Do you have a place to sleep tonight?"

"Is it all right if I stay in this little house for tonight? I will be gone in the morning. I have to see that all my troops are sent home from here."

She turned to Kevin. "Is that all right if he uses your house since you are staying at the keep tonight?"

Kevin just nodded yes; he was too stunned to do anything else. As she walked to the carriage, both Lars and Charles helped her into the carriage, and then she had Kevin join her inside as the king went back to the house with his guards. Lars joined them inside, and Catherine told Kevin that in the morning, she wanted to talk to him before he sent Jane and the children back to the house, so they should just stay at the keep for the day until she could talk to them. He looked a little panicked, and she reassured him it was something good; she was too tired to get into it tonight. After he calmed down, she laid her head on Lars's shoulder and fell asleep.

When they got back to the Keep, she had to hold both men's arms to get up the stairs to get to her room; and when she got there, it was all she could do to get undressed, put on a gown, and get into bed. She was getting too old and too pregnant to do these midnight runs anymore. Lars was going to start his tirade about that, but she was already asleep before he could start; besides, he figured she already knew. She didn't expect to be ambushed by the king, and Caroline said if she hadn't have been there, that baby would have died. She also said something weird happened; he had a pretty good idea what that was. He would ask in the morning. Caroline said she asked someone for help when the baby didn't breathe, and he knew of only one person she would ask. He took off his clothes and left a loincloth on; now they wore nightclothes to bed as they had a visitor in the mornings, but he was going to sidetrack Ian in the morning so Cat could sleep because it was almost morning.

She got to sleep in later than usual, and she figured Lars had gotten Ian so she could sleep. She got dressed and went looking for Kevin; she wanted to talk to him and Jane. Cat found Kevin working in one of the newly opened rooms, and she was astonished every time they opened a new room; they had all been so pretty at one time when there were lots of families living here.

"Kevin, come to my office, and I will get Jane. We will meet you there in a bit." She went looking for Jane and found her and the children peeking around the corner of the playroom; and as Cat walked up, Jane shooed them back away. Catherine came up and told the children, "Go on in and find you a toy to play with. There are plenty." Jane put up her hand to stop them, and Cat stopped her. "What is wrong with them playing with the other children? They will be watched. We take turns watching the children."

"Most of those children are highborn, and mine are not."

"Look again. There is the cook's children and the stableman's son and two of the guards' daughters. Caroline will start the reading lessons soon, or she will read a book to them today. I don't know which, but they will be entertained."

"You are teaching these children to read, all of them?"

"Yes, why not! I think everyone should know how to read." Then she looked at Jane strangely. "You do know how to read, don't you?"

"No, it was not thought a woman was supposed to do things like that, I was just supposed to find a rich husband and know how to sew."

"Our fathers really thought a lot of us, didn't they? Mine needed me to read so I could do the books for him so he didn't lose any money to thieves. That was the only reason I know how. Would you like to learn?"

"I am too old and stupid."

"Nonsense that is just some men talking. Don't listen to them. Women are just as smart as men, sometimes smarter. I am teaching Lars not only English but how to read and write it as well, and I can teach you."

"I won't be here that long to learn."

"We will see about that. Come with me."

As they went down to the accountant's office, they were met by Lars and Kevin; she sat down and had Jane sit by her, and then she started.

"There is a small farm a couple of miles from here, and the owner died several weeks ago. He was the last of his family. The land reverted back to this estate, and I wondered if you two would be interested in taking over it. The house needs repairs, but the land is good, and there is a good well. You could work here and stay in the rooms you are in now. Jane could help around the castle and be paid a wage, and the children would be watched and taught as we talked about earlier. Kevin, you could do repairs on the house and work here and earn a wage. Then when you are ready to plant, I will get you started. And after you start to make some money, you can pay rents like the rest of my farms. Do you have any interest in my idea?"

They both looked stunned and looked at each other. "Yes, my lady, we would be very interested. But why would you help us after what we did to you all those years ago?"

"Because it was all those years ago, and I have been getting glowing reports about your treatment of those children and your trouble finding work because of our past. Maybe if you work for me and have your own place things will get better. Besides, you stood beside me last night, and that could have cost you your life. You knew, and still, you didn't leave. And I thank people who protect me."

Jane had her head in her hands and was crying. "

Now don't do that. It is too nice a day, and Robert is going to take you out to show you the property. Kevin, you will need supplies. Put anything you need on the keep's account and I will take care of it."

He took Jane's arm and led her away as Robert took them to the stables; he too had been impressed with the way he had protected Catherine last night. He thought he would run; instead, he stayed close and snuck both of them a sword in with the firewood. Catherine didn't know it, but he would have fought for her, and that had impressed him.

"Are you sure this is how you want to handle this? They weren't very kind to you," Lars asked after they left.

"That was a long time ago, and I think she is truly sorry for what she did, not to me, but something else."

"What else could there be?"

"She tried to get Giles back by telling him she would have his children, but Marie told me she got rid of a child by an old woman, and it left her barren. I think that is a mistake she can never take back."

"So you are trying to fix a life she messed up? Don't you think she should do that?"

"Sometimes you can't fix everything you did wrong, and someone else has to step in and make your world better again. I got lucky and had two men who loved me and helped me get my world in order. Most people don't get that chance."

He kissed her, and they started out into the main hall, where they met Hanna. "What are you two smiling about?"

"Oh, your mother-in-law thinks she is Freya, and she has to fix the world."

"Oh, is that all?"

"Who is Freya?" Cat asked as they went into the hall.

"Odin's wife."

"Another Norse goddess. You are going to have to teach me who these people are. I don't know if I am being insulted or not."

Lars kissed the top of her head. "You're not."

CHAPTER 14

Catherine was in the kitchen when she heard Beth yelling at Jacques that it was a stupid idea and she wasn't going to let him do it. So she starting wiping off the flour from her hands, got up off her stool, and waddled into the great hall to see what was going on now.

"What is the problem in here? I can hear you two shouting from the kitchen."

"He is leaving to go back to France."

"All right, I thought that was the plan and he would come back at Christmas?"

Beth looked at her as if she had suddenly become stupid. "He intends to enter every jousting match he can so he can earn enough money to marry me so we won't have to live somewhere less than this. Since he is a third son, he won't inherit anything." She didn't still quite see the problem until Beth said, "He doesn't know, Mother, about me and the other children."

She looked at Beth and then at Jacques, and then it dawned on her. "Oh good lord, he doesn't know! In fact, I am not sure your brothers and sister know. Round them up and meet me in my office in a few minutes. Let's get this settled now and please stop screaming at the boy. You are giving me a headache." She headed to her office and grabbed Lars along the way and said, "I am going to need some support. Come with me."

"What is going on? I heard yelling."

"Jacques was going to enter every jousting match to win money to support our daughter in the style she is accustomed to and probably get him killed in the process. At least that is what Beth thinks."

"He doesn't know about her inheritance or the lodge and land?"

"No, and to think of it, I have never told the other children about their inheritance, except William. So we are going to do it now and have it done so they won't worry."

"No, they will think you are dying, and this is your last will. It will scare them to death."

"I didn't think about that. It still has to be done. They are making decisions without us, and they need to know they have land and money to do it with."

As the children assembled in the room, they all had a look of dread; she got them to sit down, and then she started. "I am not trying to scare you, but you children need to know that your daddy made plans for all of you. This is not coming out right. Beth and Jacques were having an argument about how they were going to live after they were married, and he doesn't know about Beth's inheritance. Beth, you will get the lodge and one hundred acres of land surrounding it as well as rents each year. Ann and Jacob, you both get one hundred acres of land and a settlement of money each year as well. Michel gets the right of the keep. He will be the new lord when he is of age. And, David, there is a hundred acres of land here for you with a yearly settlement of money as well. Your daddy set up moneys for all of you, and none of you are ever going to be poor if you take care of your land. And you will. I will teach you how. None of you will ever have to marry for anything but love. We saw to that. I just wanted you to know you are all taken care of. Giles took care of all of you. He loved you."

Ann was the first one to stand; she walked over to her mother and asked, "What about this little one?" Then she pointed to Catherine's stomach.

"This one will be taken care of as well."

"We never really worried about the money. We are just worried about you, Mama. Will you be all right, or are you telling us something?"

Lars looked at her. "See? I told you that you were going to scare them to death, and now you have."

"I am fine. The baby's fine. It won't be much longer, and everybody can stop worrying, and we can get on with a new baby and weddings—not too soon on the wedding part."

As she looked at Ann and Jacob, she could see they wanted to say something, but not here. Jacques was just stunned, so Beth took him, and they were talking in the hallway; at least they weren't screaming. It looked like Jacques was numb; he didn't realize he would be marring an heiress.

After everyone had left, Ann and Jacob came back in and sat down across from them. "We would like to go to the lodge next summer and stay there, if it is all right with you? We would like to be away from here and see how things work out."

Catherine knew they wanted to see if the feelings they had for each other would last someplace where no one who knew of their prior relationship was watching them. Lars looked at her and added to the conversation, "What would you think about going to the North Country and visiting my relatives there? No one knows you there, and you could be alone to see how this would work out between you two."

Ann just looked at Jacob and nodded. "That way, we could see if this is real or just because we have always been together. We would finally know."

She looked up at Jacob, and Catherine already knew the love she saw in her daughter's eyes was the kind for a husband, however it had started out—they were meant for each other. Whichever gods were looking out for them had been watching since they were little and still had eyes on them.

"You go do what you must do to be sure, and then you come back to me. You don't marry without me beside you, either of you—whether it is to each other or someone else. You are still both my children."

Ann just grabbed her hand and squeezed it. "So you aren't going anywhere?"

"Not a chance in hell. I have way too much left to do on this earth."

"You think they will be all right?"

"I think they need to be away from here to decide, but she has always been his since he found her as a child, and I think that is just the way it will stay. But let them find out on their own and be sure."

When Lars reached down to help her up, he noticed she had flour on the front of her dress and asked, "What have you been doing?"

She looked at him and said, "Building a barn."

So he dropped her back in the chair. "Smart aleck, it is too hot in the kitchen for you to be baking bread. You are supposed to be resting. That is what most pregnant women do."

"How would you know? You ignored your other pregnant women to have your sons by themselves. I would have kicked your butt! It is a wonder one of them didn't." When he looked away, she said, "One of them did do something. Which one and what did she do?"

He just turned and walked away.

"I will find out. You know your sons pardon me my sons will betray." He kept walking while she was laughing; he knew that his sons would tell her, and she would know by tonight. Boy was she going to gloat.

All the soldiers were gone from around the keep, and now the French soldiers were ready to go home. The fever had been gone for two weeks now, and she was sure it was just the bad living conditions and the contaminated water. Jacques said he would bring back one of his sisters with him when he came in December, and that pleased Catherine; she wanted to meet his family.

It was time for Ann's and Jacob's birthday; no one knew when their real ones were. So they decided on the day Giles had brought them to Cat at the lodge, and that was it from then on. It was in a few days, so he decided to stay until after; it would take his people that long to get ready.

Catherine was scurrying around the castle and found Kevin in one of the new rooms, and she was inspecting it; he really was a good mason.

"You are doing a beautiful job in here. It is looking good and so much warmer without the holes in the walls." And then she smiled at him. "Is Jane enjoying living here with the children?"

"Very much and she is learning to read. She says she is going to teach me when we get into our house."

"And how is that going? Was the structure as good as I thought it was, or was there more damage?"

"No, the old man had kept it up very good. There wasn't much damage at all." She continued to walk around the room and inspect everything.

"If you don't have it finished by the time the snow falls, don't worry about it. You can stay the winter here. It won't be a problem." Then she walked out of the room and was gone.

He had been worried about not having it finished for the winter, and she had just wandered in and told him not to worry about it. He sat down on the bench he had just finished and thought Giles could have killed him and Jane for what they did to her, but he didn't; and now she was helping them. Why, he would never know.

Catherine had wanted something special for Ann and Jacob for their birthdays, and it had arrived today. It was a small carriage of their own to take them to the lodge and back and anywhere else, and Lars had made arrangements for one of his boats with Doeri sailing to take them to the North Country. She couldn't fix everything, but at least they could ride in comfort. At the dinner table that night, they celebrated both birthdays and wished them well, and then she presented them with her present. Lars later told them about the boat and how Doeri and his family would take them home with them, and they would stay in his homes. She thought everything was settled, but she was wrong.

Later, she was prowling the house, as she did lately because she couldn't find a comfortable spot to lie down in. So she walked. When she went past the playroom, she found Ann in there, sitting on the floor and holding her old lamb and looking four years old again; she knew something was wrong, but she wouldn't tell her what. She went in, put her candle on the shelf, and sat on the floor with her.

"Well, there had better be a good reason to get your fat old mother on this floor?" She didn't get any further. Ann put her head on her belly and chest and started crying—not just crying, sobbing like she hadn't done since she was little. She just held her and let her cry until there were no more tears, and then she lifted her head up and asked her, "What is really going on that you won't tell me about?"

As she looked at her mother, all Catherine could see was that little girl holding that half a loaf of bread for her to eat the next day, and she knew this wasn't going to be good. "What does it feel like to be in love with someone?"

How do you explain that one?

"Why do you want to know so badly right now Ann?" The look on her face frightened her; she was so panicked.

"I don't want to go to the lodge for the summer, and I don't want to go to the North Country ever, and I don't want the land by the lodge. I don't want any of it." She was so angry, and Cat didn't know why.

"What are you so scared of, baby? You have been there before, and this hasn't been a problem."

"I am not your baby really, and I am afraid my father or my real mother might come to get me if I am there and not with you."

God, why hadn't she thought of that? She should have; she was so terrified of her mother when she was a child.

"You are my baby until the day they put me in the ground, and you don't have to go anywhere if you don't want to. If you want land around here, I can make that happen just as easily." That seemed to calm her down, so they just sat there. Catherine held her, and Lars came to the door. She shook her head no and waved him away, and he gently closed the door.

"Now let's get back to the love stuff. What was the question you wanted to know about?"

"Jacob wants to marry me, and I think I want to marry him. But some of the people in the village say things behind our backs and laugh at us. Father Marques says to ignore them. He knows we are not related, but it hurts just the same. I don't want to have to run away to have to marry him and live away from you. This is the only family I have."

So that was what was going on behind her back. Well, she could put a stop to that quick enough. "You have feelings for Jacob. Are you sure they aren't just because he has always been there for you? Has anyone else ever touched or kissed you?"

She shyly looked up at her and answered, "Eric at the lodge last summer."

She had thought as much; she suspected he had eyes for both her daughters, and Jacob wanted to kill him every time he got close to Ann. If he had known he had kissed her, he would have hurt him.

"What was that like when he kissed you?"

"Nice but nothing special really kind of boring, he was just nice to me."

"And when Jacob kisses you, is it different?"

She couldn't look at her, and she was blushing; it was all she had to do or say. Catherine had been right all along; they had been meant for each other since the start.

"So what are we going to do about it? You obviously love him and not as a brother. And as for the village people, I will put a stop to that gossip. You are not related, and you two can have your land here if you want."

From the doorway came a voice. "Why didn't you tell me any of this, Ann? I didn't know you were in such torment. I could have helped." Jacob picked her up, took her in his arms, and held her as Lars watched from the door; he must have figured out there was something going on and went to find him. She didn't know how long they had been standing at the door, but he had heard enough.

"We will do whatever you want to do and go wherever you want to go."

"I want to get married and soon, and I want to do it here with Mother at the keep. I want to live near here, not too far away. I want to be close to our family."

"We will do anything you want if you will just marry me?"

"Yes."

Then she turned to Catherine. "Can we get married here in the main hallway?"

"Of course you can! I would be thrilled. When do you want to do it?"

"In a week."

Cat almost choked on that one. Lars thought she was going to faint, but she didn't. "Of course we can. We will start getting ready in the morning. All right, let's get to bed and get some rest. We are going to need it." Lars and Jacob helped her get up, and she kissed both her children good night. They left, and it was just Lars and her.

He turned to her and asked, "What is the big rush?"

"She wants me at her wedding, and she thinks I am going to die. I will be so glad when this baby gets here and everybody stops thinking that." And then she walked to their bedroom to go to bed; he just watched her walk away. She scared him to death sometimes.

The next few days were a madhouse of activity with people everywhere and workers setting up tables and chairs. Helen had women making pies and cakes for company, and dressmakers were working from dawn to dark. Caroline and Jennie had Cat sewing in a chair so she wouldn't overdo; they didn't want that child here earlier than it was supposed to be.

Catherine had Father Marques brought to her, and they went into her solar and talked for almost two hours; then she had Ann and Jacob come in. They talked about how they were going to do their wedding vows since they both had the same last names, so it was decided that Ann would use Catherine's maiden name in the ceremony. The good father told her he would take care of the other problem of the name-calling since he had seen the children since they had been adopted by Giles and Catherine. No one would think to question his honesty about the children's bloodline. Ann was to wear a white dress with tiny pearls around the neckline, and down the sleeves were cuts where white fur showed; she looked like an angel. She also had a white veil of the finest lace they could procure, and that took some doing. Robert and James rode for two days looking for a market that had some to sell, and they bought it all. There was enough for three weddings.

The day before the wedding, a package arrived; in it were a jewelry box and a letter.

CATHERINE,

I hear one of your daughters is getting married, and I thought she should have something to wear from Marie. I hear my granddaughter is doing well under your care. Marie must have forgiven me. I sleep now. I hope someday you can forgive me as well. Thank you again.

CHARLES

Inside the box was a string of pearls with a single teardrop pearl; she had seen Marie wear it before, and now she would see her daughter wear it down the aisle. Maybe Marie had forgiven him, or she had just finished what she had to do when she helped her save her granddaughter's life. She sure didn't know what she was doing, but she wouldn't forget that little trick. Anyway, it got him off her back and away from her life; and if he thought it was Marie, so much the better for her. The night before the wedding, Cat was helping Ann in her room, and Beth was in there with her. They were just talking, and Cat asked, "Where are you going on your honeymoon, someplace special?"

"We aren't going anywhere," Ann answered.

Catherine looked at her. "Why not this is your special time, and you should go somewhere."

"Not until this baby is born and I know you are alive and everything is all right. Then we will take a honeymoon, maybe to France."

Everything was on hold; she had to be sure she was all right before she could get on with her life. Cat was so sorry she had put her children in this position; she wouldn't ever again. She wasn't going to argue. Ann had her mind made up.

She pulled out the ring box with the wedding ring she had made for her and the one she had just made for Jacob. "Now you both have something from Giles so he will be with you on your wedding day."

Giles had several other gold rings, and she had taken one and had it remade into a wedding ring for Jacob.

"He will always be with us, Mama. He was our daddy and always will be. He saved me and Jacob, and he made me his daughter when he didn't have to."

Catherine was so proud of her two girls; she couldn't even put it into words. When she walked out of the room, she looked up and said, "We did well by our children, Giles. I hope you are watching."

The duke and his daughter were still here; they had intended to leave, but Cat had talked them into staying for the ceremony. The baby was thriving, and Katie was up and about, helping with the wedding. Katie hadn't had a big wedding, so she was enjoying helping with this one.

Everything was ready, and Cat settled down for the night; she was so excited she couldn't sleep. So she went to the solar and just looked out the window at the horses and the trees.

Then Lars came up behind her. "Can't sleep?"

"Is there any such thing as being too tired to sleep? All I want to do is just sit and look at the horses."

He pulled up a chair, leaned an arm over her shoulder, and said, "Well, I will sit and look at the horses with you how about that?"

"Sounds like a good plan to me."

Then she pulled his hand to her and kissed the inside of his palm. "I know this has been a mess and a rush, but I do appreciate your help and cooperation in this project."

"It is for our children. What else was I supposed to do?"

"Thank you for that."

Lars just leaned his head on her shoulder; the moon was full, and they watched the horses.

In the morning, when she got up and started to dress, Catherine got some pains in her abdomen. She doubled over; they were becoming more, often several a day. This baby wasn't very far off, and she knew it. But not today, please not today.

"I know you are there, and you want some attention. But this is your sister's day, so wait."

"Who are you talking to in here?" Caroline asked as she came in to find her still doubled over.

"No one, just myself."

"Who do you think you are talking to? I have had a baby too, remember? How long has this been going on?"

"A couple of days, just a few a day I just need to rest more."

Caroline looked at her. "Soon, resting isn't going to work anymore, and that baby is going to decide on its own to come. And you aren't going to have a choice in the matter." She knew she was right, and she also knew she wasn't going to miss her daughter's wedding.

"Have Lars and James help me down the stairs, and I will sit in a chair for the wedding. But I am going to be there."

When Lars came into the room, he didn't like the way Catherine looked. He said, "Caroline said you didn't feel so good. What is wrong?"

"I am huge, that is all. Do me a favor and get out the emeralds for me." He just looked at her, then went to the window seat, took them out of their hiding place, and brought them to her.

"When Ann is ready, please tell her to come here. I want to see her before she goes downstairs."

Caroline was back in the room and saw the box on the bed. "You are going to have her wear those?"

"Yes. I want her to feel like a queen for the first time in her life."

Caroline finished helping Cat dress, and as they finished, Ann came into the room. She was beautiful. As she looked at the bed, there were two boxes of necklaces; one was the emeralds, and one was the pearls. Cat reached down to put the emeralds on her, and she said, "No, Mama. I like the pearls better. The emeralds were for you and the queen and should always be worn by you. But the pearls fit me and Beth better.
You and Marie are women to be reckoned with, and the one with the emeralds is your necklace—even a king understands that."

She reached down, got the pearls, and put them around Ann's neck; and they were indeed better suited for her. She asked Lars to put the emeralds back up, and then he and James helped her down the stairs; as soon as she was seated, they started the wedding. Beth came down first, followed by Ann holding Lars's arm. Ann stopped in front of her mother took out a rose from her bouquet and handed it to her mother then she walked down the aisle. Lars walked her to a waiting Jacob who, if he smiled any wider, would have split a lip.

They knelt before Father Marques and said their vows as Cat watched the first of her children marry. Lars's hand was on her shoulder as Ann and Jacob stood and turned as man and wife wearing rings from Giles. Caroline came over and told her to stay put; they had everything under control and asked if she had any more contractions. Lars had heard that last part and asked, "What contractions? What is going on here?"

"Be quiet. You are going to spoil everything. I am all right."

"Are you having this baby now?"

"*No*, so hush. I just have had a few contractions the last couple of days. I have done too much. I will slow down now, so be quiet."

He looked at Caroline, and she just shrugged her shoulders and went on to help Helen get out the food.

Everything went beautifully; the food was delicious, and there was dancing and wedding presents. Cat had a special room done for the bride and groom, whom she escorted to at the end of the night; it was one of the new rooms she had thought she would need but didn't know why. Ann seemed to love it, and Jacob didn't care as long as Ann was in it and she was his; they could have been in a barn. She hoped things went well tonight.

"Ann, look in the closet. Good night, my loves."

In the closet, she had left a gown made of white silk, like the one she had worn for Lars, and a robe for Jacob made of the finest fur; she didn't figure he would have thought of that or anything as fast as they threw this thing together. If he had, she would apologize tomorrow.

As she walked toward the bedroom, all the guests who were staying here were getting settled, and everything was shutting down for the night; she was tired and ready for bed. Then her little one made an appearance again, and she doubled over against the wall; that is how Lars found her several minutes later. He picked her up and carried her to their room and asked, "Do I need to call Gretel and the others?"

"No, let's wait and see if it happens again. Sometimes it just happens once and then goes away, and I am very tired." Sure enough, it didn't happen again, and they slept through the night.

The next morning, at the breakfast table, a very happy bride and groom were there; and she was happy to see things had gone well. They held hands, and any reservations Ann seemed to have had were gone; she was definitely in love. They ate, and then they were going riding and took a picnic lunch with them.

Before they left, Jacob leaned over and kissed his mother on the cheek and said, "Thank you for the closet. It was the most beautiful thing I have ever seen, except for Ann, and the robe was nice too." She didn't even turn around because he would have seen the blush on her cheeks. Silk and fur always worked wonders.

Several more days went by with no contraction, and she thought she was good; then when she couldn't sleep one night, she went to her solar and was watching the horses again. This time, there was no mistaking what was happening—she was in labor. She tried to stand,

and she couldn't. These were bad ones, and she needed help. So she called out for anyone. Who should come but Kevin? His room was on the other side of the wall, and Jane told him she thought she heard someone calling.

"Please go get Lars! I am in labor."

"To hell with that!" Then he picked her up and started to carry her to her bedroom before he got there he was met by Lars looking for her. A quick explanation and Lars took her, and Kevin went for the women. Soon, the whole household was up, and the women were working. She was changed, and he was told to leave.

"No, I am staying right here. I helped put it in there. I can help it be born."

Gretel just looked at him; this was a side of him she had never seen before. Ann and Beth were there as well, and Cat told them, "You two might want to leave. This isn't the most appealing thing to watch. It is called labor for a reason, and it is messy." They both shook their heads no, even though Ann was terrified

"All right, if everybody is going to stay, you are going to help. This is probably going to take a long time. So settle down, and we wait."

Catherine looked at Gretel and said, "There is something I haven't told you about my other babies. I didn't have very long labors with them."

"What do you mean not very long? How long?"

Jennie answered this time. "Six hours with Beth, five hours with Michel, and three hours with David."

Gretel just looked at her for a minute. "You are kidding, aren't you? Nobody has babies that fast."

"She does."

"Well, we had better get ready then."

At about that time, another contraction hit, and it was a big one. Gretel had her hand on her stomach when she said, "Aren't you going to tell him you found out about his son's mother and her having Doeri and what she did to him? I was surprised he was going to stay for this birth."

She was trying to take her mind off the pain even though she didn't even cry out; she was a tough lady.

"My spies tell me that you went hunting when Doeri was being born, and when you came back two days later and she presented him to you after twenty hours of labor; you threw a dead buck at her feet and said he was kind of scrawny. She went back inside, got a skillet, threw it at your head, hit you and cracked your head open. It took twelve stitches to close it up. That is one of the reasons why she wouldn't marry you."

She was laughing but had to stop when another pain hit her; they were coming closer and closer together. This baby was not far away.

Gretel had him lean down and told him, "Get behind her and hold her hands and help her, talk to her."

Lars got behind, he lifted her up so she could push against him, and then said, "Your spies? I wonder who that could be my sister or my sons." She had started laughing when another pain hit; she grabbed his arms and pulled.

Gretel said, "Catherine, I see a head. Start pushing." And she did, and in a few minutes, he had a redheaded little girl with a set of lungs on her. Gretel gave her to Beth to clean up, and Ann was watching as the other ladies in the room went about setting up again. Gretel started talking to her brother while Catherine rested as she rubbed her hand over her still-round belly.

"Little brother, did you know you had a twin brother when you were little? His name was Liam. He died when you were both barely one. There was an outbreak of fever, and it took him and almost took our mother. He had red hair too."

"Why are you telling me about this now?"

"Because you are about to become a father again right now." The women in the room began to laugh.

"You knew that there might be more than one and you didn't tell me?"

"We all knew, or we suspected you were so dead set this wasn't your child, we decided to let you wait and see. But now we have some more work to do because there is another one on the way. Ready to go again Catherine? I have got another head PUSH."

It wasn't much longer this time before they were looking at a perfect little boy with blond hair and screaming like his sister. Ann took this baby and was cleaning it up as the women were cooing over the two of them. Then Gretel looked up at Catherine and said, "We have a problem. Caroline, Jennie, get back over here now."

Catherine looked down at her, asking, "Am I bleeding too much? You need to start kneading my stomach."

"I feel another baby in here, and something is wrong. It won't turn. You know what I am going to have to do."

"Just do it before it dies."

Gretel maneuvered the baby until it was downward, and Catherine was holding Lars's arm so tight he couldn't feel his hand anymore. But she finally said, "Push now, Cat."

After a minute or so, she held in her hands a very small blonde-haired girl; and when she put it in Beth's arms, it could have been her child. But she hadn't yet cried; she just looked around, and then she cried. Everyone started to breathe again.

"Now, Catherine, let's take care of you. I think you have done enough work for one day. And I must say, brother, you were in fine form on that night. Don't ever do that again." Gretel worked on Catherine for more than an hour, but nothing out of the ordinary except three babies was happening.

Catherine let the girls name the first redheaded girl, and they decided on Rose because of her hair; and the little boy was named Liam for Lars's brother who, until today, he didn't even know existed. The two biggest children weighed maybe five pounds, but the littlest girl weighed less than that. When they put her in Catherine's arms, she just looked at her mother, and Cat said to her, "Hello, my little Marie. You have fought to stay alive to get here. Now you are going to have to fight some more. But you can do that, can't you, my tiny love?" That child acted like she understood every word her mother said, and the room was dead quiet because they all knew this baby was in for a fight. Babies this small didn't generally survive.

For the next few weeks, the women in the keep went to work in the nursery full-time, and the men ran the keep; they took care of the smaller children and any other problems. Helen took care of any kitchen duties, and Jane kept the housekeeping and maids under control and the house spotless. Upstairs, the babies were held constantly; there were two wet nurses brought in, and the children were fed whenever they would eat. Marie lost some weight in the days after she was born; they couldn't get her to eat enough. So Cat held her all the time and fed her at every opportunity, and she finally started to gain weight. None of them were hardly ever in a cradle; they were held by one or the other of the women, but after Marie stopped breathing, she wasn't put down again. It didn't take anything but shaking her gently to get her breathing again; it was like she forgot for a second to breathe.

Cat made sure Jane got to have her time at holding and being a part of taking care of the newborns because they both knew she would never have a chance to do it on her own. One night, when she was leaving the room after being in the nursery all day taking care of Rose, she looked at Cat. "You don't know how lucky you are. I gave all this away." Then she walked out of the room.

After she left, Catherine said to herself, "If you only knew how many times I have thanked God for just this."

All the babies' health began to improve, although they were never left alone; there was always someone in the room listening to them breathe and a nurse to feed them if Catherine wasn't around, and Cat generally wasn't far away.

It had been almost a month when they went to bed one night, and Lars asked her, "Well, wife, do you suppose I could get your attention for a while before our children start calling for you?"

"Oh, I don't know. We have so many now I might not have time for a father anymore."

"What, was I just for breeding purposes?" As he watched her grin at him, he swatted her bottom.

"And boy, did you do a good job! Doeri will be bragging about his father's prowess when he goes back this summer."

He didn't care what she was saying; he had been too long without her, and he was already kissing her neck and breasts and getting milk all over him. As he entered Cat, she arched up to meet him and pulled his mouth to hers, kissing him deeply. Then she looked at him. "We have got to be more careful. I can't do this again." He already knew that no more babies, except grandbabies, but he would enjoy bringing her over the top before he retreated.

They made love slowly; there was no hurry, and it rose in volume until she exploded in a million crystals in his arms. Then he came, and he held her close; she was his again, and their children were safe and healthy.

"Now what do we do? We have eleven children by my count, unless you have some hidden I don't know about," he asked as he pulled her to him, and she snuggled as close as she could get. It was nice to be able to get close again; all this breast-feeding had shrunk her body quickly after the babies' births.

"Now I think we have enough to do just raising what we have got and their children after them, don't you think? Let's get some sleep. Morning comes early around here."

When he awoke in the morning, she was gone. So he went to the next room; he figured she was with the children, but she wasn't. He asked the nurse where she was.

"She said she was going riding today."

He turned and ran to the playroom; she hadn't ridden in months, and he knew she had been waiting to get back on her beloved horses. Sometimes he wondered which she loved more, and he sure as hell was never going to ask. He wasn't that stupid. He went past Beth and Ann, and they asked, "What's the big hurry?"

"Your mother is going riding today."

"Really it is about time. Ann, go get the rest of them. We will meet you in the playroom."

Soon, all the children were in the playroom. Jacques, Doeri, and Hanna couldn't quite figure out why there was all this excitement to watch Catherine ride. But it seemed to be a big deal, so they came as well.

"Which one is she going to ride, Cloud or Khan?"

"How should I know, Ann? I don't read minds." As Beth leaned out the window, she said, "Khan, she going to ride Khan. This is going to be good. Bruce is bringing out his saddle."

As they watched, she went into the corral, and she called Khan. He soon came running to her, and she stroked him, and all he wanted was her attention. But as she stood back, she wanted something from him, and Lars could see the smile on her face from where he was.

"She promised she wouldn't do this anymore, and besides, I have never seen her do it with Khan."

As they watched, she took a step back and raised her hand; and sure enough, the stallion reared up on his hind legs and pawed the air. Bruce stood absolutely still; she had done this before. Then she put her hand down and down he came right in front of her so she could pet him just like all the other horses.

After that, all the people on the balcony got real interested in this ride. Jacques asked, "Did I just see what I think I saw, or was that a fluke?"

Beth turned and said, "No, she does that all the time it scares people to death. Papa, breathe, especially him."

"I will kill her, I swear. I will kill her."

"No, you won't. It is one of the things that make Mama what she is, and she is never going to change. Would you really want her to?"

Ann made a point; it was one of the things that made him fall in love with this woman and wait for her for all those years. She wasn't like anybody else he had ever met. Bruce had Khan saddled by now, and Cat swung herself up into the saddle

"Open the gate, Bruce. I am going for a ride. We will be back in a while."

Bruce was worried for her he had only seen her ride this horse that day when they were bringing him to the lodge. They had always had trouble controlling him. The men at the barn were standing, watching to see what was going to happen.

"Don't worry, we will be fine. We are going to go play."

Play this horse didn't play. It kicked your head in.

They walked out the gate, and he reared a little, and she said, "It is all right, baby boy. Let's go have some fun." And they were off.

Bruce just stood there; he had never watched this beautiful horse run, and she looked like a part of him. He stretched out, and he became a part of the land; it was like nothing he had ever seen. He looked back at the men at the barn, and they were stunned as well. He could hear cheering, and he looked up at her children. They were watching from a window upstairs; they knew she could ride like this. Marie knew, and now he did. Queen Marie had always told him Catherine could ride like no one she had ever seen. He wished he could have seen Marie and Catherine together; that would have been something. He wished Catherine had been with Marie when she died, but he somehow thought maybe she had been and always would be. He smiled at that thought. They were like one creature. No wonder Marie wanted her to have this horse he belonged here with her.

She had discarded the veil she had on and the ribbon holding her hair, and she was free again—just her and a horse. She headed around the keep. She was flying; this horse had been keep penned for too long. It was used to deserts and wide-open places, and everybody was afraid to just let him run. Well, she wasn't, so they ran. The children had watched her from the window and saw her go around the keep.

Ann and Beth said at the same time, "The tower! We can watch her anywhere she goes from there."

And out the door and up to the tower they all went up the stairs and out on to the platform. And sure enough, they could see her from there; it was a great vantage point. When Lars got out there, he realized this was where he saw her with Giles the night before the battle, how scared she must have been. No wonder she cooked up that little scheme of hers. He might as well tell them the rest of the story she hadn't.

"The only part of the story your mother didn't tell you at the lodge that night was about the little war between Giles an me over Beth and your mother. I came back to claim her and Beth after three years, and Giles said no to King Charles even after he said he would take away all these lands and his title if he didn't."

Beth asked, "What happened?"

"Giles told to him to take it. He would take his children and his wife to France, and I could have the keep, but not all of you."

"What happened after that?" Beth asked her papa.

"Your mother walked out onto a field of five hundred armed men and horses and told Giles and me that if we didn't work something out, she would disappear, and we would never see any of you again. It seems Queen Marie had offered her sanctuary at one of her estates, and she was going to go rather than watch us kill each other. That is the kind of woman your mother is. Right now, she is riding where she walked into an army of men, and not one horse moved against her. That was the first time I saw how horses acted for her. I was not so sure about the men."

"Well, what did you do?"

"Exactly what she wanted us to do what do you think? Giles and I were neither total fools. I just had to wait for what I wanted. I have never seen your mother ride like this. She is like nothing I have ever seen on a horse. It is beautiful. He would do anything for her."

"You don't understand, Papa. Any horse she is around will do anything for her, not just this one."

By now, she was at the front of the keep, and the men at the barn were on top of the barn. Everybody else was on the tower, watching. Jacques looked down at Beth and asked her, "Can you ride like your mother?"

"Not yet, but I will." Then Beth turned back to watch Catherine.

Jacques had been told by Catherine he was going to have to wait to marry Beth at least a year and he hadn't been pleased about that; now watching her mother and then the man beside him who had waited almost ten years, a year didn't seem so long—she would be worth the wait.

She jumped over logs and small fences and just ran this horse that hadn't been able to do this since he had been stolen for Queen Marie years ago, so they just ran. They all walked around the tower as they watched Catherine play; she rode for the longest time, and then she disappeared over the hill.

"Where did she go? I can't see her anymore," Lars said, concerned.

"She is at the cemetery. She wants some privacy now. She let us watch now we leave her alone."

She rode to the cemetery and dismounted; she had to talk to Giles; as she sat down beside his grave she looked over at his stone. She liked the headstone; she would have to compliment the man who did it the next time she was in town. There was also a small marble cross between her mother's and grandmother's stones that had no name on it; under it was a small coffin that held a small infant from years ago. She smoothed the grass on that grave as well; she had been too sick to see her son buried that day. Only Giles and Robert had been here for that funeral.

"Well, my love, I have three new babies. How about that? When I do a thing, I go all out. Now between Lars's sons and the new babies, we have eleven children. I think I have enough for now, unless another one wanders in. You know I can't turn a child away. I guess you know I kind of went crazy when you died, so your daughters took me to Lars. That was a good plan, seems it was yours. There is always a part of you with me. I see you in our sons' faces every day.

"Ann married Jacob. I hope you were there. We always figured that was going to happen. Well, it did, and they are happy. The girls wanted something of yours for their wedding, so they are wearing our rings. You would be proud of our girls. They don't want to live at the lodge. They want to live here. So we were wrong about that. In fact, even Beth wants to live close. She wants to see to the lodge only in the summertime and live around here. She has met a Frenchman from your properties, and she is pretty sure she wants to marry him. I may have to buy more property in France, but at least they want to stay close.

"I am even a grandmother by one of Lars's sons. How about that? I miss you so much it hurts, but somehow I got another chance at life. Not many people get that. You were right about the king he made a move on me, but Marie protected me even after she died. We always made a good team. Our little boy lies next to you. Watch out for him and Marie. You gave us all so much love, and you sent me to Lars, knowing he could heal me. You are tucked away in that corner of my heart now, so you are never lost or forgotten.

"I have got to go now I see Lars coming. I guess I was lucky enough to love two men in my life. Sleep in peace, my love. I will see you again. I wonder if you can have two husbands in heaven."

As she got up, she took Khan's reins and walked toward Lars and the rest of her life.